Tell It to the Bees

HAVE YOU EVER WONDERED HOW BOOKS ARE MADE?

UCLan Publishing is an award-winning independent publisher. Based at The University of Central Lancashire, this Preston-based publisher teaches MA Publishing students how to become industry professionals using the content and resources from its business; students are included at every stage of the publishing process and credited for the work that they contribute.

The business doesn't just help publishing students though. UCLan Publishing has supported the employability and real-life work skills for the University's Illustration, Acting, Translation, Animation, Photography, Film & TV students and many more. This is the beauty of books and stories; they fuel many other creative industries! The MA Publishing students are able to get involved from day one with the business and they acquire a behind-the-scenes experience of what it is like to work for a such a reputable independent.

The MA course was awarded a Times Higher Award (2018) for Innovation in the Arts, and the business, UCLan Publishing, was awarded Best Newcomer at the Independent Publishing Guild (2019) for the ethos of teaching publishing using a commercial publishing house. As the business continues to grow, so too does the student experience upon entering this dynamic Masters' course.

www.uclanpublishing.com
www.uclanpublishing.com/courses/
uclanpublishing@uclan.ac.uk

Also available by Zoë Richards

Garden of Her Heart

Zoë Richards

Tell It to the Bees

uclanpublishing

Tell It to the Bees is a uclanpublishing book

First published in Great Britain in 2025 by
uclanpublishing
University of Central Lancashire
Preston, PR1 2HE, UK

Text copyright © Zoë Richards, 2025
Cover design and illustrations copyright © Jo Spooner, 2025

978-1-916747-74-6

1 3 5 7 9 10 8 6 4 2

The right of Zoë Richards and Jo Spooner to be identified as the author and illustrator of this work respectively has been asserted in accordance with theCopyright, Designs and Patents Act 1988.

All rights reserved. No part of this publication may be reproduced, stored in a retrieval system, or transmitted in any form or by any means, electronic, mechanical, photocopying, recording or otherwise, without the prior permission of the publishers.

Set in Kingfisher by Becky Chilcott.

A CIP catalogue record for this book is available from the British Library.

Printed and bound in Great Britain by Clays Ltd, Elcograf S.p.A.

To my two E's – love always and for ever

To my wonderful bookclubbers – The Last Minute Page Turners, part of Jordan's Travelling Bookclub that meets in The Snug, Burscough – you got me through a tough time, and I'm forever grateful

1

GEORGIE

Seven Days to the Award Ceremony

THE scrape of metal against brick is chilling. The car is only a month old, for god's sake! Another thing to add to the growing list of *stuff* going wrong in Georgie's life: losing Mr Big, her beloved dog, at only ten years old; the mess the interior designer's made of their home, taking all of the heart out of it; oh, and let's not forget Ryan's latest fling. She's pretty sure there's someone new. And now she can add pranging the front wing of the bloody car to that list.

With a bit more manoeuvring whilst holding her breath, Georgie squeezes her Range Rover Sport into the remaining parking space at Pinewoods Retreat with no further harm. She sighs. She should take a look at the damage, but can't bear the thought. The car can go into the repair shop when she gets home. For now, she's got a job to do, and she's putting the prang behind her.

With a quick check of her make-up in the mirror – a long-time habit from a perpetual fear that there'll be mascara smudged under her eyes and nobody will tell her – Georgie nods at her reflection.

Everything's in place, and she looks pretty good for forty-three, even if she does say so herself. She will *more* than do.

Standing in front of the large, imposing house, Georgie gives it a quick inspection. Weeds growing out of the gutter that runs around the roof; peeling paint on the lintels above the windows; original single glazing here and there. This place has definitely seen better days. Bringing her eyes down to ground level, Georgie counts a jumble of pots on the steps. Twelve. Does any house really need a dozen small terracotta pots, filled with geraniums, lined up on their porch steps?

In the front garden, tables and chairs are set out for a café. A handful of people, some with dogs, are huddled in one area where the sun is peeking through the pine trees, hugging coffees or smoothies. There's a shrill squawk of seagulls fighting with the caw of carrion crows, and as Georgie listens she wonders if they're judging her. They wouldn't be the first, if they are.

She takes a quick snap of the front of the house and WhatsApps it to Ryan.

Gee: *Here goes. What a dump.*

"Ms Macrae?"

Georgie looks up from her phone as a laughing emoji lands from Ryan. A young woman wearing dungarees with only one side of the bib done up stands in the doorway smiling at her. Her hair, fashioned in a long plait, is similar in shade to Georgie's auburn hair, though it looks like this woman's is natural. Her face is tanned from spending plenty of time in the outdoors, with freckles spread across her nose and cheeks. Georgie looks past a scar that runs down her face – the woman is a homey kind of pretty.

"Yes," Georgie says, holding out her hand as she walks towards the woman. "Georgina Macrae. Everyone calls me Georgie. Is there someone to take my bags?" She forces herself to smile, and points a finger over to where her car is parked.

"Oh, yes, of course. I'll ask Hunter to bring them up to your room."

Georgie drops her key into the woman's outstretched hand as she walks past her into the hallway. There's a cloying scent of incense filling the space, and irritatingly ambient music is playing in a room off to the right.

"I'm Holly, by the way," the dungareed woman says, following her into the hall. "If you'd like to take a seat in the living room," she points to where the music is coming from, "Lorraine will be through in a few minutes. She likes to give all our guests a little tour of Pinewoods, and she'll show you to your room."

Georgie nods and steps into the lounge. Standing in the middle of the room, she looks around.

What is it with people who go for the maximalist look?

Two large sofas and a couple of chairs are pushed up against the walls, like an overfilled doctor's waiting room. A large, squidgy looking sofa takes up the whole of the bay window – Georgie makes a mental note not to sit there. That's not a sofa designed for elegance – anyone sitting in it would be swallowed up by the cushions, and have to fight their way out of it. To be fair, though, the room at least has some of the personality to it that Georgie's own home has lost since they got that dreadful interior design woman in. Anything that used to make their house feel homely has been replaced with the latest on-trend furniture that lacks history or any connection to hers and Ryan's life together. Was that the plan when Ryan suggested they have someone make-over their house?

Georgie brings her attention back to the room she's in. Two buddhas sit either side of the unlit fire, and an incense stick smokes away on the mantelpiece, clearly the perpetrator of the offending smell that hit her as she walked into Pinewoods Retreat. Georgie wrinkles her nose. She much prefers a Diptyque candle or Jo Malone, but then, this isn't the kind of place she generally stays at. Much more down-to-earth. In the days when she would have been forced to stay in a place like this, she couldn't afford it anyway, and by the time she could, clients were paying to put her up in far more luxurious locations.

"Ah, here you are."

A voice purrs behind Georgie, breaking through her reverie. She spins around on her heels to see a woman with a soft smile and full cheeks, dressed in cropped leggings topped with a floaty tunic, and sandals on her feet. The woman has sharp blue eyes, and a chopstick holds her slightly unruly blonde hair in place in a bun at the nape of her neck. Her skin reminds Georgie of her mum's – it's covered in fine, downy hairs that Georgie knows will be incredibly soft to the touch, and there is barely a wrinkle in sight, despite the woman's obvious advancing years. Fifty, maybe? If Georgie's not mistaken, this woman has never had a cosmetic procedure in her life, and yet she still manages to look beautiful.

"I'm Lorraine," the woman says. "Welcome to Pinewoods Retreat, Ms Macrae."

A black and tan dachshund scampers into the room behind Lorraine.

"And who's this?" Georgie asks, crouching down to stroke the dog.

"I'm so sorry, I didn't realise he followed me through. This is Moose, our therapy dog. A relatively new employee of ours." Lorraine grins. "He belongs to our yoga teacher. Ed asked if he could bring Moose in with him one day and now it seems this little munchkin has taken up residence, as if he owns the place." She laughs. "Come on, Moose, out of here. You need to wait for a proper introduction to our guests."

"No, please, I love dogs," Georgie says, glancing up at Lorraine before returning her attention to the dog. "Hello, Moose. How cute are you?" Moose rests his head in Georgie's hand. "Ohh, you charmer, Moose, we're going to be great friends."

"If he knows you like him, he'll be happy to spend time with you."

"He's gorgeous." Georgie pushes away the sorrow that jabs at her heart as thoughts of her own dog, who died a week ago, flash through her mind. She glides back up to standing, dragging her eyes away from Moose. "And I'll be very happy to spend time with him." She extends a hand to Lorraine. "Lovely to meet you. And call me Georgie, please." Ever the professional, Georgie flashes a smile, gently folds one hand around Lorraine's, laying the other on top. "I'm . . ." she clears her throat, steeling herself for the lie that Ryan is forcing her to tell by asking her to come to the retreat incognito, "booked in for a break. A week. Just what I need as a getaway from a busy life." She sighs and tilts her head. "Though I'll be honest with you, it's not like me to do a week away in England. Italy or the Maldives is much more my thing. But," she shrugs and glances around the room again, "the heatwave in Europe is a bit much for me this year." Georgie smiles to herself at the added white lie. She loves the heat, but nobody needs to know that.

Lorraine moves to the fireplace, opens a wooden box, looks back at Georgie, and closes the box again, tapping its lid three times as if she's thinking about something. "Let me show you around," she says, tilting her head towards Georgie in a slight nod. "Holly tells me that Hunter is getting your bags for you. He'll take them up to your room."

Lorraine leads the way out into the hallway, and Moose's claws clickety-clack on the floor as Georgie follows on behind. She's shown where the therapy room is for facials and massages – Georgie isn't sure if she can trust a backwater place like this to do a facial, but a massage or two won't hurt. Next they walk through the kitchen, where Georgie is greeted by an explosion of spices. *Don't say this is one of those places that over spices the food to hide how bad it is. Urgh.*

A small, curvy woman who shows signs of enjoying her own cooking stands at an old range at the end of the kitchen, stirring a pot.

"Dee," Lorraine says, "this is the last of our guests for the week, Georgie."

Dee turns, and beams at Georgie. She has rosy, round cheeks and short, cropped, pink hair peeking out from beneath a bandana. At least, thinks Georgie, it will be obvious if there's a hair in the soup. "Forgive me," Dee says. "I'm in the middle of cooking or I'd be over to say a proper hello. We can chat over dinner." She returns her attention to the stove.

"Dee's the co-owner of the retreat," Lorraine says.

"There's two owners?" Georgie's early research before she came to Pinewoods Retreat only showed up one owner. She'll need to do a bit of digging to find out more about Dee. "And she's your cook?"

"Chef. She had her own place in town for some years."

Georgie's ears prick up. "Really? Will I know it?"

"The Pea and Pod. But – er – anyway, let me show you around outside."

Taking Georgie out through the back door, making sure that Moose stays inside, Lorraine shows her the kitchen garden. It's a riot of vegetables in neat rows, with an old Victorian greenhouse running the length of one side, a few benches dotted about the place and a low building at the back with a homely look to it from the outside. A group of people are busy hoeing and weeding, and there's a faint hum of comfortable chatter.

"All these people are staying at the retreat?" Georgie's surprised that the place has enough rooms to accommodate such a large group.

Lorraine's laugh is like honey, and Georgie finds herself wanting to hear this woman laugh more often. When she thinks of the laughs she has with her friends over cocktails, they all sound far more coarse and raucous – herself included.

"No," Lorraine says. "I'd love it if I could be this busy with the hotel and retreat part of the business all the time. These are Holly's community gardeners."

"What's a community gardener?"

Lorraine points over to the greenhouse to the left. The woman with the scar who greeted Georgie when she arrived is inside. "That's Holly," Lorraine says. "She invites people to come and garden here to help with their mental health, or to simply give them some purpose in life. Some people just come to be part of a community, for the friendship." She laughs again. "And I'm sure there's some who come just for Dee's food."

"So a care in the community kind of thing for the mentally ill?" Georgie shivers slightly at the thought of being surrounded by people who are going to want to talk about their lives. Too much introspection does nothing much to help anyone, at least, not in Georgie's experience.

"I suppose you *could* call it that, though it's not the way I'd describe it." Georgie watches as Lorraine studies her, and for a moment it's like she sees deep inside her. "Any of us can have mental health issues at some point or other in our lives, can't we? Sometimes we need to be part of something outside of ourselves to help us recover." Lorraine looks back over to the greenhouse. "That's what Holly does with the garden. Most of these are locals who come down for a few hours a week. One of the women in the group, Morgan, is staying here. You'll meet her later."

"And the woman in the greenhouse? Holly, was it?"

"Yes. She's our head gardener and beekeeper. Came last year for a break, a bit like you, and stayed."

"If you don't mind me asking, what happened to her?" Georgie has a curious streak about people. It helps her to suss things out and be in the know. "That scar?"

"That's not for me to say," Lorraine answers. "But know that if you ask Holly, she will likely ask you about your scars too."

Georgie raises an eyebrow. "Really?" She laughs and shrugs. "I don't have any scars, so . . ."

"Ah," says Lorraine as Georgie's voice trails off, "we all have scars." Her beautiful smile disarms Georgie slightly, and again, she feels as though the woman has taken a peek into her soul.

Lorraine turns to her right and walks on around the side of the house where she points out a yurt where yoga sessions will be held. Georgie nods as Lorraine suggests she might want to join in, as she's booked onto the deluxe package. The yoga sessions are included.

"Ed's planning to do some beach yoga too. Oh, and tomorrow night you'll have to join us for our barbeque down on the beach. Ed has promised to bring his guitar, and we'll have a singsong around the campfire."

A little piece of Georgie curls up inside as she cringes. Her hair will stink of smoke. And campfire singalongs are hardly her idea of fun these days – maybe when she was a teenager, but the only singing she does these days is in the shower.

Finally, they walk around to the front of the house, to the garden where the café is. Georgie can't help thinking that its promise isn't fully utilised. There's no pretty flowers in the garden, besides two rows of lavender that line the path to the front door, and without any covered areas the café is only usable on pleasant days. That surely eats into profits.

"It's very popular with weekend walkers," Lorraine says, sounding a little defensive, as if she's inside Georgie's thoughts.

"Great," Georgie says, throwing Lorraine one of her networking smiles. She can see she'll be switching on her charm and networking approach a lot over the next week. Christ, really, a whole week? All Ryan's idea – she should never have agreed to it.

"I've been meaning to ask you about the name," Georgie says as Lorraine takes her back into the house through the front door.

"Pinewoods Retreat?"

"Yes. I mean, it's not exactly . . ." Georgie pauses for effect, "inventive."

"Probably not, no. The house was called The Pines when we bought it, and I wanted to give a nod to its history. We're in the middle of the pinewoods, this is a retreat." Lorraine frowns. "Seemed the obvious name for the place. To us, at least."

Georgie nods and leaves a gap for Lorraine to fill with whatever morsels she wants to give as information.

"I'll show you to your room," Lorraine says, taking the stairs rather than the hint.

2

GEORGIE

CLOSING the bedroom door behind Lorraine, Georgie looks around the cramped room. Being sent here is something else she can add to her growing list of *stuff*.

She takes out her phone. There are two calls she needs to make: one to Ryan, the other to her mum.

"Hello, honey," Dot says in her strong Liverpool accent when she answer's Georgie's call. "How are you doing?"

"I'm good. Arrived at this place I'm staying at for work."

"Nice?"

"I guess." Georgie looks around the room again. It's not particularly nice, but her mum doesn't need to hear that.

"And how are you doing over Mr Big?"

"Still finding it really tough, Mum. I can't believe how much I miss him. That dog was my best friend." Georgie sniffs, fighting the urge to cry. This is not like her. She's not a crier. And she's not going to start now, even though losing Mr Big has left a huge hole in her heart.

"I know, honey."

"And I can't keep ringing you every day to tell you how sad I am."

"Course you can. That's exactly what I'm here for. And it's only been a week. You're bound to still be upset."

"I'm hoping being away from home for a few days might do me some good. At least I'll not to be at my desk for ten hours a day."

"Do they have a spa? You could have a treatment or two. Are you at that lovely place you took me to last month?"

"That was lovely, but no, I'm not there. I'm not far away. Only in Formby. So if you need me for anything, you'll call me, won't you?"

"I'll manage."

"I'm back home for the award ceremony."

"Oh my god, girl, I'm so excited to see you getting named Liverpool's woman of the year. I've been telling everyone!"

"It's *business*woman of the year, Mum."

"Well, you're woman of the *decade* for me, honey. Got me hair appointment booked for two o'clock on the day of the ceremony. You couldn't pick me up from there at four, could you?"

"Of course I will. We can plan things out the day before. I best go, Mum. I need to call Ryan. Love you loads. And thanks for being there for me."

"Always, honey. Tar-rah."

Ending the call with her mum, Georgie clicks on Ryan's number.

"Hey, babe," Ryan says, answering her call on the sixth ring, which wouldn't be out of character if he wasn't the kind of person that has his phone permanently glued to his hand, and usually answers on the first ring. He sounds a little out of breath, like he made a dash to answer.

Georgie bats the thought away. "I'm here." She sighs and opens the wardrobe door, peering inside. The damned thing can only be about eighteen inches wide. She'll not fit much in there.

"Everything OK? You sound stressed," Ryan says.

Georgie hesitates. Yes, she's stressed. And not least because she's had to come to this godforsaken place. She agreed to come to Pinewoods Retreat to do some reconnaissance for a business associate of theirs, Mick Rodgers, a cut-throat developer who wants to buy the place at a knock-down price. Ryan was insistent that she should stay at the retreat for a week to find out all she can about the owners and how business is going for them, and he expects her to report back her findings. So yes, she's feeling more than a little irritable right now. Plus, this probably isn't the best time to tell Ryan what she's done to her brand-new car. She's not even inspected the damage herself yet. If she's lucky, it might only be a little scratch.

"I was just talking to Mum about Mr Big."

"Again? I know it's hard on you, losing the dog, but you need to move on, babe."

Georgie chews on her top lip for a second. How has he managed to forget about Mr Big so quickly? "And it's this place, too." She wants to add 'as well as you for making me come here', but now's not the time. She sits down on the bed and bounces up and down a few times. At least the mattress is reasonably firm. "You know," she continues, "this really is *not* the kind of hotel I like to stay at. The thought of putting up with it for a whole damned week is doing my head in already, and I've not even been here an hour, yet."

Ryan guffaws. "It's all for a good cause. It'll be worth it, you'll see."

"Doesn't feel worth it right now. I mean, I don't even have an en-suite room. The bathroom is out on the landing, for god's sake. And the room is so small you could just about fit our bathroom in here."

"It can't be that bad."

"It is, Ry. There's dried flowers in the fire grate, faded photographs of red squirrels on the walls, and over in the corner there's a chair that I'm guessing is supposed to be shabby chic, covered in a fuddy-duddy crocheted blanket. If you ask me, the chair's ready for the tip. Christ, most of the room needs taking to the tip. Oh yeah, and there's a bloody plant in the room."

"A real one?"

She knew Ryan would understand. She hates living plants of any kind in a bedroom. "Yes, a real one. Urgh! Why did I agree to this?"

"Because it's a spa—"

"This is so not a spa, Ry."

"And you're good at schmoozing people, which we need, and you'll have a better chance of getting away with giving the place and the owner the once over than I ever could. You know it's the only way we'll be able to scope everything out. And Mick Rodgers is impressed at your dedication to the contract, I can tell you."

Georgie stands in front of the mirror above the cast iron fireplace and immediately regrets it. It's mottled with mirror rot across its surface – what is it with people, that they like so-called vintage mirrors like this one? They do nothing for a woman's looks. "Bloody Mick Rodgers. That bastard owes me for this – big time." She pulls a face at her reflection. Their mission statement for the business proudly celebrates their integrity and authenticity. Nothing about her lies to scope out this place and snooping on the owners has integrity to it, but she's persuaded herself that she can overlook all that. But god, she'll shoot Mick and Ryan if either of them says again that the redevelopment will create an authentic retreat experience. She rolls her eyes – how the hell can you be authentic to a load of pine trees and sand?

"Honestly, Ry, this week can't be over fast enough. I've worked hard to enjoy the luxuries of life, not this . . . this . . ." Georgie has no idea what name to give to Pinewoods. It doesn't feel like a hotel, and it's not a spa. What even is it? "Hovel." She watches herself in the mirror as her lips tighten into a thin line. God, listen to her. She sounds so entitled. Someone who bemoans the lack of quality hand creams and the like, when Vaseline did her mum just fine. She shakes herself and faces back into the room, momentarily hating herself for the snob she's turned into. The Georgie of old, before she met Ryan, would have relished the idea of even one night at Pinewoods Retreat. It would have been pure luxury to her in those days.

"The bones of the place are good, though, yeah?"

Georgie brings herself back to the present and the job she's here to do. "From what I can tell. When I arrived I had a good look at the outside, from the front at least, and, like we expected, it doesn't look from the ground like there's anything major going on."

"Stuff that Mick can deal with," Ryan says. "It's all about digging up the dirt on the owner, then."

"If I find out all that we need to know in the next day or two, I'm coming home early."

Ryan laughs. "No, you're not." His tone fails to match his laughter. "It's gotta be worth the ten per cent share Mick's promised you. That's huge, babe. And just think, you'll get to stay for free at your very own luxury spa when he's done with the redevelopment."

Georgie shakes her head, still smarting at having agreed with Ryan and Mick that she would do the digging on the owners to find something, anything, that will help Mick bring the place down so he can get it for a knock-down price. Sure, it's the right business decision in some ways, but all the same, a week – a whole bloody week! She'll add *that* to the list of things going wrong in her life right now, too.

"It's not like it was Mick's idea for me to stay for a full week," Georgie says. "It was yours." Her mind ticks over the memory of the meeting where Ryan suggested the length of time she should stay. He was – she searches for the word – insistent. "Remember?" There's silence on the other end of the phone. "It was *you* who said I need to be here for a week, not Mick Rodgers. It's up to us if I come back and report early."

Georgie stops short of challenging Ryan about *why* he wanted her to stay here for so long. The trouble with her husband is that she can't trust him – she's known it for most of their time together, with his first affair starting somewhere around their fourth or fifth year of marriage. And here they are now, with Ryan eager that she stay for the week. Is he planning a little trip away with some young woman he's picked up? Is he already away somewhere?

Is that why it took him so long to answer the phone?

God, she's a fool to put up with him all these years. She can add *that* to her growing list, too. The trouble is, a big part of her still loves him, despite his shenanigans, and they work so well together in business. It would be a shame to break them up as a team. That thought leads Georgie to another niggle that's been teasing the back of her mind.

"I still don't get why we've teamed up with Mick Rodgers on this project. It doesn't make sense. Don't you think it's a bit—"

"Have you managed to find anything out about the owner yet?" Ryan interrupts.

Sleazy for us? Georgie finishes the question in her head as she walks to the window and looks out over the kitchen garden. Her and Ryan are into urban regeneration and development, helping people and businesses make something of themselves. Mick Rodgers is into land grabs and asset-stripping after getting elbow-deep into other people's businesses, and there's mutterings he's mixed up in some shady deals to get building projects through the council planning system. Georgie can't help wondering if this retreat project is a way for him to wheedle his way into QuinnEssentials to bolster his credibility. She rests her fingers on the windowpane and looks down at all the people busying themselves in the garden. "Give me a chance." Georgie laughs. "I've only just arrived."

Ryan clears his throat on the other end of the phone, but says nothing.

"They're nice enough people, from what I can tell."

"They?"

"Yes, seems there's two owners, but none of that showed up on our initial research. I'll do a bit more digging. My guess is they're maybe a bit naive, the kind of people we would give business support to if they were based in Liverpool. And they have some kind of community gardening project going on here." Georgie quickly counts the people in the garden below. "I can see eleven people outside at the mo'."

"And they're all guests?"

"No. The woman that showed me around said only one of those is staying here. I get the feeling there's not many guests this week. Going by the cars in what passes for a car park," Georgie flinches at the thought of her car, "maybe three of us, four, possibly. There could be more staff here this week than there are guests. I'll know more later. There's some kind of welcome thing this evening, and then I'm going to some blasted campfire barbeque tomorrow night, down on the beach."

"You'll survive, babe."

"Yeah, well, hopefully I can start to ingratiate myself at that, and find out a bit more about what's going on. I've met a few of the people here. Already started to soften the owner up when she was showing me around, to get her on my side. That's the woman called Lorraine, whose name we got from the early research. She's been very friendly towards me, and hopefully she'll be a pushover to extract intel out of."

"That's my girl. Switch on the old charmer-oo. Get what you can out of her, anything that could bring them down. It's the building we're interested in buying. Just use the people to get what you can out of them."

There he goes with his mansplaining, as if she wasn't in the briefing meeting with Mick only yesterday. It's convenient for Ryan to think of himself as the brains of their business, but he's nothing without her to provide balance and intuitive insight. "Sure," she snaps. "I do know how to do my job, Ry." Christ, what's wrong with her? She can't afford to be short with Ryan. His threats to throw her mum out of the house he's let her live in since they got married have been increasing in frequency of late – and he has it in him to do that, too. She's seen him ignore the law as a landlord on a few occasions over the years, when a tenant has pissed him off.

"You know how I work," Georgie says, softening her voice. "I'll find out what we need to know about the place, and the people." She pauses. Ryan doesn't fill the gap. Either he's ignoring her, or his attention is elsewhere for a moment or two. "I'll go for a snoop when I get the chance, see if there's any unlocked rooms I can check out, and I'll update you on anything I find."

"OK. Well, you have fun on your break. You've got it easy on this job, babe."

Georgie tuts. After more than twenty years, she ought to be used to him diminishing her contributions to their business, but she'll never get used to it – unlike his infidelity, that she came to terms with years ago. It's an unfortunate part of her marriage that she's chosen to accept in return for the lifestyle.

"Let's swap, then." Georgie waits for Ryan to speak. A polite, high-pitched sneeze comes down the phone in the distance, as if someone in the background is trying to stifle it.

Ryan laughs. "Chillax, babe. Sounds like you need to make use of some of the spa facilities while you're there. Get yourself a massage or something. On the house. Deductible expense. Check in tomorrow?"

Did Ryan seriously just tell her to *chillax*? Georgie rolls her eyes. She clears her throat and puts on her smile voice. She'll not have Ryan making out she can't do her job, the way he does whenever he gets a sniff of her being stressed. "I'll call when I can, Ry. Don't want to risk being overheard. Maybe leave it a couple of days? I'll WhatsApp you photos of what I find, and I'll let you know if there's anything worth talking about. Oh and hey, don't forget to pick up your suit from the dry cleaners for the award ceremony. I won't have time to collect it for you. Promised Mum I'll collect her from the hairdressers around four."

"No problem, I can go to the dry cleaners," Ryan says.

"Thanks. Love you."

He finishes the call, not even offering a 'you too'.

Georgie rests her head on the window, still looking out into the garden. It's not exactly the best timing to be at Pinewoods, with the award ceremony being on the day she goes home, but Ryan insisted it was best to get this bit of the job out of the way as quickly as possible. It would be different if she was simply sitting in the audience, or handing out one of the awards, but this year it's all about her – she's the main event, as Ryan likes to tell her at every opportunity. Although the couple jointly own and run QuinnEssentials, it's Georgie's own venture that she's being celebrated for at the Liverpool Businesswoman of the Year Awards. Some years back she established LivSmarter, supporting vulnerable women who needed guidance and outfits when going for interviews and as they started in new jobs, and she's already been informed that it's for that she's being recognised at the awards. So yes, the timing isn't perfect – the last thing she needed was a business trip away, taking her right up to the day of the ceremony.

Holly looks up at the window and waves. Georgie almost steps back, reacting to being observed as if Holly overheard her phone conversation or got into her thoughts. Must she really connect with this woman in the garden? But then, maybe Holly is exactly the type who gets enthusiastic around her, wanting to be a little bit 'Georgie'? Another worker bee, recognising her as the queen bee, just as she likes it. Although this isn't her territory, she can make the effort to fit in here at Pinewoods Retreat whilst she's here. Hesitantly, she waves back, and flashes that networking smile of hers.

And then, good grief, really? Holly motions her to come down to the garden. Where did she get the idea that Georgie looks like someone who spends time in gardens? Sure, she takes her coffee out into her own carefully manicured, landscaped garden when the weather's good, but she leaves the dirty work to the gardeners who turn up every week on a Tuesday at eleven, come rain or shine. For Georgie, a garden is something to look at from the house. She shakes her head, and Holly gives her a thumbs up.

There's time to befriend the staff, but right now, she needs to hang up her clothes in the Lilliputian wardrobe before everything in her bags gets too creased. There's unlikely to be an ironing service at Pinewoods.

3
LORRAINE

PULLING her phone out of her pocket, Lorraine checks the weather app. It's not forecast to rain for at least twenty-four hours, and even then the app suggests there's only a twenty-seven per cent chance of it. She eyes the bowls in the attic bedroom. They need emptying from the overnight shower, though thankfully there's not much in each one. Lorraine picks a bowl up, empties it into the one bucket she has to collect all the water, and repeats the exercise with each bowl, carefully repositioning them ready to catch the drips when they next get rain.

The last thing they needed at Pinewoods was for the roof to spring a leak in two of the bedrooms on the top floor. Still, it could be worse. At least they haven't had to cancel any bookings – yet. Though fewer rooms means she's not able to take more if anyone calls. She sighs. So few bookings. Things have never really picked up after the usual quiet January and February that they always experience.

Lorraine sighs again. They've put so much into Pinewoods Retreat, her and Dee, and she has to get it back on its feet so they can take bookings to fill the place. With her hands on her hips, she stares upwards at the water damage. So far the plasterboard hasn't come down in either of the rooms, but it's only a matter of time. Besides, she probably needs to remove it to take a better look at what's going on behind. For a moment, she's tempted to poke at the sodden ceiling with a screwdriver.

"Don't be silly, Lorraine," she says to the empty room. "You at least need to minimise the damage first." She pulls the duvet from the bed, removes the sheet, and bundles it all together with the two pillows, putting everything out onto the landing. As she works, she berates herself. She should have done this last week when she found the leaks. She manoeuvres the bed so that it's along the wall away from the ceiling damage, and then repeats the process in the second of the attic rooms.

"That'll do for now," she mumbles, checking her watch and seeing that she needs to get ready for the regular first-evening welcome she does for her guests. At least her wonderful friend Morgan is booked in for the month, as she has been every summer since they opened Pinewoods. They can enjoy some laughs together, and Morgan's pragmatic dose of realism will surely bring some light relief to the depressing conversations that Lorraine and Dee have been having of late.

*　*　*

As Lorraine steps down into the hall, the smell of Dee's delicious food envelopes her. She loves that woman so much, and not only for her food, but god, her cooking is one good reason never to mess up their relationship.

"What's on the menu for tonight?" Lorraine asks as she enters the kitchen. "Smells amazing."

"Starting with," Dee says, chopping up a cauliflower into small florets, "roasted cauliflower on a bed of pea and lime purée with a large drizzle of chimichurri sauce over the top." She blows a kiss at Lorraine. "But what you can smell right now is that quesadilla mix you love so much. Tonight we're having it with Persian rice."

"Mmm, can't wait." Lorraine walks up behind Dee and wraps her arms around her, kissing the nape of her neck. "Timings for tonight, then. Stick the cauli in when everyone's in the living room. We've not got many people to get around for the introductions, so we'll be ready to eat about half an hour after we get started. Plan for seven thirty."

Dee leans her head into Lorraine's for a moment before shrugging her off. "I need to get on then. Everyone arrived and settled in OK?"

"Yeah, you met the last one when I was showing her around."

"Good group?"

"Morgan's fab, obviously, and she'll help bring them together, as she always does when she comes to stay. But that last woman to arrive, Georgie somebody or other, there's ... hmmm, it's hard to say – I can only describe it as her aura being off. Seems lovely enough, all smiles, but there's something not quite right. She comes across as one of those businesswomen who uses charm to get her through every situation. She probably just needs to relax whilst she's here."

Dee laughs. "And isn't that exactly why Pinewoods attracts people?"

Lorraine pinches a piece of uncooked cauliflower from the cutting board. "Well, yes, of course it is," she says, chomping down on the floret, "but I got a feeling from her that she has no plans to relax." She shrugs. "It's . . . odd."

"Everyone else OK?"

"Apart from Morgan, it's only two others – sisters. It's August, Dee. Four people. That's everyone." Lorraine's laugh is hollow. She wants to scream out, 'Help me, Dee. Tell me what to do to keep this business afloat', but instead she wears the words as a deep furrow between her eyes as she leaves the kitchen.

4

GEORGIE

THERE'S a card in Georgie's goodie bag inviting her to a 'Friday Fizz Night' at seven on the dot, to meet the other guests and some of the staff. This will be easy for her with her networking experience.

She fingers each item of clothing that she's hung in the wardrobe, and settles on the perfect outfit of a dusky pink silk skirt and a white chiffon blouse – not too dressy, but smart, nonetheless. She pairs the clothes with strappy Dune sandals, and despite preferring her hair in carefully coifed curls, she pulls it up into a neat high bun on the top of her head, showing off her long neck and adding an air of elegance. It's important to make an effort, despite not actually wanting to be here. It's not the first time she's found herself having to engage in something she doesn't want to do, and if Ryan keeps taking QuinnEssentials into work with some of the less salubrious of Liverpool's business glitterati – against her better judgement and advice – it certainly won't be the last, either.

With one last check in the mirror to be sure that her make-up is perfect, Georgie pulls her door behind her and stands at the top of the stairs. That was something else she should have told Ryan. There's no locks on the blasted doors. Is she supposed to trust all these strangers staying at the retreat? And anyone could walk in off the street. Well, OK, it's not a street exactly, with the place being off the beaten track, but still, the front door isn't locked either, so anyone could walk in. There's a mini safe at the bottom of the wardrobe for her valuables, which is some consolation, but this is not the kind of security she likes from a hotel.

The one useful thing about there being no locks means it's easier for her to have a snoop around when she gets the chance. Standing on the landing, she takes a quick look at the doors and sees that there are six on the floor she is on. One of them is hers, obviously, and another is the dreadful shared bathroom – *god, do people still think that's OK in the twenties*? She shakes her head at the thought of having to get up in the morning and cross a hall simply to have a pee. Worse still, what if she needs to get up in the middle of the night?

Taking a quick photograph of the wine-coloured carpet and dark wood panelling on the walls, Georgie WhatsApps Ryan.

Gee: *So 1995. Urgh.*

He returns a laughing emoji and Georgie smiles to herself as she slips her phone into her clutch bag. She looks up the stairs that lead to the attic rooms, and moves to take the first step.

"Evening."

Georgie startles and leans over the banister. A man is standing at the bottom of the stairs, his hand held up in a mini wave. A raft of leather bracelets, the kind that surfers wear, covers his lower arm, and a copper band hugs his other wrist.

"It's this way," he says, one eyebrow raised as if quizzing her about where she was going.

"Of course," Georgie says. She needs to be more careful at her snooping attempts. "Hi." She flashes the man one of her networking smiles and descends the stairs with practised grace, her silk skirt swishing around her legs, and she watches as the man keeps his eyes on her – nothing unusual in that. Men always appraise her when she walks into any room. She smiles demurely and scrutinises him with every step she takes. Late thirties, strong jawline beneath a smartly trimmed beard, sun-kissed brown hair, toned body with a light tan.

"Ed," he says, his hand outstretched. He almost winks as he tilts his head and nods ever-so-slightly at her with a twitch of a smile.

Georgie takes the last step and puts her hand into his. He's slightly taller than her, despite her heels giving her an extra two inches, which puts him at least an inch taller than Ryan. His smile and the slight tilt of his head are cute – self-assured in a couldn't-care-less way. Ryan is more inclined to jut out his chin – cocky, almost arrogant, self-assured but very much caring how people perceive him. Ed's hair is shaved on the sides of his head, with the rest of it piled up in a top knot – Ryan's sharp cut has a 1950s vibe.

And then there are the clothes. In this kind of situation, Ryan would wear a blue jacket teamed with beige chinos and brown brogues; stylish, preppy. There's little to call stylish about Ed's casual wear of a pair of denim shorts and a white linen shirt – one of them may have misjudged the level of formality for the evening's event – and yet, despite his obvious faux pas, he carries the look off well, sexily even. Georgie locks eyes with him, their hands still clasped. Yes, he definitely has a rugged, sexy vibe.

"Hello," she says, tilting her head to match his, purposely not offering her name, enjoying the frisson of flirtation between them, a tactic she's used occasionally in business dealings to help her and Ryan get what they need. "The yoga teacher?"

"The one and only." Ed grins.

Georgie lets go of Ed's hand and he holds out his arm towards the living room, indicating for her to go ahead of him. She nods her thanks.

Heads turn as Georgie walks into any room. It's impossible for her to secretly slink or sidle into a populated space. Nor does she need to bounce or bound, blathering and babbling to be noticed. No. Georgie is worldly; she is wonderful. Georgie has the confidence of a woman who knows she will surpass the peering eyes of other women, self-appointed as judge and jury. Every part of Georgie's appearance is carefully curated to impress and, she admits, sometimes to intimidate, too.

On this occasion, though, when Georgie glances around the room, only Lorraine's head turns, and she sees straight away that she's over-dressed for the occasion – everyone else is dressed casually. Lorraine, standing in the middle of the room, is wearing a fuchsia pink tiered cotton maxi dress, with a wide brown raffia belt tied around her waist; two women sitting next to each other on one of the sofas, projecting a nervous energy that suggests they're new guests, are both in relaxed lounge gear; a third woman, older than everyone else and short in stature, is wearing an oversized green floaty A-line kaftan dress which she doesn't even bother to smooth out behind her before plonking herself down on the second sofa, curling her legs under her. She appears perfectly comfortable in her own skin as she rests one arm over the back of the sofa.

"Good evening, everybody," Georgie says confidently. Never one to be phased by a mismatch in attire, she accepts the drink that Lorraine holds out to her, smiles with ease, and takes one of the armchairs, despite there being space on the sofas. Georgie isn't about to let herself be inelegantly swallowed up by a squidgy sofa, and anyway, even under normal circumstances, she prefers to have everyone in her sightline. The chair is perfectly positioned to see everyone. This scoping exercise is going to require her to keep herself more on the ball than usual.

Ed settles himself on the floor by the fireplace to Georgie's left, effortlessly adopting the lotus pose with his back straight and shoulders back. He glances at Georgie, his head on a tilt and one eyebrow raised as if he's about to ask her something.

Moose, the little dachshund that Georgie met when she arrived, trots into the room and settles himself between Georgie and Ed, looking from one to the other as if trying to determine who will give him the most attention, before snuggling his head into Ed's leg.

"Hello, my friends," Lorraine says, her voice purring as it

glides its way around the room. "We're just waiting for Holly and Hunter to join us, and then we'll get started. Whilst we wait, let me tell you about our kombucha fizz. This is an alcoholic drink of kombucha and gin, and as well as being delicious and easy to drink, the kombucha has health properties that are said to be good for us."

"Mmm, ooh that's nice," says one of the loungewear-clad women on the sofa, taking a gulp of her drink. "That's good, Lorraine."

Lorraine nods at her. "Isn't it, Beth? It goes down well with all of our guests. Though we did have a . . . hmm, let's call it an incident last year," she laughs. "So these days I'm sure to tell people that it's got gin in it." It's that warm laugh again, tinkling.

There's a gasp at the door, immediately followed by a giggle. All heads turn to see Holly standing there. "You're not telling everyone about me and the kombucha fizz, are you, Lorraine?" Holly smiles as she looks around the small group of people in the room. "OK, I admit it. I was the one who got a little bit tipsy because I didn't realise there was gin in a kombucha fizz." She holds her hands up in mock defence as she walks into the room, followed by a tall, burly man rippling with muscles covered in tattoos. The two exchange a glance of familiarity as they each take a seat on the sofa next to the older woman.

"I didn't mention any names, Holly. The secret was yours to tell." Lorraine's eyes twinkle and she smiles affectionately at Holly. "Welcome to Pinewoods, everyone. I hope you enjoy your stay." There are mumbles of *'hello'* and *'thank you'* around the room, and Lorraine lowers herself onto the floor. "Usually on a Friday evening we do a little game with a Q and A, but there's so few of you this week I thought we could just have a chat and get to know each other. Would someone like to introduce themselves first?"

In situations like this, Georgie generally speaks first, being full of confidence and intolerant of awkward silences. But during her stay here she's got a job to do, and this evening she keeps her lips tightly clasped shut as she looks around the room. Ed is looking at her again as she glances in his direction, and there's a furrow in his brow. He immediately looks away.

"How about me?" It's the older woman who speaks. She has thick, chin-length hair that's almost all white, and a gap in her front teeth. As she speaks, she tucks her hair behind her ears, though it refuses to stay there long. "I'm Morgan, I live in Lancaster, and Lorraine's an old friend of mine." She smiles at Lorraine with obvious affection. "So whenever I decide a break would do me good, there's no better place for me to come. I've been to Pinewoods at least a dozen times over the years, and every time my soul is restored. I'm staying for the whole month."

"Thank you, darling," Lorraine says, holding her hands out in front of her in a cringy heart shape. "And who would like to say hello next?" She looks straight at Georgie, who smiles back.

"I'll go, if nobody else wants to," says Beth, the woman who spoke earlier about the drink. Her light blonde hair is scraped so far back, it lifts her eyebrows into an attitude of constant surprise, emphasising her angular features. "I'm Beth. Originally from

North Wales but live in Manchester now." Her tone is clipped. "Here with my sister." She nods at the woman next to her, sitting half curled into herself. "Always loved coming to Formby Point for days out when we were kids. We'd come to see the red squirrels. Hopefully I'll see some while I'm here." She finishes with a nod as curt as her words.

"Who's next?" There's silence around the room, and Georgie has to bite her lip to stop herself from speaking up.

"Erm, me?" Beth's sister, who is around Georgie's age, or maybe a little older, holds up a tentative hand. She's the antithesis of Beth, with rounded features.

"Please, Kate, yes, introduce yourself," Lorraine says, her smile warm and welcoming.

"Erm, hello. Well, er, yes, I'm Kate, and I'm here for two weeks." Pink blobs break out on each cheek as she speaks.

"And you're booked in with me," says Hunter, the man with the meaty arms, as if he's trying to rescue Kate's embarrassment. "With two weeks of personal training sessions, we'll soon get you fit enough for that run you're doing."

"Oh, lovely, a run?" Lorraine asks.

"Should I tell them about it, Kate?" Hunter smiles at her, and she nods back at him, her whole face now burning bright red.

Beth briefly squeezes Kate's hand before turning towards Hunter.

"Kate wants to get fit so that she can do the Great North Run in September," Hunter says, "to raise money for the Alzheimer's Society, after nursing her dad. I think you said he was diagnosed with Alzheimer's a few years back, right?" Kate nods a little too enthusiastically.

"Kate's been a trooper," Beth says, looking around the room. "I couldn't do much with Dad. Demanding job. She looked after him all this time. Best way I can help is to support her with this training. I run, do parkrun, half marathons and the like." Beth smiles at Georgie. "Yeah."

"Are you already a keen runner, then, Kate?" Morgan asks.

"No, well yes, but no, not far. I've got up to four miles." Kate looks down at her hands, pulling at the skin around her thumb nail.

"That's wonderful, Kate. Well done both of you," Lorraine says.

"Yes, well done," adds Holly, giving Kate a thumbs up.

"Isn't the Great North Run a half marathon?" Ed asks. Kate nods, her eyes wide, as if even the thought of it scares the life out of her. "And you've never run a half marathon?" Kate shakes her head, her eyes widening further. "That's brilliant. Happy to sponsor you."

"This week will do you the world of good, Kate." Lorraine gives her a thumbs up. "I know you're coming back again at the beginning of September for more training with Hunter, which is fabulous."

"Thank you, I mean, yes, I mean, I am," Kate says, her voice almost a squeak.

"Sorry I can't come with you then," Beth says, nudging her sister's shoulder. "Work," she adds, looking around the room.

Out of the corner of her eye, Georgie spots that Ed is looking at her again with that furrowed brow. She's about to turn to him when Lorraine claps her hands with a hint of excitement spreading across her face. "What about you, Georgie? Tell us *all* about you."

All? Georgie almost laughs. She's definitely not telling all – in fact, she'll be revealing as little about herself as possible. She carefully prepared a response before she even got here, knowing she can't give anything away. "Georgie." She straightens her back and rests both her hands on her décolletage, as if confirming that she is referring to herself. "I need some time out from the stresses of life, as you do, and here seems like a good little getaway, not far from home and close to the sea."

"And where is home?" Lorraine leans forwards and rests her arms on her knees.

"Can't you tell from the accent? Liverpool, of course." Georgie juts her chin upwards and flashes back a smile that challenges Lorraine to try to squeeze anything more from her. "Like yourself, Lorraine – and I'm guessing you too, Morgan. Going by your accent, you're not originally from Lancaster." She throws a big smile Morgan's way.

"You got me, queen," Morgan says, winking.

Lorraine pats Morgan on the knee and turns to Ed. "I know you're staff, not a guest, but do you want to introduce yourself to everyone, Ed?"

"Sure, sure," Ed says. "Well, you know my name, thanks Lorraine. And I'm your yoga teacher here. Started working at Pinewoods just over a month ago. I'm also the resident guitar player. I look forward to seeing you all down the beach tomorrow night for a bit of a sing-song by the campfire." Georgie watches

Ed as he speaks. Her eyes drop to the v of his chest that shows through the gap in his open-necked linen shirt. He's wearing a braided leather necklace with what looks like silver and wooden beads on it. Yes, he's the yoga teacher. In fact, he's the epitome of a guitar-playing, singalong, sexy yogi.

"Yes, of course." Lorraine interrupts Georgie's thoughts. "Have I told you all about the campfire barbeque? We'll have a light tea around four, and then, when the sun's going down, we'll go to the beach and have some delicious food that Dee's preparing for us. You'll all come, won't you? The forecast is perfect."

Georgie watches on silently as everyone agrees to be there. In truth, she wishes there was a way she could get out of it, but this is exactly what she's here for.

"Anything else you want to share, Ed?" Lorraine asks, bringing the conversation back to the introductions.

"I'll be doing yoga every morning and evening for anyone who wants to do some stretching and a bit of meditation. And I also do walking therapy, where we walk and talk, and for anyone who's OK with dogs, Moose, here, comes along too." As if on cue, Moose rolls over to Ed who gives him a belly rub. "If anyone wants to join me, I do a walk along the beach every morning at ten-thirty. I generally do it one-to-one, so book in for that, won't you? And then I'll meet you out in the garden café. Other than that," he says with a shrug, "I'm loving it here at Pinewoods. It's fast becoming my favourite place I've ever lived."

Lorraine leans across and rests her hand on Ed's shoulder. "It's been wonderful having you on board, lovey."

"I'm not sure Hunter agrees, with me having moved into his caravan with him." Ed cringes, bringing his shoulders close to his ears as he looks over at Hunter.

"Thankfully," Hunter says, "I have a bolt hole for if, or when, you irritate me." He winks in a way that suggests the two men have already become firm friends. "I'm Hunter, by the way. Personal trainer here at Pinewoods, in case you haven't already guessed, and Holly's partner."

Georgie shoots a look at Holly, surprised that this handsome guy with curly chestnut-brown hair and hazel eyes is with the freckled-faced woman with the scar down her face. She immediately berates herself for her uncharitable thoughts – it's not Holly's fault that Georgie's irritated about spending a week at Pinewoods under false pretences.

"Hi, everyone," Holly says. She raises her hand a little from her knee. "I'm Holly, head gardener. I run the community gardening, and you're all welcome to come and join me anytime. And I also keep bees if anyone wants to put on a beekeeping suit and help me out."

"No chance," Beth says. "You'll not catch me going anywhere near bees. Scared of getting stung, me."

"I'd like to," Georgie says. Eyes shoot to her and she notices looks of surprise. They've clearly judged her already, and probably deservedly so, deciding she's not the kind of person who will don a beekeeping suit, but hey, there's a lot about Georgina Macrae, or more accurately Georgie Quinn, that these people don't know – the name she actually goes by being only one of them.

"Great," Holly says, with a grin at Georgie. "I'll let you know when I'm checking on them next. I like to leave them alone as much as possible, but there'll be a time I'll need to look in on them during your stay, I'm sure of it."

Dee pokes her head around the door. "Dinner's ready. I've set the table in the kitchen, with there only being four guests, for all of us to eat together."

Lorraine ushers everyone through to the kitchen for dinner like a mother hen. Georgie hangs back, leaving others to go ahead of her. As he pulls himself up to standing, Ed looks at her intently. He opens his mouth as if he's about to say something, shakes his head, and walks out of the lounge.

5

GEORGIE

IN the kitchen, another maximalist room fulfilling the shabby-no-chic look, Georgie pulls out her chair, and again sees Ed staring at her. She's an attractive woman, she knows that, but this doesn't feel like it's about her looks. There's something in the way that Ed studies her, and it's making her feel uneasy. She shoots him a smile.

"So you've worked here a month," she says, hoping to distract him before he says something. If he knows her true identity from seeing her picture in the local newspaper, she'd like to at least get through the meal so that she doesn't have to cook after being kicked out.

Ed nods. "Yeah, love it. You know," he says, his hand on the back of his chair ready to pull it out, "I'm sure I know you."

Georgie's stomach flips. *Here we go.*

"I keep thinking her face is familiar, too, Ed," Lorraine says, screwing up her eyes as if she's working hard to place Georgie.

Georgie eyes Ed for a moment and looks back at Lorraine. "I get that a lot," she says, a lump forming in her throat. What an idiot she was to think she could get away with coming incognito to Pinewoods Retreat. She's so well-known in Liverpool as a local businesswoman, there always was little hope of her fooling everyone into thinking she's simply a guest like all the rest. "I must have one of those faces." She laughs. "What's for dinner, then?" Georgie looks at Dee, who places serving dishes in the centre of the table.

"Did you used to be . . ." Ed hesitates and rubs his chin. "Yeah, you are – are you Georgina Macrae?"

Georgie's eyes shoot wide open as blood thuds past her ears. "I am," she says, biting her bottom lip. It can't happen this fast. Beads of sweat prickle her hair line. Except – wait, he called her Macrae, not Quinn . . .

Ed slaps his hands on his knees. "I knew it! Gee-Gee Macrae." He points a finger in her direction, rocking back and forth on his heels, still holding the back of his chair. "You were in my class in high school." He laughs, his white teeth gleaming. "I was the maths and physics geek."

"Wow. Really?" Georgie grins. Thank goodness – this, she can work with. At least he doesn't seem to know who she is as a Liverpool business celebrity and one half of QuinnEssentials. "Dorky Dixon? Is it really you? Goodness, of course it is. Edmund Dixon." Georgie laughs, relief flooding through her. She studies Ed, and although she recognises the teenage boy from her class all those years ago, there's little of the awkward, scrawny dork about him now.

"Dorky Dixon." Ed shakes his head, lowering himself into his seat. "Yeah, took me a while to ditch that nickname. Anyway, I go by Ed these days." He laughs, a full smile covering his face.

"God, it's been years. Probably last saw you when we were sixteen."

"Eighteen, surely. After our A levels."

"Not me, I didn't stay on at school. I went to the tech."

"Really? You were a smart kid. Wow, who'da thought it. Georgina Macrae." He massages her name around his mouth. "Hey, do you remember those parties our class had? They were boss."

"I . . . never really went to any of those parties." Georgie cringes internally at the memory of always having to find excuses for why she couldn't join in with the class parties when everyone was turning sixteen.

"No? I thought everyone was there, even dorky me."

Everyone's eyes flit between Georgie and Ed. "Sorry," Georgie says, letting out a weak laugh, "we're taking over your entire evening with our catch-up."

"Not at all," Lorraine says.

"Edmund?" Beth asks.

"My granddad's name," Ed explains.

"Who would have thought you and Ed would know each other, Georgie," Morgan says. "It's a small world, particularly around Liverpool. Everyone knows everyone."

"What a lovely surprise for you both," Holly says. "I really do love how Pinewoods brings people together."

"You're biased, Holly," Hunter says, winking at her.

"Yes, a total romantic at heart." Holly laughs.

"So what little titbits can you share about Georgie, huh, Ed?" Beth asks.

"Only good stuff, I promise you. From what I remember, she worked hard and kept her head down. Never said boo to a goose."

"A goodie-two-shoes," Beth says, almost snorting.

"I suppose I knew how to keep my nose clean and not get into trouble," Georgie says, smarting a little at the possibility that Beth is judging her. She accepts the plate of food that Dee passes to her, nodding her thanks. "We'll have to catch up tomorrow sometime," she says to Ed. "Perhaps down at the beach for the campfire."

6

LORRAINE

LORRAINE slumps into the carver chair the moment the last guest leaves the kitchen. She drops her head in her hands.

"They seem a nice group," Dee says.

Lorraine doesn't move.

"You OK, Raine?" Dee leans in and as she picks up a serving dish from the table she kisses Lorraine on the top of her head.

Lorraine shakes her head. "I don't know," she says, shrugging. "Something's not right. Perhaps it doesn't help, with such a small number of guests, that two of them are sisters. They're not a group – I can't see any of these guests gelling. Can you?"

"Morgan will help them get along. Everyone always gets on with Morgan." Dee scrapes the leftovers from the serving dishes into a glass container. "What do you make of that well-dressed woman? What was her name again?"

"Georgie," Lorraine says. She leans back in the chair and folds her arms around herself. "I'm really not sure about her. When she arrived, I couldn't tell what crystal she needs. I can *always* tell what crystal our guests need, from the moment they arrive."

"You're good at that," Dee says.

"Not Georgie, though." Lorraine sits back in the chair. "I got nothing from her. Not a dicky bird. And did you see that outfit she wore for dinner?"

"That's why I asked what you make of her."

"Makes you wonder if she'd be better placed at some boutique hotel, or Champneys or the like."

"Come on," Dee says, filling the dishwasher, "this isn't like us. We never bitch about guests. Our job is to work out how to help them get the most out of their stay at Pinewoods, not pull them apart."

"No, you're right. It's just – I don't know. Georgie's unsettled me a little, and I can't work out why. Anyway, like I always say, Pinewoods finds you when you need it most. There must be some reason she needs to be here." Lorraine rubs a hand over her face. "There's an air of sadness about her. Did you notice? She hides it well behind that professional veneer, but..." She stares blankly at Dee, who leans her back against the kitchen worktop and watches Lorraine.

"But what?"

"She's totally out of balance. I know she doesn't *look* like she is, what with her perfect hair and make-up, and being so well presented. But I'm convinced that's all a mask."

"If you think she's out of kilter, Pinewoods will work its magic on her. It always does."

"It does."

"OK, so how do we help each of these guests to get the most out of Pinewoods?"

"Kate's easy. Hunter will work with her on her training, and I know he'll do a good job bringing her out of her shell, too.

I'll suggest to him that he mixes it up a bit. Some sessions with Beth, some on her own."

"And maybe he could bring in some of his regular clients to do some training with Kate, as well."

"Great idea. And talking of Beth, I know she says she's here for Kate, but we need to help her see this as time for herself, too. She's in a demanding job, though I don't know yet what it is she does, and it seems like she worries about Kate. Maybe we need to let her off the hook a bit. If we get Hunter doing some one-to-one training with Kate, Holly could get Beth into the garden, or maybe Ed could take her off for a walk with Moose. I think both her *and* Kate need some me-time. I'll suggest a therapy session or two for each of them as well."

"That might be what Georgie needs, you know."

"A therapy session?" Lorraine taps her fingers on her chin.

"Yup," Dee says. "Something that'll get her to let go."

"Hmm, that's an idea."

"What type of therapy would you suggest with her if she agrees, Raine?"

"The fact she's out of kilter suggests she needs her chakras balancing."

"Great." Dee nods slowly. "Hopefully she will agree to that. But come on. What else is going on? I'm not convinced your worry is just about our guests gelling, is it?"

Lorraine sighs. "We're in the middle of summer and we only have three guests, with the cherry on top of our lovely Morgan staying with us for the month."

When Lorraine and Morgan first met, many years ago, Morgan was down on her luck. They were at a craft market in Preston with stalls next to each other, Lorraine selling crystals and aromatherapy oils, and Morgan selling dreamcatchers and wind chimes. They bonded over the link between their products as well as their Liverpool accents. Buyers were thin on the ground and the two chatted their way through the day, but their friendship was cemented when a young lad leant across Morgan's table and pinched her cash box, immediately making a dash for it. Lorraine chased after the lad, and probably wouldn't have caught up with him had it not been for an old lady dragging a shopping trolley behind her who got in his way. Lorraine was able to grab him by his hoodie, wrestled him to the ground and snatched Morgan's cash box back. Holding the box close to her chest, she immediately let him go, in case he decided to turn on her, but he scarpered without looking back. From that day on, Morgan has insisted she's in Lorraine's debt, but in truth, they've been there for each other throughout the years, and it fills Lorraine's heart with joy whenever she comes to stay at Pinewoods Retreat.

There's a *rat-a-tat-tat* on the back door, and the postman pops his head into the kitchen.

"Hope this isn't all bills for you lovely ladies," he says, waving a handful of letters in the air before placing them on worktop.

"Thanks, Andy. Fancy a coffee?"

"No time today, Lorraine. Picked up another fella's round on top of my own. Good of you to offer. See yers."

Lorraine leafs through the post, and, spotting one with a local postmark, she opens it, just in case someone has gone old-school, asking for a booking by post. She scans the letter and laughs.

"Well I never. Did you still want to go to that Liverpool Businesswoman award ceremony thing, Dee, with you being up for café of the year?"

"I'd love to, but there's no way we can leave this place for the night and the tickets cost an arm and a leg."

"What if I said we've got free tickets?" Lorraine waves the letter in the air above her head.

"No, I don't believe it. These kind of things charge a fortune, even when you're nominated for an award."

"Well, some guy called Mick Rodgers is inviting us as his guests. Three tickets sitting at his table!"

"Mick Rodgers?" Dee's egg timer goes off, and she bends down to open the oven door. "I feel like I know that name," she says, as she straightens up with a tray of freshly baked brownies in her hand.

"Going by the letter," Lorraine says, "he's a local developer."

"That's right, I remember him. He has his fingers in quite a few pies around Liverpool. I catered for some huge event of his not long before we opened this place, in the days when I still had mousy-brown hair." She laughs.

"Well his PA, who this letter is from, says – let me read it to you – '*Every year, Mick likes to support a small business that's up for an award so that they can enjoy the ceremony and meal without worrying about the cost. This year, he has chosen Pinewoods Retreat as his guests, and I enclose three tickets so that you can bring along friends or family.*'"

A broad smile spreads across Dee's face. "Ooo, goodness, my hearts a-flutter. How exciting. Do you think we should go?" She rests her palms across her heart, as if to calm herself.

"Why not? You're being recognised for your food! Wouldn't it be brilliant to actually be there? Especially if you win."

"It's a shame it's not an award for the whole retreat."

"The more people who know about the café," Lorraine says, "the more they'll discover the retreat, too. I'll ask Holly if she wants to join us."

"I don't think it's her kind of thing," Dee says, "and you know she's going to say that we need someone here to look after the guests. What about asking Morgan to join us?" Her cheeks fill out as she smiles and Lorraine's heart swells with love for this wonderful woman.

"Great idea."

"We'll need to think about how we can get some marketing off the back of this, even if we don't win the actual award."

"I'll ask San," Lorraine says. "She might be able to help us work out how to make some media noise about it when she comes over for coffee with Holly tomorrow. I'll see if I can have a chat with her about it all. With her journalist experience, she'll know what we need to do. This has got to help us drum up some business."

The smile falls from Dee's face as she rubs her brow with the back of her hand. "I can't remember a time this quiet since we opened. Even in the pandemic, we managed to keep going, what with doing takeaway food and socially distanced exercise sessions. It really doesn't help that it's been so bad, weather-wise. You can't blame people for going abroad when it pretty much rains all year." She plonks herself down in a chair at the kitchen table. "We'll get through this, though, won't we, Raine? Tell me we will."

Lorraine walks over to Dee, engulfing her in a hug. "And now I'm giving you all of my worries. I don't want you fretting about the money side of things. That's my job. I'll find a way to make this all work for us, I promise."

Dee leans in to Lorraine. "We're in this together, remember. In sickness and health, for better, for worse, that's what we said. So, it's not *you* finding a way. It's *us*. We'll find a way together, as long as we keep talking about things. Your problem, Raine, is you always try and save the world on your own. I'm full-on with the café, feeding our guests, doing the farmers market, and making preserves and stuff for the takeaway trailer, but I can still talk things through with you. Just don't give me anything else to do, cos honestly," Dee yawns, as if the mere thought of how busy she is reminds her that she's tired, "I can't physically do anything more."

Lorraine rests her chin on the top of Dee's head and swallows the sigh that lingers in her throat. "I know you're done in, lovey. We'll see what we can do that doesn't put any more pressure onto you, I promise." Can they, though? And can Lorraine really promise Dee that they'll find a way out of all of this? Maybe not, but she has to try, for both their sakes – and there's no way she can tell Dee how bad things actually are. Not yet, not until she's tried everything she possibly can.

GEORGIE

Six Days to the Award Ceremony

THE following morning, after an unusually restful sleep, Georgie is up and ready to join Ed's yoga class, covered head to toe in Lululemon in her favourite pale pink – *strawberry milkshake*. At some point over dinner the evening before, she found herself promising Ed that she'd join him for the early morning yoga class, and having been awake since half four, after her usual four hours of sleep, with nothing else to do, she's ready.

She steps out onto the front step and breathes in the crisp, fresh air. It's the kind of start to the morning that used to excite her when she was a kid, with all the promise for a beautiful day ahead.

"Morning." Beth joins Georgie on the front step. "Dragged yourself out of bed to come along too, then?" Beth squishes her nose. "Can't believe I'm up this early on a non-work day. My body clock never switches off."

Georgie returns a tight-lipped smile. There's something about Beth that niggles her. She's too . . . in her face – direct, yes, that's it, at least in part. And those eyes, looking straight at Georgie, not flinching. But it's more than that. Georgie feels judged, something she's not used to. It's not that Beth has said or done anything – she just looks at Georgie. A lot. She can feel the woman looking at her now.

"You're very beautiful," Beth says. "Perfectly put together, even at this time of day."

Georgie nods. "Oh, thank you." That wasn't what she expected Beth to say. "It's a miracle what a bit of bronzer can do," she adds.

"It wouldn't do that for me." Beth bounces off the step and almost skips off in the direction of the yoga yurt. Georgie sighs, straightens her back and follows her.

"OK," Ed says, as Georgie ducks her head to walk through the tent door. His voice is low and calm. "It's just the three of us this morning, but that's OK." He rubs his hands together, as if he's massaging a spider. "Anyone done yoga before?"

"Years ago," Beth says, laughing. Why is the woman laughing? Georgie forces her eyes to look straight ahead at Ed to avoid giving Beth a visible eye roll, before sighing. Why is she being mean about Beth? It's not like it's her fault that Georgie is stuck here at Pinewoods Retreat – first it was Holly, last night, and now Beth. The woman hasn't even been rude to her. Georgie needs to pull herself together, and get over the list of things going around her head that are niggling her – with Ryan and what he's up to taking the top spot – and stop taking her bad mood out on churlish thoughts about other people.

"What about you, Georgie?" Ed asks.

"Me?"

"Yoga."

"Right, yes. I do it every week," she says, not wanting to reveal the four times weekly private sessions she has with her yoga coach who comes to the gym in their house. It's better to downplay how she lives her life – though she briefly wonders if the brand-new, now scratched, Range Rover in the parking space is all the giveaway that's needed about her wealth.

Georgie and Beth each sit down on a mat and follow Ed's instructions, starting with a warm-up, and moving on to one stretch after another. As they flow into yoga poses, Ed talks the two of them through the positions and makes suggestions to Beth for how she can improve her practice. Out of the corner of her eye, in the middle of Warrior One, Georgie notices Ed walk up to Beth.

"Can I help you adjust your pose?" he asks.

Beth nods. He places his hands on her hips.

"Tilt your pelvis back a little here," he says quietly. "You'll find the pose works much better for you." Ed turns and faces Georgie. "Good, good. Beautiful pose, Georgie."

For a split second, Georgie wishes her own pose wasn't so *beautiful* and then Ed would rest his strong hands on her hips, too. For goodness sake, what on earth is she thinking? She bats the thought aside, and wobbles.

They finish the yoga flows and move effortlessly into meditation, Ed guiding them with a gentle, calm warmth. Georgie soaks up his tone and soon finds herself drifting into some form of relaxation – not that she ever allows herself to go into a deep mediation. She's not one for losing control, after all. Despite doing regular yoga sessions, Georgie never lets go. And even now, as she relaxes a little, her senses are still on alert.

Next to her, Beth purrs on her in breath and her out breath, and Georgie smiles inwardly to herself. It's a comforting sound. And in that moment, a less comforting sound comes back to her. Who did that high-pitched sneeze she heard when she was chatting to Ryan on the phone yesterday? He's up to his tricks again, there's no doubt about it.

Georgie shivers with cold, and wishes she'd used a blanket to cover herself for the meditation. But this temperature drop has less to do with the meditation that she's currently failing at, and more to do with Ryan. He's changed in recent weeks – maybe even the last few months. Something is different, not least the kind of comments he's been making. A few weeks ago, he made some comment about it maybe being time for Dot to find a place of her own instead of sponging off him. Sponging off him? In more than twenty years he's never made a single comment like that, and back when he offered her mum one of his houses, for her live in rent-free, he was all smiles about how she'd never need to worry about a thing for the rest of her life. Georgie doesn't get this change in tone.

Possibly the strangest comment, though, was two weeks ago. Georgie stood up to him on something in front of a group of business associates, and when they got home he came out with all kinds about how she should be more grateful to him for how much he's done for her and Dot since he dragged them out of the gutter. Where did that come from? Hasn't she always told him how grateful her and Dot are?

Ed's words of relaxation creep back into Georgie's consciousness, and she acknowledges the intrusive thoughts about Ryan, just as her yoga teacher at home tells her to do when things keep popping into her head, before bringing her attention back to the moment. Ed's voice is soothing, and Georgie is just starting to let herself be lulled into the calm of the yurt when he asks her and Beth to wiggle their fingers and toes and bring their attention back to the room.

As she pushes herself up to sitting, Georgie makes a mental note to set her worries aside and focus more on the meditation next time she joins one of Ed's classes. Ed holds out a hand to her and levers her up from the mat, his eyes locking with hers, a twitch of a smile forming at the corner of his mouth. Beth waits, grinning up at him in a silent request to do the same for her. When he does pull her up, Beth lets herself fall gently into his chest, letting out an 'ooo', looking up into his eyes. Could this woman be any more obvious with her crush on the yoga teacher?

"Any plans for the day?" Ed asks, stepping away from Beth and dropping her hand.

"I'd love to join you for your walking therapy, Ed," Beth says, almost fluttering her eyelashes, "but I promised Kate I'll go with her for the training session she has with Hunter."

"It might do you good to do some walking with me so that Kate can surprise you with her progress. Maybe join me tomorrow or the day after?"

"I'd love that!" Beth claps her hands, unable to contain her excitement. "I'll tell Kate."

"And you, Georgie?" Ed asks.

"Kitchen garden for me," Georgie says. Her plan is to stay close to the house for the day so she can learn as much as possible about the place and the people. She wasn't able to do a recce of the first floor the evening before, with Ed interrupting her, so she needs to find time to have a little snoop whenever the coast is clear. "You've been here a month," Georgie says then, smiling at Ed.

"Just over, yes. And me and Moose have settled right in."

"How are you getting on with Lorraine? Do you like her as a boss?"

"Leaves me to it, most of the time. She says she employs experts in their field, so all she asks for is that whatever I do, I keep it aligned to the Pinewoods way of doing things." He grins back at Georgie. "It works perfectly for me."

"Is there enough business to keep you going?"

"It's a bit quiet this week, and I'll admit I do like things busier than this." Ed waves his hands around indicating the yurt, which Georgie takes to mean herself and Beth. "But I'm starting to build up a set of clients from Formby Village, so hopefully they'll help boost things."

"Are you on a contract or . . ."

"Is this twenty questions, or something?" Ed laughs.

"Sorry, just interested. I have an enquiring mind."

"Georgie's right, though," Beth says. "It is quiet."

"Apparently," Ed says, "this is unusual. I'm sure it will pick up again soon. But for now, my wonderful yoga buddies, enjoy your day. Oh, and Georgie, remember, you can join me for a beach walk if you like. Half ten." Georgie nods. Ed waves as he pulls down the canvas door on the yurt and does a little hop and skip down the garden path.

"You didn't look too pleased last night when Ed said he knew you," Beth says.

Georgie laughs. "I wouldn't say that. More surprised that he's Dorky Dixon – or that he *was*, anyway. He looks nothing like he did at school," she says, recalling his fringe hanging over his face to the point she wondered at the time how he could see anything going on around him.

"No. Nothing dorky about him." Beth walks ahead, though not before Georgie spots a little smile cross her face.

8
GEORGIE

AFTER breakfast, when Beth and Kate have left the house with Hunter for their training session and Morgan has gone for a walk, Georgie creeps upstairs before there's any sign of rooms being cleaned. When she reaches the landing for the floor where her room is, she glances back down the stairs. There's nobody in the hallway. Instead of turning right to go to her room, she turns left and walks along the landing. The first door she tries is a small single room, with a view over the front of the house. The duvet is turned back as if someone recently rose from it, and there's a jumper thrown over a chair in the corner. Clearly the room is occupied by one of the guests, and for a split-second Georgie feels a pang of guilt for snooping. The room is decorated in a similar way to her own, and it, too, feels like it's trying too hard and is missing the mark. The pictures, this time of pine trees, are too small for the proportions of the room and, again like her own room, there's no en-suite bathroom.

Quietly clicking the door closed behind her, Georgie tries another door, this time at the end of the short corridor. It's even smaller, slightly gloomy, with a view of the parking spaces below. Everything is so matchy-matchy, it's hard to tell where the walls start and the floor ends – and not in the double-drenching style that interior designers seem to favour. Georgie's never been a fan of single colour decor for a room, but there's still people, even in the 2020s, who convince themselves that having everything in one tone makes a room look like it's been pulled together well.

The next room is a mirror of her own, with a view over the back garden, only this one is slightly larger than hers, with twin beds. Facing the stairs on the landing are a further two rooms, doubles, and both occupied, both with en-suite bathrooms. Georgie quickly pulls the door shut on the last room when she hears a sound in the hall below. She peeks over the banister and, not seeing anyone, creeps back to her own room. Once there, with the door firmly closed behind her, she plonks herself down on the shabby chair and WhatsApps Ryan.

Gee: First floor has six bedrooms. Only two with en-suites. Honestly, there's really only space for three good-sized rooms on this floor – and they all need to be en-suite.

The message immediately shows that Ryan has read it. Georgie waits to see the ellipsis of his response. Nothing. She taps her fingernails on her phone screen and waits. Still nothing. A scraping noise at her door takes her attention away from her phone. Georgie stands still and listens. The scraping continues.

"Who is it?" More scraping, followed by what sounds like a whine. "Moose?" She opens her door a fraction. "Moose, what are you doing there?" She pokes her head around her door to see if there's anyone on the landing. Nobody. When she looks back down at her feet, the miniature dog is nowhere to be seen. Turning back into her room, there he is, the cutest damned dachshund sitting proud on the chair that she vacated moments before.

Picking Moose up with one hand, Georgie sits down again and settles the dog on her lap. She stares back at her phone screen and waits for Ryan to respond to her message. Eventually, nearly ten minutes after she sent her message, she sees that he's typing. He's usually all over his phone, to the point where it irritates her that he reacts to every notification the second it appears.

Ry: *There's another floor, yeah?*

Gee: *Yeah. Not had a chance to get up there yet. Like we saw on the Google satellite images, there's space at the side where Mick could do an extension. Not sure how that would go down with planning. Yurt on there at the mo and they use that for yoga.*

Moose nuzzles into her free hand, indicating that she should give him some attention.

Ry: *Check out those other houses nearby. See if any of them have had extensions. I couldn't tell from the research I did.*

Gee: *You're kidding, right? Most of them have high walls. There's little chance I'll be able to have a good nose at them.*

Ry: *Just check them out.*

"There he goes again, Moose," Georgie says to the dog. "Still dishing out orders from afar while he's . . . doing what?" She sighs. That's just it, she has no idea what he's doing, but knowing Ryan the way she does, she has an inkling he's up to no good.

Gee: *OK.*

She finishes her message with a thumbs up emoji and switches her phone off.

Georgie pulls her iPad out from her tote bag and leans it on the arm of the chair so as not to disturb Moose, who has now taken ownership of her lap. She returns to an internet search of Pinewoods Retreat that she started before coming to the place, checking the background information she's dug up in case there's anything she's missed. There are a few articles that mention the retreat that she's previously ignored – one about toads in the area, though Georgie isn't clear what that's got to do with Pinewoods Retreat, and another that's more of an advertorial than an article, all about what a great place it is to stay, with a poem included. Nothing that's any help for digging up dirt. She's previously done searches on Lorraine's name, but this time she adds in Dee's name, though she doesn't expect much, as she only has a first name.

Immediately, two articles come up. The first is an online piece about the retreat and what it has to offer, before swerving into Dee's past with a reference to her being bankrupted, then something about Hunter's life which is of no interest to Georgie, as well as some stuff about Holly and her mum campaigning to get some toy removed from the shelves when one blew up in a child's face, killing her instantly. All very interesting background information, but of no use to Mick Rodgers – except for the bit about Dee going bankrupt. Georgie sits upright, her heart pounding a little with excitement, and she quickly scans the second article.

This one is just about Dee and the restaurant business that she had in Liverpool. It tells of her restaurants in town, and confirms she had a Michelin star. Seems she was a bit of local star chef until about ten years ago. But the bit that's interesting is when the article gets into the business closing overnight, with a raft of staff losing their jobs. And there it is, right in the middle of the article – the best bit. Dee's bankruptcy. Interesting. It's not that this information will do a great deal to destroy the reputation of Pinewoods. It's already out there in the public domain. No, what's more interesting to Georgie is the hint that Dee might not be brilliant at business – and maybe neither of them is that good with money.

Pushing herself up from the chair, Georgie walks over to the window and looks out across the kitchen garden. Although she's not even been at the retreat for a full day, she keeps finding herself drawn to the view, regularly looking out of the window onto the garden with its luscious planting in something of a chessboard pattern. Something about the garden mesmerises her.

Now, as Georgie looks out, she sees Holly standing in the centre of a group of people. It's obvious from how she's directing people, handing over tools, pointing to different parts of the garden, that she's giving out jobs, and Georgie recalls that after yoga she glibly told Ed she was going to work in the garden today. She wonders what job Holly would give to her if she did go and join in. It's not like she's got any mental health problems or anything, not like the other people who come to work in the garden. She can hardly claim that being brought up in poverty scarred her for life. Except for that freezing cold night her and her mum had to spend on a park bench. Georgie gives herself a shake to rid her mind of the memory that she prefers not to think about.

Taking in a slow, deep breath, Georgie returns her attention to the kitchen garden below. It can't hurt to offer a little help in the garden, can it? It will at least give her something to do in this dreadful place, and maybe she can find out a bit more about Lorraine and Dee from Holly. One thing she's sure of is that she detests sitting around with nothing much to do. There's no way she can spend a whole bloody week just nosing around the place for Mick Rodgers.

Dressed in her yoga gear, with the nearest she has to an old pair of trainers that she pulled out of the boot of her car, Georgie walks out of the kitchen door into the garden, and crashes into Holly.

"Sorry, sorry," Holly says, stepping back. "I was lost in my own little world." She gently rests a hand on Georgie's arm. "Are you OK?"

"Yes, fine. I – thought I'd join you in the garden today. Though," Georgie holds up her hands and wiggles her fingers, "I'll need some gardening gloves, if you've got a spare pair. I don't want to mess up my manicure."

"I'll be back shortly and we can get you sorted with gardening gloves, a trowel and a job or two, if you like?"

Georgie nods and wanders through the garden to the old Victorian greenhouse. Paint is peeling off the worn wooden frame, and a couple of the glass panes are cracked. Mick'll want to do something with this wreck. It could make a lovely dining room if he did it up and finds a way to create a covered walkway from the house. Maybe if he moved the car park?

She takes her phone out of her pocket and takes a quick photo to send to Ryan later, before poking her head inside. The smell of damp earth and tomato plants fills her nostrils. She pulls back with disgust as a memory surfaces from deep in her soul – her mum's disastrous attempt at growing tomatoes on the window ledge in that horrible, musty council flat they had. The view of the city from the tower block was amazing, but the mould and damp were a nightmare to live with. Thinking back, she wonders how her mum put up with it for so long, until Ryan offered her one of his rentals, free of charge. He called it his '*welcome to the family*' gift. And now he's using it against Georgie, anytime he doesn't like something she says. She taps her fingernails on a pane of glass, chewing on the inside of her cheek.

"Here we go," Holly says behind Georgie, handing some gardening gloves to her. "Do you want to potter, get dirty, or do heavy lifting?"

"I'm – not really into heavy lifting, and you've probably guessed from my clothes that I don't do getting dirty."

Holly nods. "Pottering about it is, then. There's a patch that needs weeding over by the beehive. That's if you're OK with bees buzzing around you."

"Do I need to put your bee suit thing on?"

"No, no," Holly says, shaking her head and smiling. "We're not disturbing them so they'll not sting you. And as long as you don't hassle them, they won't even bother you. Is that OK?"

"Sure. I'm not scared of bees. Show me what you need me to do."

Holly leads the way, zigzagging across the garden, stopping towards the back at a raised bed full of flowers. "Careful of the plants, obviously." Holly points to a few of the plants. "If you could pull out some of these ground weeds and clear the soil to give the flowers some breathing space, that would be great."

"Absolutely. Happy to help."

"And any life problems or issues you're grappling with, you can tell it to the bees whilst you work."

"Pardon?"

Holly's laughter is light and relaxed. "Tell it to the bees." She turns her head and looks over at the beehive. "I'm still new to beekeeping, but I love my hive. And when I have a trouble that I need to get off my chest, I tell it to the bees."

"Interesting," Georgie says. She makes no effort to sound interested, half her mind still on Ryan.

"The tradition," Holly continues, as if she's blissfully unaware of, or couldn't care less about, Georgie's indifference, "goes back a long way. It's said that when a beekeeper dies, someone has to go and tell it to the bees. But there's another story of women in villages in Ireland telling any gossip they know to the bees to stop them from passing it on to anyone else. So, yeah." She shrugs. "I find it helps me to tell the bees about any trouble or worry I have. It always makes me feel better." Holly laughs and looks down at the ground. "I sound like an oddball, don't I?"

"No, no, not at all. There was something in the news about the royal bees having to be told when the Queen died." Georgie puts a little more effort into her words. She doesn't want to come across as rude to the very people she wants to glean her local intelligence from, and right now she keeps letting her irritation with Ryan come out in how she talks to Holly. That really won't do.

Holly's mouth twitches into an almost smile as she hands Georgie a small fork. "That's right. Anyway, this won't get the weeding done. Just make sure it's only weeds you pull, and if you're at all unsure about what's a plant and what's a weed, give me a shout."

Georgie settles herself on the edge of the raised bed. She thrusts the small fork into the ground, wiggles it from side to side, and pulls up a dandelion. She thrusts and wiggles a second time, and pulls up another weed, and then another, and another, getting into her wiggle action. Every now and then, a bee buzzes past her and sits on a flower head. She watches the dance of the bees as they collect pollen, momentarily distracted by how delicate they are, before returning to her weeding.

When she finishes the patch of soil in front of her, she manoeuvres herself around, getting closer to the beehive.

"What do you think, bees?" Georgie almost whispers. "Does this whole talking to you work then?" She rolls her eyes, almost laughing at the idea that anyone would talk to insects.

A bee that's been resting on the edge of the hive, by a small hole close to the bottom, flutters its wings, takes flight, and settles on Georgie's gardening glove before flying off again in search of pollen. Another bee flies around her head, and then dives towards the hole in the hive. Georgie laughs quietly. "Well, I guess some might say that's a message from the bees, but I'm still not convinced I buy it. I guess I could give it a go." She takes in a deep breath and quietly tells the bees what's going on with Ryan.

"I get the feeling he wants me out the way this week, and I'm not sure why. Yes, I have my suspicions. But a whole week, here, just to do a bit of digging . . ." She smiles to herself at the ironic connection between the physical activity she's engaged in and the reason she's here at Pinewoods Retreat.

One bee after another exits the hive and flies off. Another returns and hovers around the entrance before flying back in. "And I guess that brings me to why I'm at Pinewoods. Things are going to happen around here, bees. Do you need warning that things are about to change with the house and garden?" She pauses as a bee flies into the hive. "Go on, bee, go and tell your mates that news." Georgie smiles to herself, gently shaking her head at getting carried away by this ridiculous idea of telling things to the bees. She's not one for idle chatter, but the buzzing of the bees seems to have loosened her tongue.

She tuts to herself and pulls a weed out from the side of the raised bed, tossing it into the bucket by her feet. A handful of bees buzz past Georgie's ears, as if they're wanting to check they heard her right, and she resists the temptation to swat them away with her hand. Picking up the bucket, she moves along the raised bed, a little away from the beehive. The flowers are teeming with bees collecting pollen. There are fewer weeds here, but Georgie settles herself down and pulls them up one by one. "You're a busy little thing," she says to a bee that settles on a particularly large flower in front of her. "I hope all this hard work is worth it."

"Is it helping?"

Georgie jumps. Holly is standing on the other side of the raised bed.

"Shit, how long have you been standing there?" What a fool! Anyone could have been listening in on what she was saying. She should never have let herself get carried away with Holly's romantic idea of telling your troubles to the bloody bees.

"Don't worry," Holly says, a light blush spreading across her cheeks, "I've only just walked over. Wanted to tell you there's cookies and a cuppa on the benches by the kitchen door." Holly points a thumb over her shoulder in the direction of the house. "I'll – sorry, I wasn't eavesdropping. Your secrets are safe with the bees, I promise."

"No, it's OK." Georgie puts down the garden fork. "I admit it does sound crazy, you saying to tell the bees, but," she looks back at the hive, "hey, each to their own."

Holly nods, slowly. "Yes – erm, I hope you got the answers you need."

"Well," Georgie laughs, relieved at the opportunity to change tack, "you came offering cookies, so that's a good thing. Though I'm not usually much of a biscuit eater. Not good for my figure." She gracefully rises to standing in one smooth move.

Holly laughs. "I wasn't much of a cookie or cake person before I came here. It was buttered crumpets and Jaffa Cakes for me. But wait until you eat one of Dee's homemade cookies. You'll never want to eat anything else. Hunter swears by them. He's always nabbing himself a couple off the cooling tray when Dee isn't looking." She smiles, shaking her head with obvious affection. Georgie feels a pang of envy at the fondness Holly has for Hunter's behaviour. It's been a while since she was anything but irritated by the things that Ryan does. And going by his recent comments, she suspects he feels the same about her.

Georgie follows Holly down the path to the tray of cookies and drinks, and Holly introduces her to the group of locals from the village. The talk is of planting schemes and how to increase yields, with teasing and laughter about some woman who's grown the biggest courgette. The conversation turns smutty for a moment before moving on to tomatoes and whether you can use the seeds off one year's crop to grow the next year's. The group is immersed in its small, parochial, and simple life – their world of gardening. They have no idea about the plans for what's going to happen right on their doorstep. By the time next summer comes around, the size of courgettes and what happens with tomatoes will be irrelevant, as they'll not have access to this garden. And for a split second, carried along by the camaraderie of the group, Georgie feels sad for this little community of gardeners. That won't do. She can't afford to get close to these people at Pinewoods Retreat. She's in danger of getting soft over them.

Leaving the gardeners to chat, and with a cuppa in one hand and a cookie in the other, Georgie wanders back along the garden path. She settles herself down in front of the beehive again.

"You're all busy little bees, you lot." Georgie looks over her shoulder and checks that everybody is still standing around the back door with their drinks. She turns back to the bees as one buzzes in front of her face. Georgie holds her breath for a moment to stop herself from swatting it away.

She pushes herself up from the raised bed and leans in close to the beehive. "You have an easy life, don't you?" She pauses. "I bet you don't have a list of things going wrong for you. I just seem to keep adding to my list. Dog, car, the interior designer making a mess of our house, Ryan, a week here." Georgie takes a bite out of the cookie she's holding. "Mmmm, ohhh, Holly's right, Dee's cookies are to die for. I didn't expect that. I thought staying here would help me lose a little weight so I can look fabulous in the dress I've bought for the award ceremony. At this rate, I'll be busting at the seams."

Georgie turns back to the house and watches the people milling around by the kitchen door. Gardeners pat each other on the back; Holly hugs a woman on the edge of the group; Dee collects in the mugs and plates; Ed walks around the side of the house. He joins the group and starts talking to some of the gardeners, an easy smile spreading across his face. Georgie's heart flutters a little. He truly is beautiful.

"Fancy that, huh, bees," Georgie says, her eyes fixed on Ed. "How bizarre to bump into Dorky Ed Dixon after all these years. What a gorgeous man he's grown into." Georgie wipes beads of sweat from her top lip, her fingers grazing lightly over her mouth. She lets her hand stroke down her neck to the base of her throat and rest there.

Ed looks over as if he picks up that she's watching him, and waves. She tilts her head, realising she's been staring at him for some time. But then, he's bloody gorgeous, in a rough and ready way, and there's nothing wrong with enjoying what she's looking at. Men do it all the time. At least, Ryan does. He even does it in front of her, like that meme of the guy walking down the street with one woman, only to turn and watch another woman walking past him.

Georgie nods back at Ed and, smiling to herself, she lowers her eyes and finds a patch of weeds that need her attention near her feet.

9

GEORGIE

BY the time Georgie is ready to walk down to the beach for the campfire and barbeque in the early evening, the house is silent. A note is stuck to the porch door with directions to where the barbeque is taking place, telling her to unlatch and close the front door behind her. Standing in the hallway, she calls out a "Hello!" to check if there's anyone about.

Nothing. She calls again, louder this time. No response.

"Anyone else still here?" Silence.

It's the perfect time to nip back upstairs and have a quick look around the top floor. She runs all the way, thankful for her personal training sessions that keep her cardio fitness levels up. Again, she calls out to make sure there's nobody on the attic level. Holding her breath for a moment, she listens for any response or signs of movement. Even the air is still.

There are four doors. One has a Yale lock on it. Georgie knocks. No answer. She tries the handle but the door doesn't budge. Another door is closed, but when she opens it, there are shelves filled with bed linen. The next door is ajar. It's a small room in the eaves with an en-suite. For a moment she wonders why she's not been put in a room on this floor, but then admits to herself that at her height she'd spend most of her time with her head on a slant to accommodate the angle of the roof. She quickly looks around and takes in as much as she can before closing the door behind her.

Behind the final door, Georgie sees that it's a similar layout, but a few bowls are scattered randomly on furniture and across the floor. When Georgie looks up at the slanted ceiling, there are patches of damp. In one area, there's a bulge in the plasterboard, and in another there's a small hole. A sliver of light cuts through it. At last, Georgie has found what she's been looking for. There's a problem with the roof, and looking at the bowls dotted about she doubts that Lorraine and Dee can afford a full reroofing job. Does that mean money's tight? At least too tight for getting the big jobs done like reroofing.

Worried that someone might come back to the house and find her snooping, Georgie quickly descends the stairs, feeling happier that she has something to report back when she next talks with Ryan. As she turns the corner on the landing where her own room is, a noise startles her. She freezes at the bend in the banister.

"You OK up there?"

Georgie peers around the bend in the stairs. *Damn it.* Ed's standing in the hallway, a bunch of yoga mats under his arm, his face deadpan.

"Yes, fine. Thanks, Ed." Georgie descends the stairs, holding Ed's stare. She was convinced she was the only person in the house. How could she let herself get caught out like this?

"We have to stop meeting like this," Ed says, tilting his head. "You know, me standing at the bottom of the stairs, you seeming to have a particular interest in the house, rooms that aren't yours?"

"Oh, that," Georgie laughs, bouncing down the last few stairs with a lightness to her step that she doesn't feel, her legs like lead. "You know what women are like. We're all nosey." She smiles. "I find old houses like this fascinating, don't you?"

Georgie swallows hard. Ed says nothing.

"Need a hand with those?" Georgie nods at the yoga mats under Ed's arm.

"No, I'm going to run back with them. Forgot to take them down with me." He eyes her one more time, his head still on a tilt like he's trying to figure her out. Georgie leans past him and grabs the door, holding it open for him. "See you at the beach shortly?" Ed asks.

"Of course," Georgie says. "I'll follow you down now, though I'll take a more leisurely pace."

Taking her sunglasses off the top of her head and putting them on her nose, Georgie wanders down to the beach, letting Ed hurry off ahead of her. She's in no rush to spend an evening with the same people as last night. She soaks in the sea air and the last of the sunlight warming her skin. It makes a change from rushing about everywhere she goes, barely ever taking her foot off the pedal. Even on holidays, she seldom lets herself slow down. It might do her good during her stay at Pinewoods to slow things down – besides, it's not as if there's a lot for her to do whilst she's here, so there's nothing to hurry for.

In front of her on the path, a lone figure waddles along, and despite her slower than usual pace, it doesn't take Georgie long to catch up.

"Morgan," she says, as she gets close. Brilliant, a chance to talk to Lorraine's friend. This woman is bound to be a confidante for the owners and will have some insider knowledge. All Georgie needs to do is find a way to get her to open up and, with any luck, she'll be home before the weekend is out.

Morgan turns around. "Georgie! Ed said you'd be along. He just ran past me with an arm full of yoga mats." She grins at Georgie. "You saved me from being an embarrassment on my own for my tardiness. I thought I was going to be last to arrive. We can get told off by Lorraine together." Her laughter is relaxed and ripples through her whole body. "Not that Lorraine ever tells anyone off, not seriously." Morgan screws her nose up.

"You've known Lorraine a while then?"

"God, it must be twenty years now. No, wait, it could even be twenty-five. I'm getting old, as these arthritic knees and painful hips will attest."

"Has she had Pinewoods all the time you've known her?" Georgie forces her voice into surprise to hide the true inquisition that's going on.

"Goodness, no." Morgan laughs and stops, resting a hand on her chest. "Gosh, I'm going to have to get some exercise in whilst I'm here. This walk down to the beach never used to feel so hard. You walk on, if you like." She nods in the direction of the beach.

"I'm happy to walk at your speed. Here." Georgie offers Morgan her arm, and they walk along a few steps in silence. "How long has Pinewoods been going, then?"

"Let me see. I'm guessing now, but I think they opened it about four or five years before the pandemic." Morgan pauses to cough. "Maybe coming up to ten years. I'll have to ask Lorraine. If it *is* ten years, they should do some kind of celebration. That should help with marketing."

"Wow, yes, that's something to celebrate these days. They've done well to keep it going through the pandemic, and then the cost-of-living crisis. Not easy with a small business." *And ten years is likely to be all this small business will manage.*

"Remind me to ask Lorraine when we get down to the beach. At my age, I forget everything."

"Ah, you don't fool me, Morgan. You're a smart cookie. You play on this *old lady* malarkey." Georgie laughs, warming to the woman. "You're not even old. What are you? Seventy?"

"Cheeky!" Morgan laughs, squeezing Georgie's arm with her own. "Never ask a lady her age."

Georgie laughs along. "I'm not asking, though, am I? I'm saying you're seventy." She flashes Morgan a smile.

"Seventy-two, if you must know. And you, you're still a baby. Though I'll pitch my guess that you're older than you look. You've far too much gravitas to be the thirty-six you pretend to be. And, anyway, you were at school with that lovely lad, Ed. Your botox does a good job of giving you a natural, young look."

"Now who's being cheeky?" Georgie winks at Morgan. "Do your family not join you on your visits to Pinewoods?"

"I don't have any." Morgan shakes her head, but as Georgie glances at her she picks up no sadness. "Walked out on the old fella about thirty years ago, and believe me when I say that once you've lived with a man who shows you he's in charge, you never give your power over to anyone again."

"So he...?" Part of Georgie doesn't want to hear what Morgan's about to say next.

"Yes, he beat me, but it was the coercive stuff, too. Gaslighting, telling me what I could wear and who I could see. Controlled all the money. I just thank the lord I never brought any kids into the world. I'd have had to stay in touch with him just for them. But thankfully, I was able to walk out."

"Crikey." Georgie gulps. For all Ryan's faults, he's never laid a finger on her. But there's something in what Morgan says that resonates, as Georgie considers how he used to tell her what to wear, until her style met his exacting standards. And then there's the way he corrects her after meetings they've been in together, particularly of late, leaving Georgie doubting her own version of events. Is he gaslighting her? Has she simply ignored the signs?

"I got on a bus from Liverpool to Preston," Morgan continues, "with no idea where I was going next. When I arrived in the station, there was a bus about to leave to Lancaster, so I hopped on that and I've never looked back."

"That was brave of you."

"It didn't feel like it at the time, not when I left him. I was brave in the beginning, until I wasn't and it became easier to take it from him than to fight back. Then one day, when he was lying on the sofa, passed out from too many beers at three in the afternoon, his shirt gaping over his belly, I packed a small bag, took a couple of hundred out of his wallet that he'd won on the horses, and I walked. I didn't plan it, I wasn't brave. It just happened that way. I gave myself permission to expect more for me than he ever did."

"Were you never afraid your ex would come after you?"

Morgan shakes her head. "I changed my name. And we'd never been to Preston, let alone Lancaster, so I prayed he'd never think to look for me there. And if he did go looking for me, he never found me."

"Well, I like the name you came up with."

"Thanks. It gives me power, which is important to me after everything I put up with in my marriage." Morgan's breathing is short and rasping. "Are you married?"

"Yes, more than twenty years. Goodness, it could even be twenty-five." Georgie laughs. "I stopped counting after . . ." Georgie stops herself before she mentions the third affair. "After ten years."

"What do you put up with in your marriage?"

"Me?" Georgie stops and waggles one foot around, and then the other, to release sand from her sandals. "Nothing in particular. Everything's great. He pretty much allows me to do whatever I want. And I'm grateful for all the things he's done for me over the years. Not really anything much for me to put up with."

"Allows you," Morgan says, so quietly Georgie isn't entirely sure she heard her own words repeated back at her. Morgan stops at the foot of a particularly steep dune, plants her hands on her hips and blows a raspberry. "Seriously," she yells at the dune, "who put this damned thing here?"

Georgie laughs and holds out a hand to Morgan. "Come on.

You can give yourself permission to expect more of yourself, and climb over this dune."

Morgan punches Georgie playfully in the arm. "Take that back," she says, laughing.

"Nope. You can do this, Morgan. I'm right here next to you. We'll scale this mountain of sand together. Use the foot holes that others have left. It will make it easier for you."

Morgan plants one foot and then another into the sand, and slowly, with Georgie alongside, she reaches the top and thrusts her arms into the air.

"Yay!"

"Told you," Georgie says, punching the air with her fist. Morgan opens her lungs and belts out the words to Queen's 'We Are The Champions'.

10

GEORGIE

ON the other side of the dune, Hunter is half-way up, pushing his feet into the soft sand. "There you both are," he says with a smile, the setting sun giving his curly chestnut hair a halo. "Lorraine sent me out as a one-man search party in case you were lost."

"Apologies," Georgie says, holding her hands aloft. "I hadn't realised the time. And then I caught up with Morgan, and we've been strolling along, getting to know each other on the way. Lovely evening for the barbeque." She stoops down and takes off her strappy sandals which are now covered in sand.

"You're just in time," Hunter says. "Dee's close to dishing up the scran."

Georgie runs down the dune, a sandal in each hand, digging her heels in to ease the descent.

"Well done, Georgie," Hunter says. "You should come on the dune running sessions I'm doing with Kate and Beth this week."

"Maybe," she says, distracted, her eyes landing on Ed. She smiles, her eyes not leaving Ed's face, glad that her sunglasses disguise where she's looking. She watches him strumming his guitar. He's sitting with Lorraine, Beth and Kate, with the dancing flames of a campfire a few feet away from them. Holly is a little way off, walking towards the group with a pile of driftwood in her arms. Dee stands over the barbeque, preparing food that smells incredible.

"Georgie! At last." Ed stops playing the guitar and waves over to her. "Come and join us." His hair is loose, hanging in waves over his shoulders. As a strand falls over his face, he flicks it out of the way.

Georgie walks towards him, her eyes fixed on his. He was never this good-looking at school. She stumbles over loose sand, losing some of her usual elegance as she walks in his direction, and Ed laughs.

"Doesn't that feel great?" Ed says. "The sand between your toes." The sides of his eyes crease with an easy smile, no sign of the look of suspicion he gave her as she walked down the stairs earlier. "Come and sit yourself down here." Ed pats the ground next to him.

"On the sand?" Georgie's hands rest on the crepe fabric of her pants.

"Yes, on the sand." He laughs again and strums a chord.

"These are Jaeger," she says, patting her pants and shaking her head. For the second time in two days, Georgie internally scolds herself for her misjudged choice in attire. It's unlike her to make these kind of faux pas. But then, it's unlike her to be in this kind of situation, and she has nothing more appropriate with her.

"Here," Lorraine says, holding out a yoga mat. "Ed brought a couple of these down for me. You can use it."

Georgie nods her thanks, admiring how good Lorraine looks

in her red shirt. She rolls out the yoga mat, sits with her legs off to the side, and watches Ed. The sounds of the waves accompany his gentle strums on the guitar, and he adds in the occasional, intentional tap with his hand near the sound-hole. He nudges his bum around and turns his body towards Georgie.

"Do you have any requests?"

"Something from The Beatles," Beth says, moving herself to sit on the yoga mat next to Georgie, right opposite Ed. She leans forwards and rests a hand on Ed's bare knee.

"Really? The Beatles? Isn't that a bit obvious?" Ed asks. His smile is soft and kind.

"Go on, play something for me." She lets her hand linger.

Ed plays the opening bars of 'Hey, Jude'.

Georgie grins. "I used to love this song," she says. "I've just remembered. You and that other lad used to play your guitars at lunchtime and we'd all sing along." She changes position, and her foot strokes over Ed's as she moves. He strums his guitar again and locks eyes with her. A blush hits her throat.

"You'll have to update me on what's been going on in your life since the schooldays." He grins, and Georgie returns a coy smile. He's gained a self-assuredness that he never had as a teen, and it suits him.

"I thought we were singing 'Hey, Jude'," Beth says, pouting.

Ed throws Beth a smile, strums the opening chord again, and sings. Part way through, Beth joins in, her voice less than melodious, and as they reach the end of the song, she claps her hands enthusiastically.

"What next?" Beth leans forwards again, her hands clasped in front of her, and Georgie wonders if Beth seldom has the chance to enjoy company like this.

"Remember this one by The Ten and Overs?" Ed looks at Georgie and strums a chord. "*Hey hey, you're fine and you're mine*," he sings. Ed's soothing tone embraces Georgie. She leans back on her hands, tilts her head and closes her eyes. She could listen to him all night with that voice.

And then Beth joins in, with all the confidence of a singing voice that's taken a leave of absence, and it sounds dreadful. All credit to the woman, she carries no embarrassment for her inability to hold a note. Georgie's not sure she could ever be that assured in her own vocal cords, not the way she is when she stands at a lectern to make a speech.

Thankfully, Morgan picks up the cue to add her voice to the mix, soon followed by Hunter, and before long, everyone is sitting around the fire and singing at full volume. When Ed strums a chord and starts with the words "*Don't you ever doubt me, I'm here for all eternity*", Georgie smiles, and adds her voice to the singalong. Barley and Twist was one of her favourite bands when she was a teenager.

Ed laughs as he strums the last chord. "We used to sing that all the bloody time on school trips." His eyes linger on hers.

Georgie claps her hands, carried along by the group's enthusiasm. "Play it again."

"No time for an encore," Dee calls over from the barbeque. "Food's ready. Come and get it, everyone!"

"If you've not tried it," Morgan says conspiratorially, looking at Georgie whilst holding a hand out for Hunter to help her onto her feet, "you have to have one of Dee's falafel kebab pittas."

"That doesn't sound very appealing, if I'm honest with you, Morgan," Georgie says, offering to take Morgan's other hand as she heaves herself up from the ground.

"Ah, well, that's because you've not tasted it. It's that sauce she pours on top. Bellissimo." Morgan puts her fingers to her mouth and kisses them. "You just be careful with those cream pants, though. You don't want to spill anything on such expensive clothes."

"Do you not have anything sensible to wear?" Beth is standing behind Georgie. "You know, something more suitable to the outdoors?"

Georgie turns and faces her, immediately flashing her a networking smile, one that doesn't even make an effort to climb up to her eyes. "No, I'm not really one for slumming it."

"Ouch," Hunter says, laughing.

"Well, I'm not," Georgie says. The defensiveness in her tone makes her cringe. It's not like her to be sharp to other women, and yet that's exactly what she's being here, with these kind people. What's the matter with her? If anything, on a normal day, she's the one to hold women up, defend a woman's right to speak out, to own her space, to be proud of who she is. But she's completely out of sorts, staying at Pinewoods.

"Then why did you come to stay at Pinewoods?" Beth is staring at Georgie. As Georgie studies her face, she's surprised to see there's no malice behind the question; her eyes soft, her lips turning up in a gentle smile. Beth is genuinely interested.

Georgie runs her fingers through her hair. "I – well," she hesitates. Why *did* she agree to come here? Sure, there's a job to be done, but she didn't have to agree that it was to be done in this way, or by her. Silently, she agrees with Beth's sentiment – it truly does look strange that she came to Pinewoods at all, and particularly with her suitcase full of designer clothes. "Good question, Beth," Georgie continues, softening her tone. "I suppose I don't look like I fit in, do I?" She lets out a half laugh, and is met with smiles of what she can only assume is relief from the party around her. "I guess I'm here because it's close to home, something a bit different. I need time out without having to travel too far." She shrugs, and raises her eyebrows, hopeful that her response will be easily accepted.

"D'you know, it might be worth you going into the village in the morning," Ed says. "Get yourself some clothes that won't get messed up out in nature. Even your yoga stuff is that expensive posh Lulu-whatever brand." He laughs. "There's no *Primani* for you, is there?"

"No," Georgie says, grinning back at Ed. "Can't say I've ever even been into Primark." She holds back a guffaw at the mere thought of being found inside one of their stores. Designer all the way, that's Georgie Quinn. But this – not fitting in because she dresses too well – is a whole new experience. The women she mixes with look up to her, want to emulate her, including those she supports through her business, LivSmarter – her business that helps women get interview-ready. She's never needed to think of herself as not fitting in. And now, here's Ed and Beth suggesting, with no subtly attached, and equally no malice, that she needs to dress down.

"I'll take you tomorrow, if you like," Ed continues, nudging his shoulder into hers. "I need to pick up a few vitals from the village, anyway."

"Yeah, thanks," Georgie almost snorts, "but do they even have any suitable stores in the *village*?"

Lorraine laughs. "It's been called a village for years, but in truth it's a small town, and yes, we have stores where you can buy loungewear and gym gear. You don't need to pick up much – we've a washing machine you can use if you buy enough to get you through a few days."

"Thanks," Georgie says, "good to know."

"I'd offer you some of my things to wear during your stay," Holly says with a bright smile, "but you're a bit taller than me."

"Yes," Georgie says. There's always someone who has to mention her height to her, as if she's never noticed it herself. She generally wants to respond with '*Wow, when did that happen? How did I get so tall?*', but keeps her mouth zipped and simply smiles as if it's the first time someone has commented on her height.

"Trip to the village tomorrow then," Ed says, slapping his hands on his thighs.

"That's adorable of you, Ed. Well, I suppose the answer is yes, please."

"OK, enough of this stylists' convention," Dee interrupts as Georgie reaches the front of the queue for the food. "Can I interest you in a falafel pitta kebab?" Georgie nods, not even sure why she should be trying this kebab thing, and takes her plate, piled high with food, back to the yoga mat.

All around her, there are mumbles of how good the food is. Georgie takes her first bite into the pitta, and it's heaven on her tongue.

"Mmm," she says. She takes another bite. "Oh my word," she says through a full mouth, staring at Morgan. "A-ma-zing!"

"I told you, queen." Morgan laughs, wiping a dribble of sauce from her chin.

"What's in this sauce, Dee?"

Dee beams. "It's a secret recipe, but what I will say is, there's tahini and Dijon mustard and a bit of lemon, some herbs and the best olive oil money can buy, and then my two secret ingredients."

"I've never tasted food so good," Georgie says, taking another bite, "and I live the good life."

"No, darling, you live a rich life," Morgan says. "There's a gulf between the two." She smiles at Georgie and takes a bite from her own pitta, leaving some sauce at the side of her mouth.

Georgie watches Morgan for a moment, wishing that she would use her napkin. "And there was me," she says, "thinking I'm living the good life."

Morgan licks the sauce from side of her mouth. "Ah, well, only you will know how good it is." She nods at Georgie with the hint of a smile, and Georgie finds herself wondering if this trip away to scope out Pinewoods Retreat is going to end up being a week-long therapy session, whether she seeks it out or not.

As a companionable silence falls over the group, with the only sounds being appreciation for Dee's food as they eat, Georgie reflects on Morgan's words, niggled at the small part of her that wants to tell these people what her money allows her to appreciate: classy clothes, boutique hotels, comfortable cars, three-star Michelin restaurants. Pinewoods doesn't even appear to have any star rating – not even the B&B part of the business, let alone Dee having a Michelin star as the chef. But, despite the problems with Pinewoods Retreat, Lorraine, Dee and their staff all seem to enjoy life without all the trappings of wealth. Would it suit her? She's so used to having money, now, she really has no idea what life would be like with less.

Georgie takes another bite of the pitta. "God, Dee, what have you done with this food? You should be working in one of the high-end restaurants in town."

Dee shakes her head. "Been there, done that, burned the apron. It didn't suit me." Her smile is tight and thin-lipped.

"So you're a trained chef, then?"

"Oh yes, trained under Marcus Wareing. I got one star from Michelin."

"Wow, I – I—" Georgie keeps a poker face, not letting on what she's already discovered about Dee.

"Most people," Dee interrupts, her tone gentle and calm, "think I'm just a cook in some backwater place, but I'm not. I'm a fully trained chef, and I've never been happier since Lorraine and me set up Pinewoods."

Georgie blinks. "Of course, you said about the restaurant you had

88

in town. But really, this is your happy place? Here at Pinewoods? You could be earning so much more at one of the big restaurants."

"I could, if I wanted to," Dee says. She takes hold of Lorraine's hand and gives it a squeeze. "It's not all about money, though, not for us. Yes, I'm in my happy place." Lorraine tilts her head and leans it on Dee's shoulder.

"Oh, I see." Georgie hadn't considered that Lorraine and Dee were life partners as well as business partners. Does that change anything? Probably not, but it's good to know the lay of the land. "Is it Pinewoods, specifically," Georgie holds the last of the pitta close to her mouth, ready to take another bite, "that's your happy place, or the slower pace of life you get here?"

Dee laughs. "I still work just as hard, but I don't have a commute and I work with people I love. Yes, I'd say it's Pinewoods that's our happy place." Lorraine nods in agreement as she chews on a mouthful of food.

"Where's your happy place, Georgie?" Morgan asks.

Georgie thinks for a moment before answering. "Until a little over a week ago, it was walks on the beach with my dog, but he died." Food lodges in her throat at the mention of Mr Big, and she quickly takes a gulp of her drink to help it go down.

"Shit, that can't be easy," Ed says. "Sorry to hear that. I'd be lost without Moose."

"Dear me," says Morgan. "I seem to have made you sad. Sorry, Georgie. Let's do happy thoughts instead. What makes you happy?"

Georgie sniffs away any thought of Mr Big and takes in a long, slow breath. "The freedom I have to do whatever I want."

"Yeah," Ed says, extending the word, a smile working its way up to his eyes. "Me too."

"Really? But—" Georgie stops herself before she asks how anyone can be happy with no money, knowing she's already flaunted her wealth far too much amongst a group of people for whom money doesn't seem to matter.

"Sure," Ed says. "I'm really happy." He picks up his guitar and strums some seemingly random chords. "I've literally no money and hardly any possessions. It's just me, Moose and my guitar."

"And your yoga mat," Hunter adds. "And let's not forget those Tibetan cymbals of yours."

Ed laughs. "Yeah, OK, all my yoga stuff too. But that's it."

He starts picking at the strings on the guitar with his plectrum, and sings the opening bar of 'Wake Me Up When September Ends'. Hunter joins in, and the two men sing the song as a duet. Tears prick at Georgie's eyes. Of course, she knows the song is about personal loss, but it's never affected her before, not like this – but then, she's never experienced the pain of loss before Mr Big died. She pinches her nose to stop herself from crying – Georgie Quinn doesn't cry – and as the song concludes, she joins in with the chorus of clapping.

"What about another Beatles song?" Beth asks, breaking the moment of magic.

"Or The Carpenters," Morgan says. "That Carol Carpenter had the voice of an angel. Bit like you, Kate. Your voice is beautiful. Angelic." Kate blushes and looks away, as she brushes sand off the soles of her feet.

90

Ed strikes a chord, and another, and sings 'On Top of The World', grinning at Morgan before locking eyes with Georgie for the rest of the song. Morgan joins in, followed by Beth, and then Kate, and as Georgie opens her mouth to sing, her voice cracks. God, he's so sexy when he plays that damned guitar. She turns away from him and looks out at the setting sun.

Get a-hold of yourself, Quinn. There's a job to do here. We don't need any distractions. And we certainly don't need to descend to Ryan's level.

As they reach the chorus, Beth's voice rises above everyone else's, not exactly tunefully. Georgie smiles and turns back to Ed. His eyes are still on her as he sings, and her skin tingles. She feels like a shaken bottle of champagne ready to fizz over the top.

Pushing herself up from the yoga mat in one smooth move, Georgie walks a short distance away from the group towards the sea and wraps her arms around herself, watching the sun set. The cloud-scape is both ominous and spectacular, which is exactly how she feels about Ed. Christ, what is she thinking? She's a happily married woman – well, she's married, but happiness hasn't been part of the contract between them in years. Were they ever happy, her and Ryan? In the beginning, maybe, though it would be fair to say she always knew he was her ticket out of poverty. She's forever grateful to him for that. But in many ways, it's been a business partnership more than a marriage for something like fifteen years, maybe more. It's never helped that Ryan's not exactly committed to their marriage vows, what with his flings and that affair he had with the journalist for around ten years. He thought she didn't know about it for the first few years, but he was wrong. She knew — she simply didn't want to admit it to herself. Do all women know, even when they pretend that they don't?

There's no pretending to herself this time, though — she's pretty sure he's got someone else on the go, based on the perfume that was all over his suit jacket last week. It wasn't her own Coco Mademoiselle that's been her signature perfume for years, she knew that instantly. As the song nears its end, Georgie sighs and hugs herself tighter. She needs to watch herself around Ed. She didn't come to Pinewoods to get mixed up in a short fling. It's not her thing. Never, in all the years, has she done anything to get back at Ryan — never took a hammer to his Patak watch, never slashed the tyres on his car, never smashed up his wine collection, despite the intense desire to do just that a little over a year ago. The most she's done is insist on one or other house upgrade, and he has always agreed to keep her sweet.

Georgie glances back at Ed. His mouth twitches into an assured half smile as he strums the last chord. Shit, but that man is gorgeous.

"Whoop!" Beth is in her element, showing a more relaxed side to her than she displayed when they all met the night before. "Play another," she says, clapping her hands. And, in unison, the clouds clap, as if they're enjoying the singalong too.

"Ooo, that was thunder," Kate says, and Georgie realises that, beyond joining in with the singalong, she hasn't heard the woman speak all evening, leaving all the chatter to her sister. "I hate thunder," Kate adds.

Everyone's gaze turns skyward as a flash of lightning strikes through the clouds.

"It wasn't forecast to rain," Lorraine says, worry etched across her face.

"We better get everything packed up." Dee stuffs the last of her food into her mouth and jumps to her feet. "Ed, kick some sand over the fire to put it out. Hunter, gather up everyone's plates. Holly, help me with the barbeque stuff. Lorraine, the yoga mats. Here's a bin bag for someone to pick up the rubbish." Beth snatches the bin bag and the group leaps into action as huge blobs of rain plop onto bare arms.

Kate squeals as thunder claps again, quickly followed by more lightning and a gust of wind.

"You're OK, Kate," Holly says. "Come on, you come back to Pinewoods with me. We can take this first couple of baskets of plates and food that's ready." She turns to Dee. "You're all right with me getting Kate back to the house?"

Dee nods. "Yes," she calls over the increasing wind. "You two go, now. Hunter, carry the gas canister back. I'll take the barbeque."

Holly passes Kate one of two baskets, grabs her arm, and pulls her in the direction of Pinewoods.

The wind picks up, and Georgie's hair is blown across her face as she bends to pick up some rubbish that's ready to blow away, stuffing it into the bin bag that Beth holds tight in front of her.

Hunter lifts the gas canister onto his shoulder and follows behind Holly, effortlessly running up and over the dune. Lorraine stumbles up the dune behind him, with Morgan's arm through hers, and Beth helps Dee with the barbeque. Georgie stuffs rolled-up yoga mats under her arm and picks up the bin bag. Ed pushes his guitar strap around his body, sitting his guitar across his back, and picks up the last basket of food.

"Here," he says to Georgie, the two of them bringing up the rear of the group, with the rain soaking them, "pass me the bin bag. You don't want that splitting over your good clothes."

Georgie falls into step alongside Ed and laughs. "God, when are you going to give over making comments about my clothes?"

"Sorry, you're right. It's just, you know, you've gone all posh."

"That's not fair. For one thing, I'm not posh!" Georgie lets out a mock gasp and looks across at Ed, rain streaming down her face.

He's smirking. "No, you're a Huyton girl. And we all know what they say about them." He laughs.

"You can take the girl out of Huyton," Georgie starts, and together they finish the phrase, "but you can't take Huyton out the girl." They laugh.

"But, come on," Ed continues, "you're well off and you do act like you're posh."

"OK," she says. "I am well off. But I'm not posh."

"Let me ask you another question – are you happy, Georgina Macrae?"

"Of course," she says. "As much as any of us can be happy."

A silence hangs between them for a moment, and Georgie fiddles with the rolled-up ends of the yoga mats under her arm.

"And is it the kind of happiness that feels right to you?"

"I guess so." Georgie thinks for moment. Rain tickles the end of her nose. "I don't know. I mean, Ryan, my husband, he's given me and Mum so much. I'm forever grateful for his love and kindness. I couldn't be luckier."

"I'm not asking that. I'm asking about you."

"I owe Ryan a lot." Georgie glances across at Ed. The features of his rain-soaked face are more defined than they were earlier.

"Go on." Ed's voice is gentle

For crying out loud, what is Ed on about? "I couldn't have got by in life if Ryan hadn't saved me." The wind shoves Georgie in the back and she stumbles forwards, her sandals heavy with wet sand. She steadies herself, and the wind pushes them both along the path to Pinewoods.

Ed swaps the bin bag over to his other hand, further away from Georgie. His free hand brushes against her arm, and a spark runs down Georgie's spine. She squints at him, blood thudding past her ears. Ed looks down at their arms, swinging alongside each other as they stride on through the rain. This time, there's no mistaking his move as his little finger takes hold of hers. He slowly lifts his head, following the line of her arm, along her shoulder, down her décolletage, back up to her throat, her lips, and eventually settling on her eyes.

Georgie snatches her head away, keeping her eyes fixed on the others, a short distance ahead of them, nearing Pinewoods Retreat. She leaves her little finger in his. Despite the rain and the wind, warmth floods over her. Hunter and Dee turn and pass through the gate. Georgie and Ed are alone on the path now. She wants to stop, wants to turn and face him, wants to drop the basket on the ground, wants to hold his face in her hands, wants to ... no, no, stop it! Hasn't she just told Ed she's happy? A happy woman doesn't fantasise about another man. Sure, she's had many passes from business associates over the years, and that bloody Mick Rodgers has made a few too many attempts to plant a slobbery kiss on her lips that she's managed to avert to her cheek; but no, she prides herself in respecting their wedding vows. Unable to look at Ed, Georgie squeezes his finger with hers before letting it drop and picking up her pace.

"Anyway," Ed's voice, a little behind her, is hoarse. "I'll take you into the village tomorrow, then," he says. She allows herself to turn and look at him. Rain streams down his face. He smiles at her.

"Yes. Please." Georgie is surprised to hear her own voice crack. "I'd like that." Walking through the gate ahead of him, her head spins. It takes all the strength of every moral fibre in her body not to take hold of his hand and lead him up to her room.

11

LORRAINE

LORRAINE scurries back to Pinewoods, Morgan attached to her arm, feeling a little held back by her dear, aging friend being less mobile these days. She's desperate to get back to Pinewoods, and not just because of the *plip plap plop* of heavy rain soaking through her red linen shirt. The bowls she's positioned on the top floor to catch the rain could be overflowing by now, with how heavy this blasted rain is.

How could she be so stupid? A shower was forecast for overnight, that was obvious from the weather app. It's become an almost hourly habit to check for rain, just in case, even when the day is forecast to be dry. Lorraine intended to buy some buckets to put down instead of the bowls she's using to catch the drips, but . . . She purses her lips, annoyed with herself for getting distracted and not doing just that. There's always too much to do at Pinewoods and not enough people to do it all, and so yes, she forgot about the buckets and now she's trying to hurry Morgan along on those little legs of hers so that they can get back to the house as fast as possible. The last thing she needs is for the bowls to overflow and water to go through the ceiling and damage the main bedrooms on the floor below. She can't afford to lose any additional income with more bedrooms put out of action.

"Slow down, can't you?" Morgan pants heavily by her side, coughing.

"Sorry, sorry. I'm trying to get you back before you're soaked through."

"Too late for that now," Morgan laughs, wiping rain from her face with her free hand.

"I didn't expect a summer downpour like this!" Lorraine sighs. "You go on ahead if you need to."

Lorraine squeezes Morgan's arm closer to her body. "It's OK, we've not got far to go and any damage is already done."

"You worrying about that roof again?"

"When am I not worrying about it? But don't tell Dee. She doesn't know how bad it is, not yet."

Morgan leans into Lorraine. "You're all wound up, Lorraine."

Lorraine looks over her shoulder. None of the others are in close proximity. The last thing she needs is for the staff or guests to get wind of how bad things are at Pinewoods Retreat.

"It's all getting too much, Morgan. Costs have gone up, bookings are down, I can't keep up with the repairs, Dee's working flat out doing the farmers' markets as well as the café and the meals for staff and guests, I'm doing what I can with the therapies as well as doing the housekeeping and looking after guests and seeing to staff, and . . ." She fizzles out as she runs out of breath.

"I know, my love. And I wish you'd let me help you. Financially, I mean."

"That's sweet of you, but like I've said before, this place could eat up every penny you've got, and I can't let you do that."

"I could cash in my pension. I'd do that for you."

"No, you definitely can't do that. I can't ask you to do something that big."

"I want to help, though. You and Dee have done so much for me over the years. It's my time to help you."

They reach the front step of Pinewoods and stand in the porch, looking back at the rain.

"Look." Morgan steps back out into the garden and picks something up off one of the café tables. "A feather. I know it's a sodding wet feather, and it's not a white one, but still, I reckon it's a sign that the angels are looking out for you, if you'd only let them."

Lorraine leans forwards and hugs Morgan as she steps back into the porch. "I need someone looking out for us, Mor." She takes the feather and runs her fingers along its silky length. "It feels like the whole place is crumbling around my ears. Right, can I leave you to take this bag back through to the kitchen for me?" She places the feather into the back pocket of her Aladdin pants. "That's something you *can* help with whilst I go up and check on what the rain's doing to the attic rooms."

Taking two stairs at a time, Lorraine runs up to the attic. The bowls scattered across the floor are close to full but, thankfully, none has overflowed yet. She quickly empties them one by one into the sink in the en-suite, then carefully places each one back under the leaks.

Relieved that there's no further damage, Lorraine looks out the window at the grey skies, willing the rain to stop. Stuffing her hand in the pocket of her pants, she feels the feather that Morgan gave her. It's a mix of greys and grubby whites – it's not particularly beautiful to look at, but Morgan is always telling her that a feather is a sign. Well, she needs looking over through the night, because she doesn't relish the idea of having to get up every hour, on the hour, to check the bowls until the rain stops. Absentmindedly, she strokes the feather across the back of her hand and watches the rain. Within moments, a gap appears in the gloomy sky, and slowly, in the fading light of the day, it brightens. A pale rainbow appears in the distance, and within a minute, the rain stops completely. Turning back to look at the collection of bowls, Lorraine allows herself to breathe properly.

"I need a teaspoon of my Hawthorne tincture," she says to herself. "That should calm my nerves a bit." Taking a last look at the room, she returns downstairs to look after her guests.

12

GEORGIE

Five Days to Award Ceremony

A MOTORBIKE, with Ed sitting astride, ticks over as Georgie walks out through the gate onto the cinder path.

"Here she is." Ed looks her up and down and smiles. He warned her the night before that she needed to wear jeans – which she doesn't have with her – or her yoga pants, which she's now wearing, along with a suitable pair of flats. "Thought you weren't coming."

"I slept in. Almost missed breakfast. Not like me at all. I'm usually up with the lark."

"You must have needed it." Ed hands Georgie a black helmet. "This is like a reverse *Pretty Woman*," he says, laughing.

"Really?" Georgie raises her eyebrows and pulls the helmet over her face.

Ed's broad grin is squashed in the confines of his own helmet. "Yeah, the *poor* fella taking the rich woman out to shop for casual clothes." Georgie opens her mouth to protest but Ed turns his back to her and revs the engine. "Hop on," he says, raising his voice above the engine sound.

"Is this thing even safe?"

"Of course it is."

"I'm really not sure. Could we walk, maybe?"

"It's well over a mile to the village. It'll take us under ten minutes on the motorbike. Around half an hour if we walk."

"It's just . . ." Georgie cringes at the thought of getting onto a motorbike. The last time she sat on the back of a motorbike was more than twenty-five years ago, when she was a teenager, and that was with some lad – she can't remember his name now – who was desperate to display all sixteen years of his manliness with gravel kicked up behind them, wheelies performed on a thankfully empty street, and corners taken so fast she feared she would be swallowed up into the tarmac.

"It's safe," Ed says, reassuringly. "I'm a sensible biker, I promise."

Georgie lifts a leg over the back of the bike and wraps tense arms around his body.

"Ready?" he asks.

"As I'll ever be," Georgie says, squeezing her eyes shut and gripping tight hold of Ed's T-shirt, expecting him to whizz off down the road. Instead, it's a much gentler ride, as he navigates potholes and gravel with care. The ride is more of a tootle down to the village, a gentle breeze caressing her arms, and although she could probably let go of Ed, she keeps her hands where they are, enjoying the close physical contact, feeling his muscles flex through his faded T-shirt. Sparks of want thud with each beat of her heart. No, who's she kidding? This is a flood of unadulterated desire – and right now, she's feeling it far lower down than her heart. She blushes under her helmet and leans her body in closer to Ed. Surely, as long as she does nothing to follow through on her feelings, she can allow herself to enjoy a little private physical attraction.

In the village, which is definitely more of a small town as Lorraine said, Ed points out a couple of shops where she might find clothes more suited to the retreat, and they agree to meet up in a café in an hour.

In the first shop, Georgie scans the rails, decides there's nothing for her, and turns to walk out again, when she remembers that the whole reason she's here is to find exactly the types of clothes she normally wouldn't be seen dead in. A young woman sitting on a stool behind the counter, chewing gum with a phone in her hand, glances at Georgie, looks her up and down, and turns back to her phone, leaving Georgie to finger her way through the hangers of clothes herself.

* * *

Forty minutes and three shops later, Georgie carries an armful of bags into the café Ed suggested they meet at. She's managed to pick up one pair of jeans, a pair of shorts, four T-shirts, two blouses, a pair of trainers, some cheap plastic flip-flops, and even a hoodie, of all things. But her favourite item of clothing, if it's at all possible to have a favourite from a selection of clothes that cost less than the dress she bought from a boutique a couple of weeks ago that she's not even worn yet, is the cute pair of capri pants. Unbelievably, they only cost her twenty quid.

Ed turns up as Georgie settles herself into a seat in the window with a steaming latte.

"You found some suitable clothes, then," he says, nodding at the bags surrounding Georgie's feet. He places his helmet on the floor.

"Everything I could possibly need for the rest of the week."

"You'll feel much more comfortable."

"I'm not sure it's me who's feeling uncomfortable." Georgie grins at Ed as he wanders off to get himself a coffee.

"You're not how I imagined you'd turn out," Ed says, as he returns with his drink.

"You said that last night, but I don't believe you've even given me a passing thought until you saw me here at Pinewoods."

He laughs. "Maybe not. But you know what I mean. Seeing someone again after so many years brings back memories of the person you used to know."

"I guess." Georgie lifts her cup to her mouth, and pauses. "In that case, you're nothing like I'd have expected either. I mean, you were the biggest geek in the class. How come you're not working on computers?"

"There's still a geek inside here," Ed says, laughing, resting a hand on his heart. "I did a computer science degree. Got bored. I was coding from when I was twelve. Realised there's more to life than being a full-on nerd." He laughs again, shaking his head. "So I became a dorky drifter."

"Tell me more. I'd love to hear about life as a dorky drifter."

"Not a lot to tell." Ed shrugs. "Drifted around New Zealand

and then Australia after I finished my degree. Spent a couple of years in Bali doing computer work. Still do a bit of remote working stuff, like app development, website design. Which reminds me, I need to talk to Lorraine about her website."

Georgie chews the inside of her cheek to stop herself from telling Ed not to bother – Pinewoods won't be needing its website soon. "How did you get into yoga from website design?"

"When I went to New Zealand, someone at a hostel I was staying in was going to hot yoga classes. She said it was a great way to build core strength, so I gave it a try. And you know what us nerds can be like." He shrugs and playfully raises his eyebrows. "I'm ADHD, and when I get into something I hyper-focus. Have to know everything about it. I went to yoga classes, researched everything I could find about yoga and the body, became more mindful, built up whole-body strength, got into gratitude. It was . . ." he hunts for a word, "enlightening. No, well yes, it is enlightening, but that's not the word I was searching for – enriching, that's it. It's like yoga found me."

"And you decided to teach it?"

"Yeah, went to India for three months some years back," Ed goes on. "Did my yoga teacher training. Been travelling around again for a bit since then, teaching yoga in places like Portugal and Italy, came back to the UK, and," he takes a sip of his coffee, "after a bit of mooching around, I came across Pinewoods Retreat. Lorraine needed a new yoga teacher at the same time that I needed a job. Perfect timing. I'm loving it. Have a laugh shacking up in Hunter's caravan with him. Yeah, that's about it, really."

As he rests his cup back in its saucer, his fingers graze across the back of Georgie's hand. Her breath catches in her throat. "But what's your career?" She looks down at her coffee and clears her throat.

"Career? I'm not one of those corporate types, surely you've worked that out. Live a free life, that's my motto. I like being able to move on whenever I'm ready."

"You don't want to put down roots? Find yourself a nice woman, have a family, settle down?"

Ed shakes his head slowly. "I've had great relationships with a few really wonderful women. Stay in touch with most of them, too. No particular desire for a lifetime commitment."

His green eyes are piercing. Georgie wonders if she ever noticed his eyes when they were at school. "You'll never make much money as a yoga teacher," she says.

"I make enough to get by."

"Imagine if you were the one running the yoga centre, though."

"Yeah? Then what?" Ed grins and leans in closer, his face so close Georgie can feel his breath on her lips.

"You could employ a load of yoga teachers," Georgie says, leaning back in her chair, not daring to stay so close to him. "Have classes on all day long and into the evening, use your profits to open more yoga centres."

"And what would I do when I've got all these people running yoga classes for me?"

"Well, you build the business up to a point where you can sell it for big money, and then take yourself off on amazing holidays, chill, take it easy, have a good time, and never worry about anything in life again."

"So pretty much the life I have now, then." He throws his head back as he laughs.

"Except that you'll be rich and successful." Georgie is surprised at Ed's light-heartedness.

Ed shrugs. "I'm happy with the success of my life, and honestly, I've no idea what I'd do with a load of money."

"Really?" Georgie resists the urge to cross her arms, in defence of her own lifestyle choices. "I don't believe you."

"Of course not. You're loaded."

Georgie picks up a sachet of sugar and taps it on the table, turns it up the other way and taps it again. She wasn't always loaded, but admittedly, making money became an obsession for her well before she'd left school, long before she met Ryan. There's something about spending a cold night on a park bench that seeps into your bones and changes you.

* * *

When her dad walked out on her and her mum, a week after Georgie started at high school, it didn't take long for Dot to fall behind on the rent on her meagre wages as a cleaner. At the start of December, the landlord threw them out without warning, tossing Dot's tiny Christmas tree into the street behind them. They were homeless for less than a week before the council found them a damp and dingy flat, but that memory of sleeping on a park bench on their first night with nowhere to go, followed by sleeping on a friend's sofa for a few nights, is chiselled into Georgie's mind. And then there was the embarrassment of Dot being caught shoplifting a loaf of bread and a tin of spam from the local supermarket, and her court case being reported in the *Liverpool Standard News*. Thankfully nobody in school mentioned it, but for weeks Georgie lived with the fear that someone would call her out on it. The fear of the possibility of humiliation never left her.

At fourteen, as soon as she was old enough to get a job, Georgie worked alongside her mum, cleaning local offices to help make ends meet. It didn't take her long to find out how dirty people could be at work, with coffee granules scattered across the counter top, tea bags left in the sink, mugs stained from not being washed between cuppas, spilt milk left in puddles on the floor, and dishes piled up in the sink from lunch. But the toilets were the worst, a job that her mum told her was always given to the newest recruit to find out what they're made of. Georgie soon proved her worth, unblocking sinks and loos, scrubbing tiles and mopping floors until they shone.

The shift started at four in the afternoon every week day, and Georgie dashed out of school the second the bell rang at the end of class, earning her the mercifully harmless nickname of Gee-Gee Macrae. As soon as they got home at eight thirty, Dot made tea whilst Georgie got her head down and did what she could of her homework. Even though she knew she was as clever as some of the other kids in her class, with insufficient time in the evenings to apply herself, Georgie's grades seldom showed the teachers what she was capable of. None of that mattered to Georgie, though, because her sole focus was to earn her keep and help her mum. There was no way they were spending another night sleeping on a park bench or someone else's sofa ever again, and as long as Georgie could bring in another wage, it meant that there was no reason for Dot to shoplift. If cleaning offices with her mum was the only way to keep a roof over their heads, she'd take sarcastic comments from the less understanding of her teachers about her incomplete homework.

* * *

Ed takes another sip from his coffee cup. He smiles, showing perfectly aligned white teeth. "Go on, then," he says, tilting his head. "Your turn. What do you do?"

Georgie looks out of the window and watches as a woman stoops to pick up her toy poodle before crossing the road. "Ryan and I are into urban regeneration, and I help small businesses and women who need their first break in life – you know, to get their foot on the first rung of the ladder."

"Management consultant? Lawyer? Venture capitalist. Yeah, I reckon that's it – you're a venture capitalist."

Georgie shakes her head, wrapping her fingers around her latte. "Not exactly."

"What exactly, then?" Ed lifts his coffee to his lips, his hand gently touching hers in a move that Georgie is convinced is purposeful.

She quivers at his touch. "Are you always this intrusive?"

"Hey, a moment ago you were throwing questions my way."

He locks eyes with Georgie and leans in closer to her. "Are you always this cagey?" His voice is low and quiet.

Georgie wrinkles her nose. "Yes, I suppose I am."

"OK," he says, laughing. "At least it's not personal to me, then. So, this is my guess: You're a successful businesswoman; married to the man of your dreams though maybe he's not exactly Mr Wonderful; no kids, cos there's no way you'd wear silk if you had greasy fingers around the house; you've more money than you know what to do with; and," he tilts his head, gentle eyes fixed on hers, "you've popped a few miles down the road to get a break from something that's going on in your life."

Georgie watches him watching her. Warmth rushes through her. She wants him to touch her, wants his fingers to glide across her body, pull her in close to him . . . *Stop it, Georgie, just stop it!* Her breath catches in her throat.

Ed puts his cup back onto its saucer. "You know, now I've said that out loud, it just doesn't stack up," he goes on.

He's right, of course. It's so bloody obvious that her story is fabricated. There's so many holes in it – her clothes, her attitude, the fact she can afford to stay somewhere far fancier than Pinewoods Retreat could ever hope to be under Lorraine's stewardship. "Well, I – it seemed like a good idea to take a break somewhere . . . a bit different." Georgie rests her elbows on the table. She needs to get the conversation away from her staying at Pinewoods. "What's this, then?"

"What's what?"

"This – the flirting, the glances, the touches. For a loner who likes to live a free life, you're coming across . . . hmmm, a bit strong." With a hint of a smile on her lips, Georgie slowly lowers her eyes, then looks back up at him, confident in the effect she has on men.

"Ah, *this*." Ed cradles his coffee cup. He looks down at the table. Georgie sighs and mirrors Ed by lacing her hands around her cup. "*This* is both of us, you know. It takes a pair to pas de deux." Laughter lines radiate from his eyes. "You're beautiful, Georgie." He leans back in his chair, as if giving himself the opportunity to fully take her in.

For a few seconds, the coffee machine in the café is silent. There isn't even a whisper. Ed must surely be able to hear the quickening of her heart. "I – I . . ." Shit, what's the matter with her? Usually when people comment on her looks she says a simple, polite *thank you*. But right now, her mouth won't form any words.

"You've caged yourself up for too long, Georgie. I think you're ready to let yourself go."

Georgie squeezes her eyes shut and an image of herself in a cage flashes through her mind, like the paintings in a book she had as a child of Hansel and Gretel, caged by the witch. "Maybe," she whispers back, "yes."

"Hey, look, I need to go to the loo before we head back." Ed pushes his chair back and stands. "Don't go anywhere." He grins. Georgie watches him as he walks to the back of the café, amazed at how quickly he changed tack. He did come on to her, right? She wasn't imagining it?

A rapid rap on the window makes Georgie jump. She turns and

sees her best friend, Carla, who waves as she turns towards the door to the café. *What the...?*

"Shit," Georgie says under her breath, as heat floods over her. What the heck is Carla doing in Formby? How much of the staring into Ed's eyes has she seen? Georgie's heart sinks. What a fool she's been to sit in the window. She's not even told Carla about this project, so she'll have no idea what Georgie is up to, and there's no room for a slip-up.

"Who's that handsome fella you were talking to?" Carla asks as she approaches Georgie's table.

Georgie stands, air kisses Carla, and clears her throat. "Ed Dixon. We were in the same class at school. We bumped into each other. He teaches yoga near here."

"Cute," Carla says, looking to the back of the café, as if she's waiting for him to return.

"What are you doing here? Formby's hardly one of your usual haunts."

"Oh, god." Carla rolls her eyes. "Can you believe it? I promised one of the mums from the PTA that I'd pick something up for her – before she told me it was all the way out in the sticks." Carla's cacophonous laughter carries across the café. "And what about you? Is Formby the place you chose for a secret assignation with your man?" She nods to the back of the café in the direction of the loos and guffaws again.

Georgie checks to see if Ed is on his way back, and seeing that the coast is still clear, she leans in close to Carla. "I'm here doing some work for QuinnEssentials," she says, her voice low and hurried, "and a project we're working on for Mick Rodgers. I could really do with you not blowing my cover." Georgie's heart thuds.

"How exciting. Secret Agent Georgie Quinn." She laughs again, and the heads of other coffee drinkers at a nearby table turn to look at them.

"Please, Carla, help me out here." Georgie wants to add *'and don't tell Ryan what you saw'*, but daren't raise her friend's suspicions.

Carla taps the side of her nose. "Don't you worry, Georgie, I know when to keep schtum. Tell me all about it at the award ceremony. Can't wait to cheer for you. Liverpool Businesswoman of the Year! You deserve it, darling. Proud of you. Must dash. Toodles." Carla barely pauses for breath. She leans in to air kiss Georgie goodbye, and in typical Carla fashion, exits the café at breakneck speed, bumping into an elderly woman as she goes.

"Friend of yours?" Ed asks, coming alongside Georgie as she stares out of the window.

"Uh-huh," Georgie says. "Kind of. Business associate." She doesn't even know why she's lying to Ed about the woman who is the closest thing she has to a best friend.

"Funny you bumped into her here."

"Funnier still that I bumped into *you* at Pinewoods Retreat," Georgie says, picking up her helmet and shopping bags. "Ready?"

"Ready." Ed retrieves his own helmet and holds the café door open for Georgie.

13

LORRAINE

COOKIES are cooling on the rack in the kitchen, and the air is filled with a heady mix of chocolate, baking bread and roasting vegetables.

"You watch," Dee says to Morgan. "Hunter will be in within minutes to pinch himself a cookie or two. He's got a sixth sense for when I get them out the oven."

"He's a little imp, isn't he?" Morgan says, laughing.

"Imp is not a word I associate with Hunter," Lorraine says, laughing along with Morgan. "Dee always bakes more than we need because she knows what he's like." Her words are full of love. "And besides, he does so much for us, well and truly over and above what we pay him for. How can we resent him a couple of cookies each day?"

"True." Morgan opens her mouth to carry on talking but stops, picking up her mug instead and taking a sip of her tea.

"Go on, Morgan," Lorraine says. "What were you going to say?"

"Look, it's none of my business, but I do wonder where your heads are at right now. I keep hearing you both talking about how slow things are here at Pinewoods Retreat, and I can tell you're worrying yourselves sick about staying afloat." She pauses, nursing her mug between her hands. "I don't know that I've ever heard such a lot of negativity from you both, and it worries me."

"We're exhausted, Morgan," Dee says, letting out a long sigh. "I work flat out, we both do. It's all go. And before you say it, we can't afford to pay anyone to help out. Holly doesn't even get much for the extras she does selling at the farmers' markets with me."

"You know she's talking about getting a regular stall at Ormskirk Market to help us out?" Lorraine cradles her mug close to her chest. "Selling plants and seeds from the kitchen garden."

"She can't be taking on any more work."

"But Lorraine said that Holly's talking about it," Morgan says. "That sounds to me like she *wants* to help."

"They all do," Lorraine says. "Hunter's such a darling. He's always offering to do odd jobs, but as well as being on staff to do personal training with our guests, he's got his clients from the village, and then there's the bootcamp he runs. When he's not doing his personal training, he does other stuff to help out, but honestly, he really can't do anything else because he also needs time off. I won't ask him to do more for Pinewoods." Lorraine's tone is firm, and she adds a nod to punctuate her words.

"Again," Morgan says, "it sounds to me like he's offering to help without you even having to ask. And we both know you'd say that to someone else if you were supporting them."

Lorraine takes a sip of her tea. "I know." She smiles ruefully.

"You've said it to me many times in our friendship. Remember when I wouldn't accept any help at all when you found out I lost my job? All you kept saying to me was that you had the means to help me, and I'd get the chance to help you back one day."

"Oh yes, I remember. I had to force you to take food parcels, even when it was leftover food from Dee's restaurant that would have been binned if we'd not given it to you. You were so stubborn, Morgan." Lorraine smiles at the memories of how pig-headed Morgan could be in those days when times were hard for her.

"And who's being stubborn now?" Morgan winks.

"But Hunter, Ed, Holly . . . they're all doing far more than we pay them for as it is, and I won't ask them to do more. They need their rest."

"What are you going to do then?" Morgan looks from Lorraine to Dee and back again.

"There's not a lot we can do, Mor." Lorraine lowers her head to the kitchen table and rests her forehead there for a moment. "We're stuffed unless I can find a way to get those repairs done to the roof."

"What repairs to the roof?" Dee asks.

Lorraine looks away from Dee, not daring to meet her gaze. "We've got a little bit of a leak. It's OK, I'm sorting it."

"You should have told me, Raine. What else are you keeping from me?"

Tears prick at Lorraine's eyes. She should have told Dee, and she meant to – at some point, anyway.

"Well, if things don't pick up, we've not got enough money to stay afloat," Lorraine says, her voice almost a whisper. "And based on the bookings we've got over the coming weeks, I'm not sure things will pick up."

Dee covers her mouth with her hand. This is exactly why she's not told Dee. She hates to see her worry like this. "What will we do?" Dee asks, an emotional squeak in her voice.

Morgan stands up from her chair and walks over to the window, looking out across the kitchen garden. "OK, so let's consider your options. Bank loan?"

"It's difficult, with Dee having been bankrupted with her last business," Lorraine says. "And we can't afford the repayments on top of the increased mortgage."

"What about insurance for the roof?"

Lorraine blanches.

"You have insurance," Morgan says, reassuringly.

"We did." Lorraine struggles to meet her friend's eyes. "It was due for renewal back in March and I didn't have enough money to pay it, so Dee and I decided we could get by for a few months."

"Ah." Morgan chews on her top lip.

"There was nothing wrong with the roof when we made that decision. Nothing. Then we had that storm over Easter, and then the second storm over the spring bank holiday weekend, and that's when the problems started."

For a moment, none of them says anything.

"Like I said," Morgan tilts her head, her face full of concern, "you two have a downer on yourselves, and on this place. Where are your energies at right now? What can we do to manifest the success you need? You've *always* manifested everything you needed."

Lorraine shakes her head. "I'm so tired, I'm all out of manifesting energy."

"We can't positively think ourselves out of this mess," Dee says, a slight edge to her voice. "We can't positively think up a drop in the mortgage or the cost of gas and electric. And seemingly," she glances at Lorraine, "we can't manifest customers to bring in the money to pay for roof repairs."

"Look, you two are always so positive. Even when things have gone wrong in the past, you've always looked for a positive reframe. And I'm getting none of that from you now."

Dee yawns. "There's nothing left in the tank to reframe with."

"Then I really do wish you'd let me help you with your finances."

"I can't take money from you, Morgan," Lorraine says. "I won't do that to you. I don't know if we'll ever be able to pay you back, and then we'll be dragging you down with us."

"And then," Dee says, "I'd feel like I have to work even harder so that we can pay you back."

"This is me saying thank you for the help you've given me in the past," Morgan presses. "But if you insisted on paying me back, well, I'll just come and stay for free every year." She leans her back into the kitchen worktop. "Besides, I've no one to leave my money to. I want to help."

Lorraine sighs. "It's incredibly kind of you, Morgan. You're the most wonderful friend. But this is a business, and we have to find a way to make it work as a business. If we can't make it work, it's just an expensive hobby."

"So, back to manifesting," Morgan says.

Lorraine nods. "We have been." Her voice is almost a whisper. "And for once, it seems we've failed."

"Have you included yourselves in your intentions? Or have you worded it purely about Pinewoods?"

Dee looks at Lorraine. "She's right. We keep saying *Pinewoods finds a way to survive*. We need to reword our intention to manifest a positive outcome with us in it."

"Ownership," Lorraine says, letting out a short, wry laugh. "We always go on to others to make sure they include themselves in their manifesting, that they own their intentions." She sighs. "God, how stupid of us. Let's just hope it's not too late to manifest something positive out of all this mess."

"We'll find a way, Raine," Dee says, rubbing her tired eyes. "We *were* doing fine, you know, Morgan." She sighs. "Lorraine's right. We have to find a way to make this work, or we'll have to close Pinewoods Retreat for good."

14
GEORGIE

THE aromas of lunch greet Georgie as she skips back into Pinewoods swinging her shopping bags, still exhilarated from the ride on the back of Ed's motorbike, albeit a leisurely, safe one. Her mouth waters at the thought of Dee's cooking, her tastebuds ready for whatever scrumptious creation is put in front of her today. There's something magical about the food here that is beyond delicious. It beats all those Michelin-starred restaurants that she frequents with Ryan. And it's not only the savoury food. Georgie isn't generally someone who gives in to the temptations of cakes and biscuits. It's one of the ways she's able to keep her figure so trim. But Dee does something special with the flavours in everything she makes, so much so it makes up for some of the less good bits about Pinewoods Retreat, such as the lack of an en-suite, the shabbiness of her room, the relaxed way that everything works – like taking meals in the kitchen because there are so few guests.

Georgie runs up the stairs with a lightness in her step to unpack her bags and get changed before lunch. In her room, she immediately pulls out the capri pants she loves and puts them on, along with a cute little button-up blouse. She studies herself in the mirror, and wonders what Ed will think of her new outfit.

She turns from side to side, smoothing her hands over her hips, relishing the thought of being attractive to another man. No, that's not it; she's always attractive to other men, she sees it in the way they ogle her. What's exciting with Ed is that she's enjoying being attractive – and to being attracted to him, too. Her skin tingles. There's that spark of want again.

She shakes her head. *Stop it, Georgie. No need to descend to Ryan's level.* Goodness, how many times has she said that to herself in the last couple of days?

Her phone pings as she unpacks the rest of her shopping. It's a WhatsApp from Carla, which is no surprise, as that woman loves to be in the know. Georgie smiles, sure that Carla will have been itching to message for the whole of her drive home from Formby to Blundellsands.

Carla: *Hey you*

Gee: *Hey yourself*

Carla: *Spill*

Gee: *Not much to spill*

Carla: *What's this secret mission you're on? And why does it need to be secret?*

Gee: *Can't say yet*

Carla: *You can tell me*

Gee: *Can't. That's how secrets work. Haha*

Carla: *Ahhhh*

Gee: *Will fill you in when I see you*

Carla: *And the cute guy?*

Gee: *Told you, old school friend*

Carla: *And?*

Gee: *And nothing. Bumped into him. Had coffee. Back to work*

And nothing . . . Georgie looks at herself again in the mirror. Does she really mean that? She buzzes at the mere thought of Ed. But it has to be nothing. She can't behave like Ryan. She won't. Distracting herself, Georgie calls her mum.

"Hello, honey," Dot says, her voice cheery. "Everything OK?"

"Hi, Mum. Yes, all good. This few days away is doing me a little bit of good. Bumped into one of the kids from school, a lad called Ed Dixon."

"I remember him. I cleaned for his mum for a bit when she had a few women's troubles."

Georgie laughs. "You crack me up, Mum. It's like you're still back in the eighties; can't possibly say what's actually wrong with a woman."

"I never knew what was wrong with her. We didn't talk about those kinds of things in my time, not like the young 'uns today. She had an operation of some kind, that's all I can remember. Might have been a hysterectomy, with her needing me for three months. Got to know her quite well, and saw that lad of hers a good few times. He was one of those brainy kids, wasn't he? What's he up to now?"

"Teaches yoga at this place I'm staying at."

"Yoga?"

"Yes, Mum. I was surprised, too." Georgie laughs again.

"Well, listening to how chilled you sound, honey, I reckon the yoga is doing you some good. Not heard you sound this relaxed in donkeys years! And there's none of that sadness you've had in your voice since Mr Big died."

Mr Big – Georgie realises she's not even thought of her poor old dog today, and a pang of guilt momentarily waves over her.

"I do feel a little more relaxed. Maybe this place is helping me to get over Mr Big dying."

"And you've got the award ceremony coming up. Can't wait, Georgie. So proud of you."

"You keep saying, Mum." Despite rolling her eyes, Georgie's heart swells. Making her mum proud is the best feeling in the world to her.

"And I'll keep on saying. A mother's allowed to be proud of her daughter, but especially me. I mean, look at everything you have achieved. From nothing to Liverpool's Woman of the Year."

"Businesswoman, Mum. I'm not getting the keys to the city or anything like that." Georgie smiles to herself. Dot has yet to grasp that it's a business award. "Look, I've got to go, it's coming up to lunchtime. Just wanted to check in and let you know I'm doing OK. I'll call you again in a couple of days."

Georgie makes her way to the kitchen where Ed is already sitting at the large table in the middle of the room. Dee has her back to him as he talks, animatedly, about someone he bumped into in the village when he was on his way to meet up with Georgie.

"Hey," he says, as Georgie takes the seat next to him.

Dee glances over her shoulder. "You're back," she says, returning to her cooking.

"I'm back." Georgie smiles at Ed and soaks him in again.

Handsome, in a cheeky, urban, dishevelled way, the total opposite of Ryan. *And those tender, plump, soft lips, so kissable.* Another way he's different from Ryan, though Ry's got the classic cupid's bow lip of the Irish. She imagines running her finger over them, leaning in and kissing Ed, stroking the back of his neck, pulling him in to her...

"I hope," Dee says, bringing Georgie out of her daydream with a bolt, her back mercifully to them both, "Ed didn't drive too fast with you on the back of his motorbike."

"He was very careful, Dee. And he pointed me in the right direction to get everything I needed."

"Glad to hear it."

Georgie tells Dee which shops she visited, what she bought, and gives Dee a twirl of her capri-pants-and-blouse combo. Ed joins in with chatter about the jobs he did, all the while his eyes fixed on Georgie. A gentle smile spreads across his face, revealing a dimple in each cheek.

Georgie catches herself. She's staring into his eyes. "What have you been up to, Dee?" she asks, walking over to the range where Dee is working.

"The usual. I stand guard at this range pretty much the whole day, making meals that excite the taste buds." She nods at Georgie and grins. "And I love every minute of it."

As Dee natters on about food and combining flavours, Georgie's mind wanders to her feelings. It's not like she hasn't had offers for affairs in the past, but she's always prided herself on staying true to her marriage vows. So why is she reacting to Ed's obvious flirtation? There's nothing she can gain from it, and she doubts he'd be bothered if she did, anyway. But she can't deny she has feelings for Ed. She steals a glance over at him. These feelings are the most real she's had since she started dating Ryan, all those years ago.

"Georgie? Would you mind?" Dee is staring at her, and Georgie realises she hasn't the faintest idea what Dee has said to her.

"Sorry, I lost myself in thought for a moment." Georgie feels an unfamiliar blush rise up her neck.

"Can I just get into the plate warmer behind you? I'm ready to plate up."

"Oh, gosh, yes, so sorry." Georgie steps away from the range and spots Beth standing in the doorway looking at her. How long has she been standing there? Beth winks at her and walks into the room, followed by Kate, and takes a seat on one side of Ed, leaving the chair on his other side free. Georgie watches as Kate sits next to Beth, as if glued to her sister's side.

Gradually, the mix of guests and staff descend on the kitchen table, Dee serving food whilst telling everyone to take a seat. Georgie holds back. She has messed up. Beth has seen her watching Ed, and that wink has to mean she knows how Georgie is feeling. She can't afford any more slip ups. When everyone is seated, Georgie takes the one remaining chair, nearest to the kitchen door.

Part way through the meal, Beth's phone rings and she glances at it.

"Sorry, this is one person I promised could contact me during my stay. Won't be a mo." She pushes her chair back and walks into the hall, leaving the door ajar. "No, no," Beth says from outside, her voice slightly muffled. "The settlement has been agreed. If he wants a smooth divorce, he sticks to the agreement." Georgie pricks up her ears, keen to get a little insight into Beth. "Right, I'll get my paralegal to send over the final documents for signing, but your client has to get them signed in the next twenty-four hours or things are likely to get messy." For a moment, there's a lull in the conversation in the kitchen, the only sound being the scrape of cutlery on plates, Beth's words filling the silence. Kate coughs and then clears her throat, as if attempting to cover up her sister's conversation.

"No, no, can't be helped." Beth can still be heard from the hallway. There's a pause before she reappears. "Work," she says, by way of explanation as she takes her seat and stuffs a forkful of food into her mouth. There's an air of confidence about her that Georgie hasn't particularly tuned into until now, as if momentarily returning to work-mode brings out an inner strength in her.

"Divorce lawyer?" Georgie asks.

"Mm-huh," Beth mumbles through her full mouth.

"Didn't mean to eavesdrop," Georgie says, "but you left the door open."

"Sorry, yeah, I don't like taking work on holiday with me, but this has been a particularly difficult mediation, and the guy was asking for more. He's a cheater, doesn't deserve more. So many of the husbands that my clients have think they can do what they like and then take the wife to the cleaners."

"You mainly represent women, then?"

"Solely. It's been my mission since my own messy divorce, seven years ago, to only work on behalf of women who've been shafted by a husband who cheats on the wife and still wants more than his half of the marital home. Women like that deserve to have someone looking out for them. That's where I come in."

"Good on you, Beth. I admire you for standing by your principles." There's more to Beth than Georgie has assumed, and the revelation impresses her.

Beth beams back at Georgie. "Thank you. I'm here for every wife who has been badly treated by her husband." She holds Georgie's gaze, and Georgie finds herself struggling not to look away.

"Great," Georgie says. "Dee, any more of these lentil balls? They're incredible."

15

GEORGIE

AFTER lunch, Georgie returns to her room, feeling a desperate need for some alone time. She snuggles into the shabby chair in the corner of her room, bringing her feet under her, and leans her head back. With sleepy eyes, Georgie looks at the tops of the trees through her bedroom window and mulls over her years with Ryan. What's going wrong between them? Things *worked*, right from the start. It was like they were made to be together. He was good to her. More than that. He rescued her – and her mum, too. Dot would still be wallowing in a damp council flat if it hadn't been for Ryan.

And all because of a moment of luck, when Georgie overheard a conversation by the lifts of Ryan's dad's building. People ignore cleaners in offices. It's like they don't exist. One evening, when Georgie was mopping the tiled floor in the reception area, three men pressed the button for the lift. And as they waited they talked in hushed tones, though not so quiet that Georgie couldn't hear. They discussed the meeting they'd just had with Ryan, and one mentioned how easily they could screw him over. As they stepped into the lift, they laughed and patted each other on the back. The lift doors closed, and Georgie made her way to Ryan's office, mop in hand.

"Those men," she said, nervously dancing from one foot to the other as she stood at the door.

Ryan slowly looked up from the paperwork in front of him. "Hiya." He smiled at Georgie. "Not seen you about before."

Georgie wanted to say '*no, nobody sees the cleaner*', but she kept silent on that. "Those men." She thumbed over her shoulder. "They were in a meeting with you?"

Ryan nodded. "They were." He leant back in his executive office chair and let it take his weight as it tilted away from the desk.

"You can't trust them." Georgie's heart pounded. She'd never talked to the boss's son before. She'd never talked to anyone in management.

"Is that so?"

"They're planning to screw you over."

"Oh yeah? And how do you know that?"

Georgie relayed what she'd heard at the lifts. Ryan stood up from his chair, leaving it swinging behind him as he walked over to her. "You sure about that?"

Georgie nodded. "Yeah, I heard them. They think they've got one over on you. You need to work out how to get one over on them." Her cheeks burned.

Ryan invited her to sit down, and as he leant against his desk he took in everything that she said. He quizzed her, shared with her what happened in the meeting, asked her opinion. When they'd finished, he threw his head back and laughed. "Can't believe I'm taking business advice off the bloody cleaner." He rubbed a hand over his eyes. "You're the first person to talk sense around me in months. Are you doing a business degree or something? One of those MBA things?"

Georgie shook her head. "Me? Get over yerself." She swallowed a laugh. "I'm just a cleaner."

"Nah, I don't buy it. You're more than that."

"Left school last year. I'm doing a BTec at college. The rest of the time, I work as a cleaner. Early mornings and then this evening shift what I'm on now."

Ryan slowly nodded his head. "You've got your head screwed on, you have."

It wasn't long after that conversation that Ryan offered Georgie a junior admin job in his team, and a few months after that he promoted her to be his executive assistant. Ryan asked her to meet people for him, talked business ideas through with her, got her to research potential business associates and clients, and had her pulling together reports. He soon trusted Georgie implicitly, and she worked long hours to prove her worth to him.

"You wanna watch him," Dot said one evening over tea, worrying for her daughter. "Men like 'im only want one thing."

"Don't be daft, Mum. It's nothing like that."

Dot let out a rueful laugh. "You don't know men, yet, my girl. Mind my word, is all I'll say."

As time went on, and Georgie brought home good money each week, enough that they no longer lived hand-to-mouth whilst paying for things on the never-never, Dot warmed to Ryan. With each promotion, Georgie brought home more money and paid off her mum's debts. It was never enough to change their lives, but Georgie was grateful that being noticed by Ryan, and him believing in her, meant that she could help her mum.

Within a year, Ryan and Georgie started dating, and another year on they were married. Ryan's dad paid for the lavish wedding, which both Dot and Georgie were hugely grateful for, as the best their budget could have stretched to would have been a buffet in the Social Club in Huyton. One of Ryan's wedding gifts to Georgie was a small, terraced house for Dot that he allowed her to live in rent free. The house was a dump when he bought it, but he had some lads from his dad's building business do it up exactly how Dot wanted, with all mod-cons and not an inch of damp or black mould. In a little over two years, Georgie went from the hard graft of cleaning offices to enjoying an unimaginable lifestyle, and before long, Ryan helped Dot set up a little cleaning business, which he then used for all the offices that him and his dad owned. Georgie was eternally grateful to Ryan for his generosity and kindness.

Life with Ryan was filled with dinners and events, and Georgie always went with him, proud to be by his side as he talked business with Liverpool's bigwigs.

"Here," Ryan would say, handing over a bunch of money whenever they had an event to go to, "go buy yourself something nice."

"I've got nice clothes," Georgie said, pushing his fist full of fifties away the first time he made the offer.

"Have you seen the state of yourself, babe? Your second-hand clothes have a pretty unique smell to them, and your shoes are scuffed. Buy yourself something new."

Still Georgie refused, but when the two of them turned up at the restaurant that night and she saw the dresses and shoes and incredible jewellery the other women wore, she knew she needed a new wardrobe – one that fitted in with the people she was expected to mix with. Ryan's money rescued Georgie from making a series of faux pas with her charity shop finds of second-hand brands that she'd previously been so proud of.

This whole new way of life, being taken to events at posh venues, having things bought for her, receiving a monthly allowance, all felt like a fair exchange to Georgie. Ryan brought the money, along with a generous spirit, and Georgie brought an insight borne out of business naivety that complemented his experience. She had a total lack of fear when it came to the questions that nobody else around Ryan would ask, and she played on her attractive, youthful looks to get men explaining things to her in such detail that she could trip them up when it came to business deals. Over time, Ryan trusted her with more and more involvement in the business, valuing her input, and eventually they set up QuinnEssentials in partnership to give them a venture of their own.

Georgie also set up her own independent business, picking up on her own embarrassment at not owning the right clothes to fit in. Ryan still occasionally teased her about the outfit she wore for her first day at work with him when she was seventeen – an old school skirt that was shiny across her backside, and a blouse of her mum's that was at least two sizes too big and ten years out of date. She didn't want other young women to experience the same discomfort at not having suitable interview attire, and so she set up LivSmarter, an interview preparation consultancy for disadvantaged and vulnerable young women in Liverpool. Her and her team find outfits that suit their clients, and train them in how to behave in the jobs market, with mock interviews and coaching.

Many of those she supported in the early days when they were in their late teens are now over thirty and either sponsor the women in need, or are part of her coaching team, spreading the kindness and goodwill. There hasn't been a day since she established LivSmarter that she's not been proud of the work she's done, and the multitude of local women she's helped. And, best of all, it gives her an income of her own, separate from Ryan, who never showed the slightest bit of interest for her 'pin-money project', as he likes to call it.

As time went on, Ryan and Georgie's reputations grew in Liverpool for urban regeneration, and they got a name for supporting women and young people in setting up small businesses, whilst also making significant contributions to local charities. They became local 'royalty' – Georgie regularly photographed in designer clothes and Boodles bling, looking adoringly into her handsome husband's eyes. It's a life she could never have dreamt up for herself, and she could not be more thankful for Ryan's belief in her.

Ryan's first affair was when they'd been married for about five years – or at least, that was the first one that Georgie knew of. She didn't dare say anything about the first couple of women, because everything she luxuriated in belonged to Ryan, including her mum's home, and she wasn't ready to give any of that up. Besides, she's always felt that he's easy to forgive. Georgie loves Ryan, he's good to her, and to Dot, too – generous with his money and gifts, and kind to them both. His dalliances are a mere crack in her marriage that she's prepared to wallpaper over in return for all the benefits she enjoys.

When Georgie did eventually challenge Ryan, a little over ten years into their marriage, he lied at first, and then shrugged it off, saying all the men had 'a bit on the side'.

"Hey, babe," Ryan said, "this is who I am. You've known for years what I'm like, and never said a word until now." He shrugged. "If you don't like it, that's your choice. Just remember, you'd be nothing without me. If it wasn't for me giving you a job, giving your mum a place to live, you two would be nothing. If you're not happy, you can always pack your bags and leave. Oh, and Dot'll need to hand over the keys to that house of mine. Like I say, your choice."

It hurt at first, but of course Georgie couldn't complain. Ryan was right. Despite how kind and caring he could be, he also held all the cards. He was in control. Everything was, still is, in his name – their house, her mum's house, even her car. She can't imagine her life going back to what it once was, a life of hard graft and mould-ridden rented rooms. She tolerates his behaviour, and remains grateful for the lifestyle he's built for her and Dot.

Not long after Georgie started to challenge him, Ryan settled down with just one other woman, and that affair went on for ten years. It was so much easier for Georgie than wondering who he was with, and the one thing that gave her solace was that if Ryan intended to leave her, or more realistically toss her out of his house, he wouldn't have run the two relationships alongside each other for as long as he did. She made her choice, accepted – and for the most part ignored – his infidelity, and got on with her life.

And now he's possibly – probably – doing it all over again. This time, as Georgie drifts into her afternoon snooze, she isn't so sure she even wants to deal with the cracks in their marriage. She's likely to lose everything, and that's something she has to get her head around.

16

LORRAINE

PLACING a piece of cake in front of San, Lorraine takes a seat next to her in the garden café.

"I admit it," Lorraine says, grinning at San, "this is shameless bribery."

"You don't need to bribe me to help you." San tucks one side of her jet black bob behind her ear and smiles back at Lorraine.

"You're off the clock, and the last thing you need on your day off is for me to barge in on your coffee date with Holly to quiz you about marketing. I really appreciate you saying you'll help."

San pushes her fork into the cake and takes a delicate bite. "Mmmm, oh, with Dee's cakes, you can bribe me anytime, Lorraine."

Lorraine smiles at their friend. San originally came to Pinewoods Retreat a little over a year ago as part of a marketing drive. She was one of a group of journalists who came to stay at the retreat for free, in return for a write-up about their experience staying at Pinewoods. She quickly struck up a friendship with Holly, who was staying as a guest, and has become a frequent day-visitor to the retreat since. Her article in the *Liverpool Standard News* did a lot to bring in custom for many weeks after it was published, and Lorraine hopes that San can offer her advice on how to do something similar to bring people their way now.

"Here we go," Holly says, returning to the table with a tray of coffees. "I can leave you two to it, if you like. San and I can catch up later."

"Not at all," Lorraine says. "Stay. You're a great help in these kinds of conversations. Besides, this is your catch-up with San."

San takes another bite of the cake and leans her elbows on the table. "How can I help?"

"Did Holly tell you we're up for an award in the Liverpool Business of the Year thing?"

San nods.

"It's for the café. Shame it's not for the retreat, but anything is good. And I need some help in getting the word out there. What can I do to make something of this, even if we don't win?"

"Firstly," San says, sticking her fork into the cake in front of her, "you've got the right attitude. It's not about winning, it's about being nominated. Congratulations! Are you coming to the award ceremony at St George's Hall?"

"Yes, we've been gifted some free tickets. This is such a great opportunity for us to get the word out there."

"I'll be there for the *Liverpool Standard News*. You're right, we can work out some kind of marketing strategy. And it's OK that this is about the café, you know. Get people here, and then you can market the retreat to them, too."

"I was thinking that, I just don't know how to get them here." Lorraine sighs, and looks across the lawn at the half-empty café tables. Ed walks out of the yoga yurt into the front garden, holding back the flap that acts as a door so that Kate, Beth and Georgie

137

can walk through, all looking very relaxed after their yoga session. Georgie glances over in Lorraine's direction as she walks across the grass towards the front door to Pinewoods. She smiles. And then something strange happens. Georgie looks at San, back at Lorraine, and back to San again, and immediately speeds into the house, barging straight past Kate and Beth.

"That was odd," Lorraine says. "Did you see that?"

San and Holly shake their heads.

"One of our guests clocked you, San, and hurried into the house."

"Is it someone I know?"

Lorraine shrugs. "Georgie Macrae?"

"Not a name I recognise." San leans back in her seat. "So we need to get people here."

"What?" Lorraine looks back to the front door where Georgie has disappeared, before turning back to San and Holly. "Oh, yes, the café. How do we do that?"

"I can get one of our guys at the paper to do some playing around with SEO and get that article I had published last year back up the rankings. That might help a bit."

"You'd do that for us?"

"Of course. Now, what else?" San taps her chin for a moment. "How about a chef's table kind of thing?"

"You mean like where people are invited into the kitchen for tasting sessions?" Holly asks.

"Yes, exactly that," San says, "but we can do it around tables out here in the garden if the weather is good enough. Use the takeaway trailer as the place that Dee works from, instead of back in the kitchen."

"We can do something in the kitchen garden, as well," Holly suggests. "Show them where the produce comes from, like we do with guests when they have yoga and smoothie sessions."

Lorraine rests a hand on her heart. "I do love how you are both saying 'we'. This is so good of you."

"Of course it's a 'we'." San laughs. "We're all in it together."

They chat for twenty minutes about how they can set up a chef's table, using the award nomination as leverage.

"We can use the angle of 'come and find out why the judges are putting this place on the local map', or words to that effect. I can come up with something better for you over the next few days."

"You'll have to let me pay you, San."

"Nonsense. You'll do no such thing. Besides," San licks a finger and picks up a few crumbs from her plate, "you've already paid me in cake."

17

GEORGIE

As soon as she's in the house, Georgie takes the stairs. What the heck? San Sartori is in the café at Pinewoods, chatting away to Lorraine and Holly like they're old friends. This can't be happening.

"Everything OK?" Beth calls up the stairs after her.

"Yes, fine," Georgie says, closing the door to her room. She leans her back into it, her hand still clutching tight hold of the door knob.

Her heart thudding, Georgie throws herself into the shabby chair in the corner of her room. The stress of working incognito is taking its toll on her, and right now, she feels like relaxation is a world away, despite the lovely yoga session of Ed's that she joined this afternoon. She can only hope that the Sartori woman didn't spot her as she walked across the grass, but Lorraine noticed, that was obvious – and she noticed Georgie's look as she spotted San, too.

Georgie says a silent prayer of thanks that she used Macrae as her surname, and not Quinn. There's little chance of San knowing her by her birth name, though she'd know exactly who Georgie is if she clapped eyes on her, or if she heard the name Quinn. How could San not know who she is, after having an affair with Georgie's husband for ten years?

Tears take Georgie by surprise. Never, with all the affairs that Ryan has had, has she ever allowed herself to cry. So why is she crying now? San Sartori finished it with Ryan well over a year ago. She wipes tears from her cheeks, only for more to roll over her eyelashes and replace them within seconds. *Get a grip.*

Georgie tries to take in a deep breath, only for it to get trapped in her throat, replaced by an unexpected sob. Why is she crying over San Sartori? She shakes her head, and more tears flow down her face. It's not San that's she crying over, not really. It's what she represents – Ryan's infidelity, and the fact that Georgie has lived the lie of the happy marriage for years. God, she's a fool.

There's a scraping sound at her door, and Georgie immediately recognises it as Moose. She opens the door, and there he is.

"Hey, little fella," Georgie says, crouching down to stroke the dog. Without waiting to be asked, Moose waddles into the room and, despite his short legs, takes one leap up onto the shabby chair in the corner of her room. Georgie joins him, and lets him snuggle onto her lap.

"I could never do this with Mr Big," she says, laughing. "He would have smothered me." Looking at the treetops through the window, Georgie strokes Moose, enjoying having the dog for company. "Did someone send you to spy on me, Moose?" Georgie shakes her head. No, that's not something Lorraine or Ed would do, or any of the others either. "Or did you pick up the vibe that I need the company?" She rubs around his ears, and Moose rests his head in her hand, letting out a sound that is half whine, half purr, totally in his element. "You're a good boy, Moose."

Not daring to make an appearance in the house until the coast is clear, and having no idea when it will be safe to surface, Georgie stays in her room, hoping that San Sartori leaves long before it's time for dinner. Eventually, Moose makes the decision for her, leaping off her lap and scratching her door to be let out. Georgie tentatively takes the stairs and follows Moose into the kitchen garden. There's nobody about, and for a moment Georgie is unnerved. Did San see her, after all? Is she telling them all who she actually is? Warning them to be careful around her? Blood rushes past Georgie's ears.

"Well, Moose," she says to the dog, "let's take a little walk around the vegetable beds. Might as well enjoy the garden while I can." She opens the back door and weaves her way along the gravel paths, Moose leading the way – sniffing something here, picking up a scent there – until they reach the back of the garden and the beehive. Georgie lowers herself onto the raised bed that's nearest to the hive and leans closer to the bees, as Moose settles himself across her feet.

"Do you know what San Sartori is doing here, bees?" A solitary bee exits the hole to the hive, stays there a moment, and then flies away. Georgie waits for a bee or two to return to the hive – nothing. "And here's me thinking I'd found friends amongst the bees," she says, shaking her head at the reality of being completely alone, except for a dog curled at her feet.

"Hey, Georgie."

She turns, disturbing Moose, and sees Holly walking towards her along the gravel path from the back door.

"Have you been waiting long? Do you want to do some gardening?"

"No . . . I don't know. Moose was sitting with me in my room and I thought maybe he needed to do his business. Brought him out here, and I will admit I was surprised that there's nobody here. The garden's been a hive of activity since I arrived."

"It's my afternoon off," Holly says, sitting down next to Georgie on the raised bed. "A friend of mine came over for coffee and cake."

"I saw you in the garden café." Georgie hesitates before continuing. "I – the woman, black hair – there was something familiar about her." Her heart pounds. This is the best way she can think of to find out if San said she recognised Georgie, too.

"You've probably seen her in the paper and on the regional news. She's a local reporter. San Sartori. Works for the *Liverpool Standard News*."

"Ah, right." Georgie waits for whatever comes next, crossing her fingers behind her back in the hope that San made no mention of her.

"We met here when I first arrived at Pinewoods," Holly goes on. "She was here for work to do a write up on Pinewoods, I was here on a short break. We hit it off straight away, and now she's my best friend." Holly grins at Georgie, and inwardly Georgie lets out a sigh of relief. If San did mention her, it doesn't appear to have registered with Holly as something sinister.

"That's nice," Georgie says, letting out a slow breath of relief. "So, let me get this right," she says, keeping the conversation focused on Holly. "Based on what you've told us since I arrived, you came here on holiday some time last year, found a new man, *and* a best friend, *and* you got a job?"

Holly straightens her back, puffs out her chest, and grins from ear to ear. "And a few other lovely friends too, fabulous bosses in Lorraine and Dee who are like family to me, the *best* boyfriend I could ever have asked for, and a cute new home." She nods at the low building over to her right, at the back of the garden. "Who would have thought that coming to Pinewoods Retreat could change my life in so many ways." Holly hugs herself, the grin still stretched across her face. "Pinewoods does that to you, you know, when you stay here. Weaves its magic deep into your soul and changes you." Holly leans forwards and strokes Moose. "No, that's not right, Pinewoods doesn't change you." She pauses for a moment, as if contemplating what she's saying. "What it truly does is sprinkle fairy dust over you, which helps you find who you really are so that you can change yourself if, or maybe when, you're ready to be authentically you."

Georgie fights the urge to start crying again and bends down to pick up Moose, in the hope that Holly doesn't notice the emotions that are stirring up inside her.

18

GEORGIE

Four Days to the Award Ceremony

THE phone sitting next to Georgie on the kitchen table at breakfast the next morning pings. She glances down at it to see a message from Ryan.

Ry: *Can you talk, babe?*

Ed, sitting next to her, glances down at the message and back to Georgie as she turns her phone over.

"Husband?" he asks.

She nods, as she chews on her food.

"Checking in on you?" Beth asks from across the table.

Georgie shrugs.

"God, when I was married, I had to work bloody hard to persuade my fella that it was OK for me to do anything on my own. He was such a controlling grump." Beth's laugh is hollow and a little sad. "Is your old man all right with you coming away on your own to Pinewoods? What did you tell him?" She rests her forearms on the table next to her plate, a knife in one hand and fork in the other, both pointing straight up to the ceiling, and leans forward, waiting for Georgie to answer her question.

Georgie puts her fork down on her plate, dabs the sides of her mouth with her napkin, and sighs irritably. "I regularly go away to spas and the like," she snaps. "I don't need to explain myself to my husband or," she glares pointedly at Beth, "to anyone else who might want to know the ins and outs of my private life." It's bad enough when Ryan quizzes her, despite his own expectations for freedom to go where he pleases without checking in, but having Beth quiz her is too much.

Morgan tuts and purses her lips, glaring at Georgie.

Kate's knife and fork clatter as she drops them on her plate and rests a hand on Beth's arm.

The room falls silent.

Georgie's heart plummets. She just said all of that out loud – in front of a room full of people. It's rude of her to even think it, let alone say it out loud – most unlike her.

Picking up her fork, Georgie gathers some of the tofu scramble on her plate, along with a few mushrooms, and is about to put it in her mouth when she senses eyes are on her. She glances up and catches Lorraine's eye, then Holly's and – oh God, Ed's too. Guilt envelopes her. She lowers her fork. What a bitch she is. Beth is simply trying to be friendly, and doesn't deserve to be snapped at.

"I'm sorry," Georgie sighs, looking down at her plate and then back up at Beth. "You didn't deserve that." Shame sweeps over her with the blush that covers her neck and face.

Beth shakes her head, lips pulled tight, her knife and fork frozen in time. "You're right," she says, her voice high-pitched. "It is none of my business." Beth's cheeks flush into two bright, burning blobs.

Georgie swallows hard, hating herself. She's had about three hours sleep, tossing and turning as thoughts of her marriage grumble around her head. It's not Beth's fault she didn't sleep much; it's not Beth's fault that her husband is unfaithful to her; it's not Beth's fault that San Sartori turned up out of the blue at the very place Georgie has come for an undercover project; it's not Beth's fault that she feels lost; or that she really doesn't want to do a bloody phone call with Ryan. She's allowed herself to be distracted by Ed – also not Beth's fault – so she has nothing to report. And Ryan will be impatient that she's not found out anything juicy yet – when, in reality, beyond building works that Mick Rodgers will expect anyway, there's probably never going to be anything of much interest to find out about Lorraine and Dee. They're nice people, and Ry won't want to hear that. No, none of it is Beth's fault. And yet she's behaved to her as if all of it is.

Not daring to look into the eyes of everyone around the table, Georgie slowly, deliberately moves her fork to her mouth, chews her food a few times, and swallows before saying, "Dee, this tofu is amazing. It's incredible what you do with food. I don't know what you do to make it taste so delicious. I always thought tofu was bland and disgusting. You must give me the recipe." She glances across the table at Beth. Beth is looking down at her plate, her cheeks still burning red.

Dee clears her throat. "It's all in the marinating and the seasoning," she says, her tone flat. "All foods are fairly bland if you don't put time into the prep. But there's nothing more bland than tofu if you don't put some effort in to the seasoning."

The room falls silent again.

"Well," Georgie says, carefully placing her knife and fork together and pushing her chair back, "that was a delight. Now, I've things to do, calls to make, so I'll leave you all to it." Without looking at any of the others at the table, she walks out the back door, angry with herself for her uncommonly sharp tongue. She checks that the garden is empty, despite knowing that everyone is in the kitchen, and settles herself on a bench, halfway between the house and Holly's little hut in the back corner.

Ryan picks up on the third ring. "How's it going, babe?"

"OK, I guess." Georgie's voice catches at the back of her throat, as she swallows the questions that have been crashing around her head all night. She closes her eyes. "I – er – it's a bit boring here, not a lot to do. I'm struggling to find anything major that's going to help Mick Rodgers close the place down, you know. Nothing particular about the owners."

"Nothing at all? Come on, I find that hard to believe." Ryan tuts, and Georgie imagines his exaggerated eye roll that he employs when things don't go his way.

"There's some not especially significant bits that could inconvenience them, but we already know about them, or I guess they're things we'd expect."

"Great. Spill the beans," Ryan says. "What have you found?" There's an eager anticipation in his voice, an excitement like he's on the edge of laughing.

In the background, Georgie hears a distant noise down the

phone. She knows that sound but can't place it, and something about it bothers her.

"There's not many of us booked in this week or next from what I can gather, so I don't know how well they're doing financially. But then, this could just be a quiet week in an otherwise busy period." Georgie stops. It feels unfair to be sharing information about Pinewoods Retreat with Ryan. These are good, kind people, and they don't deserve this.

She gives herself a shake. *Come on, Georgie.* She didn't come to the retreat to make friends. This is a job, and she needs to focus. Ryan expects her to dig deep, find out what she can, and report back to him, so that Mick Rodgers can buy the place at a knockdown price. Once she's back home, it's not like she's going to encounter Lorraine and the rest of them ever again.

"Considering the staff they have on payroll," Georgie continues, swallowing her guilt, "I suspect they're not doing as well as they pretend to be."

"Great, we can use that. What else?"

"Well, I suppose you could check something for me. When we looked at the satellite images, the land to the side was clear, just grass. There's a yurt on there now, and a trailer that they sell takeaway coffees and cakes from. And I think they've been in position for some time. Did these people ever get planning permission to site a yurt or a trailer at the side of the property? I should have checked in my initial research before I came away, but it didn't cross my mind that they'd have erected temporary structures."

"On it. I'll text you with an update later."

"No, don't do that. It'll show on my notifications." There it is again, that background noise.

"Switch notifications off then."

"Seriously, Ry? Just wait for me to call you. I'll get an update off you then." And then it hits her. That noise is their coffee machine at home, grinding the beans. But...

"What about their kitchen?" Ryan asks.

How is it possible for Ryan be talking to her, and have the coffee machine going off in the distance? Did he set it going to make a double shot and walk away from it? There's no echo to his voice, though, so he's not in the kitchen.

"Babe?" Ryan interrupts her thoughts.

"What?"

"The kitchen. How bad is it? Can we not get environmental health to close them down for their kitchen being filthy?"

Even though Ryan can't see her, Georgie shakes her head, her forehead furrowed. "There's not a thing wrong with the kitchen, Ry. It's immaculate," she says. "In fact, things are so clean, they even have us eating in the kitchen." Her mind flashes back to sitting around the table at breakfast, and how she spoke to Beth. She has to apologise – properly. That was unkind of her. "If I'm honest," she says, returning to the conversation with Ryan, "I'm not sure our kitchen at home is as clean as Dee keeps hers at Pinewoods Retreat." The coffee machine starts up again in the distance behind Ryan. He definitely can't be making coffee, even if he is having a double-shot espresso. The fact the machine is going off a third time means that a second cup of coffee is being made. "Have you got company, Ry?"

"What? No. Go on – any structural stuff?" He doesn't miss a beat, but he's clearly lying.

She's been married to him for over twenty years, and knows that's his way – deny what he's accused of and go straight into something else. Yes, he's lying. And that means, whoever it is he's got there in the house with him is a woman. At breakfast time. Before work. The bastard. No wonder he was keen for her to come and do the scoping out of Pinewoods. It gave him the chance to get his latest bit on the side into bed – into *her* bed. Her lip curls at the thought. She might have known. It's not like he's doing anything different from his antics of most of their marriage, but at least he usually has the decency to meet his floozies in hotels. He never brings them back to the house. At least, she *thinks* he's never done that before now.

How could he do this?

The back of Georgie's throat burns as she forces herself not to be sick. She presses the phone closer to her ear in the hope she might pick out more sounds, but all she can hear is Ryan's breathing as he waits for her to respond.

"No," she says. "There's nothing structural that I've found so far." It's her turn to lie. She's not giving him all the intel so that he can pass it on to Mick like she's an also-ran. If she tells him everything before the meeting with Mick, he'll pass it all on himself *and* take the credit for it. Besides, it's only building works at the end of the day, and Mick's going to redevelop the building, so what's the point in telling Ryan about that? Now it's obvious that he's got someone in the house, she'll keep some of the cards close to her chest. He doesn't deserve to hold the power.

She looks up at the house from where she's sitting and takes it in, her eyes gradually moving to the garden around her. A couple of bees settle onto the stamen of the flowers in the terracotta pots next to her, and she watches as they perform their dance.

"Come on, babe, you've gotta do better than this. Mick expects more. You need to find something that's too costly for them to put right. If you can do that, Mick's made. The moment he knows, he'll pounce with his lowball offer."

"I did find something when I was doing a bit of online research." A bee buzzes in front of Georgie's face, hovers there for a moment, and comes to rest on her knee. "The woman who runs the kitchen, Dee, she's been bankrupt in the past. Something to do with a string of cafés and restaurants she ran. Do you remember that place called The Pea and Pod in town?"

"Nah, never heard of it."

"Probably not your kind of thing. It was huge with the students and trendy types for a while. Anyway, that was one of her cafés. It closed down about eight years or so ago, I think." Georgie rests her hand close to the bee and lets it walk onto her finger. "Do you think bees can understand what you're saying?" she asks.

Ryan lets out a hearty laugh. "What the – are you on somethin', babe?"

"Forget it, ignore me." The bee flies off in the direction of the hive.

"What do they use this yurt thing for that you said about? Is it a glamping thing?"

"The yurt? No. The bedrooms are all in the house. The yurt's where they do all the yoga. There's this guy, Ed." A warmth spreads across Georgie's chest as she mentions Ed's name. Thank goodness they're not talking on FaceTime. "He – er, he," Georgie swallows and regains her composure, "he does yoga classes for the guests, and then he does other classes for locals and some private sessions in there too. Seems quite busy from what I can tell. He's not been here long, but looking at the yurt, I'd say that was in place well before he arrived. At least a couple of years, I'd guess, so definitely longer than the twenty-eight days the council allows for a temporary structure." Georgie glances around the garden, and Holly's hut catches her eye. "One other thing you can check is change of use. They've got some kind of structure in the garden, probably a coal shed or tool shed way back when. I remember seeing it on the satellite images. Looks like it's been done up in the last, I don't know, year or two, maybe. There's a woman living in there, one of the staff. Check if you can find anything at the council for change of use for that being turned into a dwelling. If you find a plan of the place, or look at the satellite photos, angle it as if you have your back to the house. The structure's in the top right corner of the garden, south west."

"Isn't this stuff you should have researched before you left?"

"You didn't give me much time, remember? And I did carry out the research, it's just some things are more obvious when you're on the ground." Studying the hut, Georgie is struck by how homely it looks. It perfectly suits Holly's kind nature. Suddenly, guilt at revealing things about Pinewoods twists in the pit of

Georgie's stomach. "No, you're right, forget I mentioned it. I'm sure they have that sorted."

"It's OK, babe, I'll do your job for you. I'll check it out."

"No, seriously, forget I mentioned it."

Ryan tuts. "Don't go native on me." He laughs. "It won't take much for me to dig around and find out what I can about the shed thing."

Georgie rubs the knuckle of her thumb up the bridge of her nose and into her forehead. He's right, she's in danger of going full-on native, getting too involved with these people, and she can't help herself. Pinewoods Retreat is working its way into her bones. It's sprinkled that fairy dust over her that Holly talked of. She stands up from the bench and wanders towards the beehive.

"Right," Ryan continues, "that's two possible things to inconvenience them, then. But, like you said, it's not enough to close them down. Me an' Mick'll see what we can come up with our end. You keep nosing about on site and find out what you can, particularly about the owners. We need some dirt on them. Hey," Ryan laughs, "you might need to plant something, babe, like bed bugs or cockroaches or whatever in the kitchen." His laugh is bitter and it sends a shiver through Georgie. "No idea what, but Mick'll know the kinds of things that can cause problems for them, with all his building experience. How old is the house?"

"Victorian. Late nineteenth century. Built in 1898. That much I did find out from my research." There's silence on the end of the phone. Georgie waits.

"OK." More silence.

"Look, Ry, I'll leave you to it for now. You sound distracted."

"Me? Nah. Anything else to report?"

"No." Georgie shakes her head. "Oh, yeah, remember to pick your suit up from the dry cleaners. You need it for the award ceremony."

"Will do. Bye, babe." Ryan lets out a long whistle as he ends the call, and Georgie is sure she hears a light giggle in the background before the line goes dead. She makes a mental note to check the doorbell app on her phone to see if anyone walked into the house with Ryan, who hasn't yet walked out again.

Georgie kneels down in front of the beehive and watches the bees.

"I'm not wrong, am I, bees? There's someone in our house." Bees fly in and out of the tiny entrance to the hive. "What do I do this time? Ignore it? Christ, but it feels like I've done that a few times too many already. I don't know if I can go there again. But then, what are the options? You can't break up a good partnership. I just wish – I wish . . ." Georgie puts her head into her hands. "I wish Ryan'd show me just a little respect in our marriage. That's not a lot to ask for, is it? I mean, look at Holly and Hunter, and Lorraine and Dee. They all seem able to be in respectful relationships. Surely I can have a bit of that, too."

Georgie stands up and turns towards the house. The back door opens and Beth steps out, followed by Kate and Morgan. Morgan waves at Georgie.

"I'm going for a stroll whilst the other two do some dune running," Morgan calls over, pointing a finger towards the front of the house. "Come with me." Beth glares, first at Georgie, and then at Morgan.

Georgie gives a thumbs up, surprising herself that a walk with this woman she's only known for a few days sounds appealing, though part of her cringes at seeing Beth, after the way she spoke to her. She sighs as she admits to herself again that she needs to give a more heartfelt apology, and walks down the gravel path to join Morgan.

19

GEORGIE

OUT on the cinder path that runs in the direction of the beach from Pinewoods, Georgie falls into step with Morgan, keeping at her slower pace, as Beth and Kate make off down a side path to get on with their training.

A huge part of Georgie, the part that's irritated by Ryan and the probability that he's brought a woman into her house, maybe even into her bed, would like to march on ahead of Morgan until her heart beat is up, pounding the exasperation out of her with each step. Whenever she's angry or fed up, she finds the best way to handle her emotions is to stomp them out of her on a long, fast-paced walk.

But instead, she thrusts her hands into the pouch at the front of the hoodie she bought in the village – an item of clothing she would never normally be seen dead in – chews on her bottom lip, and works on slowing her breathing to match the slower pace of Morgan's stride. Admittedly, there's something about the older woman that reminds her of the aunts on her street growing up. She wasn't actually related to a single one of them, but for some reason they always called the neighbours '*aunty*'. The memory of simpler, poorer days, when life felt so much easier, softens Georgie to Morgan.

"You said on our first night that you're from Liverpool, Morgan. You don't have a strong accent, but I can still detect a hint of it."

"I never lost it," Morgan laughs. "I'm originally from the flower streets in Kirkdale. Moved away donkeys years ago, but Liverpool's my home. What about you, lovey?"

"Me? My roots are firmly planted in Liverpool. Never lived anywhere else."

Morgan nudges her elbow. "You didn't need to tell me that. Your accent's a dead giveaway. And despite all your airs and graces, you're not from one of them posh parts of Liverpool."

"I live in Blundellsands," Georgie says, laughing lightly.

"Yeah, now you do, but that's not where you grew up."

"It's that obvious?" Georgie turns her head to look at Morgan, waddling alongside her on her short legs.

"Lovey, you know what they say. You can take the girl out of Huyton, but you can't take Huyton out the girl."

Georgie laughs. "Right, it *is* that obvious then."

Morgan winks, and nudges her elbow again. "I'd be lying if I said I guessed. Ed's from Huyton. And he said you went to school together. I just put two and two together."

Georgie nods slowly. "Ahh, and there was me thinking you had an incredible linguistic ear."

"You've gone up in the world, then, living in Blundellsands."

Georgie nods, but offers up no response. She learnt many years ago that it's not necessary for her to give up information about herself if she doesn't want to – and right now, she'd rather not divulge too much about herself.

"And," Morgan goes on, "my detection skills also tell me you've got something on your mind."

Georgie looks down at the path passing by beneath her feet, a mix of cinder and gravel. She's not one for sharing what's going on in her life, not even with the closest thing she has to best friends – Carla, Ali and Sian. But there's something comforting about Morgan, and Georgie wants to be real with her, even if it's not the whole truth.

"I was rude to Beth at breakfast." Georgie sighs. "And I know I said sorry at the time, but she deserves a proper apology."

"You don't say." Morgan purses her lips. "Yes, you were rude, and yes, she does deserve a better apology than you gave at breakfast." A silence hangs between them for a moment, the crunch of their shoes on the cinder path filling the gap in their conversation. "You're woman enough to handle that, though. My question is, why you were like that to her in the first place. I don't think that's who you are, Georgie."

Georgie screws up her nose. "Not at all, Morgan. I pride myself on my brilliant networking skills. I'm the one who brings people together. Truly, I'm ashamed of myself."

"Good."

Georgie shoots Morgan a glare. "I deserve that."

"So why were you rude to Beth?" Morgan asks.

"I – er – I . . ." Georgie shrugs. "I suppose because I'm used to women looking up to me."

"Bollocks. Just because you're usually the queen bee, you suddenly turn nasty on someone who doesn't look up to you?

What a load of crap, Georgie. You don't fool me. Whatever's going on for you right now, it's bigger than Beth, but you took it out on her. That's what you need to unpick for yourself."

Georgie stares off into the distance. For the last couple of days, thoughts about her life have been hurtling around her head, colliding into this irrational attraction she's got for Ed. It's crazy that she's even spending a moment thinking about Ed because she's not going to act on these feelings. She's not Ryan, and she won't behave like him. And, talking of Ryan, as she is in her internal dialogue, she's barely ready to admit to herself that this time around, if he is having another affair as she suspects, she simply doesn't have the energy to go through the pretence again. Georgie purses her lips. Beth undeservedly became the target for all of that pent-up emotion, and truthfully, it's not about her. Georgie could have taken it out on anyone. "I should probably go and talk to Beth," she says, thumbing back to the path that Beth and Kate took.

"She's helping Kate just now. Leave it for a bit," Morgan says, and Georgie nods. "It's all right, lovey," she continues. "I'm not digging, and I'm not having a go at you." Morgan gently rests a hand on Georgie's arm. "But you need someone to talk to, and just so you know, I'm good at being discreet."

"Thank you." Georgie holds back a sigh. Morgan's right, she has plenty on her mind. Bloody Ryan and his flings; bloody Mick Rodgers and his insistence on buying Pinewoods; bloody Pinewoods itself for creeping into her heart when she least expected it to; and bloody gorgeous, sexy Ed Dixon. But there's no way she can open up about any of this to Morgan.

"I am," Georgie says. "Talking, that is. I'm talking to – shit, this sounds so stupid when I say it out loud – I'm talking to Holly's bees." Georgie lets out a sound halfway between a grunt and a laugh, and shakes her head in embarrassment.

"I've seen you doing that," Morgan says, "and you know, I'm sure it helps a bit to say things out loud. But the thing with bees is that however much you offload to them, they'll not challenge a single word you say." There's a glint in Morgan's eyes when she glances over at Georgie.

"Well," Georgie says, feebly attempting to change the way the conversation is going, "they buzz a lot. Holly does a good job with them."

"She does," Morgan agrees. "Lorraine always says that Pinewoods Retreat finds us when we need it most. It's none of my business why you're here, and whilst I suspect you're not here for the reasons you say you are, I don't need to know exactly what brought you here. What I do know is that you need something from Pinewoods. This isn't your usual haunt. You're more an expensive, exclusive spa kind of person. You can tell by those clothes you arrived in." She guffaws. "God, I don't think I've ever seen anyone look more out of place at Pinewoods than you on that first night." Her whole body shakes as she laughs. "Anyway, you need to be here, and I'm guessing it's not for the reason you think it is. Pinewoods will help you find out why, soon enough."

The ground beneath their feet changes from the cinder path to soft, dry sand, and the path takes a route over a dune.

"Here," Georgie says, holding out her arm to Morgan. "Let me help."

"I'm not decrepit, you know. Not yet, anyway." Morgan's laughter lines fan out around her eyes. "And I know you're avoiding talking openly to me." She slowly stomps up the dune ahead of Georgie. "Though it's probably more likely that you're avoiding being honest with yourself – or," she says, breathlessly, "the blasted bees." Morgan stops at the top of the dune. "Will you look at that view." She plants her hands on her hips. "It never fails to delight, whatever the weather."

Georgie stares out at the broad expanse of golden sand, before looking back at Morgan. Is she right? Is there another reason that Georgie needs to be here, at Pinewoods? She shakes her head.

"You don't like the view?" Morgan asks.

"Huh?"

"You shook your head."

"No, I mean, yes, I mean – I was thinking. Are you psychic, by any chance, Morgan?" Georgie laughs. What a ridiculous question. She doesn't even believe in psychics, but it's like Morgan has eyes on a deeper, hidden part of Georgie, that part she keeps locked away.

"Aren't we all a little bit psychic," Morgan says, "if we only know how to connect to our intuition on a soul level? My thinking is you stopped communing with your soul a long time ago. You use your intuition in a corporate kind of way. I don't think you know how to listen to your true soul any more. You're adrift."

Georgie's breathe catches, forcing her to cough. That's exactly how she feels: adrift. "You're right, Morgan. The view. It's perfect, isn't it?" She laughs, nervously. Morgan's in danger of getting too close to the truth of Georgie's life, a truth Georgie is only beginning to notice for herself.

There's something about Morgan, something so familiar, almost familial, about her that Georgie connects to, and she can't afford to let her in, just in case she gives away too much about herself.

So what is it that Georgie's wary Morgan could reveal by her inquisitiveness? There's the scoping exercise she's at Pinewoods to do, obviously. Her name; that she's no longer known as Georgie Macrae? That's something she can easily explain away. No, it's more than that. Morgan has a way of looking at people like she knows things about them – deep, soul-level things. Yet how can she know anything about Georgie? Morgan lives in Lancaster, so there's no way she'll have seen anything in the local newspapers about QuinnEssentials, LivSmarter and Georgie Quinn about to be awarded the Liverpool Businesswoman of the Year in a matter of days.

It's like Morgan knows Georgie's roots, her journey to success. Her truth.

* * *

Georgie is a mimic, always has been. She put her skills to good use at college, and when she started working for Ryan, where she soon discovered she needed to raise her game. Whilst studying her BTec course in business admin, she also studied her lecturers –

white middle-class women who dressed with little effort, and yet at the same time with every effort they could muster. They looked smart, cool, and downplayed. Their accents, still clearly from Liverpool, were softened, and Georgie practiced softening her own, slowing down her speech to sound more deliberate, thoughtful. When she was in her early teens, she had a phase when she copied the cut-glass accents of wealthy women she'd seen on the telly. Most clipped their words in a manner that Georgie's mouth wasn't made for, and some had top lips that never moved, long before botox was run-of-the-mill. The received pronunciation, refined by these women over a lifetime, was like a foreign language to Georgie. But this, the softened, middle-class accent of her own city, women who were proud to hold on to their Liverpool roots, was exactly what Georgie needed to acquire. She listened, she practiced, she copied.

Next, she changed her hair, first from its natural mousey brown to black, and then blonde, before settling on auburn. Hours were passed in front of the mirror, learning how to style it, and putting on make-up, taking it off again, applying it again, until she perfected a natural look that took her an hour to apply. For clothes, she visited charity shops in classier areas and bought the best brands she could afford at knock-down prices. Over time, when the money came pouring in from working for Ryan, along with the money he gave her for clothes, she adapted to buying brand-new designer labels.

Her transformation was complete – except for her name. Her mum called her Gina, but it always felt to Georgie like that was a name of the streets, of the poorer areas of town. At school, everyone called her Gee-Gee because of how fast she left at the end of every day, or they shortened it to Gee. But in her new life with Ryan, Georgina Macrae needed a classier name. The idea for '*Georgie*' came to her when Ryan teased her with the old nursery rhyme *Georgie-porgie pudding and pie*. Georgie; there was a name that was harder to place in the class structure she was entering – from that day, she claimed it for herself. Classy, yet individual. For working with, and then marrying, Ryan in the early noughties, it was perfect.

The auburn-haired, carefully presented, self-assured Georgie Quinn was born, and people assumed she was born into wealth.

Georgie soon discovered her skill at networking, able to persuade businessmen at event after event that QuinnEssentials, the business that she and Ryan built up from nothing, was successful and influential. She marketed them well, name-dropped when it mattered, started rumours about their business – and themselves – to get people talking about them. Within five years, her bank account went from zero to bulging – or, as she likes to say in one of the presentations that she regularly gives at business events, from *Zero to Zillions, the QuinnEssential way*.

Georgie knows she's been lucky, landing on her feet from the day she met Ryan. She's not always liked some of his business tactics, but he has a heart of gold, putting thousands into local charities each year, building up young entrepreneurs like a local 'Dragon', and that makes up for the less salubrious things he does. Has everything they've done with their business been honest?

Probably not. Has it been authentic? Well, their mission statement says they're authentic and work with integrity, but it depends how you define the words. Is it successful? Damned right it is. And Georgie relishes in the kind of success that fills their bank account and creates a wealth beyond her wildest dreams. A little bit of her still dreams of more money, enough to fill the small, dark hollow, deep within her, that she pretends isn't there – the bit that fears a night on a park bench. But yes, they're successful, they're rich, and her wildest dreams keep coming true – as long as she ignores the cracks in her marriage.

* * *

"Stop, don't move," Morgan says, interrupting Georgie's thoughts. "Look, there's a dragonfly resting on you." She points at Georgie's upper arm. "It brings you luck, you know."

"Really?" Georgie turns her head to where Morgan is pointing, and sees the dragonfly. "I've never heard anything about dragonflies and luck."

"Just you wait and see. Dragonflies landing on you signifies better times ahead. Things will turn out all right for you, I'm sure of it. Signs turn up everywhere, when you believe. Keep an eye out for white feathers too. D'you know about those?" Georgie shakes her head. "That's the angels looking out for you."

Georgie laughs. "You'll be telling me that Mercury is in retrograde next."

"It is, actually. I'll bet you've been experiencing things a bit out of sorts."

Georgie wants to scoff at Morgan, not believing that a planet in the solar system can have any impact on her life, but there's an intensity in the way the woman is talking that stops her. "Go on. Like what?"

"Well, Mercury affects us all differently, but it could be relationship issues, like someone cheating on their partner, or not being honest about how the relationship is working out for them. And it can be about travel chaos, like a car crash, or a traffic jam making you late for something important. And then there's work stuff, with all kinds going on with communication, particularly when it comes to contracts."

"I see. OK." Whilst it's comforting listening to Morgan's melodious tones, Georgie can't help the tightening in her belly at how close each of those things is to the way her life is going right now. Relationship issues, tick; car crash – well, more of a bump, but yes, another tick; and this blasted contract putting her at Pinewoods Retreat for a whole week, yes, that's a tick too. "I scraped the car when I parked up at Pinewoods on my first day. Brand new car." Georgie shakes her head.

Morgan studies Georgie before continuing. "Oh dear. Well, that's probably Mercury in retrograde. And then you can have misunderstandings, confusion about what's going on – and why, too. That's all common when Mercury's retrograde," she says.

"Hmmm." It's like Morgan is inside Georgie's head, and she bites her tongue to stop herself from opening up, telling Morgan about more than just the scrape on the car, screaming *'this is me'*, and sobbing on this wonderful woman's shoulder.

"There are good things that come out of Mercury being in retrograde, too. You might find it's a great time for reflection and being open to growth or insights. And for you and me, well, we've already benefitted from the impacts of Mercury because it's often a time of reunions."

"I've definitely had that with Ed." Georgie laughs. "Who's your reunion with?"

"Lorraine, of course." Morgan's smile is soft and warm, and Georgie feels a tug of envy at Morgan enjoying a friendship that makes her feel that way.

"Ah, yes, you're old friends." The reminder to be cautious around Morgan is timely, and Georgie swallows any thoughts of opening up and talking about her feelings.

When they reach the beach, Georgie carries on walking ahead, to edge of the sea. She takes off her shoes and steps into the cool, shallow waves that lap gently and slowly around her feet. With each wave, the sea stops a little further away from her as the tide goes out. *Just like my life, creeping away,* she thinks, taking two steps closer to the sea.

20

LORRAINE

Three Days to the Award Ceremony

LORRAINE holds the door of the therapy room open for Georgie to walk in and beams a smile at her. Georgie meets it with a strong smile of her own, and looks Lorraine in the eyes.

"Please, take a seat," Lorraine says, glad to have a reason to break the gaze between them. It's not that it's uncomfortable, exactly – but there's a sense of something unfamiliar in the way that Georgie looks at her. Lorraine resists the shiver that rests between her shoulder blades and kicks off her shoes. Having Georgie in her therapy room makes her want to ground herself, something that always calms her. For a split second, as she smiles at Georgie, she wonders what it is about this woman that unsettles her so. "What kind of treatment would you like today?"

"What would you recommend?"

There it is, that way that Georgie has of – what, exactly? Retaining control? Holding on to power? Avoiding commitment? Deflecting?

"Well," Lorraine says, thankful for the opportunity to suggest the one treatment she has felt Georgie needs from the moment she arrived at Pinewoods, "how about chakra balancing?"

Georgie smiles. "My yoga teacher is always saying I need to balance my chakras. Sure, why not? Though I've no idea what it involves."

"We all have energetic pathways, and sometimes we get a little out of balance. A chakra balance helps to remove any blocks, cleanses us, re-centres our spiritual and energy channels. You may feel very little, or you may feel a significant shift. It's different for everyone. Only you will know if it works for you."

"OK, let's do it." Georgie tilts her head and looks at Lorraine warily, despite the confidence of her tone.

Lorraine directs Georgie to the therapy bed. "If you want to lie down on your back when you're ready."

Georgie nods. She slips off her flip-flops and hesitates, forming pyramids with her hands on the therapy bed, before she turns and lies herself down on her back.

Lorraine stops the music and taps the side of one of her glass bowls. Although she generally uses the sound bath to prepare her clients for the shift in energy, today the sound bath is as much for herself as it is for Georgie. After a few minutes of using the singing bowls, she puts on some music that continues with the same energies, suitable for chakra balancing. Lorraine breathes in, long and slow, and grounds herself further. She closes her eyes for a moment, a hand on her heart, and when she opens them again she selects the crystals she feels calling to her for working with Georgie. Carefully, she places them on the table next to the therapy bed. Georgie's eyes are fixed on Lorraine's every move.

"You might find it helps to close your eyes during a chakra balancing," Lorraine says. "Simply let the energy flow through you."

Georgie blinks, but keeps her eyes open.

"Are you ready?" Lorraine asks.

Georgie nods, and this time she lets her eyes close and rests her arms by her side.

Lorraine works methodically in an almost ritualistic way, trusting her instincts. She starts by tapping the side of a Tibetan singing bowl, letting the sound wash around the room. She taps it again, this time directing the sound along Georgie's body from her toes to the top of her head. As the sound dissipates, she places crystals in a line, one at each chakra point, starting with red jasper at her feet and finishing with a beautiful piece of amethyst at her crown. She watches her client for subtle changes, and as she begins the massage at Georgie's feet, she sees her breathing slow and her face relax.

Some thirty minutes or so later, Lorraine removes the crystals from along Georgie's body. When she reaches the piece of tiger's eye at her sacral chakra, a little below Georgie's naval, the stone slips out of her fingers, as if a magnet is pulling it back to her client's body. So this is the stone that Georgie needs, then. Lorraine had been wondering when she would identify the right one for her – it's something she can usually do within moments of meeting someone, but then, Georgie has had a barrier up around her since the moment she arrived.

Carefully placing her crystals back in the box where she stores them, Lorraine keeps hold of the tiger's eye. She rests her fingertips lightly on Georgie's shoulder.

"When you're ready," she says, her low voice little more than a whisper, "you can open your eyes."

Georgie's breathing returns to normal – shallow and quick. She blinks three times.

"How was that?" Lorraine washes the crystals she used in the treatment in a bowl of water, a ritual she does to make sure she removes any negative energies that the crystals might have picked up.

"Erm, short?" Georgie raises herself up onto her elbows before pushing herself all the way up to sitting.

"Short?" Lorraine laughs. "Chakra balancing takes a little over half an hour, so . . ."

"Half an hour? Are you sure? It felt like five minutes."

Lorraine smiles and nods slowly. At least Georgie has time distortion in common with other clients. So many don't notice the time passing when she carries out a treatment. "You went into a deep relaxation moments after you closed your eyes."

"Really?" Georgie pushes herself off the bed and slips her feet back into her flip-flops. Lorraine nods. "Wow. Well it went quick. I suppose I needed it."

"I suppose you did. You may benefit from another session. You've got some unusual blocks around you." Georgie raises an eyebrow. "I'd like to give you this." Lorraine takes Georgie's hand and places the piece of tiger's eye in her palm. "It's tiger's eye, the stone of courage. It will help you ground yourself and it keeps you safe from negative energies."

Georgie stares down at the stone in her palm. "Oh," she says. "It's beautiful." When she looks up, her eyes glisten.

"I like to give everyone who stays here a crystal of their own to take home. It took me a little time to know the right one for you."

Georgie nods, saying nothing.

"Keep it with you, and it will help with any chaos around you, or anything in your life that's a bit toxic." Lorraine gently closes Georgie's hand around the stone. "Now, go and get Dee to give you a glass of water and I want you to sit and relax in the garden for ten minutes or so."

Georgie nods and walks to the door of the treatment room. She turns back and looks at Lorraine, as if taking her in fully for the first time. "Thank you," she says. It's the first time Lorraine has seen a genuine smile from her.

Left alone, Lorraine lets out a slow, free breath. Since Georgie walked into her treatment room, she's found it difficult to breathe deeply. She gives herself a shake from her head to her toes, feeling the need to remove negative energies from around her. It's not often when she does a chakra balancing that she comes across the kind of blockages and strange vibes that Georgie carries with her. The woman is pleasant enough – it's not about Georgie being someone she would rather wasn't staying at Pinewoods, but there is definitely something off about her energies.

Lorraine opens the blind and pushes the sash window up as far as it will open in an attempt to change the air. As she looks out into the garden, she sees Georgie walking down one of the paths towards the back of the garden, a glass in her hand. Eventually, she stops in front of the beehive where she sits down on a raised bed. It's not the first time Lorraine has seen her go over to the hive, and she's pleased that something in the garden is giving her a place of sanctuary.

Right, these energies in the room are not going to change themselves.

Lorraine turns her back on the garden. She picks up a sage smudge stick, lights it and watches as the flame catches. After a few seconds she blows on it until the flame goes out, leaving the smudge stick to gently smoke. She walks around the room in a meditative state, wafting the cleansing smoke into the air, spending a little longer in each corner, directing it along the line where the two walls meet. Having completed a circuit of the room, Lorraine moves the smudge stick in a figure of eight around herself in the centre of the room before tapping the smouldering ends into a bowl to make sure it is fully out.

21

GEORGIE

LATER that day, as Georgie changes for dinner, she remembers that she wants to check the videos from the doorbell app on her phone. Before she left home, she switched off notifications for the app, not wanting to get pinged about a delivery at an inopportune moment, but now she needs to check the recordings to find out who Ryan has brought into their home. With any luck, Ryan will have forgotten about it. He's shown no interest in it since the day they had the doorbell fitted, and honestly, Georgie hardly ever looks at the recordings these days. It was exciting when it was brand-new technology, when they first had it installed, but for the last six or seven years, Georgie has only checked the footage when a delivery company sends a message to say they've delivered a parcel and nothing has actually arrived.

Now, she opens the app and slides the timeline of the event history to the day she left the house. She watches as she puts her bags into the car and backs out onto the road. That's followed by the postman, someone doing a leaflet drop, next door sticking something through the door, that damned cat that always used to tease their dog by walking slowly past the bifold doors in the kitchen – and then nothing. For hours, as she slides through the video on into the early evening, there's no movement beyond a single magpie hopping across the drive, and the cat making a return trip, pausing a moment to look straight at the camera, before walking out of shot.

And then, at a little after eight on the day that Georgie arrived at Pinewoods, there it is. Ryan's car pulling up onto the drive. Ryan getting out of the driver's door, light-footed. The passenger door opening.

Georgie's stomach tightens. She peers at the recording, watching as a woman in jeans and heels shuts the car door and follows Ryan into the porch. She's laughing. As she nears the camera on the doorbell she looks straight at it, almost as if she dares Georgie to see her. Georgie flinches. She almost closes her eyes, not wanting to see the face of Ryan's latest young fling, when she realises that this woman appears older. She peers into her phone, but doesn't recognise her. And then, as Georgie's ears ring in the silence of the video, she watches the woman lean in to Ryan and kiss him on the cheek before they enter the house.

She rubs her eyes. Damn it and blast it and bugger it! She should never have looked at the video footage, because now she can't unknow, can't unsee. It was better when she only suspected, but now ... this! Not only is he seeing someone, he's bringing her into their house – and this woman is *not* his usual type by any stretch.

Her heart thumping, Georgie scrolls on through the timeline. When does the woman leave the house again? She has to know. On Georgie scrolls, her back clammy with heat. One hour passes in the footage, two hours, three; fuck it, of course she's staying the night. It's four hours since they entered the house, and it's – Georgie glances down at the timestamp – a little past midnight. Despite knowing in her gut that Ryan didn't drive the woman home after midnight, Georgie continues to scroll, just in case. The timestamp shows two thirty, and Georgie speeds forwards to the morning, shortly before eight, where she sees Ryan and the woman leave the house, hand-in-hand to the point where the car forces them to separate. She checks the next night, and the next, and the next. The same scenario plays out each time.

Anger clutches her throat. How could he? This is her house, her bed – her husband, for god's sake. And there's Ryan having a bloody sleepover with someone, playing house with her.

A pain stabs at Georgie's temples as she stares at the screen. This – *this* – is why he wants Georgie out of the way, staying at Pinewoods Retreat for a week, so he can play bloody house with his new woman. Bastard. Bloody bastard.

Another thing to add to the list of things going wrong in her life – and this one goes straight to the top of the list above losing her precious dog, Mr Big.

* * *

At dinner, Georgie is quiet, seething inside, all the earlier relaxation from the chakra balancing a distant memory. She shouldn't be bothered by Ryan having another woman. It's who he is. But that woman on the video acted like she owns Ryan, like she wants Georgie to know. Georgie feels sick at the thought.

She has little appetite, and as soon as she finishes eating she mumbles her excuses and goes for a walk, marching as fast as she can. She has to shake off this knot of frustration and anger in her stomach. Ryan's done it before, he'll do it again – and again. She shouldn't be surprised by him having affairs. It's who he is. The cheeky, self-made scouse lad – except that he isn't, because it was his dad's money that made him – with a twinkle in his eye and the gift of the blarney from his Irish roots, that gets women hanging off his arm.

But playing the part of the submissive wife is not who she is – though she has to admit that she's firmly planted herself in that role over the last couple of decades. She deserves better. Georgie won't let his behaviour and disrespect for her as his wife define *her*. She storms down the cinder path and soon veers off down a narrow track into the trees, chunnering to herself under her breath about Ryan and this blasted woman. How *dare* he let another woman lie next to him in *her* bed? It's the biggest betrayal of all.

Georgie marches on, the light fading as trees fold in around her. A man passes with a cockapoo that pushes its body up against her legs before carrying on by, but otherwise the path is empty. Gradually, her anger runs out of steam, her pace slows, and her breathing returns to normal. If she was at home, just a few miles away, walking through the woods would be the furthest thought from her mind. But here, with the earthy smell of the woods and the oily scent of pine trees soothing her, Georgie's heart slows and she takes in the beauty of her surroundings. The thick carpet of pine needles gives a little beneath her feet, evening birdsong fills the air and rays of sunlight filter through the branches. This beats pumping flesh at a networking event.

But then, everything feels different at Pinewoods – relaxing, comforting.

Safe.

It's ... perfect.

Since she arrived, she's found herself slowing down, eating simple yet delicious food, and, possibly most surprising of all, sleeping – even having a couple of afternoon naps, for goodness sake. For years Georgie has said that she has insomnia, and yet here, at Pinewoods Retreat, in a room barely big enough to swing a cat, she's sleeping deep, dreamless sleep.

There's something else that Pinewoods is doing for her, too, and it's possibly the most important bit. It's opening her eyes to her ridiculous acquiescence to Ryan's affairs. But can she leave him? Everything they own is in his name – their house, Dot's house, her new car. She has some savings, but beyond that, there's only the income she gets from LivSmarter, plus her Boodles jewellery collection, that is truly hers. Everything else is Ryan's, which always felt totally normal – until today.

He's changed since he partnered with Mick Rodgers on a few building and development projects. In the last year and a bit he's oozed this weird bloke energy, and then there's the little bag of white powder she found in the inside pocket of his suit jacket, a change from his usual poison of whiskey. Since then, his behaviour has become erratic. Some days she gets the old, lovable, kind Ryan. Others, he seems to relish in reminding her that he lifted her and her mum out of poverty, that he changed her life, that she'd be nothing without him.

And then there's the rumours she's heard recently. There's mutterings that Mick Rodgers is mixed up in dodgy dealings, and Georgie worries that if Mick's involved in shady business dealings to get building projects through planning, there's a chance that Ryan's caught up in it all, too. He's a good man, or at least he was in the pre-Mick era. But there's a lot that's changed. All the reasons Georgie used to feel safe with Ryan in the past are no longer there, and it disturbs her.

When it comes to her mum, Dot is as much a part of their marriage as Georgie is, and she adores her son-in-law. It would break her heart if Georgie told her what Ryan is really like these days, on top of the affairs. It's easier to pretend everything is rosy in the Quinn house, but being at Pinewoods, Georgie is waking up to reality. Those days of her meekly putting up with Ryan, such a contrast to the woman she is in work, may be at an end.

In the near distance a twig cracks, and Georgie swivels around expecting to see someone on the path behind her. There's no one there. She walks on, matching her breathing to the slow, purposeful steps she takes. Another twig cracks. This time, Georgie stands still for a moment and listens. There's a faint sound to her right. Slowly, she turns her head and spies a figure standing amongst the trees. In the fading light it's impossible to tell who it is, giving the figure a sinister edge. Blood pounds the hollow of her throat. Not moments ago she was thinking how safe she feels here, and now there's someone following her, walking towards her. She holds her breath and looks to the left and then the right. There's no one else on the path. When she looks back at the figure it raises a hand, and a finger of light from the setting sun filters through the pine trees, falling onto the person's face. She immediately relaxes.

"Ed!" She breathes a sigh of relief. "What were you doing creeping up on me?"

"Sorry, sorry," Ed says, pushing his way through the undergrowth, Moose tucked in under his arm. "I know how it must look. I did call out to you a few times, but I don't think you heard me. You kept powering on. I was trying to catch up with you, took a short cut and got stuck in the brambles." He laughs and joins her on the path, letting Moose nuzzle into Georgie for a moment before setting him down on the ground.

"You scared me," Georgie says.

"I can see that. My bad." He holds his hands up in defence. "God, were you in another world, or what?" Ed walks right up to Georgie and stands a matter of inches from her.

"I was," Georgie says, simultaneously wanting to fill the space between them and wanting to step away. "In another world. Needed to work something out in my head." She reluctantly takes a step back.

"Anything I can help with? You know, a problem shared and all that."

"I – my husband – I mean . . ." Georgie sighs and starts walking again. "No. But thanks anyway."

"Come on, Georgie. I'd like to help."

Georgie runs her teeth over her bottom lip. Ed's not exactly the person she'd choose to share her marital problems with. If anything, he's the man who could add to them if she were to follow through on her feelings for him. "No, it's not fair to involve you," she says.

"I don't mind," Ed says, falling into step alongside her, Moose scampering along in front of them. "Honestly, you can tell me anything." They walk on in silence for a moment, the pad of their feet on the path being the only sound.

Georgie glances across at him, on the cusp of denying her feelings for him. "The thing is, on the one hand you're my yoga teacher here at Pinewoods, and kind of a therapist, too."

"And on the other hand?" Ed asks, when Georgie takes a long pause.

"On the other there's this, you and me." She waves a hand in the air between them.

"This attraction between us?" Ed asks.

"I'm not wrong, am I? We both feel it?"

"Hey," Ed goes on, "maybe we have a holiday romance, a little fling . . . something a bit more than that, who knows."

"That's just it, Ed. I'm not ready to do that. I'm married." Georgie sighs. What she'd give for a fling, or even just a kiss, but she doesn't need more pressure adding to her life.

"Wait, I've not finished." Ed's tone is gentle. "Hear me out. What I was going to say was, we can play any of that by ear, that's not what's important right now. But what *is* important is that I get the sense you feel very alone, and I want to be here for you. As a friend, at the very least."

"What makes you think I feel alone?"

"I don't know." He pushes his hands into the pockets of his pants. "There's a kind of sadness around you. You're good at wearing a mask, I'll give you that. And it's not like you're letting your mask slip or anything. I'm . . . I don't know, I pick up this feeling from you. It makes me want to hold you tight, hug you and tell you everything's going to be all right."

Georgie laughs. "Ever since I arrived at this place, it's like I'm in one long therapy session – with all of you. Holly, Morgan, Lorraine, now you. All of you are reading me and offering to help me." She laughs again. "Not sure I've had so many people wanting to help me out with stuff in my whole life. Like you care."

Ed walks along in silence next to Georgie, slowing his pace a little, as if he's discreetly encouraging Georgie to slow down too. She bites her lip, determined not to be the next to speak, and waits for Ed to say something. Still, he walks in silence. He's right, of course. She does feel alone. This is not the kind of stuff, what's going on with Ryan, that she would ever talk to Carla about. Yes, they're close friends, but with an air of pretence around the friendship, putting on a false front that everything in their lives is rosy. The unspoken between them is better left unsaid, that's the unwritten rule that's weighed between them for years.

"God, what is it with you people?" Georgie asks, as if Ed has been talking all this time. "You're all getting in my head."

"Well, in my experience, we can only get in your head if there's something in there that our questions touch."

Georgie shoots Ed a side glance. "Pardon?" She stuffs a hand into the pocket of her jeans, and her fingers touch the tiger's eye that Lorraine gave her after the chakra balancing. Immediately, as if the stone scolded her, she pulls her hand out of her pocket again, leaving the tiger's eye where it is.

"Look at it like this," Ed says. "If I was way off the mark saying you're lonely, you'd say *'nah, nothing to see here, mate'*. Yet when we connect with something that's said to us, we can often get defensive, or protest too much, or maybe even get upset at the comment. With you, you're doing that thing you do."

"I really am being psycho-analysed." Georgie's laugh is uneasy. "What thing I do?"

"Deflecting. You change the subject. Like a moment ago, you made it all about how we're doing therapy on you, rather than thinking about what's been said. And that, Georgie Macrae, is what makes me say that you're lonely, cos you're deflecting, pushing anything away that gets too close to your heart, to your truth."

Georgie pushes her hands back into her pockets, taking care not to connect with the stone, and looks straight ahead, blinking to push back tears that threaten her. She's not a crier and she won't start now. Nope, not happening.

"Anyway," Ed continues, "I'm a friend for you to talk to, if you want to. And if you don't, I'm still a friend for you to hang out with."

"I think I prefer it when you flirt with me," Georgie says, looking up into the tree canopy.

"Of course you do. It stops you having to do any soul searching."

Ed nudges her arm. "And it's not only me doing the flirting, but I'm still up for a bit of that. Talking, flirting, anything else you want, really. I'm here for you."

Georgie leans in closer to Ed and they walk along in silence, arms touching, for a few minutes.

"I don't know," Georgie says after a while.

"Don't know what?"

"Any of it. I guess – I'm not ready to talk – not yet."

"That's a great start." Ed stops walking and grabs hold of Georgie's upper arm, pulling her towards him. "And that's OK." He leans in and gently kisses her on the cheek. Georgie momentarily closes her eyes and breathes him in. It would be so easy to turn her head, to nuzzle in close to him, to kiss him back – full, on the lips. It would be so easy . . . but no. She can't.

"Just know that I care," Ed continues, letting go of her arms.

Georgie shivers. Could he actually care?

"You OK?" Ed asks.

Georgie nods. Dot cares for her, about her – but who else? She steps away and turns her back on Ed. "I didn't expect you to say that you care."

"Well, I do. I want to get to know you, help you work out whatever's troubling you. If you'll let me. You were good to me, back in the day."

"I was?" Georgie turns around and faces him.

"You were, yes. Don't you remember?" Georgie shakes her head. "There's this one time in particular that's always stuck with me – we must have been fifteen or sixteen, I guess. A gang of lads were having a right old go at me, shoving me about, bullying me for being a bit of a wimp and a total nerd, making out it was so uncool to be clever, and you stood up to them, arms folded across your chest like a bouncer, told them that bullies are the wimps, and then – I'll never forget this – you told them that when they left school with no exams to their names, and they were mopping floors at TJ Hughes's, they'd think back and wish they'd been nerds, too."

"I said that?"

"You did. And those lads skulked off, mumbling swear words in our direction, and they never bullied me again. That's just one of the times you were good to me, but it's the one that always made me smile when I thought about it. And now, well, it's good to be able to pay that back and be kind to you."

Taking in a deep breath, Georgie turns back to Ed and flashes him a smile. "I was pretty philosophical for a sixteen-year-old, wasn't I? Thank you. I appreciate you being a friend to me." Bloody hell, it's not only Pinewoods Retreat that's getting to her, it's the people too. "And I do want more. But I can't be sure it's not this place, Pinewoods, that I'm falling for, just as much as you." Georgie looks deep into Ed's eyes, and he holds her gaze, dimples forming in his cheeks as a smile slowly crosses his face. "Come on," she says, "it's getting dark. Let's get back to the house."

"This way, Moose," Ed calls after the dachshund, who's busy sniffing in the undergrowth a few feet away from them.

Georgie links her arm through Ed's. "Tell me a story," she says.

Ed laughs. "What about?"

"I don't know. Anything. Your travels?"

Ed pauses. "Hmmm, well, there was this one time in India when I caught the wrong train. In my defence, the station was chaotic, I don't speak the language, and I didn't realise that my train was *after* the one that was already on the platform. I didn't cotton on until it was way too late to change trains, but all these wonderful women, passengers in the same carriage as me, they shared their food with me, and one ended up putting me up for the night when we reached her town."

"Do you always land on your feet, Ed Dixon?"

"Always." He grins. "Come on, Moose, keep up."

Georgie throws more questions at Ed about his travels as they walk back through the trees to Pinewoods Retreat, soaking up his stories, loving the experiences he shares. And she can't help thinking that she and Ryan have never done this.

22

GEORGIE

Two Days to the Award Ceremony

THE kitchen is buzzing with chatter when Georgie walks in for breakfast the next morning. Despite everything that's going around her head, she slept deeply and had over six hours sleep. When she woke up, she was disoriented for a minute and couldn't remember where she was, until the sound of cawing crows filled the air.

As always, the delicious aromas of Dee's cooking fill the kitchen, and, as if it's calling out for the food, Georgie's stomach rumbles loudly as she takes a seat next to Morgan.

"Someone's hungry," Morgan says.

"It's all that exercise," Beth says, glaring at Georgie across the table. Georgie's initial apology, the day before, hasn't yet made up for her unkindness, and she needs to address that.

"I'm the same," Kate says, blushing as soon as she speaks, her voice a rare addition to conversations. "Starving."

"Of course, Kate." Morgan pats Kate's hand. "You're doing the personal training with Hunter. Is it helping?"

Kate nods. "I think so. He's taking me for a run along the beach today with Beth and a couple of other people he trains. We're doing something called a crocodile run."

"What's one of them?" Morgan looks at Kate in a way that seems to encourage the nervous woman to open up.

"Well," Kate says, clearing her throat, "everyone runs in a line behind each other, and one person sets the pace for a distance and then drops off to go to the back, and then the next person sets the pace, and then they drop off to the back, and then it's the next person's turn until everyone has been a pace setter, and then you do it all again, and the idea is you run faster than you think you can."

Georgie smiles across the table at Kate. Kate smiles back and immediately lowers her eyes to the plate of food in front of her.

"Oh, I see," Morgan says. She turns to Georgie. "Are you doing these personal training sessions with Hunter, too?" Morgan pours herself a glass of orange and holds the jug up to Georgie as if asking if she would like some too.

Georgie nods. "Yes please, to the orange. And no to the PT sessions." Morgan already knows this, but Georgie says a silent thank you to this wonderful woman who is including her in the conversation. "I've not really got any desire to do any exercise during my stay. Dee," Georgie says, in an attempt to change the conversation, a small part of her still on the task to find out what she can about Pinewoods, despite her growing disinterest in sharing anything more with Ryan. "I notice you have en-suite rooms on the top floor. I wondered if I might move to one of those. That's if it's not too much bother." She isn't even sure why she's still carrying out her investigations, other than she always finishes any job that she starts. Maybe Dee will share something useful – and Georgie can decide later if she's going to use it.

Dee places a plate in front of Beth, and passes another to Morgan. "I'm sorry, we can't put anyone on the top floor right now." She rubs her nose with the back of her hand and turns to pick up the remaining plates.

"Oh? What a shame. I was really hoping..." Georgie leaves the end of the sentence hanging.

Dee puts a rack of toast in the middle of the table. "We've just got some work we need to do up there." She turns her back on everyone and busies herself wiping down the worktop – though Georgie notices there's a repetitive nature to what she's doing. Could this be their Achilles heel, that one issue with the place that Mick will want to know about? Her stomach tightens as a single word pops into her head. *Judas.* She takes in a sharp breath. Come on, Georgie – this is *not* betrayal. It's a job of work. Focus, woman.

"Really?" Georgie continues. "What kind of work?"

"Oh, nothing too major. But we'll get it sorted before we put anyone up on the top floor."

"I've a few friends in the building trade. I'd be happy to help. Make introductions, get you a good price, you know?"

"Erm – well – I – you'll need to speak with Lorraine about that." Dee throws the dishcloth into the sink. "Right, who needs a packed lunch today, and who will be back here for lunch?"

"I'll be staying at Pinewoods today," Morgan says, stuffing a forkful of food into her mouth.

"Beth and I are going to go for a walk after this crocodile run thing this morning," Kate says. She turns to Beth. "Do you fancy a packed lunch, and then we're in no hurry to get back?" Her eyes are wide and eager.

Beth shrugs. "I suppose so. Might as well. There's not a lot going on here today."

"Do you mind if I join you?" Georgie looks at Beth.

"What? On our walk?"

"The crocodile run. I'd like to help."

"Oh yeah?" Beth sniffs and wiggles her nose.

"Yes. And look, I know I said sorry for how I acted yesterday, but I'd like to show that I am and, you know, help out with the training and, well . . . shit, I'm making a meal of this." Georgie sighs. "Sorry for how I behaved towards you. It was uncalled for. Can I please help with the crocodile run to make amends?"

Beth tilts her head and studies Georgie for a moment before flashing a smile at her. "That would be good, yes, if Kate agrees."

"Hunter said it works better doing the crocodile if you have a bigger group of people," Kate says through a mouthful of food, her neck blotching red as she looks at Georgie, "so it would be a great help, thank you."

* * *

Down at the beach an hour later, Georgie stands with Beth and Kate as Hunter introduces them to three other women who are some of his local clients that he's persuaded to help Kate with the crocodile run. He barks out the orders of how everyone runs in a long line, one behind the other, with the front person being the pace setter. After a minute, they swerve off to the side and join the back of the line, leaving the next person to set the pace. Each person takes a turn at the lead, choosing a pace that suits their abilities.

After a short warm up, Georgie takes up position at the back of the line and Hunter starts the crocodile run. Kate starts at the head of the line, and as she swerves off to pick up position at the back, leaving Beth at the front, Georgie shouts out, "Great work, Kate!" Kate beams at her. Beth picks up the pace a little, and as she swerves off to join the back of the line, Georgie shouts out a *great work* to her too, and Beth returns a thumbs up.

Hunter runs alongside, shouting encouragement, and clapping his hands.

"Well done, ladies, doing great. Kate, you're a power-horse this morning."

Caught up in the collective adrenaline rush, Georgie joins in with the supportive whoops from the other runners, surprised at how much she's enjoying herself. Every now and again, jumbled thoughts of the woman on the doorbell video, and her brazen look straight at the camera, tumble through Georgie's head. She bats each thought away, returning her mind back to the crocodile run and her breathing. When it's her turn to take the front and control the pace, she picks up her speed and counts her in breaths and out breaths.

Hunter has the group run along the beach for about a mile, with the wind buffeting them from the front, and then turns them around to run back the other way. This time they're pushed along by the wind. They repeat the distance another couple of times, and Hunter gets each lead to pick up their pace a little with each mile they do. By the time they've covered six miles, he calls it a day and gets the group to do a cool down. There's high fives all round, and Kate beams.

"Can't believe I did that," she pants, looking at Hunter. "Thanks everyone for helping me."

"That was a personal best for you over a 10k distance, Kate," Hunter says, patting her on the back. "Good job!"

Beth bumps elbows with Georgie and smiles at her. "You're a good runner, Georgie. I didn't think you had it in you."

"Really?"

"You're slim, I can see that, and I reckon you go to the gym, but you don't look like a runner."

"Truth be told, I prefer gentler sports. But my personal trainer has me do a 10k every week, and he won't take no for an answer." Georgie wipes sweat from her forehead, pushing stray hairs out of the way.

"Thanks for helping. Kate needs to do this. I know she says it's for Dad, to remember him by, but it's just as much for herself."

"I'm so sorry," Georgie says. "I'd not picked up that your dad passed away."

"Yeah, start of the year. Kate cared for him for five years after Mum died. That's what I mean. This is for her, really. Getting her life started again. It's good of you to help."

"You'll have to let me know if you're doing something like this again. I'd like to help."

Beth nods her thanks and walks over to her sister, giving her a bear hug. "Proud of you, Kate."

As everyone turns to go back to the house, Georgie hangs back from the group. She walks down to the edge of the sea and watches the waves, almost mesmerised by them. She desperately wants to clear her head and work out what Ryan's latest affair means to her but the anger that still courses through her veins, despite the exercise, muddies her thoughts. As a couple of seagulls circle around her, she admits to herself that she has no idea what to do next.

23

GEORGIE

As soon as dinner is over that evening, Georgie escapes out of the back door and walks down the garden path to the beehive. It's becoming her thing to do, to commune with the bees. Looking behind her, she checks that nobody has followed her and settles herself down on the edge of the raised bed in front of the hive. She rests her elbows on her knees. A bee buzzes past her face and settles on her hand.

"Tell me what to do, bee," Georgie says, lowering her face closer to the bee. "I have it all. I really do. New Range Rover Sport, big house in one of the poshest parts of Liverpool, plenty of money in the bank. Oh yeah, handsome husband." She sighs. "Why am I not saying great husband? Wonderful husband? As if I even need to ask myself that."

The bee walks over her hand, up to her wrist, turns and flies off, landing on a piece of wood at the entrance to the hive.

"Well, you were no help," Georgie says, laughing lightly to herself. She watches the hive entrance where bees come and go with precision and purpose, one after another. Her breathing slows, and she hears the light buzz of their wings. There's barely a breeze, and aside from the bees, the only other sounds are of birds. Georgie isn't used to sitting in silence with nothing to do.

There's always something that needs her attention – working on a proposal for a contract, carrying out research, writing a report, and, of course, sorting out the house. Ryan hasn't lifted a finger beyond his own needs since the day they started dating, when she was in her late teens and he was twenty-five. They seldom go on holiday with each other – Ryan has weekends away with the boys, or what he tells her is with the boys, anyway; she has the occasional spa break with her own friends, but even then, she's not alone. And if they do go away together, to Dubai or the Maldives, Ryan soon befriends a couple in the bar, or insists they go away with their friends.

Georgie gives her head a little shake and, just as her yoga teacher would tell her to do, she thanks the thoughts and takes her focus to her breathing. With the warm sun kissing her shoulders, she relaxes a little, lowering her shoulders, letting go of tension she's been holding since she saw the doorbell video. Pinewoods is working its magic again, seeping into her heart, sucking her into its easy ways. Maybe it's the chakra balancing that Lorraine did for her, or maybe it's simply the unfamiliar sense of calm, but she could get used to this. Her breath slows even further, and time passes.

Almost minute by minute, a bee lands at the front of the hive and appears to perform a dance before vanishing through the small hole into the inner chambers. Others mimic the dance and again vanish. Georgie leans forwards, mesmerised by the bee behaviour.

"Can I join you?" Holly smiles down at Georgie.

"Please do." Georgie scoots along the raised bed to make room for Holly to sit alongside her.

"I could do with a break."

"Oh," Georgie says, "I didn't realise you were in the garden."

"I was working at the other end." Holly points a thumb over her shoulder. "Waiting for my evening gardening group to join me."

Georgie nods and looks back at the garden.

"I love how charmed you are by the bees," Holly goes on. "Do you know that one of the collective nouns for bees is a charm of bees?"

"Is it? I would have guessed at a swarm of bees."

"That's when they fly off together, en masse. When they literally swarm." Holly's smile is easy and relaxed.

Georgie nods. She leans forwards again, watching the bees enter and leave the hive. "I always thought if I got too close to a hive I'd get stung."

"You're not a threat to them, so they've no reason to attack you."

"Not much different from humans, then. Ready for a fight when they need to be, but otherwise they get on with life, minding their own business."

"I like to think there's a lot we can learn from bees," Holly says. "They communicate with each other, and they pull together to work as a team."

"How do they communicate?"

"See that?" Holly points at a bee that's moving its body. "It's called the waggle dance. That bee is telling the other bees which direction there's food and how far away it is."

Georgie and Holly both lean forwards and watch as bees perform the waggle dance on the small ledge on the side of the hive.

"They're incredible," Georgie says, her voice low and quiet like she's trying not to disturb the bees. "Magical."

"Truly, they are," Holly says.

After a moment of quiet, Georgie says, "I find it strange, here at Pinewoods."

"Really?"

"Well," Georgie hesitates, not even sure what she's about to say. "I mean, at home, in my job, I'm the queen bee. But here, I suppose what I'm trying to say is, I'm a nobody. I'm not used to that."

"Isn't that great? No pressure." Holly traces a finger down the scar on her face, and Georgie realises she's not even noticed it in the last few days.

"No pressure," Georgie says. "I didn't realise I felt pressured in normal life."

"Is that how it feels?" A bee lands on Holly's hand and she brings it up close to her face. "You know I said how bees can recognise our faces? I often wonder if I could remember all their different markings to recognise each of them." She concentrates on the bee for a moment before it flies off. "But yeah, that's your regular life, is it?"

Georgie laughs. "I love how your mind goes off on a tangent and comes right back to where you started. I'm really focused and precise in pretty much everything I do. There's no room for tangents in my conversations or in my life."

"Uh-huh." Holly slowly nods her head.

"I'm not answering the question, am I?"

Holly shakes her head. "You're not." Her eyes are soft as she looks straight into Georgie's. "Is that maybe a tangent?" She smiles.

Georgie turns her attention back to the bees and watches them for a moment, allowing a comfortable silence to rest between herself and Holly. "I do feel pressured," she eventually says. "Yes."

"To be what?"

Georgie shrugs. "To be perfect, I guess. Do the perfect job, have the perfect home, be the perfect –" she pauses, "– be the perfect wife." She blinks. Is this really how it feels? There's been no space to question her life before. At least, she hasn't allowed there to be space. There's a part of her that has maybe always suspected that if she digs too deep into her soul, she won't like what she finds.

"And are you?" Holly asks. "Perfect?"

Slapping her thighs, Georgie laughs. "Well, I thought I was until I got here, but with all this psychoanalysis I'm getting from everyone, I'm starting to question that."

"And the flirting with Ed?"

Georgie covers her face with her hands, and mocks a peek through her fingers.

"Is it that obvious?"

Holly smiles and nods. "To me, at least. It's not a topic of conversation, so I don't know if anyone else has noticed."

"I don't know what's got into me. I've never done anything like this in my life before." Georgie shakes her head. "God, why am I telling you this? I sound like I'm a right floozy, but honestly, there's never been anyone other than Ryan in all these years.

Not since I met him. He's my husband. Met just after I left school. Been together ever since."

"Oh." Holly shifts her bottom on the edging around the raised bed, as if any discomfort is physical rather than unease at listening to Georgie opening up.

"Can't say the same for him, mind you. Ryan." Georgie takes in a sharp breath, straightens her back, sighs and slouches forwards again towards the beehive. "And when I rang home, I was sure there was someone in the house with him. I mean, I know there was. I checked."

"You checked? How?"

"We have one of those doorbells with a camera that records everything. I went through the video archives on the cloud. There's someone there. In our house. A woman."

"Gosh. And how does that feel? You don't appear to be angry."

Georgie thinks for a moment. "I am, or at least, I have been. I think, though, I'm more disappointed than angry." She pulls at a weed near her feet. "Don't get me wrong, I'm used to his infidelity. He had one affair with a woman for ten years."

"Ohhh." Holly's jaw drops.

Georgie flicks Holly a glare. "You say that like you know him."

"No, I was thinking how hard that must be. Ten years is a long time. A friend of mine had a long affair with a married man, so I've heard about it from the side of the other woman. She ended it when she realised he wouldn't ever leave his wife for her. But it must be so hard being the wife in that situation, and knowing your husband is in a serious relationship with someone else."

Georgie's heart thuds. Of course, San Sartori. That's who Holly's friend is.

"I'm sorry you've had to deal with that kind of thing, as the wife of a man who – well, you know."

"Who can't keep it in his trousers, you mean?" Georgie laughs and as she glances across at Holly, she sees bright red circles on Holly's cheeks. "Sorry, I don't mean to make you feel uneasy by telling you all my woes."

Holly shakes her head, as if batting the comment away. "Why do you stay with him?"

Georgie whistles. "Now there's the million-dollar question. I know why I stayed with him in the early days. He was a good man. He still is – that is, in many ways other than his infidelity. He's good to me, and to Mum. He bought a house for her to live in, rent-free, when we got married. How many husbands do that for their mother-in-law? He saw the dreadful flat she was living in and said that wouldn't do for his second mum. Three months later, he had it all sorted and Mum moved into a lovely little place. She's still there. Yeah, he's been good to us both. Changed our lives. I've a lot to be grateful for."

"You feel in his debt?"

"No, nothing like that," Georgie says, rolling her shoulders as if persuading herself that her internal discomfort at Holly's question has more to do with how she's sitting. "I mean, no, not really... well maybe, in the early days, I guess, but it was always a partnership. He helped us, I helped him. No, I don't feel indebted. Why would I?" A throbbing pain gathers around Georgie's temple and she rubs her knuckle around the area in an attempt to reduce the growing tension in her head. "Maybe I have felt in his debt, I don't know. Or maybe it's something about what he could do – he still owns the house Mum lives in and I wouldn't want her to be turfed out. She loves living there. All her friends are nearby."

"Turfed out? Is that likely to happen?" Holly looks genuinely shocked at Georgie's choice of words.

"Listen to me." Georgie's laugh is hollow. Holly is getting too close to the things going around her head. "I don't even know why I'm telling you all this." She takes in a long, slow breath.

"That's what we're here for at Pinewoods Retreat. To help you offload stuff, deal with what's going on for you whenever you're ready, in a place where you can leave your troubles behind. I'm not as good at this as Lorraine and Dee. They've lots of experience. I generally help people by getting their hands into the soil rather than talking like this. I'm sorry I'm not better at supporting you."

Georgie gently rests a hand on Holly's arm. "You are good at this. Don't put yourself down."

"You should have met me a year ago," Holly says with a smile. "This is the new, improved me."

"Thank you, Holly. Having someone to talk openly with helps. I'm not one to open up to anyone."

"Do you not have friends you can talk with?"

"Hmm, friends. Well, yes, I've got Carla who I'm close to, and a couple of other friends, Ali and Sian. But there's no way I'd say anything about my marriage with any of them. Our friendships are based more on . . ." Georgie tilts her head back and looks up into the nearby pine trees, assessing for the first time what her friendships are about. "They're totally focused on work, alcohol and clothes." She lowers her head into her hands for a moment, and as she lifts her head again she bursts out laughing. "And shoes, too. Shit, that sounds so shallow. I really am the epitome of a workaholic who uses shopping and wine as a coping mechanism." Georgie shakes her head. "What about you? Do you have friends, Holly?"

Holly nods. "I'm lucky. I've got Hunter, of course, and friends here at Pinewoods, and I also have other friends, too. One of them, Jen, she's an old school friend. We lost touch for a bit when she had a baby, but we meet up again now, which is lovely. And then I have two really close friends that I met here last year. I think I've said to you before, Pinewoods Retreat brought us together."

Georgie looks over her shoulder, back at the house. "This place does something – it's . . . look, I'm going to sound mad, but it's doing something to me, like it's magic, or . . . I don't know. It's definitely doing something to me. And I'm talking about it like the house is a sentient being. But I kinda feel a bit like I'm in rehab without being an addict, and Pinewoods is my therapist. There's something going on here . . ." She looks wistfully across the kitchen garden, as if she's taking in the place for the first time. How could she have thought Pinewoods was a ramshackle dump when she first arrived? "It's that fairy dust you mentioned."

"It is," Holly says, grinning. "Thank you for trusting me, Georgie. I know from my own experience that it's not easy to open up. If you want to chat again, let me know."

A couple of people walk around the side of the house into the garden, followed by another couple.

"Oh, here we go. This is my evening gardening group from the village," Holly says. "Fancy joining in?"

Georgie shakes her head. She pushes herself up to standing in one smooth move, learnt from her one-to-one yoga sessions where she works hard on her mobility. "No, thanks. I'll leave you to it." She rests a hand on Holly's shoulder. "I know you're not actually my friend, but thank you for being a friend to me this evening. I needed that."

24

GEORGIE

One Day to the Award Ceremony

THE following morning, after a full night's sleep, early morning yoga, and more breakfast consumed than she'd generally eat in a week, Georgie wanders off for a walk down the cinder path. She lets her feet guide her down woodland paths, along narrow trails, up and down dunes, until eventually her feet guide her back to Pinewoods. As the house comes into view, she smiles to herself. Pinewoods has worked its way into her heart. It might be a bit shabby around the edges, but it has a good soul.

Georgie steps in through the front door and is met by Dee, standing in the hallway, hands on her hips, brow furrowed.

"You didn't see Lorraine out there in the garden café, did you?" Dee asks.

Georgie shakes her head. "No. And I've just come along the cinder path. She wasn't there either." She smiles at Dee. "Have you lost her?"

"Yes." Dee shrugs her shoulders. "I never lose Lorraine. I always know where she will be. She's not in the kitchen or out in the garden, her therapy room's empty. I've no idea where she is. Ed's checking the yoga yurt for me. And," Dee lowers her voice, "her next client is waiting in the living room." She points a finger at the closed door. "She's never late for her clients," Dee says. "Never."

Georgie sticks her head into the dining room. It's empty. "Is she in your flat?"

"There's no reason for her to go up there during the day. We tend not to see our rooms from early morning until late in the evening. There's always too much to do for the retreat." Dee pokes her head around the living room door. "Sorry about this. I'm sure Lorraine will be back in a mo. It's not like her to go awol like this." She pulls her head back again and shakes it at Georgie. "This is so unlike her," she says in a whisper. "I honestly don't know where she could have gone."

Ed walks in through the front door, shaking his head. "I checked, she's not in the yurt." He lifts his chin in the direction of the stairs. "Shall I check the bedrooms for you?"

"There weren't many rooms to clean today so she got that done straight after breakfast."

The three of them stand in the hallway facing each other. Georgie has no idea what to say, and isn't even sure this is a problem for her to get involved in, when she hears a strange sound coming from upstairs.

"Did you hear that?" she asks the others.

Dee and Ed shake their heads.

"Listen." Georgie pauses, and holds a finger in the air as if to emphasise the need for silence. "There it is again."

"I heard it that time," Ed says, running to the stairs, taking two at a time. He pauses on the first landing, turning his head one way and then the next, before vanishing from sight as he takes the next flight of stairs up to the attic rooms. "Bloody hell," he shouts.

Dee runs up the stairs after him, and Georgie follows on behind. "What is it?" Dee shouts. As she turns on the final half landing, she lets out a whimper.

Georgie peers past Dee. Lying on the floor, Lorraine is covered in debris and roof tiles. One arm is twisted at an odd angle, the fingers of her other hand tightly gripped around the jumper she was wearing at breakfast. Her hair is splattered with dry plaster, and her face is barely recognisable beneath a coating of dust.

"Oh my god, Raine! What happened? You OK?" Dee's voice wobbles as she kneels on the floor next to Lorraine, who lets out a dry cough. "Raine, my love, speak to me."

Lorraine slowly moves her fingers, letting go of the jumper. "I hurt." Her words are faint.

Ed swiftly moves roof tiles from her back and legs.

"Careful," Dee says. "Don't hurt her."

"I'll phone for an ambulance," Georgie says, knowing there's little else she can offer in terms of assistance. Dee nods wildly, gently wiping dust from Lorraine's face. Georgie dials 999, asks for the ambulance service and explains what little she knows from the scene in front of her. She passes on the information that Lorraine is slipping in and out of consciousness, and that yes, she appears to have broken at least one bone, hard to tell if there's any other damage. Every now and again she asks Dee questions the operator throws at her – Lorraine's date of birth, the postcode for Pinewoods, the code for the gated entrance at the end of the road. As she puts the phone down, Georgie relays the instructions the operator gave her, including that Lorraine is not to be moved, and that someone needs to stand at the end of the lane to make sure paramedics know where they are coming to, with Pinewoods being in a remote location.

"I'll go, if you like," Georgie offers, and Dee nods. "I'll get you a damp flannel first, so you can wipe Lorraine's face."

"And an ice cube, too," Dee says, "to moisten her lips. There's some in the freezer."

Lorraine's tongue slowly laps her lips, as if the mere mention of moisture reminds her how dry her mouth is.

* * *

Down at the gate at the end of the road, Georgie feels like she's been waiting for ever, but when she checks the time on her phone, she's only been on the lookout for the ambulance for twenty minutes.

"Hey."

Georgie turns and sees Ed walking towards her. She smiles. "Hey yourself."

"There's nothing more I could do back at the house. Thought you could do with the company, cos it could be ages yet."

"Is she OK, do you think?"

"Hard to say. That arm looks . . ." Ed lets out a low whistle and shakes his head.

". . . weird," Georgie finishes for him.

"Yeah, I didn't know arms could go in that direction, even with all the yoga I do." He grimaces. "I told Holly what happened. She's with Dee and Lorraine now. Hunter's still out with Beth and Kate doing their training session." Ed puts an arm around Georgie and pulls her in close, kissing her forehead. "You've got some good ears to hear that whimper from Lorraine all the way up three flights of stairs."

Georgie stiffens in Ed's embrace. How does he think this is OK? Sure, she's flirted with him, but she's not given him any hints that she's ready for this level of closeness. Despite the thrill of being held by Ed, Georgie takes a step away from him. She can't lead him on, it's not fair on him. "I – it . . ." Her voice is husky. She clears her throat and wills herself back in control of her body. "It was just an odd sound," she says. "I didn't even know what I was hearing. Did she say what happened?"

"No, she only said a couple of words when I was up there. Scary, isn't it?"

"That roof is going to need some urgent work on it."

"I don't think they've got the money to get someone in."

"I know a guy . . ." Georgie stops. What's she doing, offering to help when the whole situation of the roof falling in is exactly what Mick Rodgers needs to be wrong with Pinewoods?

Ed laughs. "Of course you do. I bet you've got connections all over the place." He winks at her.

"Only because of the line of business we're in. But you're right, Lorraine and Dee probably can't afford it."

A siren interrupts their conversation, and Georgie quickly

enters the code into the keypad by the gates. The ambulance eases its way through.

"We'll see you down there," Ed says to the paramedics when he's finished telling them where Pinewoods is, and where to find Lorraine on the top floor. He takes hold of Georgie's hand, but she wriggles it free. "What?"

"No," she says.

"No, what?"

"I'm married, Ed."

"I know. And I also know that you feel the same way I do."

Georgie shakes her head and strides towards the retreat at a fast pace. Ed hurries to catch up with her, falling into step by her side. She daren't look at him. It's getting increasingly hard to resist him.

"You can't deny it, Georgie," Ed says. "I know you feel the same way about me that I feel for you."

Georgie says nothing. If she tells Ed how she really feels, her resolve might weaken. Every moment she spends with him, her desire for him deepens. She's desperate to stop walking, take him in her arms, pull him in to her, and . . . No, she has to stop this. She's going home tomorrow, and she doesn't need this complication in her life. Instead, she marches on in silence, fighting to shake off her growing desires.

Georgie clears her throat. "What do you think they'll do?" she asks, as they get closer to Pinewoods.

"About what?" Ed asks.

She points to the roof of the house that has come into view in a gap in the trees. "The roof. It can't be left like that."

He runs a hand across his jaw. "God knows. Me and Hunter will need to do some kind of repair jobby for now, I guess, and see how that holds."

They round the corner to the retreat, and Georgie stops at the archway into the garden. "I'm sorry, Ed."

"For what?" he asks.

"Ignoring what you said earlier." She hesitates. "I do – feel the same." Her voice is almost a whisper. A wave of desire rushes through her veins. She leans in close to him, wanting so much to feel the touch of his skin close to hers.

Ed steps closer. There's barely space between them. Before Georgie can stop herself, she lets her cheek glide alongside his, gently kissing the side of his face, longing for so much more of him.

Ed turns his head and lets his lips brush hers. Georgie's breathing stops. One small move, that's all it will take, and she can kiss him. They stand there, nose to nose, their lips just touching. Ed closes the gap and his lips cover hers.

Georgie gasps, pulling away from him. "I can't. Sorry." Shit, what was she thinking? She can't do this. Georgie turns and rushes into the house, not daring to look behind her. If she does, she will rush into his arms, kiss him full on his lips, run her hands over his body and . . . no! *Stop it, Georgie.*

She could tell herself that it's not fair on Ed, that Dee needs their help to clear up the mess from Lorraine's fall, but truthfully, she simply cannot give in to these feelings. She won't. Annoyed with herself for letting her desire get the better of her, Georgie shakes her head and vanishes through the front door, all the time feeling Ed's eyes on her.

25

LORRAINE

LORRAINE winces as she attempts to move on the gurney in A&E. Despite the painkillers, she's in agony, and the pain is so bad she feels like she might be sick. She'd love to sit up, but she's been told to stay on her back for now.

A nurse taps something into a tablet that's resting on her arm, and as she looks up at Lorraine she smiles. "You'll live," she says. "But we're going to get you into theatre as soon as we can to reset that dislocated shoulder. Then they'll put your lower arm in a cast for that broken wrist. And then it appears that everything else is just bruising, though the doctor will confirm all that when she's back in a bit. The one thing we are a little worried about is you might have concussion, what with going in and out of consciousness." She smiles. "You don't do things by half, do you, lovely?"

Lorraine attempts a weak smile. No, she definitely didn't do things by half when she fell from the top of the ladder. How stupid could she be? That's all she's said to herself since the paramedics put her into the back of the ambulance. Stupid, stupid, stupid. All because she had a hot flush and unbalanced the ladder when she yanked off her jumper. What a fool she was to grab hold of a loose roof baton to steady herself.

"Someone will be down in the next hour or so to take you

to pre-op. Any questions?" She looks from Lorraine to Dee.

"I'm guessing it's not good," Dee says, her knuckles white from gripping hold of the metal sidebar that's been left in place on the gurney since Lorraine was wheeled back from X-Ray.

"Like I said," the nurse says, "she'll live, but it's going to take some time for her to be using that arm again." She turns back to Lorraine. "You won't be doing much for the rest of this year, that's for sure."

The rest of the year? Oh God, stupid isn't even the half of it. If she's out of action for that long, they've no chance of surviving. Lorraine's breath catches as the weight of their predicament pushes on her chest.

The nurse pulls the curtain behind her as she leaves the bay, giving Lorraine and Dee a little privacy. Dee squeezes Lorraine's hand again and leans down to kiss her on the forehead.

"We'll manage, Raine," Dee says, answering Lorraine's unasked question.

Tears fill Lorraine's eyes. "We won't. I've left a huge mess in the roof, we've no money to repair it. Those rooms on the top floor are unusable. I can't see my therapy clients or clean the rooms in this state. We've not got enough guests booked in to see us through to the end of the year." The words tumble from her. Tears run down Lorraine's temples into her hair. "And I want to sob," she whines, "but I can't because I already hurt too much and I'll only hurt more if I move even an inch."

"Shhh, it's OK, we'll find a way through this. We've got through far worse."

"I've messed everything up, Dee. I've ruined us. We can't even look after the guests we've got with me lying flat on my back and you here holding my hand."

Dee rubs her free hand across Lorraine's face, wiping away the tears. "We'll manage," she says, biting her top lip.

"You don't even believe it yourself. I can see it in your face. You're as worried as me."

Dee shrugs. "That doesn't mean we won't find a way out of this."

"Well, for now, you need to go home and look after our guests."

Dee shakes her head. "No, I need to stay here. I trust Holly to organise everything. She'll make sure that the guests are well cared for, and I know she'll be sensible enough to get Hunter and Ed helping her out."

"It's OK, you go." Lorraine winces again.

"I'm going nowhere, Raine. I don't care what you say to me. I'm staying put."

26

GEORGIE

GEORGIE sits back on her heels and rubs her lower back as she waits for Morgan to brush a pile of rubble her way. Holly has given them each jobs to do, and Georgie's is to brush piles of rubble onto a small dustpan. An eighties playlist blares out of a bluetooth speaker, filling the silence and hiding the worries wheedling their way around the group. Words go unspoken as slate tiles and bits of plasterboard are piled up to take downstairs and outside.

As the paramedics drove off with Lorraine and Dee in the back, Holly wasted no time. She swiftly organised the army of helping hands and now, an hour later, she's checking in with everyone.

"Do you need a break, Morgan?" Holly asks. Morgan shakes her head, her lips pursed with doggedness.

"Beth, Kate," Holly continues, "please don't do too much. You've already been exercising today and I don't want you to tire yourselves out."

"We're OK," Kate says, brushing a few loose hairs out of her face.

Georgie watches Holly with admiration. When she first arrived at Pinewoods Retreat, she'd assumed the dungareed woman was maybe a little meek, but the more she's got to know her, the more she sees her quiet determination and caring nature.

"I thought we might have heard something from the hospital by now," Morgan says, leaning over her brush.

"Is no news good news?" Holly asks.

"Not with a wait in A&E," Hunter says. "More likely she's not even been seen yet."

"I felt sick when I saw the angle of her arm," Georgie says. "I've never seen anything like it."

"Didn't look good," Ed says. "She's not going to be back working for some time."

Holly claps her hands. "Come on, enough of this. We can't do anything about the hospital, but we can keep things ticking over at Pinewoods." She nods around the group, her tight-lipped smile failing to offer any solace. "I need someone to go and check on the staff in the café, please. They've been managing everything on their own down there, and I expect by now they'll need someone to do the KP-ing."

"KP-ing?" Beth asks.

"Sorry, Dee's got me talking her language." Holly laughs. "It's from her days working in restaurants, when she had a kitchen porter who would do the washing up for her and keep the place clean and tidy."

"Ah, well, if it's washing up that needs doing, that's a job for me." Morgan straightens her back, groaning at the effort. "I'll do that and I can make sure the staff are OK with keeping the café going. You're all better with the heavy lifting that needs doing up here now. That's not a job for me and my old bones."

"Thanks, Morgan. And then who can help us get these bags of rubbish downstairs?"

"I'll do that," Georgie offers.

"I can help," Ed says, looking squarely at Georgie.

"How about," Beth says, "we create a bit of human chain to move the bags?"

"Great idea, Beth." Holly pats her on the back and organises how the chain will work. "Hunter, will you be OK joining the chain for now, and then we can be quicker getting on with the next stage of the clean-up?"

"Suits me," Hunter says, leaning forwards to wipe some dust from Holly's nose. He winks at her, and Georgie feels a pang of envy at the gentle love between these two people she barely knows. She can't recall when Ryan ever looked at her the way Hunter looks at Holly. Has Ryan ever truly loved her? He loves being loved, she knows that. And he's always been in love with business success.

Georgie glances at Ed and, catching him looking at her, she whips her head around in the opposite direction. Taking a deep breath, she takes up her position in the human chain as they swiftly move the rubble down the stairs.

* * *

It takes until mid-afternoon to clean up the debris, and there's a dust cloud filling the air as Georgie and Ed brush up the last of the mess. Beth coughs, and wafts a hand in front of her face, and Holly shakes bits of plaster from her hair. Just as Hunter checks the weather forecast to see if they need to fit a tarpaulin to the roof before nightfall, to protect the rooms overnight, Holly's phone rings.

"Dee!" Holly almost shouts down the phone. "How's she doing?" Her head nods furiously as she listens, and everyone gathers around, waiting for news. "OK," she says. "Uh-huh," she adds. "Oh dear." Her eyes almost pop. "No!" She gasps. "Oh god." Holly walks through the group, and settles herself down on the top stair, her free hand covering her mouth. "She's OK, though, yeah?"

There's a moment's silence, and Georgie feels herself hold her breath along with everyone else. Beth rests her hand on Georgie's arm, and Georgie in turn places her own hand on top. It's not like she even knows Lorraine that well, but there's something about the camaraderie of the group that pulls her into the concern that everyone is feeling.

"Thank god. That's something." Holly turns her head to the group and nods at everyone, tears in her eyes. There's a universal sigh of relief. "OK, yes, I'll let everyone know. We'll see you later. Do you need anything bringing in?" There's another pause. "All right, well let me know if you do." And another pause. "Love you too."

"Is she OK?" Hunter asks.

Holly nods, biting her top lip as if trying to hold every emotion in. "The tears are just relief." She smiles. "Lorraine's on her way down to theatre for her shoulder to be put back in place. She dislocated it."

Beth visibly cringes. "Ouch!"

"She's broken her wrist and got ligament damage in that arm as well. And there's some concern that she might have concussion. But, as you'd expect, the hospital has no beds, so Dee says they've been told it's likely she'll be bringing Lorraine home sometime later this evening. Hunter, Dee asked if we can set the therapy room up as a bedroom for Lorraine to use."

"Me and Ed will do that, won't we, lad?"

Ed nods at Hunter. "Sure. She's lucky she didn't do anything worse. That was a nasty fall."

"So that's the good news," Holly continues, taking in a long, slow breath.

"What's the bad news?" Morgan is standing on the half landing with a tray in her hands, filled with drinks and cookies.

"She'll be out of action for months, probably to the end of the year."

"Right," Hunter says, clapping his hands together. "All the more reason for us to pull together to help." He leans over and takes a cookie from the plate on Morgan's tray. He breaks it in two and stuffs half of it straight into his mouth.

"I know a guy," Georgie says, keen to help in any way she can. "He owes me a favour or two. I'm sure if I ask him, he'll be down here in no time to get the roof sorted." God, Mick Rodgers will have her guts if he finds out, but honestly, these people deserve all the help they can get.

"It's good of you to offer his help, Georgie," Morgan says, "but sadly Lorraine and Dee don't have the money to pay someone to fix the roof for them."

"Ed mentioned that," Georgie says, "but I thought . . ." She steals a glance his way.

"And it's not really our decision to make on their behalf," Morgan adds.

"OK," Hunter says, speaking through the second half of the cookie. He wipes his hand on his jeans. "Here's the plan. Me and Ed can get up onto the roof. We'll get some tarpaulin and fix that to cover the hole. My mate who works for the Woodland Trust will have some we can borrow. I've checked the weather forecast, and it's dry for the next few days." He turns to Ed. "You all right with heights, mate?"

"Better than that. I climb. Bouldering. The kind of climbing you do without ropes. I'll be great on the roof. Thing is, we'll need a way of getting up there."

Hunter laughs. "Getting *onto* the roof isn't the issue." He juts his chin upwards. "We can do that through the bloody great hole in the ceiling. It's getting back down again after we're done that worries me."

"I can help," Georgie says. She takes the cup of tea that Morgan offers her, along with a cookie. It's not like her to eat between meals, but being at Pinewoods has given her an appetite she's never experienced before.

"Seriously? On the roof?" Ed asks, grinning. He nudges Georgie in the arm.

"You don't think women should be up on a roof, huh?" She raises her eyebrows and nudges him back.

"Yeah, sorry, I guess it did sound like that. No, I just can't imagine you on a roof, you know, based on the clothes you wear."

"I'm full of surprises." Georgie laughs. If he only knew the half of it. "I know a bit about roofing. I've been on many a building site, worn plenty of hard hats, been up on a good few roofs in my time. My husband and his dad are in the building trade, amongst other things."

"All help gratefully received," Hunter says, grinning at Georgie. "You good for actually getting onto the roof?"

Georgie nods eagerly. "I'm used to climbing up scaffolding, rather than step ladders through a hole in the roof, but yeah, I'll be fine up there. Done it before." How will she explain this away to Mick Rodgers if he finds out she helped to make the roof secure? There's no way he'll actually find out, unless she blabs about it herself, but she's going to have to come clean about the state of the place when she meets with him in a couple of days to tell him everything that's wrong with the building. This is the kind of gold he's expecting her to find.

* * *

Water runs downs Georgie's back, cleaning all the dust and dirt from her hair, but the shower does little to ease her aching muscles. It was hard work with Ed and Hunter up on the roof, but they managed to secure the tarpaulin that Hunter borrowed from a friend of his, and they're all pretty sure that any rain will be kept out until a roofer can be found to do the necessary repairs. Only time and rain clouds will tell if they did a good job.

As she towels herself dry after her shower, a calendar reminder flashes up on Georgie's phone. Her heart misses a beat. When she leaves Pinewoods early the next morning, she's going straight to the hair salon to get her hair and nails done for the night of her career. In twenty-four hours it's the dinner for the Liverpool Women in Business Award ceremony. Georgie was told a month ago that she's being recognised for her contributions to supporting disadvantaged and vulnerable young women in the city with the presentation of the Liverpool Businesswoman of the Year Award – or as Ryan likes to call it, LiBWoTY, as if it's an actual word.

Everything about the award ceremony excites her, including a part of her being ready to get back to normal life – though she half wonders if normality is what she really wants. There are things that Georgie's going to miss about Pinewoods, and she surprises herself that, in some small way, she doesn't actually want to leave. It's only been a week, so it blows her mind that she's had something of a life-changing experience here. She's not sure she's ready to let go of the person she's becoming here, and then there's the friendships she's started to form with everyone. Add to the mix this sense of betrayal to Pinewoods that is setting up home in her gut, and honestly, she's not entirely looking forward to the check-in with Ryan and Mick Rodgers that's already booked into her calendar for the day after the award ceremony. Sure, it's what her whole trip was about, but the moment she tells them everything she's uncovered, she'll be letting Pinewoods down – and she's not convinced she's ready to do that.

Giving herself a shake, Georgie pulls out her bags ready to start packing for her return home the next day. She opens the wardrobe and pulls out the clothes that have lain in there, unworn, the whole of her time at Pinewoods. There are only two of the outfits she brought with her that have even seen the light of day. She fingers the beautiful fabric, so different to the clothes she's been wearing for the last week that it takes her a little by surprise. She's worn expensive clothes for so many years that she forgot to appreciate the beauty of them.

27

LORRAINE

Thirteen Hours to the Award Ceremony

THE blinds in the therapy room let in slivers of morning light, waking Lorraine much earlier than she'd have liked, having only got home from the hospital a few hours ago. The room is filled with scents of oils from therapy sessions with her clients, and she breathes it in, glad to be home from the hospital. Although the aroma isn't a blend, as such, as Lorraine uses whatever aromatherapy oils are right for each client, it's a familiar combination that soothes her whenever she walks into the room, and right now, she welcomes its familiarity.

Lorraine attempts to push herself up in the bed with her good arm, and gasps, the pain in her other shoulder reminding her why she's here on the ground floor rather than upstairs in her and Dee's apartment. She swallows a yelp, not wanting to disturb the rest of the house, and lowers herself back into the pillows, accepting that, after the accident, there's no way she's sitting up in bed without help, let alone taking the three flights of stairs to their apartment for a day or two.

The door opens and Dee walks in with a tray filled with pastries, fruit and a smoothie.

"To build up your strength," Dee says, holding the tray aloft before she places it on a table on the other side of the room. "I've put together a feast for you. You didn't get to eat much yesterday, so you're going to get all the goodies to help your recovery."

Lorraine tries again to move in the bed, but winces as the pain shoots through her body. She squeezes her eyes shut, refusing to cry out.

"It's OK, I've got Hunter coming to help. He'll be here in a mo, and then we can help you sit up."

Lorraine nods, laying her head back on the pillows, and a tear gently runs into her hairline. "What are we going to do, Dee?"

"Everyone's being a great help. They cleared up the mess in the attic room. So I don't want you getting all upset about it."

Tears stream down Lorraine's face, and she angrily brushes them away.

"Come on, Raine, crying about it won't change anything. Like Morgan says, we need to put positive energies out into the universe. We have to find a way to make this work. And we will." Dee turns away from Lorraine, but not before she wipes a tear from her own cheek.

Lorraine closes her eyes, trying to shut everything out. She's brought this on them both. She's ruined everything, and now there's nothing she can do to put it all right. "I'm so sorry," she says, sobs wracking her pained body. "I've ruined everything. I've destroyed Pinewoods Retreat."

Hunter walks into the room, and stops in the doorway. "Christ, I've timed that wrong, haven't I?"

Dee sniffs and rubs her nose. "No, it's OK, we need your help to get Lorraine sitting up in bed."

"And," Lorraine says between her sobs, "to help me get out of bed so that I can go to the loo."

"When you're done with that, Raine," Dee says, "we need to talk about this blasted awards thing. You're not fit enough to go."

"You're up for an award, of course we're going." Lorraine speaks with more determination than she feels, but she's not letting Dee down.

"You're nowhere near well enough."

"Dress me up as best we can, drug me up to the eyeballs, and dump me in a bloody chair when we get there." Lorraine glares at Dee as she points her finger at the wheelchair. "My knees might be a bit bruised from the fall, but my legs are still working. We're going."

Dee folds her arms across her chest. "I'm not happy with you doing anything so strenuous when we're still watching you for concussion."

"If I don't feel up for it later, you and Morgan can go without me. Maybe take Holly in my place. But honestly, I'd be gutted if you won and I wasn't there. I'd rather put up with the pain for one night and watch you pick up that award you deserve so much."

"No, Raine, I don't—"

"Ah-ah-ah," Lorraine interrupts, putting her hand up to Dee. "I'll not hear any more of this. Anyway, what else will I do with myself? It's not like I can get on with the cleaning or roof repairs in this state. No, we're going tonight, and that's that."

Dee gives Lorraine a peck on the nose, and as she walks out of the room Lorraine hears a quiet '*daft sod*' being muttered under Dee's breath. She sinks back into her pain, and grimaces. Yes, she's a daft sod, and it's going to take every bit of energy she's got, but this could be Dee's moment, and she wants to be there for her at the award ceremony.

28

GEORGIE

The Day of the Award Ceremony

HUNTER hands Georgie's car key back to her.

"Everything's packed into your car."

"Thanks, Hunter." Georgie holds out a hand to him. "I'm all paid up, so I guess that's that, then." She looks around the hall, as if soaking up the last of the fairy dust that the retreat has to offer her. "I've not said goodbye to the bees."

"You're as bad as Holly, with those bloody bees." Hunter laughs. "You best go and bid them farewell. And I think Holly's out in the kitchen garden, so you can say goodbye to her, too."

Georgie nods and turns her back on the front door, making her way to the garden. Holly is in the greenhouse, and lifts a trowel to wave. Georgie smiles and weaves her way to the back of the garden and the beehive.

"Hey, bees. I've come to say goodbye." She takes her usual seat on the raised bed opposite the hive and leans forwards, resting her arms in her lap. "I've loved getting to know you and your habits. Thanks for listening to my ramblings. You've given me space to open up about stuff." Georgie smiles to herself. "Well, you and

Holly have. She's a good woman – but then, you already know that about your beekeeper, don't you?" She sighs. "Wish I could stay longer and sample some of your honey. I hope you're all OK with the changes that are going to happen here. Hold on tight, it's going to be quite a ride." One bee after another exits the hive and buzzes past Georgie. As she pushes herself up to standing, her phone buzzes in her pocket. Carla is messaging her.

Carla: *Hey you, time to spill the beans. Coffee?*

Gee: *Just on my way home, will call from the car in a mo*

Carla: *OK*

Pocketing her phone, Georgie pops her head around the greenhouse door.

"Thanks for everything, Holly. I've loved spending time with you and your bees."

"Anytime, Georgie. You're welcome to come by whenever. You don't need to wait until you come and stay at Pinewoods again."

"That's good of you. I – I'll be back, for sure." Georgie turns away, conscious that she's blushing. Of course she'll be back, just not in the way that these lovely people expect. As she makes her way to her car, her throat tightens. A piece of Georgie wants to turn around and say to Holly '*don't let me go home*', that if she does go home to Ryan, it's going to ruin everything, that the retreat's future is in her hands. She hangs her head as she turns the corner to her car.

"Now, that's the face of someone who doesn't want to go home, if you ask me," Ed says, smiling at her. He's leaning his back into her car, his arms folded across his body, Moose laid across his feet.

"I didn't want you leaving without saying goodbye." Moose lifts his head as if it's an effort, but seeing Georgie, he scampers over to her, nuzzling her ankles, and whining to be picked up.

Georgie crouches down and picks up Moose, stroking his head as she does. "We said goodbye over breakfast." She feels the pull towards Ed, but holds her ground. She can't afford to let her heart rule her head. Biting her upper lip, as if stopping herself from saying something she'll regret, Georgie stuffs her hand into her pocket. Her fingers stroke the piece of tiger's eye nestled there. She pulls it out and looks down at it. What was it Lorraine said it was for? Something about grounding herself and dealing with chaos. She closes her fingers around the stone – yes, in this moment, she has to stay grounded.

"Look, Ed, I – it's just, I . . ." What's the matter with her? She's never tongue-tied.

"I know," Ed says. "You're married. You've said it a few times." He looks down at the ground and scuffs the gravel with the toe of his shoe. "I'd like to see you again." Slowly, Ed raises his head and looks her straight in the eyes.

Georgie shakes her head. "I can't do this, Ed."

"You can if you want to." He pushes himself off the car and takes a step towards her. "But you gave me the impression you want something more."

"Why won't you take no for an answer, Ed?"

"Because I don't think you've been saying no. You've not said no, you've said you don't know and that you're married, and I don't think you're happy in your marriage." The words fall out of his mouth in a rush. "And this feels real between us and I don't think you're being honest with me." Ed stops and takes a breath. "Or with yourself."

Georgie looks down at Moose and strokes his head. She squeezes her eyes shut. Every cell in her heart wants Ed, and every cell of her brain is telling her to get in the car and drive away before she acts on her feelings. "All of that's true, Ed. Every word."

Ed reaches for her hand and Georgie opens her mouth to tell him that she just needs to get the next couple of days out the way, that if this is what he wants, she's willing to give it a try, that they can meet up at that café they went to in Formby, that she's open to seeing where this takes them – when chatter quickly works its way towards them from the other side of the hedge that wraps around the car park. Beth and Kate round the corner, followed by Hunter. Georgie pushes Moose out towards Ed, masking the fact that they were almost holding hands, her smile lopsided. Ed takes the dog from her, raising his eyebrows, as if he knows she was about to say something and is still keen to hear it, despite the company they now have.

"Are you off, Georgie?" Beth asks.

"Yes. Back to real life. You both, as well?"

"Only me. I've a couple of work things to do, and then I'll be back in a few days. Kate's here for the whole of the next week."

"Of course, more training to do, Kate. Keep it up, you're doing really well."

Kate nods eagerly at Georgie. "Thanks for helping."

"I'm not sure I want to go back to reality, even if it is only for a few days," Beth says. "Fallen in love with the place."

Georgie looks up at the house. "Yes. Seems it's easy to fall in love here." As she looks back down from the house her eyes catch Ed's and she realises what she said. They hold each other's gaze for a moment. "I best be off." Georgie clears her throat. "Good luck with the run, Kate. Nice to meet you both." She chucks Moose under the chin before squeezing herself down the narrow gap between her car and the wall, and as she eases herself into the driver's seat, she recalls the scrape she did on the wing when she arrived. She'll need to get that sorted when she gets home.

* * *

As soon as she's on the main road, Georgie calls Carla.

"You took your time," Carla barks as a greeting.

"Sorry, sorry, took a bit longer to get away than I expected."

"Come on, darling, spill. What's this secret trip all been about?"

"We're working on something for Mick Rodgers." Georgie pauses as she checks for traffic before pulling out at a junction.

"And?" Carla presses.

"He's found this place he wants to buy, but you know what Mick's like."

"Oh yes," Carla says, "always after a bargain."

"So he sent me off to do some digging. I was booked in as Georgie Macrae, and I've spent the last week seeing what I could find out to help him get the place as cheap as possible."

"How exciting. You went undercover. Our Georgie, the mole." Carla guffaws. "What fun."

"It didn't feel much like fun."

"And did you find anything out?"

"A bit. I report back to Mick tomorrow. Not sure it's going to help him all that much." Georgie finds herself saying a silent prayer that her information won't help him at all. "It doesn't feel right, though. They're such lovely people."

"Mick won't care about that. Come on, I was looking forward to a bit of goss. There must be more you can tell me. What's this place called?"

"Pinewoods Retreat. It's in Formby, which is how you came to bump into me in the village."

"Ah yes, you were with that gorgeous hunk of a man. And how did *that* school reunion go?" Carla snorts as she laughs.

"It was nice to see him again after all these years."

"Nice? That's a bit tame for such a dreamy bloke, isn't it?"

Georgie laughs. "I'm married, Carla, in case you've forgotten."

"To a man who can't keep his dick in his pants."

"Carla!" There's an unspoken rule between them that they never talk about Ryan's infidelity, not since Carla gossiped, many years ago, about Ryan being with an acquaintance of theirs, only for Georgie to find out it wasn't true. But by then, the woman had heard that her name had been paired up with Ryan Quinn's, and she blamed Georgie for spreading rumours to hurt her business reputation. After that, Georgie made Carla swear she would never get involved again, and they've not talked about any of Ryan's affairs.

"I'm right, and you know it," Carla goes on. "Ryan Quinn

doesn't deserve you. You're a fool to put up with him."

Georgie flinches at the tone of judgement in Carla's comment. "We're fine. Our marriage works perfectly well for us." Even as she says it, Georgie isn't convinced by her own words.

"For him, you mean."

Georgie taps her finger nails on the steering wheel. "Can we talk about something else, Carla?"

"What about tonight? Got your speech prepared?"

"Yes, all done, though it won't hurt to go through it again when I get home."

"Can't wait to cheer you on. Being given this award is huge. Our Georgie, mole extraordinaire and Liverpool's Businesswoman of the Year."

"It is huge, isn't it?" Georgie smiles to herself. When the letter arrived informing her that she was being honoured as Liverpool's Businesswoman of the Year, she didn't believe it at first. But as the weeks have passed, she's come to realise that it's a great opportunity to get the word out about LivSmarter and the work she and her staff do to support vulnerable women wanting to get into the workplace after a break, for whatever reason. She'll leverage the award to get some much-needed funding in, and to raise the profile of what LivSmarter does for women in the region.

"What time will you get there? You know me, I'm bound to be late." Carla guffaws again, and Georgie finds herself rattled by the sound of her friend's laughter after the peace she experienced at Pinewoods.

As soon as she can, Georgie ends the call, saying she's just pulling into her driveway, even though she has another couple of miles or so to cover, and she enjoys the last part of her journey in silence.

***

A little after four, Georgie pulls up outside her mum's hair salon. Dot waves from the window, and moments later places her garment bag on the back seat before easing herself into the car next to Georgie.

"Is that a prang on your new car?" Dot leans over and kisses Georgie on the cheek. "Did someone crash into you?"

"No, Mum, I did that all by myself." Georgie cringes. "And I've not told Ryan yet, so don't you go and say anything when you see him. I'll need to pick my moment."

"I'll not say a word. How's my girl?"

"I'm good, Mum. Feeling relaxed after my week away."

"And ready for your big award. I was telling them all about it in the salon. Everyone is so excited for you. Liverpool's very own Deborah Meaden."

Georgie laughs, slowly manoeuvring the car into traffic. "You're biased, Mum."

"Of course I am. If a mum can't be proud of her daughter's achievements, well." She claps in excitement. "D'you like me hair?"

"Love it. You're going to look a million dollars tonight."

"And what about you? Tell us about this week away. You look a lot brighter than you did before you went to this place."

"It was . . ." Georgie searches for the right word. *Relaxing? Tranquil? Restful?* "Heavenly," she sighs.

"Oo, I say. Heavenly. Maybe I need to book in there. Where is it?"

"Only in Formby, so not far."

"And this is where you bumped into little Eddie Dixon?"

"Ed, yes." Georgie feels a light blush spread up her neck, and hopes Dot keeps her eyes looking ahead at the road. "And he's not a little lad any more." She laughs, recalling how surprised she was when she realised the gorgeous man at the retreat was one and the same as the class nerd from school.

"Lovely lad." Dot turns and looks at Georgie. "And I'm guessing from that smile on your face that you fancy him." She winks and gives Georgie a cheeky smile.

"Hmm, quite possibly, Mum. It was great to see him again. But – I'm married." How many times has she said that today, let alone all the times she's said it in the last week? And every time she says it, there's that word – *but*. It's like she's screaming out to everyone that she wants to hold Ed, kiss him, touch him, and that she'd do all that and more, if only she wasn't married. Georgie shakes her head.

"And if you weren't?"

Taking her eyes off the road for a second, Georgie glances at her mum, eyebrow raised inquisitively.

"I am married, so it's not up for debate."

"Being married doesn't stop that husband of yours."

Georgie gives the traffic her attention for a moment as she takes the filter lane to turn right onto quieter roads. "Don't go reading anything into me bumping into Ed, Mum," she says as she waits for the traffic to clear. "It was nothing. I was only there a week, and besides, I hardly even saw Ed." She'd love nothing more than to agree with her mum and tell her that yes, she definitely took to Ed Dixon, to tell her how gorgeous he is now, that there was a mutual attraction between them, that she wishes she could see him again. Damn it, she wants to tell her mum that she wishes she'd not been such a goody-two-shoes, that she'd let herself have a week of fun with Ed. But she won't say any of that. She won't say anything that changes the status quo, because if she does that, she might open up about other things to her mum, too, and if she's too honest, it comes down to her not being prepared to put their lifestyle at risk. No, she's best saying nothing. "It was a great week of relaxation, Mum, that's all."

Georgie feels Dot's eyes lingering on her for a moment, before her mum returns her gaze to the road ahead.

"I'm glad you had a lovely time, Georgie."

"Me too, Mum. Now then," she speeds up now they are through the worst of the traffic, "let's get back to mine and have a quick snack before we get our glad rags on for tonight."

29

LORRAINE

The Award Ceremony

LORRAINE, Dee and Morgan study the seating plan for their names, or at the very least for the name of the guy who invited them as his guests.

"Christ, there's a lot of tables," Dee says. "I didn't realise it was such a big event."

"There's lots of people too," Lorraine says, adjusting her arm restraint and already regretting her decision to come. She should have let Holly come in her place, like Dee suggested, but she's here now, and she's just going to have to make the most of it. "I'm suddenly very conscious of how close everyone is getting to my arm, even with this restraint on," Lorraine goes on. "It's like they don't even notice I'm wearing a sling."

"I knew we shouldn't have come," Dee says, giving Lorraine a disapproving look. "It's stupid. Could we just turn around and go home, do you think?"

"No." Lorraine smiles, working hard not to show any signs of pain on her face. "We're here now."

"Have you got that invitation, again, Lorraine?" Morgan asks. "Let's see if we've got that fella's name right."

Lorraine passes it over to Morgan who glances down at the information embossed on the card in a script font. "I'm not even sure this helps. I still can't see us on the table plan. Or him. We need to find someone to help us."

It takes a couple of the events team to eventually locate their seats, after someone realises the table is booked in the name of the man's business, rather than his own name. The three of them are guided through the throng of people and shown to their seats. They're the first to arrive at the table.

"Thirteen," Morgan says.

"What?" Lorraine asks.

"There's thirteen seats at this table. Us three, and another ten people."

"I hope they're not total bores," Dee says. "You know, business bores who talk shop, slap each other on the back and guffaw at things that aren't the slightest bit funny." She pulls a chair out for Lorraine and indicates for her to sit down. "I'll need to chop your food up for you, Raine. And I know your name card shows you sitting at the end of us three, but I think it's better I sit there so that nobody knocks into your arm."

"Matthew Crane," Morgan says, reading the label at the seat next to hers. "And next to him is Carla Crane. Presumably husband and wife.

"And it's someone called Annabelle Rodgers next to you, Dee," Lorraine says. "That'll be Mick Rodgers's wife."

"Drink?" Morgan asks. "I'm going to the bar."

As Morgan goes off to get the drinks order in, people start filling up the tables around them and the noise in St George's Hall goes up a notch. Lorraine focuses on her breathing for a moment, in the hope it takes her attention away from the pain she's feeling, and she watches as Dee's eyes wander around the room.

"I don't know why we came, Raine," Dee says. "We don't fit in at these kinds of places these days."

"We came to celebrate you and your food being nominated for an award," Lorraine says. "But I do agree. Look at how dressed up all these people are. I feel a right old frump in my version of my Sunday best, with my arm in this ugly restraint." She nods down at the black sling holding her arm tight to her body.

An announcement is made via the microphone on the stage that the meal will be served in twenty minutes, and in the meantime everyone's to enjoy '*a bit of a boogie*'. The DJ starts with an old favourite, and women force their way to the dance floor.

"Dance, anyone?" Lorraine says, laughing.

"We could do a one-handed hand jive," Dee says, rhythmically moving the upper half of her body in time to the music.

"That was a bit of a bun fight at the bar," Morgan says, setting the drinks down on the table. "Six deep, at least, so I doubled up on the order to keep us going."

"Lorraine, Dee. You're here." San comes up behind them and gives them a hug, and Lorraine cries out in pain. "Oh god, what did I do?"

"Squeezed her too tight, San," Dee says, standing up and

hugging their friend. "She had an accident, and that arm is in a right old mess."

"Bloody hell, Lorraine. What are you even doing here?"

"How could I not come? What if Dee wins, and I miss it?"

"You're a silly fool," San says, smiling at Lorraine. "And you decided the best thing you could do was to come to this event after doing that to yourself?"

"You tell her, San," Dee says, raising her eyebrows with a look of disapproval directed at Lorraine.

"You'll have to tell me more when I pop over to Pinewoods, but whilst I'd love to stay and natter, I'm here for work tonight. Reporting on the awards for the *Liverpool Standard News*. We'll catch up in a couple of days to work out what we do for your marketing off the back of this." She leans in and kisses Dee on the cheek. "Not sure I dare get close to you again tonight, Lorraine." San cringes. "I don't want to hurt you again. Speak soon." She blows Lorraine a kiss and walks off purposefully in the direction of a woman with a clipboard resting on her arm.

More people fill the hall, and Lorraine takes in the event. This is the kind of thing she regularly attended in her old life as an account manager for a huge pharmaceutical company, wining and dining important clients with the bosses, taking whole tables at charity events and the like. She thought nothing of spending the night out until well gone one, and was still at her desk before eight the next day, copious cups of coffee giving her the appearance of being wide awake and bushy tailed. Eventually it took its toll, and Lorraine burnt out. She has no regrets for any of that life, particularly as the money she earned and the knowledge she gained about big pharma brought her to the life she loves. And seeing people around her now, already high on adrenaline and drink and lord knows what else, she's glad she's moved on from that high octane lifestyle.

"Evening, ladies," a voice booms behind Lorraine. "Who do we have here, then?"

Lorraine looks up at a man standing with his hands on his hips, looking for all the world like he owns the place. This must be Mick Rodgers. Dee stands and offers her hand, introducing the three of them, and Lorraine recalls Dee telling her that she's met Mick Rodgers before.

"Great to meet you all," the man says, still failing to introduce himself as he takes a seat at the table, arms stretched out across the two chairs either side of him, and assuming a universal knowledge of who he is. "Glad to see my PA organised your tickets. Big night." He points at Lorraine's arm. "Been in the wars?" he asks.

"I took a bit of a tumble when I was doing some DIY," Lorraine says.

He grins back at Lorraine. "Not a fan of DIY myself," he says. "Always best to get someone in, if you ask me." Something about his grin makes Lorraine feel a little uncomfortable, but out of politeness she smiles back. "Unless you can't stretch to paying contractors, I guess."

Another man comes up behind the grinner and pats him on the shoulder.

"Mick, mate, how're you doing?"

Mick stands and the two men enter into a back-slapping dance that's clearly familiar to them both.

"And who do we have here?" the second man asks, a look passing between the two of them.

Mick throws his head back and laughs, despite there being nothing for him to laugh about, before introducing Lorraine, Dee and Morgan. He makes a point of telling this man that Lorraine has had an accident.

"Sorry to hear that," he says, the broad smile across his face oddly contradicting his words.

"Forgive my manners, ladies," Mick says, his voice booming across the table. "Mick Rodgers, local developer and your host this evening, and this is my associate, Ryan Quinn. Delighted to have you here as my guests this evening."

30

GEORGIE

THE cacophony in St George's Hall assaults Georgie after the peace of Pinewoods Retreat. A few weeks ago, she would have relished the mishmash of music and revelry, but now it feels overwhelming, like she's jumped into the deep end of an ice-cold pool before acclimatising to the water temperature.

Despite being unsettled by the noise, she's buzzing from the attention she's receiving about her award. It's already public knowledge that she's being honoured as Liverpool's Business Woman of the Year, and even though the presentation bit has yet to happen, and she's still to give her acceptance speech, it took her a good twenty minutes to reach the loos, having made a beeline for them the moment she and Ryan arrived at St George's Hall. She's fairly well known in Liverpool, and woman after woman that she passed stopped her to congratulate her, or to get a selfie, or to tell her how much they admire her – one woman after another telling her how great she is for women of the city, that she deserves this, that she's an inspiration to entrepreneurs everywhere. Ever the professional, Georgie doesn't let on that she's more than a little overwhelmed at being bombarded by so many women, and instead she thanks each person as if they're the only one in the room to congratulate her, and moves on towards the toilets only to be stopped by more women, more congratulations.

When she eventually reaches the toilets, she's relieved to have the space to herself, a moment to collect her thoughts before they eat and before she takes to the podium and delivers her speech. She slowly breathes in, a smile spread across her face, and checks herself in the mirror before walking into a cubicle.

She settles herself down to pee as sounds of laughter and cheering on the other side of the cubicle door fills the Ladies. Georgie smiles at the sounds of fun from the women.

"I wanna be like Georgie Quinn when I'm successful," one of the women says. Georgie's heart swells with pride at being held in such esteem. Never in a million years, when she was in her teens and cleaning offices, did she ever expect to become someone that other women would admire like this.

"God, yeah," another woman adds, "who wouldn't?"

"Christ, not me," someone else says, and Georgie flinches. "I mean, what the frig is her fella like, doing that to her?" The woman's voice is loud, as if she's failed to adjust her volume now that she's away from the dance music playing in the main hall. Georgie stands up from the toilet and adjusts her underwear.

"Ryan Quinn's always been like that, to be fair. I don't know how she puts up with him."

Georgie's heart thuds. She steadies herself against the toilet door. These are not voices she knows, but they talk as if familiar with her, as if being in the public eye of Liverpool's business community gives them ownership over her.

"Yeah, but come on, bringing your frigging latest fling to an event where your frigging wife is being honoured. That's gotta take some frigging nerve, that has."

Beads of sweat form at Georgie's hairline. What the heck? Ryan's brought that woman to the award ceremony? Georgie gasps for air, wiping a hand across the back of her neck, lifting her hair with a vain hope that the act will serve to cool her down.

"That Faith Jacks is nothing like his usual bits on the side. She's gotta be older than Georgie, yeah?"

Faith Jacks. So that's the woman's name. Georgie searches her memory banks but nobody of that name springs to mind.

"Well, Ryan Quinn is flaunting it tonight. Did you see him just now on the dance floor? I'm guessing Georgie's gone to the . . ." There's a long pause.

Silence.

Georgie imagines all eyes trained on the cubicle door. Barely able to swallow, she pushes her shoulders back, unlocks the door, and opens it wide.

"Ladies," she says, with a tight-lipped smile, her heart thudding. She counts her breath in.

Mouths turn to 'oo's and she walks through the group of five women, straight to the sink, slowly counting her breaths out.

"Shi-i-i-t!" It's the voice of the woman who brought up Faith Jacks's name.

Georgie turns, water dripping from her hands, and follows the group's gaze. A woman stands by the door, letting it swing shut behind her.

"Faith fucking Jacks," another of the group of women says, her voice almost a whisper.

Shit, indeed. Georgie takes a good look at the woman. She's wearing a black 1950s-style dress, tight at the waist with a sweetheart neckline, her long blonde hair curled down her back. She's understated pretty, and yes, a little older than Georgie.

"Let's get out of here," one of the women says.

"But I desperately need a pee."

"Then use the frigging disabled loo."

They bundle themselves out of the Ladies, leaving Georgie and Faith facing each other. A spark of tension in the air speaks for them.

The toilet door opens again, and in walks a woman wearing an oversized, long green floaty A-line kaftan dress that Georgie's seen before. It takes her a split second of confusion to realise it's Morgan.

"Really?" Georgie says, rolling her eyes and throwing her hands up in exasperation. Is the universe conspiring against her? Moments ago she was soaking up the joy of being at an amazing event where she'll be crowned Liverpool's Businesswoman of the Year, and now she's looking at Ryan's new fling, Faith Jacks, and an out-of-place Morgan, who looks like she's just walked straight out of Pinewoods and into St George's Hall. Georgie lets out a short, weary laugh, suddenly feeling breathless. She turns and rests her hands on the edge of the sink. When she looks into the mirrors in front of her, Faith is closing a cubicle door. Morgan takes a step towards Georgie, her hand outstretched. She stops a couple of feet away and lets her arm drop back to her side.

"Georgie?" Morgan looks as confused as Georgie feels.

Georgie shakes her head and studies her reflection in the mirror. There's no hiding who she really is from everyone at Pinewoods Retreat any more. It's not exactly like it matters now that her cover is blown, but she'd far rather not have to explain things to Morgan right now.

"I didn't expect to see you here, Morgan."

"Dee's up for an award for the café. We're here as some businessman's guests. What about you?"

"Officially, I'm here to pick up an award myself." Georgie lets out a sarcastic laugh. "Unofficially," she rolls her eyes, "seems I'm here to meet my husband's latest fling." She squeezes her eyes shut for a moment and takes in a long slow breath.

The toilet flushes behind her and Faith reappears, steps towards the sink next to Georgie, wets the tips of her fingers and, as if thinking better of it, turns on her heels and leaves the Ladies loos.

Morgan stands there, looking at Georgie, saying nothing.

"What?" Georgie squeezes her eyes shut for a moment. She absentmindedly washes her hands for a second time.

Morgan shakes herself, as if she'd been lost in the previous moment.

"Go on," Georgie says, "you might as well say whatever's on your mind."

"There's nothing on my mind, beyond being very confused about what's going on." Her voice is quiet and gentle.

"Well, to bring you up to speed, I'm Georgie Quinn, I'm married to Ryan Quinn, here to pick up an award – and *that's* the third person in my marriage." She jabs the air in the direction of the door that Faith Jacks just walked through. "That's who my husband is having an affair with. And apparently the whole of Liverpool knew before me."

"Wow." Morgan's eyes are wide. "So, let me get this straight. You're telling me you're not who you said you were when you stayed at Pinewoods? And you've just bumped into the other woman you didn't know exists? I don't get why you needed to hide who are from us, Georgie, but hey, this thing, bumping into that woman, that can't be easy for you." Morgan looks over her shoulder at the closed toilet door. "Did you know about her before tonight?" She turns back to Georgie.

"No," Georgie says, her voice barely a whisper. She closes her eyes. "I mean, I kind of had a feeling," she opens her eyes again, "and then when I was at Pinewoods I checked the doorbell video and saw her going into our house. At night. But I didn't know who she was until a few minutes ago." She shakes herself. For goodness sake, what is she doing discussing her marriage with Morgan? "Anyway," she straightens her back and forces her voice into professional mode, "life goes on." She smiles, inspects herself again in the mirror, teases a strand of hair back into place, and calms her breathing to regain her composure. She's not having this conversation with Morgan. She's not having it with anyone.

"You can't be happy, though." Morgan's words slice through the mask that Georgie is desperate to wear so that she can get through the night. "He can't care about you, not enough, not when he's treating you like this. Where's the respect?"

Georgie turns to face Morgan, expecting to see malice written across her face. Instead, she sees kindness, concern, and for a moment Georgie thinks she might crack. She blinks, once, twice.

"Honestly," Morgan continues, resting a gentle hand on Georgie's arm, "you deserve better than a man like him will ever give you."

Not daring to stay and hear any more of Morgan's words, Georgie marches out of the Ladies toilets. As the door closes behind her, she plasters a networking smile on her face and goes off in search of her table, more women stopping her along the way to congratulate her and tell her how much they admire her.

By the time Georgie arrives at the table, food is already being served. She says a quick hello to her friends, Carla, Ali and Sian, along with their husbands, and then takes her seat between Mick and Ryan. Looking across the table to say hello to Mick's wife, Annabelle, she takes in the guests sitting opposite her, the ones that Ryan told her would be joining their table as Mick's guests this evening. Her stomach lurches. There, on the other side of the table from her, Lorraine and Dee stare at Georgie, wide-eyed, half smiles across their faces. What the heck? It's not just that Lorraine, Dee and Morgan are at the awards, they're sitting at the same table. As Mick's guests. Seriously, what the ...

The little appetite Georgie had immediately vanishes.

"Am I seeing things?" Lorraine asks, laughing. "Or is it the medication I'm on? It is you, isn't it, Georgie?"

"Lorraine, Dee," Georgie says, forcing a networking smile. "Nice to see you again. How – how's the arm?" She leans in to

Ryan. "We need to talk," she whispers into his ear, "now!" She looks back across the table. "Excuse us a moment, ladies."

Georgie stands and grabs hold of Ryan's jacket sleeve, forcing him to follow her. They weave their way through the tables and when they get close to the bar, she turns to him.

"What the hell, Ryan." She rests her palm on her forehead. "You said Mick invited some guests, but you omitted to say it's the very people I've been staying with?"

"Mick thought it would be a bit of fun," Ryan says. He lets out a nervous laugh and clears his throat. "A bit of an entrée for what's to come." He attempts to laugh again. "Maybe not, huh?"

"Damn right it's not. Why invite them at all? I don't get it."

"They think they've got a chance at winning an award tonight. For their café, I think. They haven't. Got a chance, that is. Mick rigged it. So when they don't win, he's going in with his offer."

"How, Ry? How can he even know what his offer is yet? I've not updated you both on the latest of what's going on there."

Ryan shrugs. "He's decided you'll be the best person to take the offer to them after our meeting."

"Why me?"

"Cos you've met them already, struck up a relationship with them."

"And he's that sure of himself, is he? That he's already worked up an offer before he's even got all the information he needs?"

Ryan shrugs again. "You know what Mick's like." He tugs at his ear.

"So if he didn't need to wait for my input to draw up his offer,

252

why did I need to go and stay at Pinewoods Retreat for a week, then?"

"Anything you found out will help Mick's case. I'm sure of it." Ryan rubs his hands together and gives her a cheeky grin. "Anyway, food's getting cold and I'm starving. Come on, babe." Ryan walks past Georgie, nudging her shoulder as he passes her and returns to their table.

Georgie follows him, fuming. How many more surprises is he going to spring on her, tonight of all nights?

"Well done, Georgie," a woman's voice calls from one of the tables she passes. Georgie raises a hand in a half-hearted wave, working hard to control her thumping heart before she gets back to her seat.

31
GEORGIE

ONE by one, each of the award categories is announced, with the winners going up on stage to be applauded. When it gets to the café awards, Georgie glances at Lorraine and Dee and sees them exchange a look of excitement. The names of the nominees are read out, with polite applause accompanying each café name and the description of why it's been nominated. A place on the Wirral is given a 'highly commended'. And as the winner is announced as a place in Aigburth, Georgie sees Lorraine and Dee's shoulders slump. She's been to the place in Aigburth. It's nice enough, but the food isn't a patch on what Dee makes, and Georgie's heart goes out to the two women she's spent the last week with. From what Ryan said, they were never going to win, however good Dee's food is.

"Oh god," Carla says, leaning over towards Lorraine. "Was that you, the garden café at Pinewoods Retreat?"

Dee's eyes glisten as she nods back at Carla.

"Shame," Carla says. "And Georgie said your food was amazing, too."

"There'll be other awards," Lorraine says. "Our turn will come."

Carla guffaws. "Doubt it," she says, before taking a sip of her wine. If Georgie was sitting next to Carla, she'd be giving her a big old shunt with her elbow to remind her friend to be careful with what she says. As it is, she has to hope that at the very least nobody else heard what she said, or, if they did, they won't understand what she means.

There's a gap in the handing out of the awards as the event photographer asks all the winners to come on stage so that she can take a few pictures. A hum of chatter grows around the room, and Morgan leans in towards Carla.

"Did I hear you say that you doubt Lorraine and Dee's place will ever get an award?"

Carla bays. "From what I've heard from Georgie, they've not got much of a future."

"Carla?" Georgie cuts through her friend's words and frowns at her.

"What? I've not said anything." Carla takes a slug from her glass of wine.

"And what exactly," Morgan asks, "did Georgie say about Pinewoods?" She scowls at Georgie.

"Nothing," Georgie says. "I said nothing. Just, you know . . . nothing." She struggles to swallow. Obviously, Lorraine and Dee will know exactly who she is in a few minutes, that she lied to them about her name, and within a matter of days they'll know exactly why she was at Pinewoods, but tonight is not the time for the truth to come out, not when it's only moments before she goes up on the stage. "I think Carla's maybe had a drink or two too many." She looks pointedly at Carla, who immediately empties her glass before filling it up again.

With the photos done, the compère returns to the podium.

"If you'll all take your seats ladies, it's now time to move onto the climax of the evening." There are murmurs as people take their seats again, and Georgie's heart pounds as nerves momentarily take over. "Tonight," the compère goes on, "we are here to honour one of Liverpool's most enterprising businesswomen, Georgie Quinn."

The compère clears her throat and smiles at Georgie, who almost rises from her chair before remembering she was told to stay in her seat until after a short speech about her.

"This is a woman," the compère continues, "who needs little introduction in Liverpool. She's all over the press with the work she does to support women who need a bit of a leg-up. And many of you here tonight will have had first-hand experience of her generosity of spirit, guidance and, in some cases, money too. Her business, LivSmarter, was born out of a deep understanding of how important first impressions are for women going to interviews. Georgie's team works tirelessly to source suitable interview attire, help women pick out an outfit appropriate to the job they're going for, and then coach these candidates to be able to answer any questions with confidence. I can only say, I wish there'd been something like LivSmarter when I went back to work after having my little brood of kids." Light laughter in recognition of life with kids ripples around the room.

"But Georgie Quinn doesn't stop there. When a woman gets a job, her and her team of coaches then provide help for those first day nerves, again providing an outfit or two so that they can turn up looking the part in their first week, and coaching them in how to fit into the world of work, be that with an update in computer skills or how to read the room in a meeting, and so much more. With the help of LivSmarter, we have women in senior positions in the council, in local business, working as managers of retail stores, and running hotels and bars. There are two women here who have written their own books about their experiences of going from addiction to the board. And we've got more than a handful who have set up their own ventures, some of which Georgie has personally invested in."

The compère pauses and looks around the vast hall. "I'm sure that those of you in the room tonight who have personally benefitted from Georgie Quinn's guidance will want to join me in a particularly warm and heartfelt welcome to the stage – ladies and gentlemen," her voice rises in volume, "I give you, Georgie Quinn."

The applause is deafening. Georgie gets up from her seat and climbs the steps to the stage, clutching tight hold of her speech in one hand as she takes her award with the other. Her heart swells with pride for all that she has achieved to get here, to this moment of recognition.

"Thank you, thank you," Georgie says into the mic, and as she waits for the clapping and whistles and whoops to die down, she looks over at her mum. Dot blows her a kiss, before placing her hands over her heart. Georgie beams back at her and holds up her award, a large glass Liver Bird, before placing it onto the podium next to her, letting her hand settle on top of it.

"Ladies and – er – gentlemen? Do we have many men here tonight?" She smiles. "I know there's at least one. My darling husband, Ryan." She cringes inside as she nods over at Ryan. Out of the corner of her eye she sees Lorraine, Dee and Morgan staring at her, their mouths open in what Georgie can only assume is surprise at discovering who she actually is.

"It's a great honour to receive – ah, heck, you expect me to say all that kind of crap." Georgie looks out at the audience, and there's a ripple of laughter around the enormous space at St George's Hall. "As many of you know, I'm one half of QuinnEssentials, our business that is headed by my husband, Ryan Quinn, that has built our reputations as project managers for developments across the city. And, as with many businesses headed by a man, pretty much everything you know about QuinnEssentials will include Ryan's name. But tonight isn't about Ryan." She puts her hands over her eyes and peers out into the bright lights hanging over the audience. "Sorry, babe." The audience follows her cue and laughs. "Tonight, this award," Georgie holds the Liver Bird up for a moment, "isn't even about me. I'm just the figurehead. It's really about the women of Liverpool who dare to dream, the women who dare to achieve, who dare to succeed."

Applause erupts around the Hall.

"I started LivSmarter two decades ago for young women who don't get the same opportunities I had. Intelligent women who are judged by how they look, or judged for the nerves of being in unfamiliar environments. My mum – where are you, Dot?" Georgie waves to her mum, knowing exactly where to find her, and Dot waves back, blowing her another kiss. "My mum had a tough life, but she taught me to believe in myself, to dream big. She's been my number one fan, always in my corner. Thanks, Mum, love you. And because of my mum, Dot Macrae, I dared to dream big for me and for other women too. I had a dream to be a guardian angel for women who have nobody in their corner, all those women who don't have a Dot Macrae in their lives, and I'm proud, so proud, that I've seen that dream to fruition – and then some."

There's a ripple of '*whoop*' and '*go girl*' from the crowd.

"I remember when I was told 'stay in your lane, woman' – and apparently, according to one big-wig a couple of decades ago, my lane is firmly in the kitchen. But I say to you, each and every one of you smart, driven women here tonight who has worked harder than any man around you just to prove you're their equal, and still doubt if you're good enough – I say to you, don't you *dare* settle for small." Rapturous applause breaks out again and Georgie has to wait for it to die down. "You get out of your lane, you stand in your power, you claim your place in the boardroom." More applause, with some women jumping to their feet, hands above their heads as they clap.

The room calms down again. "And if you don't yet know your place, if you've not been given the opportunities others ahead of you have had, I can tell you now, it's there, reach for it, because you deserve better." Georgie's voice catches. Those were Morgan's words to her little more than an hour ago, and she's right. That Ryan would dare to bring his new fling to *her* night, dare to disrespect her, his *wife*, on the biggest night of her career . . . She takes a sip of water from the glass on the podium. Applause trickles around the room, filling the moment of silence. "You. Deserve. Better." Georgie repeats her line, fighting to stay in the moment, stay strong, own the room. She looks out at the women and handful of men in front of her. These women *do* deserve better. Damn it! *She* deserves better.

"People talk about manifesting. If you dream hard enough, raise the frequency of your energies, everything you wish for will be yours. That might be true. And I've just told you that you deserve better. Know this." Georgie pauses and looks to the left, looks to the right, eventually settling her eyes on the tables directly ahead of her. "If you sit on your backside and do nothing, you'll get nothing. If you believe you don't deserve the best, you'll never get the best, however much you put a manifesting mindset out into the universe. But if you *make* it happen, if you give the universe a helping hand, you can do anything you dream. Manifesting *is* making it happen. Believe in that, and the world is yours for the taking."

Georgie's own words hit her in the heart. Is this what she's done? Manifested the life she's living, with a husband who thinks nothing of his serial infidelity and shows her no respect? She clears her throat and looks down at her award.

"You know," Georgie says, looking back up and jabbing a finger at the crowd. She ignores her well-rehearsed, pre-prepared speech laid out on the podium in front of her. "I spent my whole career with an eye on the money. Every disadvantaged young woman who has been helped through LivSmarter, every one of the businesswomen I've mentored who is here tonight – you know I've encouraged you to keep your sights on the money. I told you, it's all about the profit, the bottom line. I've given speeches on how, at QuinnEssentials, we went from 'zero to zillions'." She mimes quotation marks with her fingers. "But when it's just about the money, something's missing. Heart. And. Soul. The essence of you and who you are at your core." Georgie lays a hand on her chest and steadies herself.

"I recently stayed at a place in the woods, the pinewoods in Formby, with the original name of Pinewoods Retreat." Georgie smiles. "Their café was up for an award this evening, and even though they didn't win, I can tell you, I've never tasted food so good as you'll get at Pinewoods Retreat. Get yourselves over there and give it a try. You won't regret it. Anyway – well." She runs her top lip through her teeth, and looks over in the direction of Lorraine, Dee and Morgan. "I'm going to sound like I've lost my mind," she laughs, and there's a light ripple of laughter around St George's Hall, "a total nut job. I *found* myself there; my heart and soul. As a woman in business, I can tell you all," she pauses, her eyes scanning the room, "I tell you, when we fight to be the female embodiment of men in business we leave the biggest part of ourselves on the sidelines. It's our very lifeblood as women, who we are at the core, what we bring of ourselves to the table that delivers change in the boardroom. So yes, stand proud in your female power. Get out in nature and go fucking find yourself. Go to Pinewoods Retreat in Formby. Reconnect with your soul, your true self, and bring the heart and soul of what it means to be truly you, authentically you, as a woman in *your* enterprise. Because together we are Liverpool's Businesswomen of the Year."

The audience erupts. Every woman is on her feet, cheering, hands above their heads, clapping, and the standing ovation goes on, and on, and on.

As the room settles, Georgie leans into the mic. "So women, my final words to you: make it happen. Go forth and be fucking fabulous." Georgie beams at the crowd, buzzing with the adrenaline coursing through her veins. This is probably the best moment of her life, and she couldn't be prouder of herself – for what she's achieved, and for that fucking fabulous speech she just gave. With cheers and applause ringing in her ears, Georgie picks up her award, holds it aloft like a champion, and leaves the stage.

"Fucking fabulous," Ryan echoes as she takes her seat next to him. "And I fucking love how you got a plug in for Pinewoods. Mick's gonna love that, though you maybe went in a bit strong on the café. We're trying to destroy the place, remember?" Ryan laughs and kisses Georgie's cheek before walking off in the direction of the bar. Georgie makes to follow him, but Dot steps in front of her and throws her arms around her.

"God, honey, am I proud of you." She pulls Georgie in for a tight hug. Georgie glances over her mum's shoulder and spots Lorraine, Dee and Morgan looking at her with what she can only describe as awe spread across their faces. A smile spreads across Lorraine's face and she gives her a thumbs up

"Thanks, Mum," Georgie says, pulling out of their hug. "I'm

the woman I am today because of the mum you've been to me." She kisses her mum on the cheek. "Love you, Mum. I – I just need to go and sort something out, OK?" She nods in the direction that Ryan has taken.

"Not right now, Georgie," Dot says. "Whatever's going on between you two will save for later." She gives Georgie a knowing look.

"There's nothing going on."

"I'm your mum. I'm not daft. I'll get a taxi back to mine. If you two need to sort something out, then do it when you get home, not here."

Georgie feels the threat of tears, and as her friends gather around her she brushes them away. "Look at me," she says to Carla, who pulls her in for a drunken squeeze, "I'm all emotional for getting an award."

As Dot starts to walk away, Georgie leans over and grabs her hand. "Thanks, Mum."

32

LORRAINE

One Hour After the Award Ceremony

THERE'S a queue for the taxis, even though Lorraine, Dee and Morgan have left the event early.

"I can't believe there's so many people waiting," Dee says, planting her hands on her hips.

"Looks like something's just finished at the Empire across the road," Lorraine says, cradling her arm, the pain now intense. "Maybe it's more to do with that than the event on at St George's Hall."

"That was odd," Morgan says, "Georgie being here at the awards. Did you know she's a bit of a local celebrity?"

"Years back, when I worked in town," Dee says, "I heard about the Quinns. They're well known. But I never associated Georgie as being one of them."

"Why would we think of her as a Quinn?" Lorraine says. "She was booked into Pinewoods under the name Macrae. That was quite some speech she gave. Really inspirational."

"Maybe she wanted a bit of privacy so that she could totally relax before the award ceremony," Dee says.

Lorraine pulls her shawl tighter around her shoulders. She nods her head and yawns. "Manifesting is making it happen," she says, repeating Georgie's line from her speech. "If only that was true for us right now." She yawns again.

"You're bushed, Raine. I shouldn't have let you come."

"I'm OK. I just need to be home now, tucked up in my bed. These kind of events are not my thing any more. I don't think I have the energy for them. Too much peopling."

Morgan rests her hands on Lorraine's shoulders. "I'll send you some healing reiki energy to keep you going until we get back to Pinewoods."

"Thanks, Mor," Lorraine says. "That will help." She looks back at St George's Hall behind them. "Wasn't that sweet of Georgie to mention Pinewoods in her speech?"

Dee pulls her phone out to check the time. "Such a surprise. I felt very proud to know her. And to hear her big up Pinewoods."

"By the way, I never got the chance to tell you earlier," Morgan says, moving her hands onto Lorraine's back and resting them there, letting reiki energy flow through her palms. "You know I said I bumped into Georgie in the Ladies? Well, she'd just come face-to-face with some woman her husband is having an affair with. In the loos. On the night she was getting an award."

"Bloody hell," Dee says.

"Jesus, Mary and Joseph," Morgan goes on, "but that was awkward. Can't have been easy for her."

"That's dreadful," Lorraine says. "Poor Georgie. She did incredibly well to keep it together for her speech. She must have been in so much pain. Makes me even more proud of her that she held it together."

"A true professional, that one," Morgan says. "The show-must-go-on type of person."

"Nice of that Rodgers fella to put us on his table. Georgie's husband seemed to be a good friend of his."

"I had an odd chat with one of Georgie's friends," Morgan says. "Carla. The woman sitting next to me. She said something strange about Pinewoods not having much of a future based on what Georgie had told her, but then Georgie denied it and . . . I don't know. I still kind of get the feeling there's more to her than she's letting on. Don't you?"

Dee nods, as a taxi parks up in front of them. The driver jumps out of the car and, after checking where they're going, he opens the doors, inviting Lorraine to sit in the passenger seat next to him so that she can be a little more comfortable on their journey back to Formby.

33

GEORGIE

Two Hours After the Award Ceremony

ON the drive home from St George's Hall, Ryan is hyper. He's had more than one for the road, and what with the whiskey mixed with adrenaline, he's driving erratically. Georgie would offer to drive but she's also over the limit, and with a heady concoction of alcohol and anger in her bloodstream she won't drive much better herself. If he gets done for speeding again, she's not saying she was driving, not this time.

"What was all that about this evening, Ry?"

"All what?" Ryan turns his head and meets Georgie's glare.

"Keep your eyes on the road, will you?" Georgie sighs. "Being proud of me." The words almost stick in her throat.

There's a slight pause as Ryan pulls out of a junction. "'Course I'm proud of you, babe."

Is he really going to pretend he doesn't know what this is about? "Please don't play this game. I know."

"Yeah, I told you. I'm proud of you. You saw me in the audience, yeah? Clapping for you like a loony." He shoots her a broad smile.

"Your speech was *boss*. And that bit about Pinewoods – legend. Fucking genius."

"That's not what I'm on about. I *know*." Georgie's tone is flat.

"What?"

"You and Faith Jacks."

Ryan laughs. "What about her? She's doing some PR stuff for the new co-working space me and Dad are setting up on Water Street."

A moment of silence hangs between them, filled by the *clack, clack, clack* of the indicator. Georgie looks over at her husband of more than twenty years and considers how little she knows him these days. When did they become married strangers? It used to be that they could trust each other implicitly, *'in it together'*, as they always say to each other, but he's changed over the last year or so. She's no longer sure she likes him.

Georgie puts her hands over her face. "Are you having an affair with her?"

"What *are* you going on about?" Ryan snaps his head around as he spews out the words, swerving the car. "For fuck's sake." Ryan speeds up, ignoring the signs for thirty miles-an-hour.

"I saw her. On the doorbell video." Georgie lowers her hands from her face and turns to look at Ryan's profile, his jaw twitching, eyes fixed firmly on the road ahead, even though they've come to a sudden stop at traffic lights.

"Give it a rest." Ryan takes a hand off the steering wheel and puts it onto bare flesh part way up Georgie's thigh. She flinches and slaps his hand away.

"What's got into you tonight? You're so uptight."

As Georgie keeps her eyes on Ryan's profile, she spots a telltale twitch he used to get at the side of his eye when he lied. She's not seen that in many years. Fighting the anger and frustration bubbling up inside her, Georgie turns her body away as far as she can in her seat and stares out of the side window, watching the dark streets flash by. The silence is charged, and Georgie almost expects street lamps to flicker as they pass. "You're having an affair with her."

"Come on, babe. Lighten up, will yer?" Ryan says. "Tonight's one big cel-e-bra-tion." He drags the word out with a sing-song lilt to it. "Let's talk about it in the morning, hey?"

"We're talking about it now."

"Sure, if you want. And while we're at it, I'll give your mum a call, should I? Hey Dot, pack your bags, you're on the street. Your daughter's had enough of me."

"Not this again," Georgie snarls. "You can't keep threatening me with throwing Mum out when you don't like me bringing up your flings. Don't do that to her. It's not even about her."

"What is it about, huh?"

"You know what it's about, Ryan. You promised after the journalist, no more sleeping around. Not that I believed you. But I never expected you to flaunt it. Tonight, of all nights."

Ryan stops the car at traffic lights, turns on the radio, and stares ahead. "Give it a rest."

"D'you know how I found out her name?"

Ryan keeps his eyes on the road in front of him, tapping the steering wheel to the beat of the music.

"I overheard a conversation in the ladies' loos," Georgie continues. "They all knew about Faith bloody Jacks, and you being seen around town with her. You on the dance floor with her this evening. They knew because you flaunted your relationship with her. You don't give a damn who knows what you're up to." Georgie swallows a sob. "It's humiliating."

They sit in silence as the car pulls away from the lights.

"Mortifying," Georgie says, her voice a near whisper.

"You can have a divorce if that's what you want," Ryan snaps, his top lip curling, "but you get nothing, and Dot's out on her ear. She's sponged off me for way too many years as it is. Yeah, I'll drop by tomorrow and I'll have a little chat with her."

"Please don't, Ryan. Leave Mum out of this." Georgie cringes as she hears herself begging him. This is how it's gone every time he's threatened to throw Dot out.

"Cool, if that's what you want." He shrugs. "You give it a rest about who I choose to see, how I choose to live my life, and I'll leave Dot alone. She's tickety-boo for now. We wouldn't want to spoil things for her, would we? Not now she's retired. OK?"

Georgie purses her lips. Ryan never lets her forget that he pulled them out of the gutter, but recently he's made more and more of it, letting her know he holds most of the power.

"Good, good," Ryan says. "Glad we've got an understanding. Right, we need to focus on the job in hand. Let's concentrate on this contract we've got with Mick Rodgers, huh?"

"I'm calling veto on the contract." Georgie sits up in the car seat, surprised with herself. It's a bit late in the game, but this is the one bit of power she does have left. They always said that either of them can call veto on any contract if it doesn't feel right. She does a quick mental check to be sure that her veto isn't coming from a place of anger. Sure, part of it is, but she never really wanted them to take on this contract in the first place, and – and . . . Pinewoods deserves better than the plans Mick Rodgers has for the place.

"No, you're not," Ryan says, furrowing his brow. "No veto, babe."

"We always said we each have the power of veto. Well, I've never used mine on any contract before. I'm using it now, on this contract. I'll call Mick tomorrow and tell him we're cancelling the contract." Georgie returns her gaze to the streets she can see through the passenger seat window, hoping Ryan doesn't ask her to explain her change of heart. She wants to tell him about the soul at Pinewoods Retreat, and how its heart beats. She wants to tell him about the people, and how they put community ahead of wealth. She wants to tell him about the food, the smells, the feel of Pinewoods Retreat. But she can't. He won't understand. Heck, she didn't understand when she first arrived there. It changed her – and she wants to tell Ryan that, too. How Pinewoods Retreat opened her eyes, how it woke her up to what she puts up with from him, how being with Ed who showed her he cares woke her up to seeing that she deserves so much better. But she can't tell him that, either. He'll laugh, and she's not ready to be laughed at for allowing herself to change.

"We're not cancelling the bleeding contract." Ryan thumps the steering wheel, and Georgie jumps.

"We're in it together, we always said that. And as a partnership we agreed that we each have the power of veto over a contract. I'm using mine today." Her stomach knots. Is this how it's going to be? Is she really prepared to risk QuinnEssentials for a place she's only known for a week? Does she really have to choose between betraying her husband and their business, and Pinewoods Retreat?

Georgie holds a hand across her mouth as the truth unfolds inside her – she won't let Mick Rodgers get his hands on Pinewoods Retreat, and if vetoing the contract is the only power she holds, she has to use it. She's got to do what little she can to save the haven that Lorraine and Dee have nurtured by the sea.

"No way," Ryan says, shaking his head and letting out a half laugh as if she's a fool for even suggesting she'll use her veto. "Not happening, babe. We're in line for a lot of cash on this one."

Georgie looks out the passenger window, biting the inside of her cheek. It's no surprise he doesn't agree, but she's standing firm. "I'm calling Mick tomorrow. I'll tell him we're pulling out." A sense of calm waves over Georgie now that she's made a decision she's comfortable with. Lorraine and Dee will never know how close they came to losing the place they love, and they don't need to. For once, Georgie can say she's aligning her actions to the business values of integrity and authenticity they spout. This is the right decision.

"You're deadly serious, aren't you?" Ryan roars with laughter. "Well, I've got news for you. We can't cancel the contract. There's a penalty clause that prevents us from walking away without paying a hefty fee."

"That wasn't in the contract when I signed it." Georgie's heart thuds. What the hell has he done?

"Yeah, well, Mick wanted it putting in there, so he added it in on the day I handed our signed copy over. Said it was in exchange for you getting your ten per cent share in the place when he's finished the development."

"He can't do that," Georgie shrieks. "I'd already signed the contract."

"He can and he did. Stapled the page with our signatures onto the back of the new version. With the amount we'd have to pay in penalties, it's not worth cancelling."

"And you let him do that? Christ, Ryan, what have you done?" Georgie can barely swallow as a lump forms in her throat. She can add Ryan going rogue to the ever-increasing list of things going wrong in her life.

"Besides," Ryan goes on, "this is a good contract. We're writing our own cheque on this job." Ryan puts on his indicator and pulls off the main road. "And don't forget, you personally benefit with your ten per cent."

So that's it? The ten per cent was always intended as a means to shackle her to this job? God, she's a fool. There has to be some other way she can stop Mick Rodgers bulldozing his way into Pinewoods Retreat. She can't give up on Lorraine and Dee, not now. But what the hell can she do?

As they pull onto the drive, Georgie says, "I saw her get out of the car."

"What?" Ryan puts the car into park and undoes his seatbelt.

"On the doorbell video."

Ryan laughs. "Shit, are we back onto that? Something's deffo got under your skin tonight, hasn't it? Go take your man-pants off. You're not the boss of me." Georgie watches as he gets out of the car and crunches across the gravel to the front door. As she follows him, he calls over his shoulder, "Great bloody end to the night." He slams his palm into the doorbell.

Georgie seethes as she walks into the house, gripping tight hold of her award in one hand. She lets the front door click behind her and slowly climbs the stairs to take a shower.

With water cascading down her back, Georgie's head is a mess. She's drunk far too much to think clearly, but she can't shake two intense feelings. First, her marriage is over. Ryan has shown that it's not just their marriage vows that he's happy to break – he's also prepared to engage in dodgy ways of working to get his own way in their business dealings. There's no way she can trust him any more.

And the second feeling is her own betrayal. When she walks into Mick Rodgers's office in the morning and tells him about the problems with the roof at Pinewoods Retreat, she'll be planting a Judas kiss on the place she's grown to love over the last week.

Georgie opens her mouth and lets out a silent scream. Her decision about Ryan is simple. At some point over the next few weeks they'll sit down together and be all business-like over ending their marriage, she's pretty convinced of it. But Pinewoods, that's a different story. On the one hand, she's tied into a contract that she's signed. But on the other, well, the place will be spoilt the moment Mick gets his hands on it, and all she can wish is that some kind of solution will present itself so that doesn't need to happen.

Yawning as she towels herself dry, Georgie fights with her prosecco-pickled thoughts. There has to be some kind of solution, if she could just think clearly – come up with something before the meeting that could seal the fate of Pinewoods Retreat.

34

GEORGIE

Two Days After the Award Ceremony

As soon as she arrives back at Pinewoods with a heavy heart, having failed to come up with a scheme to save the place from Mick Rodgers, Georgie makes her way around the side of the house to the kitchen garden. The offer letter for the retreat that Mick has instructed her to deliver to Lorraine and Dee is weighing down the bag that sits on the crook of her arm.

Seeing Holly with some of the community gardeners, Georgie makes her way over to her.

"Holly, hi," she says.

"Georgie!"

"I've come to see Lorraine and Dee, have a chat with them. But I wondered, do you mind if I have a chat with your bees first?" Georgie can't believe she needs some Dutch courage from a hive of bees.

"My bees?" Holly raises an eyebrow. "Of course. I'll keep everyone away from that part of the garden. You go and do whatever it is you need to do."

Holly turns back to her community gardeners and gives out instructions for where people are to work today. Georgie takes the gravel path to the back of the garden. She settles herself down in her familiar spot on the raised bed opposite the beehive and watches. There's a smooth, steady hum from the hive as bees come and go. Georgie smiles to herself, watching how busy the entrance is. It's like the platforms at Central Station in rush hour.

"Hey, bees," she says, leaning forwards, her elbows resting on her knees. "I missed you." A few bees buzz past Georgie's head in search of nectar, and more come and settle on the landing board at the entrance to the hive. It's mesmerising, and for a few minutes Georgie loses herself in the bee activity.

"What am I even doing here, bees?" Georgie purses her lips. "On the one hand, this could be exactly what Lorraine and Dee need, someone to come in and rescue them. On the other hand, we all know that Mick Rodgers will destroy everything that Pinewoods is about." She shakes her head and takes a quick glance over her shoulder to make sure she is still alone. "It's not right, bees. These are good people. I don't want to break their hearts, but what else can I do?" A couple of bees do the waggle dance on the landing board. "Am I fooling myself to say their hearts are already breaking?" Georgie buries her head in her hands. "There's nothing I've done in business in all these years that feels as wrong as this does." She sits in silence, wrapping her arms around herself, as if she's holding tight onto what Pinewoods is, what it has done to her. "What other choice do they have? The place is falling down around their ears. This offer has to be better than that, surely?"

Georgie pushes herself up to standing, as if a huge force is holding her down. "Well, I can't keep putting it off," she says. "Good to see you, bees. Keep on buzzing."

* * *

Georgie coughs as she stands in the doorway to the therapy room. Lorraine, Dee and Morgan turn to look at her.

"Georgie," Dee says, with a smile. "We weren't expecting you, were we?"

"I've got – I mean – look, can we talk?"

"Congratulations," Morgan says, grinning at her. "Quite something, you getting that award."

"Thank you," Georgie says, looking down at her feet.

Morgan walks towards her and, taking hold of her elbow, she guides Georgie to the kitchen. "Let's put the kettle on," she says. "I must admit, we were all a bit surprised to see you. Had no idea you were a big shot businesswoman. Let's leave Lorraine for a moment. Dee's about to help her out of that bed for an hour or so. It'll do her good to move about. Cup of tea?"

Georgie nods, relieved for a short reprieve before she must pass over Mick Rodgers's offer to Lorraine and Dee.

"I knew you were holding something back," Morgan continues, filling the kettle. "Didn't I say I could tell there was something? What a delightful surprise that was. I felt proud to know you. We all did."

"I didn't know you were going to be there. It never crossed my mind that you'd even know anything about the award ceremony."

"That was another shock, you knowing that Mick Rodgers fella who gifted Lorraine and Dee the tickets at his table. How do you know him?"

"Business associate." Georgie can't help wondering if the reprieve is worse than getting the whole thing over and done with.

"Georgie!"

She turns to see Ed with his arms outstretched towards her.

"You're back," he says, a grin spread across his face. Ed walks over to Georgie and pulls her in for a hug. Georgie tenses in his arms. "Everything OK?" Ed asks.

"I'm waiting to talk to Lorraine and Dee." Moose dances around her feet, and Georgie fights hard not to engage with the dog.

"You seem a bit tense. Fancy a yoga session whilst you're here?" He flashes her a smile. "I've got one starting in half an hour."

"I . . . doubt I'll be here long after I've spoken with Lorraine and Dee."

Morgan puts a pot of tea on the table just as Dee walks in, immediately followed by Lorraine. Dee pulls out a chair and nods to Lorraine to sit down, and once Lorraine is seated, she leans down and plants a loving kiss on the top of her head.

"What can we do for you?" Lorraine asks, wasting no time.

"Mick Rodgers – he – er – asked me . . ."

"The guy who gave us the tickets? The one whose table we were all sat at for the dinner?"

Georgie nods like her head has become a yo-yo. She pulls out a seat further down the table, and turns to face Lorraine.

"What about Mick Rodgers?" Dee asks.

"I've been asked to bring you this." Georgie's stomach knots as she pulls the envelope containing Mick's offer out of her bag. "It's an offer for you."

"An offer?"

Georgie traces a fine crack in the kitchen table with a corner of the envelope. "To buy Pinewoods. Mick wants to buy it."

"It's not for sale," Lorraine says.

"I know. He wants to buy it anyway." Georgie holds the envelope up.

"I don't understand," Dee says, her brow furrowing.

"Hang on a mo," Morgan says, pulling a chair out from the table, its feet scraping across the floor. She tilts her head, thought etched across her face as she eyes Georgie. "Is this . . . ? Were you . . . ? That's it, isn't it? I reckon that's what you were doing here all of last week. You were doing some kind of reccie for him. I'm right, aren't I?"

Georgie nods again, slower this time, half closing her eyes, desperately wanting to shut this conversation out. It was always going to be difficult, but this is horrid. These people have done nothing to her and here she is, shattering their world.

"You were here spying on us?" Lorraine asks, her usually beautiful voice coming out low and hard.

"God, this isn't good," Ed says. He pulls his arms tight around his torso.

"What's not good?" Holly asks, walking into the kitchen from the garden with an armful of courgettes and carrots.

"Georgie's working for that man who had us sit at his table at

280

the award thing at St George's Hall," Dee says, her top lip curling as if the words disgust her.

"I don't understand."

Georgie doesn't wait for someone to bring Holly up to speed. "Could you at least look at the offer?" she asks, holding the envelope out towards Lorraine. It flutters in her hand.

"It's not good, is it?" Lorraine asks.

Georgie hangs her head, shaking it. It stings to look at these lovely people, knowing she's hurting them. "Can I at least leave this . . ." She holds the envelope in the gaping space between herself and Lorraine.

"And that's his offer, is it?" Lorraine snaps. "No, just no." She glares at Georgie.

"You're embarrassed to even give that to us," Dee says. "I can tell."

Lorraine shifts in her chair. "I agree, Dee. She knows it's an insulting offer." She winces, pain etched across her face.

Georgie nods. "According to Mick Rodgers, it's twenty per cent above market value, but, you're right, I don't think it will be even close to matching your expectations."

"How can you do this to us?" Dee asks, planting a hand on her chest. "You've planned this, to throw us out of our home. How could you?"

"The only thing I'm doing is passing over the offer." Georgie's cheeks burn. Dee's right – they all are. She's a snake in the long grass. "I don't agree with it, but I'm doing what I've been told to do." It's hard to swallow, and the heat from Georgie's face spreads across her body like a wildfire.

"Look, just get out of my sight," Lorraine says. "I don't want to see you again. Someone, get her out of here." Her voice wobbles, her unwavering glare through narrowed eyes full of anger, her nose twitching with disgust.

Georgie can't hold Lorraine's stare any more. Cringing inside, she looks away.

Ed thrust his hands on his hips, as if he's making himself appear wider, like he's taking on the role of bouncer. "You heard Lorraine," he growls, and Georgie's heart breaks at the look of disappointment on his face.

Holly holds open the back door and, chewing on her top lip, she jerks her head at the door, her eyes fixed on Georgie. Georgie gently places the envelope on the table and walks out the back door, not daring to look at anyone as she leaves, unable to lift her eyes from the ground in front of her.

This was so much worse than she imagined it would be, and now she's hurt people she's grown fond of.

35

GEORGIE

ALTHOUGH it's still August, the weather has changed, and a cold wind has got up. Georgie shivers as she stands at the back door of Pinewoods. Feeling a pull to go and talk to the bees again, she starts to walk down the garden path and then stops, suddenly. She can't do that. It wouldn't be right. For one thing, everyone will be able to see her talking to the bees from the kitchen, and Lorraine's made it clear that Georgie is no longer welcome.

She shivers again, as much with disgust at herself and the woman she's become, as with the wind that blows through her thin linen jacket. If she was still staying at Pinewoods Retreat, she'd go for a walk to march out her emotions. Georgie nods to herself. That's what she'll do. Ignoring her less than suitable loafers, she walks around the house and turns down the cinder path towards the sea, holding the lapels of her jacket across her throat in a hopeless attempt to stave off the cold from the bitter wind.

The sea is in when Georgie reaches the beach. She walks up to the waves and stares into the dark waters, brushing away a rogue tear. Squeezing her eyes shut, she takes in a shallow breath, and loses herself as wind-whipped waves lap around her feet. Georgie takes a step closer to the sea, puffs out her cheeks and forces what little air is in her lungs out through pursed lips.

She's stuck – so incredibly, stupefyingly stuck. In her marriage, in their business, in life, and there's nothing she can do about it.

Another step towards the water. Another rogue tear courses down her cheek, this one left for the wind to dry. She wants to shout, to scream, to let the universe know it got this all wrong – her life, Ryan's. She opens her mouth to let out a scream. Nothing. No sound escapes, like it, too, is stuck.

Another step forwards. Waves splash against her green loafers.

What has become of her? She's a huge success, just as she planned to be. But at what cost?

A dog barks somewhere behind her.

And again, she steps forwards.

She doesn't like who she is. She doesn't like who Ryan is.

Another step. Waves snap at her ankles, and still she steps forwards.

More barking.

Georgie presses her knuckles into her temples. Ryan's betrayed her. She's betrayed Pinewoods Retreat. She's as bad as him.

Another step.

And then there's Faith Jacks, yet another affair.

She steps forwards again . . . and again . . . and again . . . and again . . . until she hears voices behind her, mixed up with the barking.

They sound . . . anxious, alarmed.

She feels frozen. Numb.

"Georgie, Georgie! Come back."

She knows that voice, yet strangely can't place it. Slowly, she lifts her foot and drags it through the water, and then the other foot, moving in slow motion. The uncommonly cold August wind whirls and whistles around her, like it's calling her – *come with us, join us.*

She moves deeper into the sea.

The noises around her get louder. Two voices now, shouting her name.

Splashing and shouting and shouting and splashing and the barking of a dog. Hands grab her arm from behind, and still the voices say her name, over and over.

"Georgie, oh my god, Georgie. It's OK, really, it's OK."

Gently, Georgie is guided through the water, back towards the beach, the hands still holding onto her. She shakes her head – she's in the sea. How did she get here? What the hell? How long has she been here?

Her body shakes uncontrollably as she's led ashore. When the hands loosen their hold, her arms hang limply at her side, her empty eyes staring into the distance, enquiring eyes staring at her, intently. She has no answers, for those eyes, or for herself.

"Georgie," one voice says, as arms wrap around her and hold her tight. "You're soaked to the skin. Come on, let's get you back to Pinewoods."

Georgie slowly turns her face to one of the voices. Ed.

She turns to the other. Holly.

That's who was shouting her name. She gives Holly a weak

smile. "Sorry – I-I," her teeth chatter, "d-d-don't know what happened. Sorry."

"You're frozen," Ed says. "Let's get you back to Pinewoods and out of these wet clothes."

"Is there someone I can call for you?" Holly asks.

Georgie lets herself be led back over the dunes and onto the cinder path.

Who would she call? Carla? Ali? Sian? None of them would know what to do. "No," Georgie eventually says.

"Are you sure?" Holly asks.

Georgie's voice wobbles as she speaks through chattering teeth. "Nobody. There's nobody."

"Should I call your husband?" Ed asks. He's carrying Moose under his arm.

Georgie slowly shakes her head. She can't trust her husband; her best friend almost dropped her in it at the awards ceremony; and there's no way she can burden her mum with this. She's all alone.

"I think we should call him," Holly says. "It's not right, you walking into the sea like that. I'm worried about you, Georgie."

"Don't. Please don't."

As they near Pinewoods Retreat, Hunter is standing at the arch into the garden café.

"Where'd you go?" he asks Holly, walking towards the three of them.

"After Georgie walked out, Moose was barking his head off at the back door. I thought he got himself locked out when she left, but when I went to let him back in he ran off. For a dog with tiny legs, he can move at some speed when he wants to. I mentioned it to Ed, and we were both a bit worried that Moose had scarpered, so we followed him and he led us down to the beach. Moose was standing at the water's edge, barking like crazy. And that's where we found Georgie – in the *sea*, Hunter."

"Shit," Hunter says, letting out a whistle. "Good call, Holly. She OK?"

"We need to get her inside," Holly says.

Hunter walks ahead, and Georgie is vaguely aware of the concerned voices around her. Someone puts a blanket across her shoulders as she's bundled through into the kitchen.

"I'm OK," she says, her whole body shaking uncontrollably. "Please, just leave me. I can drive home. I'm OK." She grabs hold of the blanket tight around her and lets herself be guided into a chair by the range, baffled faces staring at her. But what can she say to these people? She's as shocked as they are that she walked into the sea. She's happy, isn't she? Only a few days ago, she had one of the best nights of her life. What was she doing, standing in the water like that?

Georgie shudders. One thing she is sure of, possibly the only thing, is that she has no intention of ending her life. But if anyone was to ask her what's going on, she honestly has no idea.

She just doesn't know.

36

GEORGIE

THE kitchen buzzes with activity. Georgie barely registers as Lorraine, cradling her arm, dishes out instructions.

"And Ed, get one of those blankets we use for the café out of the basket in the porch, will you?" Ed nods and dashes out of the room. "Holly, make up one of those turmeric teas. Do you remember how to make it? Half a lemon, a chunk of ginger root chopped into slices, and a chunk of turmeric, also chopped up. Steep that in the teapot for ten minutes before pouring a cup out for Georgie. And she can keep drinking it as it cools down in the pot too."

"On it," Holly says, grabbing a lemon out of the fruit bowl that sits on the Welsh dresser.

"Here we go," Morgan says, walking into the kitchen with a couple of towels. "Right, let's get you out of these wet clothes."

Georgie slowly shakes her head from side to side.

"She could have drowned," Hunter says, taking Georgie's sodden shoes from her feet.

"God, don't, Hunter," says Holly. She sets the teapot on the kitchen table and places a mug next to it. "This'll be ready in ten minutes, Georgie. It'll do you the world of good. In the meantime, Morgan is right, we need to get you out of your wet clothes. Ed, hand me that blanket, and you and Hunter go and wait in the hall until I call you back in. Dee, grab something from my basket of clothes under my bed, please? Maybe a jumper and dungarees that Georgie can put on until her own clothes are clean and dry."

Lorraine walks over to Georgie and rests her good hand on her shoulder. "I'm sorry I was cross with you. Though that was no reason to go and walk into the sea. We'd never have known if Moose hadn't alerted Holly with his barking."

Georgie slowly turns her eyes to Lorraine. These people are being so kind. She doesn't deserve it, not after betraying them.

"I promise I'll look at the offer," Lorraine goes on. "I saw you left the envelope on the kitchen table. I'll take a look at it. OK?" Lorraine nods her head expectantly at Georgie, who turns her head away and stares blankly at the range. She gives Georgie's shoulder a light squeeze. "OK?"

Georgie blinks. After everything she's done; Lorraine, Dee, Holly, they're all looking after her, caring for her. A hiccuppy sob escapes from her throat.

Holly drags Georgie's soaked linen pants down her legs and passes them to Morgan to put into the washing machine along with the rest of her clothes. Dee returns from Holly's hut in the garden with an armful of clothes. Georgie lets them pull her to her feet and dress her, and, as she falls back into the chair, dressed with a blanket wrapped around her shoulders, tears plop over her long eyelashes and roll delicately down her cheeks.

"It's fallen apart." Georgie looks around the group in front of her as if searching for someone. Her eyes settle on Morgan. "Everything's broken."

Morgan nods, and rests a hand over her own heart.

Over the next hour, the room quietens down, except for the occasional order for the café, and gradually Georgie's cheeks regain their colour. She wanders to the back door and looks out over the kitchen garden.

"Better?" Ed is sitting outside on the bench, leaning his back against the wall of the house, a shaft of sunlight warming his face.

"I've stopped shivering now," Georgie says. "Mind if I join you?"

Ed shufties along the bench to make room for her, and Georgie sits down, the blanket still draped over her shoulders.

"Sorry if I scared you," she says. "Down at the sea."

"Want to talk about it?"

Georgie sighs. "Yes. No. I don't know. Maybe."

Ed laughs. "So that's all options covered then."

"My life is in tatters." Georgie screws up her face. "My marriage is over."

"I heard a little rumour about your husband."

Georgie leans her head back onto the brick wall behind her and closes her eyes. "He's never crowed so openly about any of his previous affairs." As if on cue, a crow lets out a series of low rattles in the trees at the end of the garden.

"And how does that feel?"

"God, are we back to that? My feelings." A single tear seeps out between Georgie's eyelids and slowly glides down her cheek. She brushes it aside, and sniffs. "It feels shit, Ed. I think – maybe I know . . . god, I don't know what I think."

"He's had a lot of affairs."

"Too many."

"And you've stayed with him."

"For too long."

"Because . . . ?"

"We're married." Georgie taps her little finger, counting each item, like she's ticking off a familiar list, though she's never voiced any of this out loud before. "I love him. We're used to each other. We're in business together. We understand one another. He's been good to me all these years. And to Mum. I owe him a lot. Everything we own is because of him. Though it's all in his name."

"I'm pretty sure I've heard you say that before, about you owing him a lot. Tell me, is that you meaning it, or does he expect it of you for everything he's done?"

"Wow, now there's a question." Of course she's owes him. Ryan changed her life. There's so much he's allowed her to do. If he hadn't let her have a go at admin in his company all those years ago, if he hadn't helped her out with promotions, if he hadn't let her join him in business a few years later, then she would never have grown into a successful businesswoman – into the woman who received such a prestigious award a couple of nights ago. So yes, she pretty much owes him everything.

Ed stands and stretches his arms above his head, revealing a sliver of flesh. He bends at the waist, first to his left, and then to his right. "My guess?" He stretches his arms up for a second time and holds them there. "You're conditioned to be grateful, like you're embedded in a practice of being indebted to your husband. I've got to tell you, it's not OK to be pressured to be grateful."

He sits back down on the bench. "In contrast, I use gratitude, a practice of respect and appreciation. No pressure, no obligation. I feel enriched through gratitude. I suspect you might feel beholden to your husband – maybe not so enriching?"

Georgie leans forwards and rests her elbows on her knees, dropping her head into her hands. "You could be right. He reminds me regularly how good he is to me and Mum. Don't get me wrong, he's incredibly generous to us both. I'd be nothing, have nothing, if Ryan hadn't given me a chance."

"You don't know what you'd be without him." Ed's voice is tender, and, although his words are direct, Georgie appreciates his compassion and honesty. "You know there's more to life than money and material things, Georgie. You don't have to hold onto that life, not if you don't want to. You can step away from your past anytime, whenever you're ready."

"I'm not sure I like who I've been in the past. Who I've become."

"It's OK to dislike who we were in the past and still like who we are now, who we're going to be in the future."

Tears stream down Georgie's face. She's a fool. How can she be strong and confident as a businesswoman and then a total wimp in her marriage? Ryan holds all the power in their relationship, and she lets him. Who is she, that she let this happen? She's been lying to herself, to her mum, her friends, everyone here at Pinewoods. She puts out this persona of knowing her place in the world, being comfortable with herself, a queen bee, and yet, in truth, she's not even sure she likes the woman she has crafted over the years.

"You're at an impasse, Georgie," Ed goes on, interrupting her thoughts. "I think you're ready to heal, and it's OK to heal in your own way, in your own time. You walking into the sea today, that was your unconscious mind taking you on a symbolic cleansing, readying you for your future. I just want to say one thing to you. As you choose your next steps, please be compassionate for who you've been, so that you can love who you will become."

Sobs rack Georgie's body, the bench rocking beneath her. She opens her mouth to speak, but no words come out.

Ed lays a gentle hand on her back. "Let it out," he says. "Let it all out."

They sit like that for a few minutes, the only sound, beyond the cawing crows, being Georgie's sobs, that eventually give way to sniffles. She eases herself back up, taking her hands away from her face and goes to check her pocket for a tissue, before remembering that she's wearing Holly's dungarees, not the linen pants she arrived in. Ed vanishes inside the house for a moment and returns with a piece of paper towel from the kitchen. Georgie wipes her face and blows her nose. When did she last cry like that? Maybe the night her dad left, and the days after, when she was eleven years old. She didn't even let herself cry when her dog, Mr Big, died a couple of weeks ago. Georgie Quinn doesn't cry, and she *never* sobs.

"Thank you," Georgie says, pushing herself up from the bench in one graceful movement. A single white feather lies on the path in front of her. She picks it up and strokes it across her cheek. Signs turn up everywhere, when you believe. That's what Morgan told her. Is this her sign to accept that her marriage is over? A sign that she's ready for wherever her life takes her next?

Pocketing the feather, Georgie doesn't even look at Ed as she turns and walks back into the kitchen. Ed follows behind. Dee is elbow deep at the sink, Morgan is at the kitchen table peeling potatoes, Beth is leaning with her back against the Welsh dresser, Kate is eating a bowl of soup at the table, and Holly and Hunter are huddled together, wrapped up in each other's arms.

"I need to get home," Georgie says.

"I'm not sure you're in a good state to drive." Dee picks up a towel and wipes her hands.

"I can drive you," Hunter offers, pulling himself away from Holly. "Holly can come with me, and we'll get the train home together. Or," he says, grinning at Holly, "we can run back, if you fancy it? Along the beach?"

Holly laughs. "Maybe not the beach today, but yeah, we can take that path that goes alongside the railway line, the one that leads into the Fisherman's Path."

"Your clothes won't be dry yet," Morgan says. "I only put them on the line about twenty minutes ago."

Georgie shakes her head. "It's OK. If Holly doesn't mind me borrowing her dungarees, I'm ready to go home. I can pop by tomorrow, drop these off and collect my own things. But I'd like to go home. There's . . ." She swallows the small sob that's ready to escape. The words she's about to say have a finality to them. "There are things I need to take care of."

As she moves to walk out of the room, Beth takes a step towards her.

"Here," Beth says, "my card." She pops a business card into

the bib pocket of the dungarees. "In case you need it. You know?" The side of her mouth twitches into a half-smile. "I might be able to help."

37

GEORGIE

Three Days After the Award Ceremony

GEORGIE stands in the hallway at Pinewoods Retreat. The excitement she felt at home bubbles inside her, and she wants to call out for everyone to join her in the kitchen. But this isn't her territory. She's not the queen bee here, and for her idea to work, she needs to tread carefully, bringing Lorraine and Dee along at a pace that encourages them to work with her, trust her.

Holding her breath, she eases the kitchen door open and peers inside. Dee is standing at the range with her back to the door, and Morgan is nursing a mug at the kitchen table. She clears her throat, and Morgan turns to look at her.

"The cat dragged you back again," Morgan says, a gentle smile on her lips.

Georgie laughs. "I brought Holly's clothes back." She holds up an Ocado plastic bag as if it's proof of her errand.

Dee turns, a wooden spoon in her hand. Her eyes are narrowed. "Thank you. You can put them down on the table and go," she says. "I hope you'll understand that we've got a lot to process at the mo, and with your connection to Mick Rodgers, it's not a good idea for you to stay around."

Georgie frowns. "I hoped . . ." She trails off as Dee continues to stare at her, saying nothing. She totally misread the kindness they all showed her when Holly pulled her out of the sea. How could she be so stupid? Of course Dee's still angry with her. This will be harder than she thought, but it's got to be worth a try. "Look, I come in peace," she says, stepping fully into the kitchen, holding the bag of Holly's clothes up in front of her. "Can I talk to you, Dee? Please?"

"I don't know that you've got anything to say that we need to hear," Dee says, still brandishing the wooden spoon.

"I think I have a solution for what you're going through at Pinewoods." Georgie steps over to the table and puts her hand on the back of one of the chairs. "May I?" she asks, indicating to the chair.

Dee nods, and sighs. "I suppose so." Her tone softens. "I'm useless at staying mad with people for long. Come near the range. It's warmer over here."

Georgie does as she's told. "Let me tell you my idea," she says. "Is Lorraine around?"

"She's resting, still recovering from her accident."

"Of course. Should I wait until she wakes?"

Dee slowly shakes her head and Georgie sits down at the kitchen table, close to the range. Dee takes a seat opposite her. With excitement bubbling inside her, Georgie leans forwards and rests her elbows on the table.

* * *

The day before, after Georgie left Pinewoods, she steeled herself to tell Ryan it was over between them. The house was quiet when she got home, and she sat clutching a cup of tea until a film formed on the top of the milk. She made another at about five o'clock and drank this one, keeping one eye on the clock above the oven. At six, hunger rippled through her stomach and she made a quick cheese sandwich. Around seven, she put the radio on for a bit of company. By eight, Georgie accepted that Ryan wasn't making an appearance, at least until much later. Based on past experience, she was sure he'd declare that he had a meeting that went on, and took some clients out for dinner – that was one of his regular excuses for spending a night with some woman or other.

She took a long, hot shower, and by nine, Georgie was in bed in the spare room. Ryan woke her when he got in around midnight, slamming doors, banging into things, and cursing loudly. Georgie considered getting up and telling him her decision, but by the sound of things, he was in no fit state for an adult conversation. Instead, she lay on her back in bed long after the house fell silent again, eventually drifting in and out of sleep.

Georgie kept out of Ryan's way in the morning, having decided in the night that she needed to talk to her mum before ending her marriage. She owed it to Dot to warn her that she was likely to end up homeless. As soon as Ryan left the house for a meeting, Georgie phoned her mum.

"What took you so long to come to your senses, honey?" Dot asked, letting out a long, slow sigh. "He's been taking the piss for years. I mean, I love him to bits, and he's dead good to us an' all, but you haven't half put up with a lot of his crap for way too long."

Georgie gasped. "You knew, Mum? Why didn't you say?"

"Nothing to do with me. Anyway, what do I know about making a marriage work, hey? Your dad walked out on me years ago and I've heard neither hide nor hair of him since. I'm not exactly an expert on matters of the heart, am I?"

"I'm sorry, Mum."

"What for?"

"You love that house, you've made it your home. Ryan's sure to turf you out when I tell him it's over."

"Let him, that's what I say. Just let him. I've a small nest egg, what with not having to pay any rent in all these years, plus the bit of money your gran left me. Don't you worry about your old mum. I'll be just fine. I mean it."

"You sure?"

"Yes. Now you do what you need to do for your own happiness, honey, and don't you worry about me."

"I've some money too, Mum, so I'll help you out. I won't leave you without a roof over your head."

"You're a good girl, Georgie. But I can look after meself. You're not to worry about me, OK?"

Georgie fought back the mounting tears of relief at not needing to worry about her mum's future, and set her mind to her own. She took herself off to the beach, and walked and walked and walked, not going anywhere near the water's edge, keeping it far off to her left. She needed a plan for her future, and all the while she walked, she played with one thought after another. It wasn't until she looked at the doorbell camera as she let herself back into the house that the idea struck her. Sitting down at the kitchen island with a coffee, she pulled out the business card that Beth handed to her the day before.

"I . . . don't know where to start, Beth," Georgie said.

"Well, you've probably got a question that led to you picking up the phone, so let's start there."

"You're a divorce solicitor, right?"

"I am, and hearing what Morgan had to say about what happened at the award ceremony, I figured you might be in need of a good one."

"Thanks, Beth. Can I talk to you about what happens when a house is in only one person's name?"

"To start with, you're entitled to half, even if your name isn't on the deeds." Beth talked on, taking her through the technicalities of divorce, and gave Georgie enough information for her to be able to get her head around things. When she got off the phone, Georgie did some rough calculations of what money she could pull together, transferred some money out of the QuinnEssentials bank account into a private account that she's never told Ryan about, and scribbled a note telling Ryan she needed some space for a few days. She threw a few clothes and essentials into an overnight bag and slammed the front door shut behind her.

***

Dee and Morgan lean back into their chairs and cross their arms in unison. "Go on," Morgan says. "Let's hear it, then."

Georgie takes in a slow, deep breath. "I – well . . ." Georgie hesitates. For once in her career, she has no fully prepared presentation at the ready, she's not thought about the best part of her idea to lead with, and she's got no sense of whether the people she's talking to will even like her proposal. She straightens her back and slaps her hands on her knees. "OK," she says, taking in another slow breath. "Things for me have fallen apart. And that's OK. I'm actually fine with that." Dee and Morgan exchange a look. "At the same time, things have been falling down, quite literally, for you. We could fight each other as I deliver on the contract for Mick Rodgers, whilst I try to save my marriage and my role in QuinnEssentials, but the truth is, the most likely outcome for you and Lorraine, Dee, is that you'll lose Pinewoods, and when it comes to me, I'll still lose my marriage. Probably the business too." Georgie pauses and looks from Dee to Morgan and back to Dee again. "I'm not even sure I care that it's the end of my marriage," she adds. Dee opens her mouth to speak. "Sorry, sorry," Georgie says, before Dee can interrupt, "this isn't about me. Well, in one way it is, but it's more about Pinewoods and me. I'll tell you now, you'll not win against Mick Rodgers. That man can, and will, play dirty. Believe me, he's not even got started yet. "

"My head aches almost as much as my arm." Lorraine is standing at the kitchen door. "Why am I having to listen to this?" Georgie's breath catches at the back of her throat. "I've read the letter from Mick Rodgers. The offer is an insult. We've nothing more to discuss." Pain is stamped over Lorraine's face. She walks into the kitchen, and is followed by Holly, Ed and Hunter.

"I forgot," Dee says. "We've got a staff meeting this morning."

"What are you doing here, Georgie?" Lorraine's voice is gravelly and thick with exhaustion.

"I brought Holly's clothes back," Georgie says.

"And apparently she's got some kind of solution for you," Morgan says, screwing up her nose.

"I'm not interested in hearing anything more about this offer from Mick Rodgers."

"This isn't about Mick Rodgers," Georgie says. "I know what Mick plans to do next. He's going to bring Pinewoods down using the council. He'll have them declare the building unfit for habitation, and unfit to run a business from here."

"He can't do that." Lorraine's mouth gapes.

"The games he plays, he probably can. His way of working is to get you thinking he holds all the cards, even when he doesn't. You've got to remember, he's not interested in playing by the rules. Mick Rodgers is bent. If I'm honest, I've suspected for a long time that my husband is, too. They've got people in their pocket. Ryan and his dad were always into some deal or other, and when Ryan hooked up with Mick," Georgie sighs, "well, let's just say that the two of them can always find someone who's prepared to take a backhander to help make one of their projects work."

"And you've been fine with this?" Morgan asks.

"I admit I've turned the other way, but that's my biggest sin. I'm not proud of that, but there was little I could do. Ryan's the one who holds the power, and I'm only involved in one of his businesses. I've no idea what he gets up to beyond the backhanders."

"Back up a bit," Ed interrupts. "You were saying that this Mick Rodgers guy is going to declare Pinewoods unfit for habitation."

"It's scare tactics," Georgie says. "There's no actual power in such a declaration, at least not permanently, but this is the kind of power play that Mick Rodgers does. He wants you to *believe* it's sufficient to close you down. And it's those mind games that he's good at. People who believe his lies end up giving away far more than they need to, but that's the way he works. I think we can pre-empt all of that, though."

"We?" Dee scoffs.

Morgan rests a hand on Dee's arm. "You two were manifesting a way that Pinewoods can survive. Let's hear her out, huh? This might be it."

"I think it is," Georgie says, nodding enthusiastically. "I can get someone in to do the roof repairs."

"Here we go again." Lorraine throws her one good arm into the air. "We've no money to pay for the repairs. We didn't even have money for Hunter and Ed to put the tarpaulin across the roof." She shakes her head.

"Georgie helped too," Hunter says. "She was up there on the roof with us."

Lorraine's eyes open wide as she stares at Georgie. "I – sorry, I didn't know you did that to help us out."

"I was happy to help," Georgie says.

"Go on," Holly says, leaning forward and resting her elbows on the table. "Your solution has to be more than getting the roof done."

Georgie smiles at Holly. "Yes, it's definitely more than that. I'm sure you could go around your friends with a begging bowl, or do a funding page, and eventually be able to pull enough money together to get the roof done, but I don't think that's enough for you. I mean, I've got favours I can call in, so we can keep the repair costs low. I'll pay but," she holds up a hand to stop Lorraine from jumping in again, "I need somewhere to stay because I think I've just walked out on my husband. So, getting the roof done quickly gives me an en-suite room I can stay in."

"I'm not sure it's a good idea for you to stay here again, lovey," Dee says.

"I get that. I only need somewhere for up to a month so I can sort myself somewhere more permanent. But wait, this is distracting us from what we really need to talk about."

Lorraine shakes her head and sighs. "Seriously, Georgie?"

"Come on, Lorraine," Holly says. "I know you're in pain, but this isn't like you." Lorraine rubs her fist across the bridge of her nose. "You said it yourself last night," Holly goes on. "The only option you're left with is to accept the offer from that Mick Rodgers bloke, even though it's way too cheap. So maybe it's worth listening to everything Georgie's got to say." Holly nods at Georgie to continue.

"My husband is having yet another affair, and I won't take any more of this, so I'm telling him it's over. I had a chat with Beth this morning, about divorce settlements, which has helped me with my calculations. We've cash in the bank, the house, and my half of the business we have together. Plus I have a couple of businesses myself, too. That'll give me more than enough. Lorraine, Dee," she looks from one to the other and back to Lorraine, "what you need right now is an investor. Businesses like yours can't survive without an investor. I want to be your investor."

"No." Lorraine purses her lips together, looking like she's ready to explode. "I'm not touching your money."

"Think of it like *Dragon's Den*, without having to go through the rigmarole of selling your idea to the dragons. You already sold it to me when I was staying here."

"I. Said. No!" Lorraine glares at Georgie, her eyes glistening.

"With my investment," Georgie goes on, her heart pounding, sure that she can bring Lorraine around, "you get to keep Pinewoods. Sure, I get a share in the business, but you get to keep this place that you're created. And more than that, you'll have the money to do the works on the building to keep it going. With you still at the helm. And you'll have enough money to do some targeted marketing to get more paying customers. You'll have money to market Pinewoods in all the right places, and I'll use my contacts to spread the word further."

Lorraine shakes her head continuously. "I'm not handing control of Pinewoods to you. This is my baby, mine and Dee's. We've built it from nothing. There's no way I'm handing it over to you."

"You'd rather Mick Rodgers buys the place from under you for less than it's worth, then?" Georgie fights the urge to roll her eyes.

"Of course I'd not prefer that!"

"This is infuriating," Dee says, walking over to Lorraine and leaning into her. "We're stuck between a rock and a hard place. Hobson's choice."

"I've no idea who Hobson is," Holly says, "but I think Georgie might be onto something here. We do need an investor. People like me, Hunter, Ed – we can help around the place, but none of us has any money. Even if I sell Nan and Grandad's house, it's never going to be enough for what you need to keep Pinewoods going. You need proper money. Do you know anyone other than Georgie who's likely to make an offer like this?"

Georgie sends a mental thank you to Holly through the ether as an uncomfortable silence hangs in the room.

"Of course not," Lorraine eventually says. "But I don't want her to be the one who rescues us. She brought this mess on us."

"She didn't, though," Holly says, her voice soft. She rests a hand on Lorraine's arm. "Nobody brought this mess on us. It just is."

"I'll, er . . ." Georgie pushes herself to standing in one graceful move. "I'll go and chat to the bees." She points a finger to the back door.

"It's raining," Holly and Dee say in unison.

"Right, yes, no. It's OK, I don't mind getting a little wet. I'll leave you all to talk."

Morgan passes her an umbrella and she walks out through the back door, feeling all eyes on her. The networking part of her wants to turn around and flash a smile at them all, but this isn't the time. These people need time to work out whether her proposition will work for them.

"Wait," Holly calls after Georgie as she walks down the gravel path. "I don't want to sound crass, but how much are we talking about here? The investment."

Georgie shrugs. "I don't know, Holly. Whatever it takes, I guess. Half a million, maybe – that's around the ballpark of what I'm expecting."

Holly nods and turns back into the kitchen.

38

LORRAINE

THERE'S a mix of irritation and resignation running through Lorraine's veins as she waits for Georgie to get out of earshot. Being beholden to an investor is not the way she wants to do business. But the only alternative facing her and Dee is to sell up – and she doesn't want to do that to the retreat, either. There's only one thing she feels certain of right now, and it's that she doesn't trust Georgie Quinn. From the moment she arrived, Lorraine felt something. It's hard to put her finger on what, but her energies are . . . odd. That's not a word she usually applies to people, but it's not exactly that Georgie has negative energies. It's less that she's got any negativity surrounding her, and more that there's an absence of something deeper in her soul.

"You always tell me to look for the glimmers," Holly says, as she walks back into the kitchen. "Seems to me there's glimmers in this offer."

"This isn't the kind of situation I mean when I say to look for the glimmers, Holly." Lorraine sighs. "When I say to look for the glimmers, I mean to look for something positive out of the day rather than focusing on the bad things that happen. This isn't something I can look for glimmers in." She rubs her hand up and down the wood of the table in front of her.

"But her offer will save Pinewoods. That's exactly what you said you need – some kind of miracle to save the retreat."

Lorraine shakes her head. "No. I'm not taking money from her. I know she won that award for all the work she does helping vulnerable women, but honestly, it doesn't feel like she cares about people like us."

"Do you really think that?" Holly tilts her head to the side. "You taught me that it doesn't matter who someone has been. Surely that means it doesn't matter to you who Georgie was before today. What truly matters is that she's trying to be a better person than she was before. Should we punish her – punish Pinewoods – because we don't like who she used to be? Should we wait for someone else to come along, too late, to save the retreat?" Holly plants her hands firmly into the pockets of her dungarees. "Georgie Quinn isn't going to change overnight. It's taken her a lifetime to become the person who came here and deceived us. But I saw the glimmer of a good person in her, and I think you did too. She's trying to change, and she's making you the exact offer that you need – that Pinewoods needs."

A silence hangs in the room for a moment.

"Holly's got a point," Morgan says. "And you and Dee have been manifesting a solution that means you don't have to sell up. Even if Georgie's offer simply makes you think differently, there's a glimmer in that, surely. Her offer could make you think of other options available to you."

"There *are* no other options, though," Dee says, irritation stamped into each word.

"That's defeatist," Holly snaps. "I can't believe that of you two. You don't do defeat. You don't give up." Her eyes glisten with tears, ready to plop over the edge of her eyelashes. "You're your own worst enemy. It's all because you won't accept help that you're in this mess." She pushes the heels of her hands into her eyes.

"That's not fair, Holly. We're in this *mess,* as you call it, because the mortgage and the cost of gas and electric has gone through the roof," Lorraine says, pursing her lips.

"And," Morgan says, pointing a finger upwards, "because your *actual* roof has fallen in."

"We've all offered to help you," Holly says, sniffing, "and you pushed us all away. Hunter and Ed said they'd help with the building work, but before they could get anywhere near it, you went up there on your own and ended up having an accident." Holly leans forwards and rests her hands on the kitchen table, her chin jutting out at Lorraine. "So yes, you did bring some of this mess on yourself."

"That hurts, Holly."

"I'm sorry, Lorraine, I don't want to hurt you. You know I love you dearly. But you're being too stubborn for your own good, turning away every offer of help that stares you in the face."

"Holly's right," Morgan says. "I offered you financial help and you turned me down."

"You don't have the kind of money we need, Mor, and even if you did, I can't afford to pay you back."

"And I told you that you don't need to pay me back. How much do you think you need?"

"I looked it up on a website, and with the scaffolding and the size of our roof, we'd be looking at over twenty thousand. We'd have to close the café for the duration, so there's loss of earnings there. Then there's not having any income from the bedrooms when the job gets done. I'm guessing that's going to cost us at least another ten thousand."

"Making a grand total," Ed says, "in excess of thirty grand."

"If I cash in my pension I have that, and more. Or I can sell my house, move somewhere smaller."

"No, Morgan," Lorraine says. "We've already talked about this. We're not taking your money. We have to accept it. We're ruined."

Lorraine and Dee sigh in unison.

"Aren't you the band of merry women," Hunter says, walking over to the cooling rack on the kitchen worktop. He selects a cookie, breaks it in two, and points one half at Lorraine. "You're acting like you're all out of ideas. Let's go back to the beginning. What are your options?"

"Sell up or sell out." Lorraine lowers her head and closes her eyes, as if trying to hide from the truth. "The thing is, I'm not sure I have the energy any more. I'm exhausted."

Hunter shrugs. "Any other options?"

"Let *me* be an investor. I can give Lorraine and Dee a little bit of money," Morgan says. "I've got nearly twenty grand in savings."

"It's not enough," Dee says, a tremor in her voice.

"Well, we've got Georgie's offer, of course, which is enough," Hunter says. "But what else? Let's go bonkers and just throw any idea that comes to mind onto a piece of paper."

Neither Lorraine nor Dee moves. Holly gets a notebook from the Welsh dresser, and Morgan, Ed and Hunter throw out ideas from crowdfunding to diversifying to getting the community involved to closing down. Still Lorraine and Dee stay on the edge of the group, their heads bowed in resignation to their fate.

"Phone San," Holly blurts out.

Hunter laughs. "I don't think she's got a spare wad of cash, but sure, give her a call."

"No, I mean, one of the reasons Lorraine doesn't want to accept Georgie's offer is because we don't know if she can be trusted." Holly plants her hands on her hips and looks from person to person. "San might know of her. She might be able to fill in any gaps that will help Lorraine and Dee to make a decision."

"It's worth a try," Dee says, speaking for the first time since they started throwing ideas around. "Come on, Raine, there's nothing to lose, and besides, San might have some ideas of her own."

Lorraine nods slowly and pulls out her phone. She pauses before going into her contacts. It's pointless. There's nothing San can say that's going to change things. She glances up at the group to tell them it's the end, but the sea of faces looks back at her expectantly. OK, she'll show willing, talk to San for them. But it's like they missed the bit where she told them how exhausted she is – there's nothing left in her energy bank any more. Even if she accepted Georgie's investment, can she really muster up the enthusiasm to keep on going? After talking to San, she'll tell them it's over. Mick Rodgers has won. They're going to have to accept his offer.

"What do you know about a woman called Georgie Quinn, San?" Lorraine, her voice low and monotone, doesn't even wait for any niceties of conversation when San picks up on the second ring.

"Oh shit, what's going on, Lorraine? You sound like crap."

"Hang on," Lorraine says, moving the phone from her ear. She presses a button and puts the phone onto the kitchen table. "You're on speaker, San. Dee, Holly and the others are all here with me." Lorraine sniffs as everyone says hello to San. "We're in trouble, San, and we might have to close Pinewoods down."

"No! Really? You can't do that!"

"Georgie Quinn's offered to invest," Dee blurts out.

"Wow. QuinnEssentials wants to invest in Pinewoods?"

"Is that her business?" Lorraine asks.

"Yes, she runs it with Ryan," San clears her throat, "her husband."

"We met him at the awards." Lorraine sighs. It all feels such an effort, even talking to San, who she loves.

"You were on the same table as him and Georgie at the awards," San says. "What was that all about?"

"You know them?" Lorraine asks. "Georgie was the woman staying here who I asked you about."

"You said her name was Macrae, not Quinn. Yeah, I – er – I know the Quinns, well, Ryan, anyway."

"The three of them," Dee says, "Georgie, Ryan and that developer, Mick Rodgers, have been working on a sneaky takeover. Mick Rodgers made a lowball offer to buy Pinewoods."

"Bloody hell." San whistles down the phone.

"But now," Hunter says, "it looks like Georgie is going rogue and she's made a counteroffer."

San's laugh has an edge of sarcasm to it. "I'm kind of not surprised, you know. Everyone's talking about what happened at the Liverpool Women in Business Awards the other night."

"You mean that other woman," Morgan says, leaning in towards the phone on the table.

"You know about it?" San asks.

"I was there when Georgie bumped into her in the Ladies. God, it was humiliating. For Georgie, that is."

"Her husband – Ryan – he, er . . . let's say he has form." There's a long pause.

"He's had a few affairs. I was . . ." San clears her throat. "I was with him for ten years. Remember when I was staying at Pinewoods last year? He was the toxic relationship I just came out of."

"Ohhh," Holly says, her eyes wide. "It was *him*."

Lorraine laughs. "Now I didn't see *that* coming, San. So you know him well, then, I'm guessing."

"Very well. He's got charisma like you've never seen. Very generous guy. Kind. But he always went home to his wife. So I kicked him into touch last year."

"Good for you, San," Morgan says.

"Poor Georgie." Holly folds her arms around herself.

"What were you wanting to know about her?" San asks.

"She's made us an offer," Dee says. "To invest in Pinewoods Retreat. Said she's got the cash, along with plenty of contacts and favours she can call in to do the repairs."

314

"What repairs?"

"Long story, San, we'll bring you up to speed another time," Hunter says.

"We want to know if she's right to have as an investor," Dee adds.

"God, yeah." San laughs. "She deserves that award she got the other night. You honestly couldn't have anyone better on your side when it comes to business. Not so sure about her taste in men, mind you, but hey." Everyone looks at Ed, who rolls his eyes with a smile.

"She's right, what she says," San goes on. "She's got loads of contacts, and I'm sure she'll have more than a few favours to call in. But it's more than that. Georgie Quinn is well connected with the right set. She'll get everyone talking about Pinewoods Retreat. You might need to bring some of the rooms up to date for the type of clientele she'll bring you, but only from the first impressions perspective. That woman will turn things around. Her reputation is second to none in Liverpool. I'm surprised it's taken this long for you to come across her, but I suppose you move in different circles."

"You don't think she'll screw us over then?" Dee taps her lips with her fingers.

"I can't make any promises," San says. "I know I'd not trust Ryan, any more. Not sure how I got lost in such a long relationship with him now I look back. Hindsight, and all that."

"But you think Georgie's sound?" Ed asks.

"From what I know about her, yes. Whereas with Mick Rodgers, if you agreed to any deal with him he'd get you so far along and change something on you – maybe add a clause to a contract or drop a worse offer on you, so late in the game that you're in no position to refuse. I wouldn't trust Mick Rodgers as far as I could throw him. I've been researching for an article me and another journalist are doing about Rodgers. It's obvious that Ryan's become his lap dog, does his dirty work for him. Georgie Quinn, though, I can't find anything where she's involved. It doesn't seem like she's connected to any of it. I reckon she'll see you right."

"That sounds hopeful," Holly says.

Lorraine looks over at Dee, barely daring to breathe. They hold each other's gaze.

Morgan squeezes Lorraine's shoulder. "I think you might have your answer, Lorraine."

Lorraine chews the inside of her cheek. "I think we might."

With the call ended, everyone around the kitchen table talks at once.

"Stop," Ed shouts. "Let's not go too fast with this. We need to do this the logical way. Are we sure this is the right decision?"

"I was thinking we were ready to take Mick Rodgers's offer, but listening to San, I don't know," Lorraine says. "Maybe Georgie is our solution, after all."

"Let's check the list." Ed picks up the piece of paper with everything they brainstormed earlier and waves it around the group. "There are solutions here. Let's go through them again. Crowdfunding. That's an option. Can that work?"

"It'll take too long, mate. We can't rely on anything on that list,"

Hunter says, taking the paper from Ed. He runs his finger down everything they came up with and lays it down on the table. "Lorraine and Dee have to make this decision for themselves. Only they know what the right one is for them."

Lorraine looks over at Dee again. "Are we in agreement, then?" Dee nods. "OK. I tell you what, let's have a cup of tea, and if we still feel the same way after that . . ."

"Well, as it's been raining," Dee says, "and we're unlikely to get many customers in the café today, who wants a cookie?"

Hunter picks up the cooling rack of cookies and places it in the middle of the table. He nabs another cookie for himself, grins at Dee, and takes a quick bite out of it.

39
GEORGIE

THE beehive is quieter than usual when Georgie reaches the back of the garden. She looks up at the clouds. There's a hint of brightness and a change in the weather. Hopefully she won't need to stand in the rain for too long after all. With no bees to watch, Georgie paces between the little hut that Holly lives in, and the shed in the opposite corner of the garden as she waits. Her phone rings. She ignores it without even looking to see who is calling her. It rings again. She ignores it again. And the same the third time it rings. On the fourth call, Georgie pulls the phone out of her pocket to see who is so desperate, and accidentally presses the button to answers it.

"Hello? Hello? You there, babe?"

Georgie sighs. "Call me by my name, Ryan. I'm not 'babe' any more."

"Ah, hey, come on, babe. What's going on?"

"You brought another woman into our house. Our bed." Georgie's voice is flat, measured.

"I – well – yeah, I did. I won't lie to you."

"You already lied, though, Ryan. I asked if you had someone there with you. You said you didn't. And it was that Faith Jacks. Wasn't it?"

"Yeah, yeah, you got me. You know how it is. Doesn't mean a thing."

Georgie waits for the usual apology that Ryan comes out with when he's been found out, though she already knows she's got no interest in hearing it, let alone accepting it. There's silence on the other end of the phone, and for a moment Georgie wonders if they've been cut off, until she hears Ryan sniff.

"You coming home, or what?"

"No, Ry. It's different this time." A finger of sunlight breaks through the clouds, skimming the top of the beehive.

"Oh yeah?"

"I can't do this any more. I've had enough."

"Really? Right, I'll get onto your mum, then, shall I?"

"I've spoken to her, Ryan. She's packing boxes as we speak. She's cool with it."

"Like fuck."

Bees exit the small hole at the bottom of the beehive, and Georgie watches as they unfurl their wings and take off in search of nectar. "All this time you had a hold over me because of Mum, and there she was thinking I should have left you years ago. It's over, Ry." She lets out a deep sigh, as if letting go of two decades of holding her breath.

"Don't believe you," Ryan says.

"It's over. Coming to Pinewoods woke me up and made me see what our marriage has become."

"That's the end of you. You'll have nothing."

"That's not true, though, is it. The law's on my side. You can't keep everything after nearly twenty-five years of marriage. It's matrimonial assets."

"How do you know that?"

Georgie laughs. "I researched it, Ryan. It's there in black and white. The house is half mine." She turns to sit down in her usual spot on the raised bed, realising just in time that it's still wet from the rain.

"I'll get the locks changed," Ryan says. "You'll not get in the house again."

"I've already packed what I need."

"You can forget about all your jewellery."

"When you check the safe," Georgie says, brushing away a couple of pine needles from the landing board at the front of the hive, "you'll find it's empty." Does he really think she's that naive? The value of her jewellery alone is the price of a small house. She made sure to take it all with her, stuffed deep in her overnight bag along with a couple of weeks' worth of clothes.

"Your mum."

"It's over." Georgie holds her breath.

Ryan is silent on the other end of the phone, like he's calculating his next steps. Georgie slowly, quietly, lets out her breath, waiting for him to speak. And then the line goes dead. Has Ryan hung up? She looks at her phone to check her service – three bars, so it's not an issue at her end. For a moment she toys with calling him back, but she has nothing more to say to him now that can't be said through a solicitor. She stares at her phone. That's it. What is she supposed to feel at a time like this? Happy? Elated? Deflated?

Georgie does a quick mental check-in – her shoulders are up near her ears, so she's carrying some stress around there, but she feels . . . nothing, really. Or is it a nothingness? Like she's empty of any feelings, ready to fill up again now, with something better, something more in keeping with who she'd like to be.

"Well, I've only gone and done it, bees," she says, addressing the whole hive. "I've left him. My marriage is over." Some bees perform their waggle dance on the landing board, as if congratulating her on what she's done. Georgie leans down to watch them closer, the mellow sun warming her neck. "I'm taking inspiration from you busy little bees. When your honey is taken from you, you make more. No matter what Ryan does to me, I'll make more money. I'm going to be just fine."

Georgie watches the bees for some time, and only notices the crunch of the gravel when the sound gets close.

"You're mesmerised by those bees, aren't you?" Holly stands alongside Georgie and watches the bees with her. "I hope you don't feel we left you out here for too long. Sorry. Any chance you can pop back in, Georgie?" Holly locks eyes with her. Her nose twitches, almost as if she's working hard to stop herself from smiling.

"Thanks." A trill of nervous energy runs through Georgie's body, the way it does when a contract she's put months of effort into comes together.

Georgie follows as Holly walks away from her, back into Pinewoods. She stands for a moment at the door, praying that Lorraine and Dee are ready to accept her investment, controlling her excitement, getting herself back in control, the way she likes to be when she's entering into negotiations for QuinnEssentials. This is the biggest decision of her life, and yet she's put the least thought and effort into it. Every big business decision they've made, she's conducted a mass of research, talked Ryan through the pros and cons, and he's then played devil's advocate to be sure they're doing the right thing. And yet with this decision, she didn't even know when she got out of bed this morning that she would offer to invest in Pinewoods Retreat.

Her stomach is in knots. Despite this idea being impulsive, and despite not having put much thought into it, this is possibly one of the most auspicious decisions of her career, and she's desperate to hear a 'yes'.

Please let Lorraine and Dee say yes. Please.

40

LORRAINE

LORRAINE shifts her weight in the uncomfortable chair, keeping her narrowed eyes on Georgie who puts her hand on a chair on the other side of the kitchen table. Georgie looks around the group, before settling her eyes on Lorraine. There's a slight uplift at the side of the woman's mouth, Lorraine notices, as if she's forcing herself not to smile. *Yeah, she's won, and she knows it.*

"How do I know," Lorraine starts, before Georgie has chance to lower herself into a seat at the table, "this isn't just some scheme for that Mick Rodgers fella to get his hands on our business?" Lorraine breathes slowly, maintaining her calm. Even though her and Dee have agreed to tell Georgie that they'll accept her offer, she wants to avoid coming across as an eager underdog. Georgie needs to know that whilst they're in need of help, they're not pushovers.

"Mick Rodgers isn't interested in investing in you or the business. He wants the house and the land around it, and he doesn't want any of you to be part of what he intends to do with the place. You'll all lose your jobs."

Gasps fill the air.

"So he'd destroy what we've created here?"

Georgie nods, clamping her lips together.

"And you say we'd all be out of jobs?"

Georgie nods again and looks at Holly, Hunter and Ed. Ed stuffs his hands into the pockets of his shorts and shakes his head.

"I love it here," he says.

Hunter lays a hand on his shoulder. "Me too, mate."

"Well," Lorraine clears her throat, "we're stitched up. We've no choice, have we?"

"I suppose not," Georgie says, eyes flitting between Dee and Lorraine.

"We either to take your offer of investment, or sell up and lose everything we've created here."

"Yes. I'm sorry."

Lorraine's upper lip curls with disgust, trying hard not to blame Georgie for the imperfect situation they find themselves in. It hurts so much to have to admit that they need help to save Pinewoods Retreat. "Answer me one question. I need to know, honestly."

"OK," Georgie says.

"Was this your plan all along? When you first came to Pinewoods?"

"No, not at all. I didn't even know myself that I'd make this offer until this morning."

Lorraine nods her head thoughtfully. Georgie appears to be telling the truth, and Lorraine's usually a good judge of character.

Holly walks over to Lorraine and hugs her. "Should I make us all another cup of tea?"

Lorraine pats her hand, shakes her head, and purses her lips together, not trusting herself to speak for a moment.

"If you're going to accept Georgie's investment," Morgan says, "I want you to accept my investment too. I know it's not much, but I can put about twenty grand in the pot."

Georgie nods. "That's sensible. And then the three of you can retain sixty per cent of the business, and I'll own forty per cent."

"Thirty," Dee shouts out.

"No, that's not enough for me, Dee. But I tell you what, I'll drop my share down to thirty-five per cent when my investment is repaid."

"It's like *Dragon's Den*," Holly says, grinning, her hands clasped under her chin.

"I really am sorry," Georgie says. "I know what it's like to birth a business. I know what it's like to struggle. I promise you, my investment will help you. Along with that, I'll support you with my business expertise and my contacts. I want to be involved in decisions, but I'm not here to take over."

"Are you sure?" Lorraine shakes her head again and takes in a slow, deep breath, reminding herself of what San told them earlier. Georgie's going through her own difficult times. This must be hard for her, too. It's not even Georgie's fault that they've got themselves into this situation. She closes her eyes for a moment and rests her hand on her heart, working to balance her energies and release the negativity she's holding on to.

"I think," Dee says, taking the seat next to Lorraine, "that what Lorraine means, is that we need to get a few things ironed out so that this can be a successful process." She gently places an arm around Lorraine's shoulder, immediately moving it when Lorraine flinches with pain. "Right, Lorraine?"

Lorraine looks deep into Dee's eyes. Love pours out, giving her strength. She nods, and turns back to Georgie. "Yes," Lorraine says. "I'm sorry. It's . . . hard." A sob escapes, and she grapples with a flood of emotions.

"Of course it is," says Georgie, pulling a notebook and pen from her bag. "Tell me some of the things that are important to you both so that we can work on those first."

"What like?" Dee asks. "You mean jobs around the house and stuff?"

"That kind of thing, yes, and your values, though I think I have a pretty good idea of those. And any ways you want us to work together."

Lorraine frees her hand from Dee's and crosses her arms, ignoring the stab of pain in her shoulder. "You see yourself as a partner, then? I don't know about that."

"No, not a partner. I'm your investor. I'm here to guide you so that I can look after my investment, but I'm not your business partner, no."

"What does that even mean?" Frustration pounds through Lorraine's veins and she sighs deeply. "I'm sorry. Look, I've never needed to have this kind of conversation before. We need to keep it simple so that there's no misunderstandings."

"Let's start again. First things first, what jobs need doing on the house? Once we know that, I can work out how much money

I need to invest just to get the building to a state where you can take more guests in."

"Good idea," Holly says, picking up her notebook and pen again from the Welsh dresser. "Start with the roof, and we can add things from there."

"Gutters," Hunter says. "They're in a right state and might as well be sorted along with the roof."

Even though Holly is making notes for Lorraine, Georgie scribbles things down in a notebook of her own, with an expensive-looking fountain pen that scratches over the paper as she writes. One by one, jobs are added to the list, and Georgie nods with each new item.

"OK," Georgie says after a few minutes. "That's quite a list. At a guess, I'd say we're looking at somewhere in the region of £100k just to sort this lot out, before we even talk about other things. I'll get one of my contacts to check everything out and come back with a price. We'll at least get mates' rates with it being through me, as I've put a lot of business his way. What else?"

"You'll not be able to have guests when you have builders on site," Morgan says, wagging a finger in the air towards the ceiling. "Add in the cost of lost business for however many weeks that goes on for."

"Hmm, Morgan's right." Georgie taps her fountain pen on her lips. "Let's aim for getting the work done in three to four months. We'll base our calculations on it taking four months, and then if it's not that bad we can get things up and running again much sooner."

"We can't close for that long!" Lorraine snaps. How can Georgie not see how exasperating this is?

"You can't work anyway for the next few months," Georgie says, pointing her fountain pen at the restraint on Lorraine's arm. "I'll cover everyone's wages and all bills during the time you're closed. It'll be part of the investment I'll put in. Does that help?"

Everyone's eyes are on Lorraine, waiting for her to respond. She sighs. This is not what she wants for the business, but there's no other way to keep Pinewoods Retreat afloat during these extended unprecedented times. She gives one sharp nod.

"Is that a yes?" Georgie looks at her expectantly.

Lorraine nods again. "Yes." Her voice is a near whisper. "You're right. We need to close. But none of the staff can suffer. They're good people."

Georgie nods and smiles. "They are good people. You've chosen well, Lorraine."

She looks around her staff. Yes, she's chosen well. And she can only hope that San is right about Georgie, too.

41

GEORGIE

An hour later, Georgie takes her bags up to the room she vacated only a matter of days ago. She left a list of what needs to be done in the middle of the kitchen table as a reminder of the agreement between them, before the legal papers arrive.

She unpacks and settles herself down in the shabby chair in the corner of her room. Her phone pings.

Ed: *Can we talk?*

Gee: *In an hour? We can walk and talk.*

The answer is a simple thumbs up.

* * *

There's something about walking alongside someone that makes difficult conversations much easier – or at least, that's what Georgie was thinking when she suggested to Ed that they should walk and talk. She's unsure why she thinks this might be an awkward conversation, but her gut tells her it could be.

They've been strolling through the woods for coming up to ten minutes, and, for a man who asked if they could talk, Ed's been very quiet.

"So," Georgie says, as if the word is a complete sentence.

"So," Ed replies, pushing his hands deeper into the pockets of his shorts.

They walk on again in silence, following the woodland path as it weaves its way through the trees.

"No Moose?" Georgie asks.

"No Moose," Ed says. "I left him back at the house."

They continue on a little further, in silence again.

"So," Ed says again, clearing his throat. "I was wondering – where does this leave us?"

"I'm not sure."

"I'm guessing you've left your husband?"

Georgie nods. "I'm guessing that too." Her laugh is weak.

"And will I be the rebound guy?" Ed asks.

Georgie stops walking. She rubs her hands over her face and waits for Ed to stop walking too, and turn to face her. "I've only ever dated Ryan," she says. "I don't know if you're the rebound guy or not. I've no idea if I'm having a rebound. I like you, Ed." She takes a step towards him. "A lot."

"And?" He shifts from one foot to the other.

"I'm not sure there is an 'and'." Georgie laughs. "I never meant for this, us, to happen – not that anything has even happened, yet. I didn't even know I'd bump into you when I came here."

"Would it have been easier if you hadn't bumped into me?" Ed tilts his head, looking for a moment like the young teen at school where they first met.

Georgie shakes her head. "I'm confused, Ed. The last time we talked, you were so sure of yourself. You supported me, I got the impression you were confident about our feelings for each other. But now... I don't get it. What's going on?"

He rolls his eyes again, and smiles. "That was about *you* – I'm good at helping other people. But right now, I'm feeling nervous as shit, totally vulnerable, which makes me uncomfortable, and I'm cringing deep inside cos even though you've not said that this," he waves his hands in the space between them, "is coming to an end before it's even begun, I've told myself that's what you want." He looks off down the path before bringing his eyes back to Georgie's. "I'm half expecting you to tell me that what we had was sweet – but you need to get back to your life now, thank you very much." He sucks in a lung full of air.

Georgie laughs. "OK, *this* I can work with. You're a great guy—"

"Uh-oh."

"Nothing about what's happened over the last few days changes the feelings I had for you."

"Had? Past tense?" Ed's jaw tightens.

"Had, and have. I'd love to see where that takes us. Right now, though, I've no idea what's going on inside my head. I've asked Ryan for a divorce. I don't want my feelings about that to get muddled with how I feel for you. I – look, yes, I do have feelings for you. Strong ones, believe me." She turns away from him, aching for him, whilst also pained by the sadness in his eyes. "The last thing I want to do is hurt you, Ed." Her throat is tight. "You're a great guy. I'm not sure I deserve you."

"Well, you can stop that right there, Georgie Macrae – Quinn. You're a wonderful woman. You absolutely do deserve me, just as much as I deserve you."

Georgie turns back to face him. "Thank you. But you've already seen how underhand I've been. I'd like to say that's not the real me, but it must be – I came here incognito, to deceive you all. And I don't want you thinking that I used you when I was staying at Pinewoods. The flirting between us, that was real." Georgie combs her fingers through her hair, the way she used to when she was an insecure teenager. "I can't tell you how much I'm attracted to you, how much good you've done me. You awakened the authentic me – god, I hate that word. But you did, Ed. You opened my eyes to who I became with Ryan – indebted to him, relinquishing my power to him – and I don't like that woman."

"What you were is not who you are."

"Well," Georgie laughs, "it kinda feels like I'm in rehab being at Pinewoods, so yeah, maybe the same way it is for an addict, a part of me will always be that version of Georgie Quinn. It's just, I want to change. I don't want to be her any more. I want to get back to being Georgina Macrae. And – well, maybe you could be part of that?"

Ed steps towards Georgie and stops. He studies her for a moment and looks away into the thicket. "Let's walk," he says.

Georgie falls into step alongside Ed, waiting for him to speak. He says nothing, but every few steps she feels him looking at her. She wants to look back at him, but whatever's going on between them in this moment needs to be at his pace. They walk on in silence.

"This way," Ed says, taking a path that Georgie's not been

down before. The path narrows, forcing her to walk behind him for a while, before opening out onto a wider path. A couple of dog walkers pass them, deep in conversation.

As Georgie and Ed walk on, side-by-side, he nudges her arm with his elbow. "We need to start over. Maybe take things a bit slower this time." Ed wraps his little finger around Georgie's.

"Maybe we do."

"Maybe." Ed laughs. He stops walking and turns to her. "Can I kiss you, Georgina Macrae?"

Georgie closes the gap between them. "And how exactly is that taking things slower?" She smiles.

"I guess because I asked this time?" He pulls her into him and folds his arms around her, kissing her hair. "I'd like to see where this takes us, but yeah, it doesn't need to be quite so intense."

"Then let's get to know each other. Properly."

"As friends."

Georgie nods, holding Ed tight to her. "As friends. But," she pulls her head back and looks into his eyes, "friends who cuddle and kiss and hold hands, and maybe, sometime soon, friends with benefits."

"Yeah, I reckon that's the kind of friendship I can go for." Ed leans in and kisses Georgie tenderly on her lips. "Come on, friend, I've got a yoga class to get ready for."

He takes her hand and they walk back to Pinewoods Retreat.

42

LORRAINE

Two Weeks After the Award Ceremony

IN all her life, Lorraine has never seen so much money in her bank account. A part of her didn't believe Georgie would follow through on the promise she made just a couple of weeks ago, but now the money with all those zeros on the end is staring back at her from her banking app. With her heart pounding, she gently lays her mobile phone down on the kitchen table in front of Dee and points at the line that shows the amount sitting in their business account.

"Shit, she's true to her word."

Lorraine nods. "The first payment. And a guy's coming this afternoon to work out how much scaffolding we need for getting the roof done. He told me on the phone that they'll be putting it up first thing tomorrow. So this afternoon's job for me is to get on the phone and cancel the handful of bookings we've got. Georgie said I can use some of this first one hundred grand to sort out repayment of the deposits for those customers. And it should cover the scaffolding, roofing materials and initial payments for the contractor. She'll give us more as things progress."

The kitchen door swings open with force and wallops into the wall. A well-dressed man stands there as the door begins its return swing. He puts out his hand to stop it hitting him in the face.

"Oh." Dee pushes herself up to standing. "Ryan Quinn, isn't it? We met at the awards thing."

"Where is she?" His tone is aggressive, his face dark and menacing.

"We don't have many guests staying this week. Can you be more specific so that I can help?" Lorraine asks, fully aware he means Georgie.

"Don't play games with me." He steps forwards into the kitchen and lets the door swing on its hinges.

Lorraine takes a few steps towards him, her heart pounding as Ryan Quinn towers over her. Where's Hunter when she needs him? "Mr Quinn," she says, forcing herself to sound more confident than she feels, "you really need to leave."

"I've no beef with you. Tell me where Georgie is, and I'll get out of your hair."

Lorraine says nothing, struggling to think on her feet.

"I know she's here," Ryan continues. "Her car's out front." He thumbs over his shoulder.

"Yes, well no, I mean..." Lorraine takes in a deep breath. "She's here, but she's gone for a walk."

"Where to? How long ago? When will she be back?"

"I – don't know. An hour ago, maybe. She didn't say how long she'll be."

"Can I offer you a cup of tea whilst you wait?" Dee asks.

Lorraine shoots her a side glance. They don't need to encourage this bully to stay any longer than he needs to.

Ryan ignores the question. "What direction did she go in?"

Lorraine looks down at his expensive shoes and toys with sending him off on the muddiest trail. She opens her mouth to speak when the sound of laughter fills the hall. Georgie and Ed are back from their walk.

"Don't worry," Ryan says, "that's her now." He turns on his heels and stomps out of the room.

Lorraine follows him out into the hall, Moose scampering ahead of her, just in time to see Georgie drop Ed's hand.

"What are you doing here, Ryan?" Georgie asks. Ed looks from her to the man standing in the middle of the wide hallway, as Moose sits in front of the two of them, as if on guard.

"Fuck me, Georgie," Ryan says. "You didn't think to tell me you had a bit on the side." Lorraine can't see Ryan's face, but she can hear disgust in his tone. "You've played me for this divorce."

"I've not played you, Ry," Georgie says. "Look, let's go in the living room." She indicates to the room on her right.

"Nah, might as well have it out right here in front of your cosy little group of friends." There's a sneer in his voice, and whilst Lorraine is wishing she could sidle away and leave them to their argument, she remains glued to the spot, mesmerised by what's happening in front of her.

"I'll put the kettle on, then," Dee says with a false cheeriness from behind Lorraine.

"You stitched up Mick Rodgers good and proper, you did.

And clearly I came just in time to see that you've stitched me up too, blaming me for having an affair when you're up to no good yourself." He brushes his jacket back and thrusts his hands onto his hips, as if making himself as broad as possible.

Neither of them speaks for a few moments, simply standing in the middle of the hall glaring at each other.

"Go on then," Ryan says, his voice low in contrast to his aggressive stance.

"You mean Ed?" Georgie glances in Ed's direction and back to Ryan. "I knew him when we were kids, and bumped into him again here."

"And?"

"That's all there is to it," Georgie says. "Nothing—" She stops herself. She won't lie.

"And he's why you want a divorce?" Ryan stabs a finger in Ed's direction.

Ed stuffs his hands into the pockets of his shorts. "It's not like that, mate."

Lorraine shifts from one foot to the other. Does she stay put or would she be better skulking back off to the kitchen? With the door wedged open, she'll still be able to hear this argument, with Ryan's booming voice.

"No." Georgie shakes her head. "This, us, it has nothing to do with Ed. I've had enough of you having affairs."

"We had an arrangement."

"We didn't, Ryan. You had an arrangement. I put up with it."

"None of the women ever bothered you before."

"You never flaunted your relationships in front of me before Faith Jacks. You know we have a video doorbell, and still you brought her into our house, and then you arranged for her to be at the award ceremony too. My guess is you wanted me to find out. Anyway, it doesn't matter. I've had enough. We're getting that divorce."

"And then," Ryan says, switching the conversation, "you screwed me over. I was in line for a lot of money with that deal, and you knew it. It's like – like – like insider dealing." He throws his arms in the air, letting them drop down hard by his side. "You had privileged access to intel that wasn't yours to use. Double-crosser. You kicked Mick Rodgers and his plans into touch."

"We were never going to sell to him," Lorraine says, recalling how close she actually was to accepting the offer.

Ryan switches his head around, as if noticing Lorraine for the first time, his eyes popping. He quickly turns back to Georgie. "You knew you were going to put the money into this dump," he snaps.

"Aye, aye," Ed says, taking a step towards Ryan.

"Shut up, mate, this has nothing to do with you."

"Maybe not, but this place is no dump."

Ryan lets out a snort.

Hunter appears in the porch behind Ed and Georgie. He steps up into the hall, and stands directly behind Georgie, as if protecting her. "Everything OK, mate?"

"Butt out," Ryan says. "This has nothing to do with you."

"As long as you're standing in Pinewoods, it has everything to do with me." Hunter folds his arms across his chest, his biceps bulging.

"This is between me and my *wife*." Ryan spits out the word.

Hunter unblinkingly holds Ryan's stare. Lorraine is impressed with the appearance of calm from Georgie in the face of her husband's rage. Georgie walks into the living room leaving the door open behind her.

"Don't you dare walk away from me," Ryan says. He stomps the few steps to the doorway and stands, almost as if he's refusing to cross the threshold.

Moose goes to follow Georgie, but Ed stoops down and scoops him up in his arms. Lorraine hears faint mumbling that sounds like '*get in here now and shut the bloody door*'. Ryan steps into the room and slams the door behind him.

"Damn," Lorraine says, her voice a near whisper.

"Do you think she's OK in there, on her own?" Ed asks.

Lorraine shrugs, immediately regretting it as pain shoots across her shoulder, reminding her of her accident.

Hunter leans his ear into the door and holds a finger to his lips. He shakes his head. "Their voices are too muffled. I can't make out what they're saying."

"Ed's right," Lorraine says. "One of us should be in there with her."

"She'll be fine," Hunter says.

"I'm going to stay here," Ed says, lowering himself onto the third step up on the stairs. "Just in case."

Hunter pats Ed on the shoulder and gently guides Lorraine back to the kitchen.

43

GEORGIE

GEORGIE looks out of the large picture window onto the garden café, the grass already cleared of tables in readiness for the scaffolding going up.

"I don't get it, Georgie," Ryan says, his voice a little calmer now he doesn't have an audience. "Why screw me and Mick over? What's in it for you?"

Georgie wraps her arms around herself. "I honestly don't know how to describe it, Ry. This place does something to you when you stay around for more than a few days." She runs a hand through her hair. "I've never felt like this before. I feel free to be myself here at Pinewoods."

"You were yourself at home, in QuinnEssentials."

"Not really. You were in charge of everything. Except LivSmarter."

"Was this your plan all along? To invest in this hole? Mick offered you ten per cent in the improved version. You'll not get that good a deal without him."

Georgie turns back to face Ryan. "It's not a hole, Ryan. I mean, I know it needs work doing. But honestly, if you stayed here a few days it would do the same to you, too. It changes people. Mick Rodgers isn't the right person to save the place. He'll rip the spirit out of it. I can't let that happen."

Ryan lowers himself into the same chair that Georgie chose to sit in on that first night just a few weeks ago. "Mick's livid, you know." He rests his elbows on the arms of the chair and forms a pyramid with his hands, a classic power pose that Georgie has seen him use in negotiations to unnerve the opposition.

"I'll bet."

"Your name's *mud* in Liverpool," Ryan snarls.

"Did you make sure of that?"

He snorts. "Me and Mick, yeah."

Georgie shrugs. "Say what you like about me. You can't hurt me any more." If she's learnt anything at Pinewoods Retreat, it's that she's no longer bothered by what Ryan's contacts think of her.

"How can you throw everything back in my face? I've done everything for you. You were nothing before—"

"Stop!" Georgie holds up a hand. "I've heard it too many times before." She shakes her head. "You want me to be grateful. I've been grateful. You want me to think I owe you something. I've paid my dues. Being at Pinewoods, I get it now. I want something more. I want to live my own life. I want to be happy."

"You'll have nothing."

"I don't need anything." A giggle bubbles up from Georgie's stomach. "I'm learning what that dreadful word '*authentic*' actually means for me. This place," she beams as she twirls in the centre of the room, "lets me be authentically me."

"Shit, babe." Ryan throws his head back and lets out a bitter laugh. "You've turned weird, for sure. You're even wearing fucking crystal bracelets." He steps into the middle of the room, standing just in front of her. "There's no way I'll square any of this with Mick Rodgers, you know. He'll not keep his trap shut. He wants to ruin you. And I'm happy to help him."

"But don't you see? I don't care, Ryan." A broad smile spreads across Georgie's face. "I'm making my own future. And remember all those women I've helped through LivSmarter over the years? They all want to be part of my future with Pinewoods. I reckon that's Karma. There's nothing you can do to hurt me now, Ryan. You won't ruin me."

"I'll find ways, mark my words." Ryan nods, like a Churchill dog. He looks around the room, like he's assessing it. "I see it's still the original windows. They'll cost a pretty penny to replace. I'll have to have a chat with all the replacement window guys I know. Make sure you can't get anyone to do the job." His laugh is hollow. "What a dump." He turns, and without looking back, he walks out of the room and slams the front door of Pinewoods Retreat behind him.

***

Dinner is a quiet affair, despite San's attempts to keep conversation going. She popped over to visit Holly towards the end of the afternoon on her way back to town from an event she was attending, and Dee invited her to stay for dinner. Georgie looks across the table at San as she takes a mouthful of food. Ten years, her husband was with this woman. She never expected to sit down for a meal with her.

San looks across at Georgie, as if aware of her stare, and smiles, hesitantly. Georgie half smiles back and returns her attention to the food on her plate. Being part of Pinewoods Retreat means she's going to be seeing much more of San Sartori – something it might be good to chat to the bees about.

As soon as the dishes are cleared away, Georgie goes outside and walks purposefully to the bees, a cup of tea in hand.

"I think I know what you bees are going to tell me," Georgie says, no longer embarrassed by her conversations with the bees. "San Sartori and I need to clear the air."

There's a crunch on the gravel behind her and, right on cue, San is walking towards Georgie.

"Can I . . . ?"

Georgie nods. "We need to talk, don't we?"

It's San's turn to nod as she lowers herself onto the raised bed next to Georgie. They sit for a moment, watching the bees return to the hive.

"Sorry," San says, her voice barely more than a whisper.

"Thank you," Georgie says. "And this is something I never expected to hear myself saying, but here goes. I forgive you."

San lets out a weak laugh. "Nope, not something I expected to hear you say, either. Where did that come from?"

"I've come to realise that no woman steals another's husband. You can't steal a person. A man who has affairs makes choices. Ryan did that. If he'd truly loved me, and was batting for our marriage, he would never have cheated on me."

"No, true. But still, I'm sorry for the part I played in that."

"It hurt me, I'm not going to lie. Particularly as he was with you for so long." Georgie stands up. She walks along one of the garden paths and looks back, indicating for San to join her. "Ten years. That's got to have meant something to him. To you."

"It did. I – sorry to say this – but I thought he was the one, for a while."

"I felt sorry for you, you know."

San nods. "I don't blame you."

"It was the only way I could cope." Georgie wraps her arms around her.

"I hate myself for putting you through that."

"Good," Georgie laughs. "That sounds cruel, but I am kind of glad. If you didn't hate yourself it would mean we've got no chance of finding a way to make amends."

"You're prepared to do that?" San's eyes are open wide.

"I'm going to be heavily involved with Pinewoods for a while, and these people are your friends. We need to find a way to get over our past."

"Thank you, Georgie." San lets out a long breath, as if she's been holding it in for the last hour.

"I'm not saying it's going to be easy. I know there's a little bit of me that's going to want to make you suffer at times. But I promise to do my best to hold those feelings at bay."

"And I promise I'm not a serial husband-snatcher. In fact, I've not had another man in my life since I broke it off with Ryan. I'm not sure, yet, if I can trust men again."

"You will, when the right *single* man comes along." Georgie stops walking and turns to face San. "I don't know if we'll ever be friends, San. But we can at least be friendly. For Lorraine and Dee's sake."

"Yes. Thank you. Pinewoods and all the people here, they mean so much to me. I'd do anything for them."

The two of the turn their faces to the house and stand, side by side, for a moment.

"Right then," Georgie says. "Maybe we start with a chat about marketing the retreat for when the works are all done? Come on, seeing as you're here we might as well get some paper out and throw down some ideas."

Georgie strides resolutely back to the house, not even stopping to check if San is following on behind.

44
LORRAINE

Nine and a Half Months After the Award Ceremony and Two Hours Until the Ten-Year Celebrations Begin

SUMMER comes early to Pinewoods the following year, with the sun making a perfect promise for the celebration weekend. The house looks good in the sunshine. It was Holly's idea to incorporate a bee theme for the open house that they're having as part of their ten-year anniversary, and Lorraine loves it. The golden yellow of the bunting across the front of Pinewoods contrasts perfectly with the new blue-green café parasols, sporting the white pine tree logo that Georgie's graphic designer came up with for the new-look retreat.

Lorraine glides through Pinewoods, having just finished giving reiki to a client in her new therapy room, which has taken over the living room at the front of the house. It's become a daily ritual for her to walk the floor, soaking in the changes that Georgie's investment and know-how have brought to the retreat. She starts, as always, at the rose arch that leads into the café. Every table is taken this morning, and there's a queue for the takeaway trailer.

Ed pops his head out of the yurt. "Lorraine, come and see what we've done with the yurt." He waves her over to him, a huge grin across his face.

"Georgie came up with the idea," he says. "You'll love it."

Lorraine walks into the yurt behind Ed, and where there was once an open space up to the centre of the yurt's high roof, now there's midnight blue voile draped across it and down the walls.

"Beautiful," Lorraine says. "It feels so much cosier in here. And you're all set up for your yoga sessions."

"I've made a sign," Ed says. "Look." He holds up a small chalk board. Across it there are times for mini yoga sessions throughout the afternoon, with a meditation to finish the day off.

Lorraine gives his arm a squeeze. "Brilliant, the perfect end to a perfect day. And how many have you got staying overnight in the yurt tonight?"

"Me, Georgie, Hunter, Holly and San, with her new fella, James. I know Hunter and Holly could have gone back to the caravan, with guests staying in the Shepherd's Hut, but we thought it would be good fun having a bit of a midnight feast and a good old chinwag."

Back out on the front lawn, there's a buzz in the garden café. An organised team takes orders and delivers food to tables, bobbing in and out through the open French doors into the dining room, which is now part of the café. It has a direct route through to the kitchen, with extra seating, and gives them the perfect spot to serve customers who don't like the sun, or for whenever the weather's bad. Georgie's suggestion to convert the hall that used to lead to the kitchen into toilets means that the café is now self-contained. Since they opened back up to the public at Easter, it's busier than it's ever been.

The kitchen, now enlarged through into the old therapy room to create what Georgie has dubbed '*the long room*', is humming with activity. Dee and her new sous-chef are cleaning up after serving lunch to the retreat guests, who sit around the large refectory style table that used to be in the dining room and now takes up one end of the long room. Every chair is taken. Mountains of food are piled in front of them, and, as serving dishes are passed around, comfortable conversation fills the air.

Holly and Hunter come in through the back door, arms laden down with jars of honey.

"This is what's left from my first honey harvest," Holly says. "All ready for the open house." She carefully places each jar into a basket on the old, familiar kitchen table. The basket handle is wrapped with a yellow gingham ribbon to match the ribbon around the neck of the honey jars.

"Good," Lorraine says. "Place that next to the basket with Dee's relishes in it. It's on the sideboard by the French doors. And here," she passes Holly a card, "try and stick the price card into a gap in the wicker handle."

Lorraine leans against the door frame, chuffed to have a full house. This is everything she ever imagined for Pinewoods Retreat.

Georgie comes up behind her and rests her chin on Lorraine's shoulder.

"Ready for the open house celebrations this afternoon?"

"Ready." Lorraine nods. "Ten years. I'll admit, there were times

I thought we'd not survive to this point."

"I'm glad you did."

"Me too. Thank you."

"Glad I could help," Georgie says. "But honestly, it's all down to you. Happy?"

"Very happy," Lorraine says, resting her head onto Georgie's. "And look at Dee. She's in her element, feeding our wonderful guests. This is exactly what I wanted us to create for her, so as many people as possible can enjoy her food."

"Perfect," Georgie says, quietly. A smile spreads across her face. "Then, is now a good time to talk about you and Dee taking some time out? Holly, Hunter, Ed and me, we're all here to look after Pinewoods. Start thinking about where you'll go?"

"We already know," Lorraine says. "Now this arm of mine is fully healed we thought we'd do a walking trip in Italy, in the Apennine mountains. We just need to work out when is best to do it."

"Don't take all the Pinewoods magic with you when you go." Georgie laughs and walks on into the long room to greet the guests around the table.

"We'll tell you more after the open house," Lorraine calls after her.

The phone on the Welsh dresser rings. "Pinewoods Retreat," Lorraine says in her honeyed voice.

"Oh, hi," says the voice on the other end of the phone, "we're looking to book in, please. A group of six for mid-July for four days, if that's possible."

"We're booked up solid until the last week of July. Are your dates flexible?"

"Hang on," says the voice. There's some mumbled chatter and then she comes back on the line. "We can do the last week of July."

"Great. I can fit the six of you in, each with your own rooms and all of them en-suite, for that last week." Lorraine smiles to herself as she works out the details with the caller, booking them all in for the deluxe package. It's less than a year since she turned a group of five people away because some of the rooms were unusable. Georgie's wisdom and investment have secured the future for Pinewoods Retreat.

45

GEORGIE

GEORGIE works her way around the refectory table, spending a few minutes with each couple or small group, laughing with them, engaging in their conversations, suggesting places to visit, and always recommending therapies, including spending time in the community garden with Holly. It's important to her to spread warmth around groups of guests as her way of contributing to the Pinewoods way of working into people's souls.

As part of the marketing strategy she developed with San, Georgie has people taking photos during their stay at the retreat, uploading them to their social media accounts, and then she immediately shares them from the retreat's account, spreading the word of how people feel blessed to have found this little corner of paradise. One of the guests hands over her phone.

"You have to take my photo with this smoothie," the woman says. "I want all my friends to be insanely jealous that I'm staying at Pinewoods Retreat." She grins as Georgie takes the photo and passes the phone back.

"Remember to tag us when you put it up on Instagram," Georgie says, resting a gentle hand on the woman's shoulder.

"Knock, knock." Someone is standing in the doorway, their face hidden by a huge bunch of flowers.

"Oh my goodness," Lorraine says. "Are they for us?"

Beth peeps her head around the bouquet, and Kate peers over her shoulder, grinning from ear to ear. "A gift from Kate and myself," Beth says, "after everything you all did to help her with her runs."

"Beth!" Georgie almost skips over to her, and after passing the flowers to Lorraine, she pulls Beth into a tight hug.

"I know we're early for the party," Beth says, "but we figured you could probably do with some help."

"Hiya," Kate says, raising a hand in a half wave.

"I'm so glad you could both make it," Georgie says. "Now, Beth, I can thank you in person for sorting everything out with my divorce. You're so good at your job."

The phone rings for the fourth or fifth time that day. Every call has been someone booking in for long weekends, week long breaks, and, in one woman's case, a whole month so she can finish writing her novel. As Lorraine answers this latest call, the doorbell chimes.

"Well, aren't we the busy ones," Dee says. "What's that saying?" She grins.

"That one about being careful what you wish for?" Georgie asks, smiling back. "You stay here, I'll get the door."

San is standing in the porch.

"San, darling!" Georgie pulls her in for a hug. "You could have let yourself in, you know."

"I'm early," San says, eventually releasing herself from Georgie's hold. "Give me somewhere to dump my overnight bag, and then use and abuse me for the rest of the day."

"We have a luggage hold for our guests now, so let me put your bag in there, and then you can grab some lunch before we put you to work."

Georgie leads San into the long room, where there are more hugs from Lorraine, Dee and Holly.

"It all feels very exciting," San says. "And Georgie, I've exciting news for you, too. Hot off the press. In fact," she says, lowering her voice, "the article has probably only just gone live online as we speak."

"Intriguing," Georgie says.

"I wasn't going to say anything until later, but I want you to hear this from me. You too, Lorraine, Dee." San rests her bottom against the Welsh dresser, crosses one ankle over the other, and folds her arms around herself.

"Come on," Lorraine says, laughing. "You're stringing this out, whatever it is."

"Well, thanks to some smart investigative journalism from none other than yours truly," she points her thumbs to her chest, "and a journo mate of mine, the police have just arrested Mick Rodgers in connection with an investigation we've been doing into building and development contracts in Liverpool over the last two years."

Georgie lets out a long, low whistle.

"Two others have been arrested with him."

"Woah," Georgie says, biting her bottom lip. "And is one of them . . . ?"

"Yup, Ryan Quinn. Since QuinnEssentials folded, he's been pretty much exclusively working with Mick."

"The bloody fool." Georgie runs a hand through her hair. "I suspected he was up to something since he got into bed with Mick Rodgers. Stupid idiot."

"The evidence proved that Ryan's been doing pay-offs for Mick Rodgers to a guy working at the council."

"And that's presumably the third arrest?"

San nods. "It all has to go to court yet, but the evidence is there."

"Is there any chance someone will cry foul, San," Georgie says, "with your – you know, conflict of interest, because you had an affair with Ryan?"

"That's why I did the investigation with this other journo. She's got the by-line in the *Liverpool Standard News*. My name is nowhere near it."

"I'm guessing that, like me, you'll have all kinds of emotions mixed up in this."

San nods. "You did well to get out when you did, Georgie," she says.

"Pinewoods woke me up. I discovered I deserve better." Georgie's bottom lip trembles.

Lorraine puts an arm around her. "You OK, lovey?"

A tear runs down Georgie's cheek. "That could've been me along with Ryan and Mick. I wasn't mixed up in anything, but I so easily could have been dragged into it. I'm bloody lucky we went our separate ways and that Beth sorted everything out so quickly with the divorce." She smiles at San. "It came through last week. I'm now Georgie Macrae, again." Georgie brushes tears from her cheeks with the heels of her hands. "Am I glad I came to Pinewoods Retreat last year."

"Well," Dee says, "Lorraine always tells us that Pinewoods Retreat attracts people when they need it most."

Georgie and San lean in and hug each other. "Thank you," Georgie whispers into San's ear.

"Right," Lorraine says, clapping her hands, "we've more than enough jobs to do before this celebration begins. Dee, get those snacks on the kitchen table, and Georgie, get your list out. Let's start checking things off."

Minutes later, the team is busying themselves with jobs, with the final preparations to get Pinewoods Retreat ready to welcome guests from the past, along with a group of women whose careers Georgie helped kickstart with the support she gave them through LivSmarter.

Later, when time allows, Georgie sneaks off into the garden and settles herself on the chair that she had Hunter build for her so that she can sit next to the beehive. She leans in and updates the bees, before filling them in on all the new faces they are going to see throughout the celebrations. It's been a while since she needed to share her troubles, but with every change they make at Pinewoods Retreat, Georgie always tells it to the bees.

ACKNOWLEDGEMENTS

THE difficulty with writing acknowledgements is that there's always the chance of missing someone – so firstly, I thank everyone who has helped me get where I am today, with two books published. How did this dream of publishing one book manage to double in number?

There, does that do as a catch all?

But there are people I want to acknowledge by name. My wonderful agent, Clare Coombes of The Liverpool Literary Agency, who gets me and my writing. Thank you for believing in me and nudging me in the right direction. My publisher, UCLan Publishing – Hazel, Jasmine, Kathy, Becky, Becky, Charlotte, thank you all for believing in Pinewoods Retreat so much you let me go there again for this story. My publicist, Karen, illustrator Jo Spooner (isn't this cover gorgeous?), and everyone else who has helped get this book in front of readers.

Which brings me to the most important acknowledgement of the lot – you! Yes, you, the reader holding this book in your hands (or ears – now there's a visual!). Thank you for reading *Tell It To The Bees*, and if you also read *Garden of Her Heart*, thank you for loving Pinewoods Retreat so much you came back for more. I cannot believe the love and support that Pinewoods Retreat has received – I wanted to touch one heart, and it seems I touch many, many times that. Without readers, I probably would still write, but you make it all the more worthwhile, and your messages of support for *Garden of Her Heart* got me through a difficult year. And please forgive me for Pinewoods not being a real place. I'm sorry.

Talking of that difficult year, I lost my mum in 2024. She never got to know that *Garden of Her Heart* was received with love by readers all around the world – though she knew you'd love it, because she loved it so much. In part, this book is for her. Writing *Tell It To The Bees* became a bit of therapy for me after her death. I was fortunate to be able to chat with Lee B, a wonderful garden designer and beekeeper friend, about all things bees for this novel, which was also great therapy – Lee, it's always a delight to natter with you, and even better when it's to help with my research. You even helped me come up with the title to the book, without even knowing it! Any errors about bees and their culture are all my own.

I dedicated this book to my fellow readers in The Last Minute Page Turners, part of The Travelling Bookclub in Burscough, Lancashire. Summer '24 was tough for us all, some more than others, and I'm not sure we'll ever fully recover, but our new home in Burscough is wonderful and cozy. Thanks for setting up this wonderful bookclub, Jordan – I love the friendships that have been borne out of our love for books. How wonderful that books has brought us together. Without this group of nutters, I'd maybe not have laughed quite so much straight after my mum died. And no, Last Minuters, you can't write spicy scenes for my books!

So, this book is for all of you, Jordan, Becca, Grace, Jacqui, Jen, Laura, Lorna, Maja, Nikki, Sammy.

Onto writers, there are so many I want to thank, and I will miss people from this list, I'm sure. The writing community is incredible. I've yet to come across a writer or author who isn't kind, and generous and supportive. Particular mention goes to Stephanie Butland for your love, direction and guidance. I adore your retreats and your washing line of wisdom. Thank you from the bottom of my heart. Thanks also to my penguin sisters, SJ and Kathryn, to all my beta readers, to my wonderful friend Sarah J (finish writing your book!), to Mark Stay for knowing so much, and sharing that knowledge, to Emma Claire Wilson for our quick catch-ups that never last less than two hours – how can two people talk so much? Then there's the Liverpool writers who support me, headed by Sarah Moorhead and Caroline Corcoran – thank you for championing writers at every stage of our careers and writing journeys. I've missed other writers and authors, but know that you – yes, you there – when you touched my life over the last twelve months or more, it meant so much to me. If we've met at festivals or book events, if you came on my podcast, if you sent me messages of support on social media, all of it helped, and continues to help. Thank you for being part of my life and my writing journey.

Then we get to the local and independent bookshops. I'm forever thankful to Jo from Broadhurst's in Southport for believing in me when *Garden of Her Heart* came out and for giving my book a whole window to itself for a display – and I'm still gutted that the shop closed. Thanks to Amy from Pritchard's in Crosby for supporting me, and to Sarah at Waterstones in Liverpool too. Then there's Bob at Write Blend, and so many other independent bookshops that have nudged my book along. Without your support, writers like me might not get the chance to be seen on the shelves of bookshops, and it means more than you'll ever know. Readers, choose local. Booksellers know their stuff!

And finally, thanks to my long-suffering husband, Rob, and our incredible daughter, Ellie. Our family means the world to me – and I love that I get to play Nanny with our mini-E. Who knew I could love another E as much as the first. Right, I'm crying now, so I'm going to stop. Love you all, each and everyone of you for being there for me. Thank you. xxx

ALSO AVAILABLE